The Complete Series

My Fox

Series

MY FOX ATE MY HOMEWORK

MY FOX ATE MY CAKE

MY FOX ATE MY ALARM CLOCK

MY CAT ATE MY HOMEWORK

MY FOX BEGINS

MY FOX ATE MY REPORT CARD

MY FOX, MY FRIEND FOREVER

David Blaze

For Zander...

Wow! That's Awesome!

Other Books
for Junior Readers
by David Blaze

Epic Kids

Janie Gets a Genie for Christmas

MAIN CONTENTS
Quick start pages

MY
fox
ATE MY
HOMEWORK

DAVID BLAZE

CONTENTS

FRIDAY MORNING

My teeth clicked and clacked when I stepped into my new school. Goose bumps popped up all over my arms like hot air balloons. I wasn't nervous—just cold. I knew I'd never wear shorts and a T-shirt there again.

Okay, I was a little nervous.

"Come on in," the sixth grade English teacher said when I stepped into her classroom. She was standing in front of a chalkboard with the name Miss Cox written across the top of it. She was older than any of the teachers I had in the city, and she had a high-pitched twang in her voice that made me shudder. "Don't be shy." She waved for me to come to her desk.

Twenty or thirty kids stared at me from their seats. My hands felt sweaty. "Can you dance?" one of the girls shouted at me. I felt ashamed to shake my head no. I did the chicken dance once at a birthday party. I knew that didn't count.

"Class," the teacher said, wrapping an arm around my shoulders, "I'd like to introduce you to Jonah Johnson."

"Joe," I said right away. I didn't like being called Jonah. I didn't expect anyone to understand, but I didn't want to feel like a little kid.

Miss Cox chuckled. "Of course, Joe. Whatever you prefer." She motioned toward the class. "Go ahead and find a seat. We only have a few minutes left."

Some kid in a tank top jumped out of his seat and shouted, "He has to sing the song!"

I had no idea what he was talking about. My mom begged me not to sing in public after she heard me singing in the shower one day.

Miss Cox shook her head and told the other

kid to sit down. "This is Joe's first day, and he doesn't know the rules yet. I think we can give him a pass this one time." She winked at me. "Anyone who's late has to sing a song in front of the class. We'll teach it to you later, Joe. Besides, I'm sure you have a good reason for being late on your first day."

I had a really good reason. It was Friday and I didn't want to be there at all! Why couldn't my mom let me start this school on a Monday like everyone else? She had to pry me out of my bedroom kicking and screaming. Maybe that's not completely true but it sure felt that way.

I walked through the rows of desks to the back of the room. I didn't want to sit near the front because that's where you get asked all the questions.

"Not here," some big kid with wavy blond hair growled at me before I could sit in the only open seat. He was so big he looked like he was supposed to be in the ninth grade. He stared at the desk when he spoke. "That seat is reserved."

The desk had dust on it, so I knew no one had sat there in a long time. "I'll find another seat next week. Let me sit here for now."

"Maybe I didn't make myself clear, Jonah," he hissed. "This seat is reserved, Jonah."

My face felt hot when he called me that name twice. "It's Joe," I reminded him. "Call me Joe."

He stood straight up, kicked his chair back, and waved a fist at me. I gulped. He was the tallest sixth grader I'd ever seen. He was wearing a gray T-shirt and gray shorts.

Miss Cox appeared by my side out of nowhere. "Do we have a problem here, Shane?" The kid snickered, shook his head, and sat back down.

Miss Cox took a deep breath and motioned for me to follow her. She led me right back to the front row of desks and an open seat. I had been there for less than five minutes and I was already embarrassed out of my mind. It was going to be a long day.

"Don't forget about the paper due on Monday morning," Miss Cox said to the room. "I want to see three paragraphs about your best friend. I'll be grading for grammar, punctuation, and speech."

I raised my hand. "Speech?"

Miss Cox smiled. "Yes, Joe. In this class we work on presentation skills. Anything you write you say in front of the class." She lowered her voice. "I know it's short notice, but is this something you can do by Monday? I heard you're a writer."

I didn't have any problem with writing three paragraphs. I was a writer for my other school's newsletter. But making a speech in front of the class? I gulped. I'd never done that before. I looked up at Miss Cox and said the only thing I could say to save myself from more embarrassment. "Sure, no problem."

The class bell rang, and everyone jumped out of their seats. There was so much noise and talking in the room I couldn't concentrate on how scared I was about Monday morning. I knew I shouldn't have started this school on a Friday. I mean, who starts school on a Friday?

"Are you okay?" the girl next to me asked. She had two ponytails and big dimples.

I stood up and slung my backpack over my shoulder. "I don't know yet."

She chuckled and stood next to me with a huge smile. "My name's Melissa."

I pulled my new class schedule out of my backpack. "Do you know where Room 104 is?"

She snatched the paper out of my hand and headed toward the door. "Yeah. That's my next class too. Follow me."

At least there was one friendly person at the school. She had a bit of a twang in her voice but not as bad as Miss Cox. I'd have to get used to it in the country.

"Where are you from?" Melissa asked when we walked into the hall.

"Orlando," I said proudly. She had to be impressed with a city boy like me coming to this small country town in Alabama. She smiled and kept walking.

I felt obligated to ask her some questions back. I wasn't a big talker, but I knew most kids liked talking about themselves. Melissa was the only person willing to be my friend so far. I couldn't risk losing that. "Where are *you* from?"

She stopped in front of Room 104, looked directly into my eyes, and said, "I came from my mama." She burst out laughing.

She didn't stop laughing, and it was so contagious I couldn't help but laugh with her.

The laughing stopped when Shane appeared by my side. I'm not short, but he was at least four inches taller than me. He was trouble—I couldn't show him any fear.

"We need to talk," he blurted out. He didn't look angry like before. I didn't know how much I could trust him, and I didn't know how much time there was until the next class started. "It'll only take a minute," he pleaded.

I glanced at Melissa. She shrugged her shoulders and walked into the classroom. "I'll save you a seat," she promised.

I looked back up at Shane. "It's fun to mess with the new kid. I don't want any trouble."

Shane frowned like he was hurt. "I'm sorry about earlier," he confessed.

I wasn't sure how to respond. All I could say was, "Oh. Okay."

He smiled for the first time and punched my shoulder playfully. "So you're a writer?"

This was going a lot better than I expected. It wouldn't be hard making friends after all. "I dabble here and there," I proclaimed. "I won an award at my other school."

Shane's eyes got big. "That's awesome!" he shouted.

Another kid wearing a tank top joined us. His hair was cut like a sailor's. It took me a second to realize he was the kid from Miss Cox's class who had tried to make me sing a song.

"Hey, Joe," Shane said to me. "This is my best friend, Sam." They pounded fists. "Isn't it funny that Miss Cox wants us to write a paper about our best friends?"

My stomach churned. I had a bad feeling this wasn't going so well after all.

"Sam and I grew up together," Shane continued. "We like to go fishing and hunting."

I tried to step backwards toward the classroom. I already knew what he was going to ask me.

"Say," Shane said to me, "you're a writer and we're friends now, right?" He followed every step I took. I was pretty sure we weren't friends.

He reached out and grabbed my shirt collar with one hand. "Where are you going?" He tightened his grip. "I'm gonna need you to write my paper for me, Jonah."

I love to write but not under threats and not for someone else. "My name is Joe."

Shane and Sam both snickered as he released

my shirt and straightened it out. "This is going to be a long year for you if you don't write it. And you'll be very, very sorry." He shoved me into the room. I stumbled and fell flat on my back. Shane towered over me, smirked, and said, "Make the right decision."

The two bullies high fived each other and disappeared down the hall. The teachers were monitoring the halls and none of them saw what happened. I stared up at the ceiling and wished I was invisible.

"Are you okay?" Melissa asked after I got up and sat next to her. "Shane is a big bully. If you give him what he wants, then he'll never leave you alone."

She was right, but to be honest, I was scared to death of the big kid! I didn't know yet my whole world would be turned upside down after school that day, but I knew right then and there what choice I would make about writing Shane's paper.

FRIDAY AFTERNOON

I went straight to my room when I got home and lay on the bed. It was so lumpy that my back had hurt all morning after tossing and turning in it all night. It's weird to call it my room and my bed when just yesterday I was living somewhere else.

My mom knocked on my door. "Is it safe to come in here?"

This was my great-grandma's house, and it had been built in 1930. The floors creaked, and the walls smelled like smoke. I wasn't sure any room in this house was safe. "It's open," I told her.

She sat on the edge of the bed. "It's hard leaving everything behind. But I have to do what's best for us." She glanced around the room. "Right now this is it."

I sat up and stared at the dirty white wall in front of me. "I know." She had lost her job, and we had nowhere else to go. Great-grandma had left this place to my mom in her will. "Thank you, Mom." She was a warrior and she'd never give up.

She leaned against my shoulder. "Now you're talking to me?" We both laughed. "How was your first day of school, mister?"

All I could think about was Shane's order to write his paper. It made me feel sick. How could I write three paragraphs for him anyways? He had only told me that he and the other guy liked to hunt and fish. I definitely did not want to write it. On the other hand, I definitely did not want to get beat up.

"It was okay," I told my mom. "I get to do some writing—like I did for the other school." I thought about telling her the truth, but she already had too many things to worry about.

She hugged my shoulders. "That's great, Jonah! You're a wonderful writer." She was the only one allowed to call me Jonah.

We both jumped when a knock at the front door echoed through the walls. My mom stood up and asked me, "Who could that be?"

"Maybe it's the pizza delivery man," I said with high hopes.

She shook her head and walked out of the room. I followed her to make sure everything was okay. My mom had spent a lot of summers in this town many years ago, but she didn't know anyone there now—except for my uncle.

She opened the door. "Hello," said a big, chubby man in a striped suit. He smiled wide and waved a smelly cigar. "Miss Johnson?"

"Yes?" she replied. "Can I help you?"

"I'm sorry to disturb you on such a beautiful day." He bowed slightly to reveal an almost bald head. "My name is Mitch Connors, and I'm from the IRS." He cleared his throat. "My condolences for the loss of your grandmother." He sounded sincere.

"Thank you," she said. She pulled me forward. "This is my son, Jonah."

Mr. Connors extended his hand to me. As I shook it, I said, "Please call me Joe." He nodded.

The man returned his attention to my mom. "Miss Johnson, we need to discuss your late grandmother's property taxes. She never paid them."

I had no idea what he was talking about, but my mom didn't have any money. Mr. Connors seemed like a nice man, but I didn't want him to be there anymore.

"Jonah," my mom said, "go out back and make sure the chicken coop is locked before it gets dark." I wished I could have said I didn't know what she was talking about, but I had spent enough time there to know my great-grandma kept a bunch of chickens out back.

I didn't want to leave my mom stranded there with that man. I was scared he was going to give her more bad news. She looked at me and winked.

"Go on now," she said. "Everything's going to be okay." I wanted to believe her, but I knew it wasn't true.

"It was nice to meet you, young man," Mr. Connors said as I walked away. I didn't respond to him. I shook my head and marched straight to the back of the house.

I could still hear him talking before I slammed the door. "This house will belong to us on Tuesday unless you can pay the $14,112.00 that's due."

I already knew we'd be living somewhere else next week. That was a good thing because I wasn't a big fan of the mosquitoes out there. And now I didn't have to worry about Shane or the paper about my best friend, which was another good thing. I didn't have a best friend.

I stood in front of a wooden shack outside the back door. It had a half moon carved into it. This wasn't the chicken coop—no sir. This was the outhouse.

My mom used to tell me how houses didn't have indoor plumbing in the old days. The toilets were outside in these outhouses. This house was upgraded years ago and there was a toilet inside now, but this magnificent building was still there.

I passed the outhouse and headed for the chicken coop. A large area of land around it was fenced in so the chickens could come out to eat and get some exercise. The chicken coop reminded me of the tree house I had in the city (except it was on the ground). It was made out of wood and had a door so a person could walk into it. The chickens laid their eggs in there.

They were already in the coop. There were only twelve chickens left. Great-grandma used to have a lot more, but she always said one disappeared every now and then—like a magic trick.

Right there in the back was Old Nelly. She was my great-grandma's favorite chicken. As my great-grandma got older, she swore Old Nelly talked to her and laid golden eggs.

Now, let's get one thing straight—Old Nelly didn't lay golden eggs. None of that chicken's eggs could be sold and they were not safe for human consumption. Old Nelly only laid rotten eggs!

I froze when I stepped out of the coop, half in fear and half in amazement.

An animal I had never seen before stared at me. It looked a lot like a dog, but it had to be something else. It wasn't very big, the size of a Scottish terrier like our neighbor in Orlando had. It was a bright brown color, almost orange. The end of its tail was white, just like its chest. All four paws were black.

There were two things about this animal I would never forget. It had the bluest eyes I had ever seen, like the ocean. And it was smiling at me.

I bent down slowly and picked up a stick. I

wasn't afraid of the animal. I had always wanted my own dog, and this was my chance. I tossed the stick to the side and shouted, "Fetch!"

The animal jumped like it was going to run away. Then it looked over at the stick and back at me. I don't want to sound like a crazy person, but I'm telling you this creature shook its head no at me.

"What are you?" I whispered. "You're not a dog. If you were then you'd have a collar." I took a step toward the animal with my hands out to show I wasn't a threat. Something told me this creature could be my friend. "This is nuts. You've got to be some kind of dog. Where's your collar?"

I stopped a few feet in front of the animal I hoped was a dog. It stared at me with its blue eyes and then looked around like it wanted to make sure no one else was watching. It stood up slowly on its two hind legs—just like a human! What it did next took my breath away.

"I don't know," the animal said like a child. "Where's *your* collar?"

I fell flat on my butt and scooted backwards with my hands. My great-grandma had said Old Nelly talked to her; now that dog-like animal was talking to me. Maybe that land made people crazy.

"Jonah!" my mom screamed from the back door. "Where are you? You better not be in the outhouse!"

I couldn't move anymore when the animal walked up to me like a human. "I'm a fox," he said. "Don't tell anyone you saw me here." It winked at me and raced toward the fence. I stood up and watched in disbelief as it jumped over the fence and ran out of the yard.

LATER THAT AFTERNOON

"You locked the chicken coop, right?" my mom asked when I walked back into the house. I couldn't remember, but that didn't matter at the moment, so I nodded.

"We're going to stay with Uncle Mike for a while," she said.

I could barely understand what she was saying. All I could think about was the talking fox. It was the most amazing thing I'd ever seen, but I couldn't tell anyone about him, not even my mom.

"We have to be out of here by Tuesday morning," she continued. "So we'll make the best of it for the weekend."

I sat at the dining room table and tried to process what she said. Uncle Mike grew up in this town and never left. I'd still have to go to the same school and face Shane. But, more importantly, we had to stay here in case the fox came back. "We can't leave," I begged.

My mom sat next to me. "What are you talking about? You don't even like it here." All I could do was look at her and plead with my eyes. "Don't give me that look, mister. I already feel bad enough as it is."

I put a hand on her shoulder. "It's not your fault," I assured her.

She wiped her nose. "So I was thinking we could go to the farmers' market tomorrow morning and sell some eggs. It'll be fun. I used to do it in the summers every Saturday with my grandma." She paused and smiled at me. "This is our only chance to do it together."

There was a sparkle in her eyes. She looked excited about it, and I couldn't disappoint her. "Sure, Mom. We can do that."

She stood up and wrapped her arms around me. "It's a shame, really." She looked out the kitchen window and into the yard. "I had some of the best times of my life here."

I wondered if she had ever seen any talking animals there. I wanted to tell her about the fox so bad, but I couldn't for two reasons. One was the fox told me not to. He didn't threaten me, he was trying to protect himself. The other was I didn't want my mom to think I was losing my mind.

"Did you have any homework?" she asked.

My stomach churned when I thought about the paper due in Miss Cox's class. I consider myself a writer, but I didn't have a best friend to write about. It would have to be about my mom—not a smart move for a new kid like me. Shane and Sam would tease me all year about it. I couldn't believe he had told me to write his paper!

"I have to write something for my English class," I told her. It wasn't a lie, and it kept me from having to explain everything that had happened in school.

"Okay," she said. "You should go ahead and do that. We may not have a lot of free time this weekend." I agreed with her and stood up to head for my room. "Just a second, mister," she commanded. "What would you like for dinner?"

I didn't have an appetite. My head was swirling with so many thoughts that it began to hurt. "I'm going to lie down for a while. I'm not hungry."

She nodded her head. "Come get me if you need anything."

I jumped into my bed as soon as I closed my bedroom door. The mattress was so lumpy that I was sure there were bricks inside of it. It wasn't uncomfortable to lie on, but after eight hours of sleep it always left my back in pain. There was no reason to complain about it—we were only going to be there for a few more days.

I was exhausted and needed a power nap before I wrote anything. Every time my eyes shut I could see the fox's blue eyes staring back at me. I wondered if I'd ever see him again.

FRIDAY NIGHT

I jumped out of my sleep when I heard a ruckus outside. The room was dark so I knew the sun had gone down. I looked at my watch and saw it was midnight!

I only felt half awake, and my back was killing me. I wished I could sleep on the floor, but that place had roaches that came out at night. I had heard them crunch under my feet when I got up to use the bathroom the night before. They disappeared the moment I turned the lights on.

I jumped again when a door banged shut from outside. *The chicken coop!* I suddenly realized I did forget to lock it.

I hopped out of the bed and shuddered every time I felt a crunch under my shoes. I walked down the hall and into the kitchen. My mom was nowhere to be found, and I didn't expect her to be—she was sound asleep. I grabbed a flashlight off the kitchen counter and walked out the backdoor and into the yard.

The outhouse looked scary in the dark, like a haunted house. The moon that night was shaped like a trimmed fingernail and not giving off much light. I flicked the flashlight on and marched toward the chicken coop. I had to lock it before the chickens got out and put themselves in danger.

I dropped the flashlight when it focused on two blue eyes. The fox was walking out of the chicken coop. I was happy to see him again, but what was he doing in there?

"You don't want to go in there for ten to

fifteen minutes," the fox said. "And you might want to light a candle." He waved a paw in front of his nose like something stank.

And it did.

The putrid odor made me feel sick. The fox was covered in something wet and slimy. I knew exactly what it was.

"Old Nelly," I whispered.

The fox shook its body rapidly from side to side so the rotten egg yolk flew off of him in every direction. "That crazy old chicken threw her eggs at me! She attacked me for no reason."

I suspected Old Nelly had her reasons. She had never thrown her eggs at me. "Maybe she got nervous," I explained. "You shouldn't be in there at night."

The fox smiled and said, "I like you, Jonah. I think we're gonna be good friends."

I couldn't help but smile back. It didn't feel weird talking to the fox, and he was nice. "Wait a second," I said. "How did you know my name? And please call me Joe."

The fox turned and walked toward the fence area he had jumped over earlier that day. "The other human with you yelled your name earlier.

She said something about the outhouse."

That made sense. "Where are you going?" I asked. "I have so many things I want to ask you."

The fox stopped walking and faced me. "I need to get some dinner." He looked back at the chicken coop. "I missed my last meal." He shook his head like he was disappointed. "And there's a river down the road. I need to wash up."

I had to agree with him on the last part. "That's a good idea. You smell like farts."

He huffed, crouched on all four paws, and raced out of the yard.

I locked the chicken coop and went back into the house. I felt a lot better after talking with the fox. I wondered how old he was, probably the same age as me (eleven), maybe a year or two younger. And I wondered once again when I would see him next. He liked the chicken coop. I'd try to meet him there again tomorrow.

I turned the kitchen and living room lights on—not a roach in sight. I was wide awake now, and it was the perfect time to write my paper for school. I grabbed two sheets out of my backpack and a number 2 pencil. That was funny. *Number 2*. Made me think of the outhouse.

I titled the first page *My Best Friend.* There were only three paragraphs to go. I couldn't think of anything. Why was this so hard? I loved to write and could probably write a book. I could warm up by writing Shane's paper. I knew who his best friend was, and I could make everything else up.

No. That was a horrible idea. I crumpled the second piece of paper and threw it in the trash. I didn't want to entertain the idea of writing Shane's paper for him. But still, my life would be easier at school if I did it. And I wouldn't have to walk the halls scared for my life.

I gave up for the night and pulled out a magazine for boys. It had articles about nature and science. Maybe I'd write for that magazine one day.

I fell out of my seat when something rapped on the kitchen window. My heart felt like it was going to explode. It thumped against my chest like it was trying to escape. I tried to ignore the noise in the kitchen, hoping it was only my imagination—but it happened again.

There's no reason to be afraid. I took a few steps toward the kitchen and peered around the corner at the window. I didn't see anything. It had to be nothing more than a branch scraping against the window. It was windy outside.

I nearly fainted when a small face pressed against the window. Once I caught my breath, I realized it was the fox. He laughed, stuck his tongue out at me, and pointed a paw toward the front door.

Was he asking to come in? He disappeared from the window as quickly as he had appeared. I scratched my head and walked to the front door.

I had misunderstood him. Why would a fox want to come inside? I opened the door to find him standing there, smiling. "Did you miss me?" he asked. He walked right past me and into the house. "I've never been inside a human's den."

I sighed and closed the door. It was pretty awesome to have him there. Thankfully, he didn't smell like farts anymore. He was used to being outside, and I had to lay down some rules. "Just make sure you don't pee on the carpet," I warned him.

He jumped on the couch and sat up in the corner. "I won't if you won't."

I laughed and sat on the couch with him.

"It's a shame I won't be here much longer. You're the coolest animal I've ever met."

He narrowed his eyes. "What do you mean?"

"We can't stay here," I confided in him. "We don't have enough money. We're leaving in a few days to stay with my uncle Mike." Why was I telling him this?

The fox looked confused. "I don't know what that means, but in my neck of the woods, if you don't have enough of something then you work as hard as you have to until you do."

He was a fox, so I didn't expect him to understand. "I'm a kid," I told him. "I don't have a way to make money."

He huffed and pointed with one of his black paws to the magazine I was reading earlier. It was upside down on the floor. "What about that?"

I threw my hands up. "What about it?"

The fox jumped off the couch, grabbed the magazine, and handed it to me. "Those kids look like they're getting enough of what they want."

What kids was he talking about? I studied the back of the magazine. I saw exactly what he meant, and I knew he was right. The kids in the picture had fistfuls of dollars and were surrounded by toys. They got all of that by selling candy the company in the advertisement gave them.

"My mom won't let me do it," I told him. I wanted to sell the candy before, but my mom said no. She didn't want me going door to door and meeting strangers. She said it wasn't safe. I tried to argue with her, but she was right. Meeting new people was too scary.

"The other human?" the fox asked. I nodded. "If this could help you get enough of what you need, then I don't understand why it's a problem."

He was making too much sense. I couldn't make enough money selling candy to pay for the house, but I could make enough to help get it back for my mom.

I went to the laptop computer my mom had set up in the corner of the room. It was already connected to the internet. I typed in the web address on the back of the magazine.

The website was filled with pictures of money and prizes. I felt excited and confident about this. If those kids on the website could make a lot of money then so could I!

I whipped my wallet out of my back pocket when the website asked for a credit card. I don't have my own credit card, but my mom had given me one of hers for emergencies only. This was definitely an emergency!

"I'm gonna do it," I turned and told the fox. "I'm gonna get a box of candy and make a lot of money to help my mom."

"Sounds like a good idea," he said. "But if one box can get you all of that (he was pointing to the money and prizes on the screen) then imagine what you could do with two boxes."

I agreed with him and changed the quantity

to two. We needed the money as soon as possible, so I opted to pay extra for overnight shipping. "I'm glad you're here, fox," I admitted to him. "I think we'll be good friends."

His blue eyes glowed brighter and his tail wagged. "It's time for me to go home, Joe." He walked to the front door on his two hind legs and waited for me to open it.

"Will I see you again?" I asked as I opened the door and let him out.

He rubbed his chin. "It depends."

"It depends on what?" I wondered aloud.

He took a step back. "It depends on if you take a bath or not. You're the one who smells like farts now."

I smelled my armpits. I didn't smell anything. I wanted to ask him what he was talking about, but he ran off laughing. "Made you smell your armpits!"

SATURDAY MORNING

I made coffee and bacon for my mom before she woke up. She could barely walk or talk until she had her coffee. And as far as the bacon—that was for me.

We collected all of the eggs that day to take to the farmers' market.

"Thank you for locking the chicken coop last night," she said before we got there. "Have to protect them from wild animals."

I nearly choked on a laugh. I couldn't imagine the fox as a wild animal.

***

"This is our table," my mom said after we got into the park at the farmers' market. She pointed to one in the middle of dozens of others. Some of the other tables were covered with fruits and vegetables. One had a massage chair next to it with a sign that said it cost five dollars for five minutes. My first thought was,

This is where all the health nuts shop.

People were everywhere—wearing jeans and overalls, walking from table to table and talking to each other like they were having the best time of their lives. That place was as crowded as the theme parks in Orlando.

Someone blasted country music from a speaker overhead. I could smell hamburgers being grilled from a booth further down the park. This place was awesome!

"Put those right there," my mom said. She was pointing to the middle of our table. I knew she was talking about the eggs we had hauled there. Our arms were full of cartons that were cut in half.

"Good morning, ya'll," said an old guy wearing a straw hat and staring at the eggs. He had a strong country accent. "Glad ya'll could join us. My name is Jim Bob."

My mom wiped her hands on her pants. "Hi, Jim Bob. We're happy to be here. My name is Julie, and this is my son Jonah."

"Call me Joe," I told him right away.

He gave me a weird look, shook his head,

laughed, and pointed to the eggs. "How much?"

"It's six dollars for half a dozen eggs," my mom said proudly.

Mr. Bob whistled. "That's too rich for my blood. I can get a whole dozen at the grocery store for half that price."

My mom crossed her arms. "You're right, Jim Bob. But the chickens that laid the eggs you get at the grocery store were raised on an overcrowded ranch. They were stressed out all the time. They may have ingested pesticides and ate each other's poop."

Mr. Bob scrunched his face in disgust. I did too.

"Now *my* chickens were raised on a small farm by my grandma," my mom continued. "She hand fed them every day and talked to them like they were her own children." She put a hand on my back. "Those chickens were loved. They're happy. Happy chickens make better tasting eggs."

FARM EGGS

Jim Bob walked away with two dozen eggs!

"That was amazing, Mom!" I looked at her with nothing but respect. I hoped I could be like her one day. "You've gotta teach me how to do that."

She took a deep breath and laughed. "Don't get used to it. They really are overpriced." She leaned against the table. "Your great-grandma never came here to make money. She just wanted to interact with people."

I didn't know a lot about my great-grandma, but she seemed pretty cool. I couldn't help but wonder how she survived all those years by selling eggs. She never had a job, and my great-grandfather passed away long before I was born.

"How did she do it?" I asked my mom.

"How did she do what?"

"How did she live without any money?" I wondered aloud. She left this world without a penny to her name.

My mom shrugged her shoulders. "I'm sure she had government assistance. And your great-grandfather Ray made sure she was taken care of before he passed away."

An elderly couple stepped up to our table and smiled. "What do we have here?" the woman asked. Her hair was gray in the front and the rest of it was brown. The man with her was bald with a long, gray mustache and bushy, gray eyebrows.

"Don't be silly," the old man told the woman. "I'd know these eggs anywhere." He stared at me and squinted an eye. "These are Rita's eggs. What are you doing with them?"

I had no idea who Rita was or why this guy thought the eggs were hers. He was a lunatic, and I didn't want to deal with it. He scared me. "Mom?" I said, looking up at her and swallowing hard.

My mom laughed. "My name is Julie, and this is my son, Jonah," she said to the couple. She patted me on the back. "Rita was my grandma."

"Call me Joe," I whispered.

"Oh, dear child," the old woman said in a comforting voice. "I'm so happy to meet you. Your grandma was a wonderful person." She stared at the table for a minute like she was lost in memories. "My name is Martha Hunter." She pointed to the man. "This is my husband, Jonathan."

My mom stepped around the table and shook the couple's hands. "Did you know her well?" she asked Mrs. Hunter.

Mr. Hunter cleared his throat. "Are you kidding me?" he laughed. "The two of them never stopped talking!" He looked at me and winked. "I had to get a new bottle of aspirin every week."

"Don't listen to him," his wife said. "He's old and bitter." She shook her head and grabbed my mom's hands. "I miss her dearly. We must get together and talk sometime."

My mom smiled. "Thank you."

Mr. Hunter grabbed his wife's hand and pulled on it. "Let's keep moving, Martha. The sun is hotter than a bonfire right now." He wiped his forehead. "Let these young people work on their tans."

I half waved at Mr. Hunter as they walked away. He was scary at first but overall a really cool guy.

My mom patted her pants leg. That meant her cell phone was vibrating. She answered the call and held up a finger to me, signaling

40

she needed a minute.

Her conversation went like this: "Uh huh. Uh huh. Yeah. Uh huh. Okay."

She put a palm over the receiver and looked at me. "It's Uncle Mike. Something about a job." She took her palm away from the receiver and spoke into it again. "Yeah, I'm still here. Just a minute."

I loved listening to these kinds of conversations where I could only hear one person. *Not.* It was like trying to put a puzzle together and all the pieces were the wrong sizes.

"This is going to take a few minutes," my mom said to me. "I need to step away. Can you handle the table?"

I looked around at all the people at the farmers' market. There had to be hundreds of them. None of them were coming to our table. "Yeah, I think I'll be okay."

She stepped through the crowd to the other side of the park where there were empty benches. I hoped it was good news for my mom. She loved to work and be around people.

"Hello, Orlando," some girl said to me. I looked across the table and saw my only friend at school. I thought her name was Melissa. Yeah, that was it. She was the one with big dimples. She gave me a wide grin.

"Hey," I said. "What are you doing here?" I was happy to see her but tried not to show too much excitement.

"I like to get crazy on the weekends," she said, bobbing her head to the slow country music playing overhead.

I laughed because I knew she was kidding. At least I hoped she was kidding. She frowned like she was hurt then burst out laughing. "Got ya!"

"I'm glad you're here," I told her with a smile.

She smiled back. "Are you selling a lot of eggs?"

I was too embarrassed to tell her we had only sold eggs to one person. "We're doing okay," I lied.

She shook her head. "No, you're not." I shrugged my shoulders like I was confused by what she had said. "Everyone who comes here on a regular basis knows these are Rita's eggs."

"What's that supposed to mean?" I asked with my arms crossed. I didn't know my great-grandma very well, but the people around here better not have said anything bad about her.

Melissa picked up a half carton of eggs and studied them. "Rita always had rotten eggs in her cartons."

"She thought they were golden eggs," I whispered.

Melissa put the carton down. "So, did you start on your paper, Mr. Writer?"

I shook my head. "Not yet. I'm working on something big."

"Can't wait," she said and clicked her tongue. "Do yourself a favor and stay away from Shane. He doesn't do any of his own work." She turned to walk away. "Someone has to stand up to him."

I had to agree with her. I just wasn't sure if I was the right person to do it. I had never been in a fight, and I wanted to keep it that way.

My mom came back to the table with a smile on her face. "Okay, so… Uncle Mike's job had a position open up, and they want to see me right away."

"Today?" I asked, holding up my hands.

She sighed. "I hope that's not a problem."

It wasn't a problem at all. I had another chance to talk to the fox, and I didn't want to pass that up—but there was one thing I had to do before we left.

"Those hamburgers smell good," I said, holding my stomach as it growled. I don't know how long we were there, but I had smelled the hamburgers grilling the entire time with spices like garlic and pepper.

"I could use one, too, but I'm not sure we made enough money for that," my mom said, picking up the egg cartons.

I was so desperate for a hamburger that I pleaded with her. "We made twenty-four dollars. How can it not be enough for two hamburgers?"

My mom smirked and spoke in a very serious voice. "People around here are crazy. They charge six dollars for half a dozen eggs." She shook her head like it was an unfair price. "If they charge for hamburgers the same way…" She started to laugh and couldn't finish the sentence. So she tried again. "If they charge for hamburgers the same way, then it'll be six dollars for half a hamburger." She snorted and laughed like she had just told the funniest joke in the world.

All I could do was shake my head. Maybe we had been in the sun too long.

SATURDAY AFTERNOON

As soon as we got home, I opened the back door to see if I could find the fox. He was nowhere to be found. Maybe he was by the chicken coop again. "I'm gonna check on the chickens," I told my mom.

"Not right now," she said, buttoning up a fancy dress shirt. "Close the door and come here." I sighed and closed the door slowly, hoping to catch a glimpse of the fox.

Nothing. Nada.

"Listen to me carefully," my mom said when I joined her in the living room. "I need to go take some tests for this job. I may be gone for a few hours."

I didn't have any problem with that. It would give me more time to find the fox. It could also be my only chance to use the outhouse.

"Do not leave this house for any reason," my mom stressed. "I want you to stay right here and write your paper for school if you haven't done it yet." She nodded her head slowly like she wanted me to nod with her to show I understood.

"Okay," I murmured. It wasn't fair, and I couldn't tell her why, but I did need to write the three paragraphs about my best friend. This would be the perfect time to do it.

She put on some lipstick and headed for the front door. "Call me if you need anything. Don't forget there's a pizza in the fridge." She hesitated after she opened the front door. I thought for sure she wasn't going to leave.

"Love you, Mom," I encouraged her. "See you when you get back."

She smiled and said she loved me too before closing the door. I waited until I heard the car pull away before I rushed out the back door. The chickens were roaming their fenced area. The coop was empty. I searched the entire yard. My heart sank when I knew for sure the fox wasn't there.

I went back inside and grabbed another two sheets of paper from my backpack. I sat on the couch and placed the paper on the coffee table in front of it. I didn't know what had happened to the one from the night before, so I started over again with *My Best Friend* written across the top of one sheet.

I couldn't go any further. I wasn't sure if I even had a best friend.

A large car or truck skidded in the driveway in front of the house. A loud horn honked. I didn't move because I had no idea who it was. My heart stopped when someone banged on the front door. I tried not to move, hoping whoever it was didn't realize I was there.

They banged on the door again. I shook every time their fist hit the door. "Delivery for Jonah Johnson!" a man's voice shouted from outside.

Me? I had a delivery?

Oh yeah! The candy!

I jumped up and raced for the door. I was scared I was too late when I heard the delivery truck start back up. I threw the door open and yelled, "Wait!"

A big man wearing shorts jumped out of the truck. "Jonah Johnson?" I nodded my head. "Almost missed you, buddy."

He walked over to me with a large box in his hands and a tablet shaped like a clipboard. He set the box on the ground by me. "Sign here." He was pointing to a spot on the tablet as he handed a pen to me.

I signed it, thanked him, grabbed my box of candy and went back inside. I couldn't wipe the smile off my face because I was so excited about all the money I was about to make. I ripped the box open and pulled out two smaller boxes full of chocolate candy bars.

I'd have to write my paper later because it was time to get down to business. I stepped out of the house with the boxes in both hands and closed the door. I didn't have a key so I couldn't lock the door. I doubted it would be a problem since we lived in the country and there were only a handful of houses on this road.

My mom said I couldn't leave the house, but I had to do it for both of us. She was going back to work to make some money, and now I had the chance to make some money too. She'd have to be proud of me for helping out. Together, we could get this house back.

I walked out of the yard with my candy and headed down the dirt road. There were two more houses on the right side and three on the left. I'd stop at each one and sell as much candy as possible. If it went well, and I sold all the candy, I'd do this every Saturday.

No one was home at the first house. I was disappointed, but I refused to give up this early.

Maybe they went to the farmers' market. I

could check back later.

No one was home at the second house either. Now I was getting worried. There were only three more houses on this street. I wasn't willing to go down any other streets because I didn't want to get lost.

A young man opened the door at the third house. He was wearing a motorcycle jacket and had earrings in both ears. There was a cigarette in his left hand. "Yeah?" he said.

I gulped. I couldn't say anything. I had pictured this moment perfectly in my head. I was supposed to introduce myself and be friendly. That didn't happen.

"Are you okay, kid?" the guy asked.

I cleared my throat and held up one of the boxes. I could only say one word, and it was in a squeaky voice I didn't recognize as my own. "Candy?"

The man sighed. "Ah, man. I bought a box of chocolate the other day from another kid."

Strike three. This was the third house, and I still hadn't sold any candy. I lowered the box and turned to walk away. I felt embarrassed for some reason.

"Hold on, kid," the man said. He threw his cigarette down and stomped on it before blowing a puff of smoke out his mouth. "How much?"

I faced him and cleared my throat again. "A dollar a bar."

He huffed. "Give me five of them." His voice was raspy like he didn't want to do it. He reached for his wallet and pulled out a five-dollar bill.

I handed him the five chocolate bars and accepted his money. "Thank you!"

He just said, "Yeah," and slammed his door.

Okay. Now I was getting somewhere. There were two more houses to go. Thank goodness I didn't give up earlier. Things were looking up!

No one was home at the fourth house. I rubbed my forehead and panicked. The two boxes had twenty bars of chocolate each. Forty bars in all! What was I thinking? I had thirty-five bars left and there was no way I could sell them all at one house.

I still had to sell as many as I could. My mom would be home soon, and I'd have to explain all of this to her. I did not want to do that. I couldn't give up.

I knocked on the sixth door. No one answered. It was over. It was *all* over. I was going to be in so much trouble.

"Hello," said an old man's voice before I turned away. "I don't believe it. You're the kid who stole Rita's eggs." He waited a second, laughed, and then turned to someone behind him. "Martha, come here. It's Rita's great-grandson."

Mrs. Hunter was by his side within

seconds. She smiled. "Oh, dear child. Come in, come in." I wasn't supposed to go into strangers' homes, but I had met these people with my mom just a couple of hours earlier. Not that it mattered—I had to get home before my mom did.

"I can't stay," I told them.

Mr. Hunter narrowed his eyes. "What brings you here, Joe?"

I was surprised he remembered my name and said it right. "I'm selling some candy and wanted to see if you wanted any."

Mr. Hunter shook his head. "I love chocolate, but my doctor won't let me touch it."

And there it was. Did you hear it? It was the sound of my complete failure. I did everything I could to keep from crying. "Thanks anyways," I told them. My mom was going to kill me.

"Wait a second, child," Mrs. Hunter said. "Why are you selling the chocolate?"

I hesitated. "I want to help my mom."

Mrs. Hunter made a sound from her

throat that sounded like *awwww.* "You're a good boy." She turned to her husband. "It's up to you," she said to him. "Rita was my best friend." She walked away and left Mr. Hunter in the doorway facing me.

"Come to think of it," Mr. Hunter said, "I never liked my doctor much." He pointed to the boxes in my hands. "How much is the chocolate?"

"One dollar each," I told him. He was only going to buy one, so it didn't matter. I wished he'd hurry up though. My mom could already be home. She'd call the cops because the door was unlocked, and I wasn't there.

"How many do you have left?" he asked. He needed to stop wasting time and just ask for a bar.

"Thirty-five."

He whistled. "That's a lot." *No kidding.* I needed him to tell me how many he wanted or I'd have to leave and race home.

He said the one thing I never expected. "I'll take them all." He pulled out his wallet and handed me thirty-five dollars!

I didn't know what to say. I couldn't move. Never in a million years did I think someone would buy all my chocolate. I certainly didn't think Mr. Hunter would be the one to buy most of them.

"So now you've got my money…" Mr. Hunter said, rubbing his chin. I knew he was going to ask me to do something for him, like wash his car or lick his boots. I won't lie—I was willing to do it. He had saved me from certain death.

"Are you going to give me my candy?" he asked.

I looked at the two boxes in my hands and realized in my excitement I forgot to give them to him! I shoved them in front of me. "I'm sorry. Here you go."

He grabbed them and said, "These are mine now, right? I can do what I want with them?"

That was a silly question. Of course he could do whatever he wanted with them. For all I cared, he could throw them in the trash. "Yes, sir. They're yours."

He smiled. "I'd like to welcome you and your mom to the neighborhood with these two boxes of chocolate." He handed them right back to me.

I wasn't sure what to do. I already had his money. Now I had the candy back too? I stared at him, confused.

"Please take them," Mr. Hunter pleaded. "I'll never hear the end of it from my wife if you don't. There's not enough aspirin in the world for that." He smirked. "Trust me; you're doing me a favor."

"Thank you," was all I could say to him. He wasn't a bad guy. I was liking the neighborhood more and more and wished we didn't have to leave.

SATURDAY NIGHT

My mom wasn't home yet when I got back. I was drenched in sweat and out of breath from running home. It was worth it though. My mom would be so proud of me.

I heard her car door close in the driveway. She came inside and didn't even see me. "Hey, Jonah," was all she said before she went straight to the computer.

"Mom, what's going on?" I asked her. I looked over her shoulder and saw she was on the bank's website.

"I got an alert on my phone from the bank," she said. "It says the account balance fell below twenty dollars." She sounded frustrated. "I don't know how this happened."

I smiled because I was about to make her day. "I can tell you what happened." I held the two boxes of chocolate in front of her like a trophy.

She stared at me and shook her head. I don't think I've ever seen her look so disappointed. "You used my card to buy candy?" She put her hands on top of her head. "Please tell me this is joke. Because I know you would not use that card unless it was an emergency."

I swallowed hard. She was speaking slowly again, and she never spoke that slowly unless I was in trouble. I had a feeling I was in trouble no matter what I told her. "It's okay. I know you didn't want me selling candy door to door, but that's what I did while you were gone. And I made a lot of money!"

Her face turned red.

I reached into my pockets and pulled out the money I had collected. "Look. I sold it all and even got to keep some." I showed her the money, but she wouldn't stop staring at me.

She said something she had never said before. "I don't know what to do with you. Go to your room until I can figure it out."

I handed her the money, but she wouldn't take it, so I set it on the desk next to the computer. I marched toward my room with every intention of slamming my door shut and locking myself in. I went out of my way to help, and that was the thanks I got for it? Never again!

"Jonah, wait," I heard my mom plead. I stopped and turned around. What else was she going to yell at me about?

She stared at me and grinned. "I got the job."

I couldn't help but grin back. "I knew you would."

She stood up and shook her head. "I don't want to be mad at you. Things are hard right now." She walked over and hugged me.

"Thank you for trying to help out."

As I lay in my lumpy bed that night, I wondered how much more our lives would change. We didn't have a lot at the moment, but at least we had each other.

SUNDAY MORNING

I woke up to a rap on my bedroom window. I smiled when I saw the fox's blue eyes staring back at me. He was standing outside with his face pressed against the window and his tongue sticking out again.

I sat up and stretched, trying to get the kinks out of my back. The sun was out, so there wasn't any crunching under my feet as I walked to the window. I unlocked it and pushed it up.

"Good morning, fox," I told him. My voice was shaky because the air outside was cool.

"Wanna have some fun today?" he asked, wagging his tail. His smile was so big I had to laugh. He made me feel good about myself for some reason.

"I don't think I'm allowed to have fun today," I told him, hoping I was wrong. I had never seen my mom as mad as she was the night before. And I didn't know what she had planned for me that day. "I'm in trouble."

The fox's smile disappeared, and his tail stopped wagging. "I hate to hear that." He looked around the side of the house. "Don't forget to unlock the chicken coop. Gotta make sure they're happy and healthy." He licked his lips for some reason.

"I may never see you again," I confided in him.

"Jonah!" my mom yelled from the kitchen. "Come get some breakfast!"

"Wait," the fox said. "What are you talking about?"

I shrugged my shoulders at him. "I've gotta go."

I closed the window and waved to him. I was never good at goodbyes. I had left Orlando without telling any of my friends I was leaving. It hurt too much.

The fox looked sad and confused with his ears down and his tail between his legs. Did he not want me to go either?

"Jonah!" my mom yelled again.

"Coming!" I yelled back.

I turned from the window and marched

out of my bedroom. I felt weak and tired. I did not want to leave my new friend behind.

***

"I'm going into work this morning," my mom said when I sat at the kitchen table. She had a plate of pancakes waiting for me. "I won't be back until tonight." That got my attention. I would have time with the fox after all.

"I've asked your uncle Mike to check in on you this afternoon if he can." She stood behind me and put her hands on my shoulders. "The only reason you're not going over there is because I'm making him clean up his place before we move in with him." I could feel her shaking her head. "It's littered with beer cans and cigarettes."

She walked around the table and sat across from me. "I may have overreacted yesterday, and I apologize for that." She nodded her head slowly again. "You know what the rules are, and I'm going to trust you." She stopped nodding. "Please don't make me regret it."

I couldn't help but notice one of my chocolate boxes was empty in the trash can. "What happened to the candy?" I asked, pointing to the box.

"I don't know," she claimed, shrugging her shoulders. "Someone must have eaten them." I knew she loved chocolate, but fifteen bars eaten since last night? That had to be a world record!

"I'm not judging," I said, shoveling the pancakes into my mouth. They were perfect with butter melted over them and maple syrup dripping over the sides.

She smirked and stood back up. "I'm taking the other box of chocolate bars to work with me. I want to make sure they feel loved." She stood next to me and kissed my cheek. "Write your paper and stay out of trouble today." She tightened one of her earrings. "I baked a pan of chicken for the day. Save me a couple of pieces for when I get home tonight."

And then, just like that, she was gone. I rushed to the bathroom to wash my face and brush my teeth. I didn't want the fox to get a chance to say I smelled like farts. They're the worst kind. Usually silent. Always deadly.

I ran out back and passed the outhouse. I didn't see the fox anywhere out there—he'd be back soon. I went ahead and unlocked the chicken coop my mom had locked the night before. Old Nelly looked like she was asleep in the back. I wondered how many rotten eggs she had laid in her lifetime. Hundreds? Thousands?

"Glad you could make it," came the fox's

familiar voice from outside the coop.

I stepped out to greet him. "I'm glad I could make it too." I realized I had never asked him the most important question of all. "What's your name?"

The fox rubbed his chin. "I don't know. You're the only person I've ever talked to."

I couldn't help but smile and feel proud. He was the only fox in the world who could talk, and he chose to talk to me. "We should call you *Fox,* just to keep things from getting confusing."

His blue eyes lit up. "Sounds original." He was trying to hide it, but I could tell he was excited to be named and recognized. It wasn't hard to figure it out. His tail was wagging like a jet fan.

"Did you get enough of what you need?" he asked me.

I wasn't sure what he meant. I kept thinking it was odd none of the chickens came out of the coop. They were hiding from something.

"You said you didn't have enough

money," he reminded me. I remembered our conversation a couple of days earlier. That's when I had decided to sell the candy.

"Not quite," I admitted. Forty dollars wasn't enough to fill up the gas tank in the car. My mom always made me fill it up. She paid for it, of course.

"There's another way you can get more money," Fox said. He stepped up close to me and whispered like he had a secret to share. "If you dig a hole deep enough over there," he said, pointing to the fence line out of view, "you'll reach China. And you know what they have in China?"

Call me crazy, but I was pretty sure Fox was trying to play a practical joke on me. I decided to play his little game. "What?"

"Gold!" he shouted. "Lots of gold!"

I laughed at him so hard my stomach hurt. He wasn't smiling anymore and seemed disappointed I didn't believe him. "Fox, everyone knows you can only find gold at the end of rainbows." *Duh*!

His blue eyes shifted from side to side.

"They have lots of rainbows in China." He waved his paws overhead in an arc. "Tons of them. Every day."

I thought about it for a second and wondered if it could be true. "How long would it take to get there?"

Fox wagged his tail again. "An hour at the most." That wasn't bad. Even if he was pulling my leg, it was only an hour of my life. But I couldn't escape this nagging feeling in the back of head that none of this was true. That it was impossible.

"Jonah!" a man's voice yelled from the house. "Where are you?" I recognized it as my uncle Mike. I heard the back door shut and shoes or boots walking through the leaves toward us. What was he doing there so early? My mom said he wouldn't be there until the afternoon!

"You should run," I urged Fox. "Meet me later." Uncle Mike liked to hunt and I had a feeling foxes were on his list.

Fox dashed off on all four paws.

"There you are," Uncle Mike said moments later, walking up to me with his arms extended. I hugged him, looking over his shoulder to make sure Fox was out of view. "Missed you, pal."

"Missed you too," I admitted. I led him back toward the house so there was no chance of Fox being spotted. I hadn't seen my uncle in more than a year. He looked like he had aged twenty years in that time. Most of his hair had turned gray, and wrinkles covered his face. My mom always said it would happen one day with all the smoking and drinking he did.

"Your mom wanted me to check on you," he said. "Make sure you're okay." He looked over my arms and legs. "I don't see any broken bones."

I shrugged my shoulders. "I'll try harder next time."

He laughed and patted my arm. "We're gonna move you and your mom into my place tomorrow night. That way you don't have to miss any school tomorrow."

Yeah. Thanks a lot.

"Are you gonna be okay today?" he asked. "I've got a lot to do, but you can come with me if you're bored."

Not a chance. If this was the last day I could talk with Fox then I wasn't going anywhere. "I'm fine. I've got your number if I need it."

He patted me on the shoulder. "My man. See you tomorrow night." He went back through the house and left.

I fell flat on my butt when I turned around and Fox was standing right behind me. His paws were raised in an attack position. "You gave me a heart attack!"

He burst out laughing. "Sneak attack!"

It took a minute for me to catch my

breath. I realized how hot it was getting as the sun rose higher. "We should go inside and cool down," I tried to persuade Fox.

He looked back at the chicken coop. None of them had come out yet. Maybe they didn't like the heat either. "Okay. But just for a little while. I'll catch some lunch later."

SUNDAY AFTERNOON

"What's that sound?" Fox asked, jumping when the air conditioner turned on and began pumping cold air out of the kitchen vents. He crouched on all fours like he was ready to take off running.

I held out my hands and tried to calm him down. "It's just the air conditioner. It keeps the air cool in here when it's hot outside."

"You can change the air?" he asked in awe. I laughed at the fact he didn't know things like that. "Witchcraft," he muttered as he stood back up on his two hind legs and eyed the room suspiciously.

I was happy to have him back inside. There were so many things to learn about him. And it looked like there were a lot of things he could learn from me. "What do you want to do? My mom's not here."

"The other human is never here," Fox observed. "This is your own den." I could only shrug my shoulders at him. My mom was there when I needed her and that's what counted. "What did you mean when you said you'll never see me again?"

I didn't want to talk about it, but I owed him an explanation. I took a deep breath. "I'm leaving with my mom tomorrow night."

Fox's tail was between his legs again. "You're leaving? Is it because of me?"

"It has nothing to do with you," I tried to convince him. "I begged my mom to stay here, but we don't have enough money." I felt tired and weak again, telling the one creature in the world who I wanted to spend time with that I'd never see him again after that night.

He didn't say anything and sat at the kitchen table. His eyes were a darker shade of blue.

"Anyways," I told him, walking to the refrigerator and trying to avoid this conversation, "I'm going to make a sandwich."

"I'm a wild animal," Fox said in a low voice. "I'm dangerous. I take what I want when I want it. I'll never be cold and I'll never be hungry."

I had no idea how to respond to him. He was hurting as much as I was. "You want a sandwich too?"

"That'd be great," Fox said, his eyes lighting back up. "I'm so hungry I could eat anything. And can you turn the air conditioner off? It's freezing in here!" I smiled when he broke out into laughter.

I sat back down at the kitchen table and slid a ham sandwich to him. He stared at it like it was an alien. He pulled the top piece of bread off and tossed it to the floor. Then he yanked the slice of ham off and ripped it apart between his teeth before swallowing it. It was the most awesome thing I had ever seen!

"Chicken is better," Fox muttered.

I remembered what my mom had said before she left. "There's a whole pan of chicken in the fridge. You want some?"

Fox sat up straight and stared at the

refrigerator like it was a magic box full of locked secrets. "You keep chickens in there?"

I laughed at his misunderstanding. "Not live chickens. It's just their legs and thighs."

He licked his lips. "You cut them up then store them in that magic box?" He jumped out of his seat and walked toward the fridge. "This is amazing. I've got to get one of these."

"I guess," I said, scratching my head. It wasn't amazing to me, but that's because I had always had one. Fox, on the other hand, looked like he was going to pass out.

"Let me see," he pleaded, standing in front of the fridge. "I have to see it."

I didn't know what the big deal was, so I went ahead and opened it in front of him. His face changed from excitement to confusion.

"Where are the chickens?" he asked, looking through every shelf desperately. "You said there were chickens."

I shook my head. "I said there were chicken legs and thighs." I pointed to the foil-covered pan on the bottom shelf. It had ten chicken pieces on it.

"That's not chicken," Fox complained. "Where are the feathers? You tricked me because I tried to trick you about the gold in China." He huffed and stepped back. "Well played, Joe. Well played."

I tried my best not to laugh at him. "All the feathers are pulled out first, and then it's cooked."

He slammed the refrigerator door shut and stomped into the living room. "More witchcraft!"

I couldn't stop smiling when I joined him in the living room. There were so many things I could teach him. He had learned a lot of things in life—he even learned how to talk! But there were so many things people did and had in their lives every day that he'd never seen. Why did we have to leave tomorrow? I needed more time.

"What's this thing?" Fox asked, banging his paws against the TV remote control.

I snatched it from him before he broke it. I pointed the remote at our fifty-two-inch TV and pressed the power button.

I swear to you, Fox's head touched the ceiling when the TV blasted on at full volume, and he jumped sky high. I turned it down right away. He scurried behind the couch and poked his head out every few seconds to look at the cartoons playing on the TV.

"It's okay," I assured him. "It's not real."

I couldn't think of a way to explain it to him without him just watching it. I sat on the couch and waited for him to come out.

It took another hour before he walked around the couch and joined me on it. "I wasn't scared," he said, shaking his head. "No, sir."

Right. It took him a while to warm up to the cartoons, but a few hours later he was laughing at them with me. At one point I glanced at the table in front of us and saw the paper I started writing last night.

"I need to write something for school," I explained to Fox, leaning toward the table so I could write the three paragraphs. "It might take me a while. Are you okay?"

He stared at the cartoons and brushed a paw at me. "Yeah, yeah. Do whatever you have to do." He laughed at the TV. "They're so silly."

I'd only known Fox for a couple of days and I just showed him some modern technology that day. Was I a bad person because I already had him addicted to TV?

I'd have to worry about that later. He was having a good time, and I was hanging out with him. Now, if I only knew what to write about my best friend.

I had no idea, so I came to the only logical conclusion. I had to write about Tommy. He was my best friend in the second grade. I was new at my school and no one knew my past. Tommy was the perfect answer.

I wrote three paragraphs about him in less than an hour. It only took that long because I went back and double-checked the spelling and grammar. That left one question in my mind because I had plenty of time left. *Do I really want to write Shane's paper?*

Fox tapped me on the shoulder. "Where did the cartoons go?" The TV screen had a message flashing on it.

WE'VE EXPERIENCED A TEMPORARY INTERRUPTION OF YOUR SERVICES.

I'd only seen that message once before, and that's when my mom forgot to pay the cable bill. I had an idea what was going on this time. "My mom had it turned off since we're leaving tomorrow. Sorry."

He huffed and looked at my paper. "Did you finish?"

I did, but I still had the other decision to make. I had butterflies in my stomach just thinking about it. "I think so. I'm not sure."

"You know what I do when I'm not sure about something?" he asked.

I had no idea. "What?"

"I go ahead and do it," he said, smiling. "There's no rule that says I can't change my mind later."

He was a fox, but his advice made complete sense. I went ahead and wrote Shane's paper for him right then and there in record time. They were the best three paragraphs I'd ever written—what a shame to waste them on someone else! I didn't know if it was the right decision, but I could always change my mind before class started the next day.

"Thanks, Fox," I told him.

My mom's car squeaked when it stopped in the driveway. *Oh no!* Was it already time for her to come home? That day had flown by so fast. I did not want it to end.

"You have to go, Fox," I urged him, pointing behind me. "Out the back door."

He jumped off the couch and landed on all four paws. What he said next left me speechless. "If you ever need a friend, just look for me." He dashed out of the living room and through the kitchen before I could say anything. I knew he was already out the back door and where he was supposed to be. I couldn't believe he was gone and I'd never see him again.

SUNDAY NIGHT

"I'm so glad to be home," my mom said, taking her shoes off and lying on the couch. She looked exhausted. "I had the longest day."

I half smiled. "I'm glad you're home too." I loved my mom, and I was always happy to see her, but I wished she had stayed at work a little longer.

"I see you finished your paper," she said, waving a hand at the table.

I looked at the table and freaked out. There was only one sheet of paper on the table. I had written two! One for me and one for Shane! Where was the second one?

"Can I read it?" my mom asked.

I picked up the paper and lost my breath. It was the one I had written for Shane! I wiped away a bead of sweat from my forehead. "I'm still working on it."

She stood up and stretched. "Let me know when you're done. I'm going to eat some of the chicken in the fridge and head to bed." She winked at me and walked toward the kitchen. "Big day for everyone tomorrow."

I waited until she was out of the living room then sprang into action. My paper had to be around there somewhere. I searched the entire living room floor and looked beneath the couch. It was nowhere!

I felt sick when I sat on the couch and remembered what Fox had said. *I'm so hungry I could eat anything.* Did he snatch it before he ran off? Why was this happening to me? It was Sunday night, and I was out of time to write anything else. My night couldn't get any worse.

"Jonah Johnson!" my mom yelled from the kitchen. "Get in here right now!"

What was she yelling about? I hadn't done anything wrong. I gulped because she only used my full name when I was in big trouble. I took a deep breath and went into the kitchen.

My night *did* get worse!

The refrigerator door was wide open, and the chicken pan was on the floor. It was empty—the ten thighs and legs were gone!

"Please explain this to me," my mom said in a low voice. "I could swear I asked you to save some chicken for me tonight." She shook her head and stared at me with wide eyes. "What's going on with you? First you disobeyed me with the candy. And now this?"

I stared back at her as I tried to think of an explanation. Fox had decided to eat the chicken after all. Did he gobble it all down in record time before he ran out of the house?

"You've written your paper and you've had plenty to eat," she said, pointing to the empty pan. "Go to your room and think about what you've done. I don't know what to do with you."

That's when I came to the only decision that could save me. I told her the truth. "It was the fox." I told her the entire story from when I met Fox up until that moment.

She put a hand on her forehead. "Now you're telling lies?" she asked with a broken voice. She couldn't stop blinking. Was she crying? "Go, Jonah. Just go. Go to your room."

I tried to plead with her to believe me, but she waved me off. I marched out of the kitchen, through the living room, and straight to my bedroom. I slammed the door shut and jumped on my lumpy bed.

It was a good thing we were leaving the next day. Fox was my friend and he was awesome, but I'd never been in as much trouble as I was since I met him.

I grunted when I realized I had left Shane's paper on the living room table. I did not want my mom to see it because she was already in a bad mood. I got out of bed, cracked my door open, and listened to make sure she wasn't around.

It was safe. I'd grab the paper and rush back.

I could hear my mom talking on her phone in the kitchen, so I grabbed the paper off the table and tiptoed my way back. Before I got out of the living room, I overheard her.

"I don't know what to do with him," she said to the other person. "I didn't raise him to be a liar. Maybe I made a mistake moving him from the city to the country. I want him to be happy."

My heart broke because I wanted my mom to be happy too. I went back to my room and stared out the window. For all the trouble Fox had caused me, I still wanted to see him again. He made me happy. My mom didn't make a mistake bringing me there. I never wanted to leave.

MONDAY MORNING

I clutched my backpack as I walked through the school halls. It still felt odd to me as I'd only been there once before. I was surrounded by kids I didn't know and none of them acknowledged me. I felt invisible.

"Hey, Jonah!" someone shouted from behind me. I didn't have to turn around to know it was Shane. I didn't bother to correct him about my name that time.

He stepped in front of me and put a hand on my chest to stop me. Sam was by his side. "Not so fast. Where's my paper?"

I had tossed and turned all night in my lumpy bed, trying to decide if I should give the paper to him. I didn't want to get beat up, and I didn't want him to take advantage of me for the rest of the year. I couldn't get Melissa's voice out of my head from the farmers' market: *Do yourself a favor and stay away from Shane. He doesn't do any of his own work. Someone has to stand up to him.*

I pulled my backpack around and held it in front of me. I looked at the big kid and thought about it for a second. Fox had told me that I could change my mind if I wanted to. I decided to go with the decision I had made the night before.

I unzipped my backpack, pulled the paper out, and handed it to Shane without saying anything. His face lit up when he grabbed it, and he pushed me back.

"That's what I thought, Jonah." He laughed and looked over at his best friend, Sam. "Sam has something he'd like to ask you."

Sam looked like a soldier with his sailor's haircut. "I've got a science project due in Mr. Wheeler's class next week." He cocked his head and smirked. "I'm gonna need you to do it."

I didn't bother to answer him because I had no intention of doing it. Besides, I was never any good at science.

The class bell rang, and all the kids scattered into their classrooms. Shane pulled Sam back toward Miss Cox's class. "What a loser," he said.

I followed them into the class and took the same seat in the front I had on Friday. Melissa was next to me again and smiling with her big dimples.

"Hi, Joe," she said. "It's good to see you again." I believed her, so I smiled back. I didn't want to tell her I had written Shane's paper for him, but she'd figure it out.

"Good morning, class," Miss Cox said to all of us. She was sitting behind her desk and smiling. It was going to take some time to get used to her high-pitched country twang. "Did everyone finish their papers?"

I was embarrassed to admit I didn't have a paper, so I didn't say anything. I was hoping it would take the entire class time for others to read their papers and Miss Cox wouldn't get to me. It would give me time to write my paper that night and bring it in the next day. Was that too much to hope for?

"Who wants to go first? Any volunteers?" Miss Cox asked, scanning the room. Everyone fell silent. "Anyone?"

Melissa raised her hand. She was brave. "I'll do it."

"Thank you, Melissa," Miss Cox said. "The class is yours."

Melissa stood up and walked in front of the chalkboard then turned around to face the class. She cleared her throat and smiled at me. For the first time I realized how cute she was.

"My best friend is my cousin, Millie," she read aloud from her paper. "We grew up together and like the same things. She goes to a different school, but we see each other all the time."

I don't have any cousins. My uncle Mike never got married. He always said girls were the devil. Except for my mom, who was his sister—she was an angel.

"That's why Millie will always be my best friend," Melissa finished. The class clapped for her. Had I missed most of what she said? I hated getting lost in my thoughts and losing track of time. My mom had the same problem and said it was a sign of being a genius.

"Thank you, Melissa," Miss Cox said when Melissa handed the paper to her. "That was very well done." She looked at the paper for a minute then set it down on her desk.

"Who's next?" she asked the class.

The room was silent again.

"No volunteers?" she asked like she was surprised. I was only eleven years old, but I knew no one volunteered to do something they didn't want to do. What was so shocking about that?

"Shane," she said. "Come on up."

I didn't turn around to face him because I didn't want to see the stupid smirk on his face. It was too late to change my mind, and it made me feel sick. My heart was racing.

"You're the next lucky contestant," Sam said, laughing as Shane passed by.

Shane stood in front of the chalkboard and winked at me. I wasn't sure if that meant he was grateful or if he was trying to show he was better than me. It's not fair if you think about it. He didn't do any of the work and was about to get all of the credit for that paper.

"You're gonna love this," Shane said to Miss Cox. "I put a lot of work into it."

"Go ahead, Shane," Miss Cox said. "We don't have a lot of time." I was glad to hear that. He could take as much time as he wanted.

He held the paper in front of him dramatically. "My best friend. By Shane Connors." He looked around the paper and winked at me again.

And then he read exactly what I wrote for him.

"My best friend is my mommy. She dresses me every morning and changes my wet sheets."

The class burst out in laughter.

As I was tossing and turning in my lumpy bed the night before, I realized I could never let someone else take advantage of me. I had to give him the paper.

Shane stared at me like he was trying to burn a hole through my head. The class was still laughing at him, and Miss Cox was trying to make them stop. "I didn't write this," Shane said while he was staring at me with hatred.

Miss Cox looked back and forth from him to me like she was trying to figure out why Shane wouldn't take his eyes off of me. She focused on me and shook her head like she knew exactly what was going on.

"Shane," she said to him, "are you saying someone else wrote your paper?"

He smiled because he must have realized Miss Cox figured everything out. "That's right."

Miss Cox cleared her throat and stood up. "Someone's in big trouble." I gulped. I was already in so much trouble with my mom. Once she found out about this my life was over.

"Shane," Miss Cox continued, "you're already behind in this class. If you're telling me that you didn't write that paper, then I'm gonna have to fail you." I think she winked at me from the corner of her eye.

Shane lowered the paper. His mouth was wide open.

"I'm going to ask you one more time," she said. "Did you write that paper?"

Shane rubbed his forehead like he couldn't think of the right answer. After a minute, he stopped and stared at the floor. "Yes. I wrote it."

"Keep reading!" Sam shouted. "We want to hear the whole thing!"

The class cheered and broke out into laughter again. Shane stood there, hanging his head.

Miss Cox held up a hand for the room to be silent. She looked like she wanted to laugh but did everything she could to keep from doing it. "Shane doesn't look like he feels very good. I'll go ahead and take that paper."

He looked grateful when he handed it to her then headed back toward the class. He made sure to stop by my desk. "You're dead meat," he whispered.

I ignored him and stared at the chalkboard like I didn't know what he was talking about. I was scared out of my mind because I had no doubt he had every intention of beating me up after school. Now I just wanted to go home.

"Joe," Miss Cox said. "Let's hear your paper. I'm sure it's very entertaining."

I couldn't move. She didn't know I didn't

have a paper and I didn't want to admit it. She knew I was a writer and had faith I could do it over the weekend. I swallowed hard. "I don't have it." I whispered my only excuse. "My fox ate my homework."

A couple of kids snickered. "I hate it when that happens," one kid complained.

"I see," Miss Cox said. "Do you remember what you wrote?"

The truth was I did. It was about my friendship with Tommy in the second grade. I wrote it in minutes because it flowed out of my mind with ease. "Every word."

She motioned toward the chalkboard. "Come up here and tell us about it. I can at least give you some of the credit."

I was leery to do it, but if it kept me out of trouble then I didn't have any other choice. All I had to do was get out of my seat, walk up to the chalkboard, and tell everyone about my old best friend Tommy.

There was just one problem. I was scared out of my mind to speak in front of a bunch of people I didn't know yet. I had once heard it was easier to speak in front of a crowd if you imagined everyone naked. I doubted it was true because I didn't want to imagine *anyone* naked!

"What's it going to be?" Miss Cox asked.

Melissa leaned across her desk and touched my arm. "You can do it, Joe. I believe in you." The way she said it made me believe in myself.

I stood up, took a deep breath, and walked to the chalkboard. When I turned around, all I could see were hundreds of eyes looking back at me. There were less than thirty kids there, but it felt like a lot more! The room seemed so small at that moment.

"Go ahead, Joe," Miss Cox said. "We're

almost out of time." That was just great. I was going to be the last one making a speech that day. If only one other person could have gone before me!

"My best friend's name is…" I froze when I remembered what Fox said to me the night before. *If you ever need a friend, just look for me.*

I started over again with words I never wrote. "My best friend's name is Fox. I've only known him for a few days, but I feel like I've known him my entire life. He's taught me a lot of things about myself, and there are many more things I want to show him."

I looked through the class with more confidence. "Fox has taught me to laugh at myself and not take life too seriously. He's taught me to go after the things I want in life and achieve what I never thought was possible." I smiled when I thought of one other thing. "He's taught me to stay away from rotten eggs because they smell like farts."

Everyone in class laughed! Even Miss Cox couldn't keep a straight face. I did my best to keep talking without laughing with them.

"I don't know if I'll ever see Fox again,

but he'll always be my best friend." I remembered how Mrs. Hunter got her husband to buy the chocolate from me. My great-grandma had been her best friend, and even though my great-grandma wasn't around anymore, Mrs. Hunter would always do what she could to help her family. That was true friendship.

"He feels like family to me now," I said to the class. "Maybe that's what a best friend really is."

Miss Cox stood up and smiled. "That was very nice, Joe. Thank you." Some of the kids clapped for me.

I went back to my desk and sat down. Melissa told me that I did an amazing job. I didn't know if it was amazing or not, but I meant everything I had said. I didn't want that day to end because, when it did, I knew I'd never see my best friend again.

MONDAY AFTERNOON

My uncle Mike picked me up from school that afternoon. I was glad I didn't have to take a long trip home with my mom while she was mad at me. I should never have told her about Fox. I don't know why I expected her to believe such a crazy story.

My stomach churned as we got closer to the house. We were going to pack up our belongings and leave forever.

"How was school?" my uncle asked.

It turned out to be a pretty good day. I didn't get into trouble for not having my paper. I became better friends with Melissa. Shane went home early because he told the school nurse he had never felt so sick in his life. I knew the real reason he left was because he was too embarrassed to stay at school. "It was okay."

When we got home, I walked as slowly as I could inside. I felt drained.

"There you are," my mom said when we walked in. Mr. and Mrs. Hunter were sitting on the couch with her. They both said, "Hi," to me.

My uncle Mike put a hand on my shoulder. "I'll load some of these boxes in the truck." He pointed to the boxes along the wall that he and my mom must have packed. There weren't many because this house had already been furnished the way my great-grandma had left it. We mostly had clothes and kitchen utensils packed up.

"Use the restroom if you need to," my mom said to me. "We're leaving in about an hour."

I put my backpack down. I hadn't eaten anything all day with the butterflies in my stomach. I didn't have an appetite. "I'm good."

"We hate to see you leave, dear," Mrs. Hunter said to my mom. "I wish you had more time."

So did I.

Mr. Hunter's knees cracked when he stood up and came over to me. "Maybe it's for the best," he said to everyone. "This house is older than I am." He grinned and chuckled. "It even survived the Great Depression of the thirties."

I remembered learning about the Great Depression at my last school in the city. The stock market had crashed, and a lot of people lost their money. It affected everyone and made life really hard.

Mr. Hunter stood in front of me. "We came by because we were going to ask you if you could watch our place for us while we're gone. Mow the lawn. Water the plants." He shook his head. "We're going up to our home in Wyoming for the spring and summer. Oh well."

Now I knew for sure life wasn't fair. They would have paid me to do it!

"Let's go," he said to his wife. She said her goodbyes and joined him by the door.

He knocked twice on the wooden doorframe. "Yep. Older than dirt."

"Thank you for the money," I told him as they walked out. I was referring to the thirty-five dollars he gave me for the chocolate.

He winked at me and looked over the house from the outside. "She really is old. Back when she was built, people didn't have a lot of money and didn't trust the banks." He shook his head and pulled his wife along. "A lot of them kept their money under their mattresses."

I froze.

My lumpy mattress.

I rushed inside and told my mom to meet me in my bedroom. I was breathing hard, and she asked me if I was okay. I didn't know yet.

Was it possible? My great-grandma had died without a penny to her name. She didn't have any bank accounts, but she survived for decades selling rotten eggs. Did she have money hidden all along?

I stared at my lumpy mattress when my mom walked into my room. "Is everything okay?" she asked. "We need to finish packing and get on the road."

My heart wouldn't stop racing. I felt like I was going to faint. "I need your help. We need to push this mattress up against the wall."

She made a tsking sound with her tongue. "We're not taking that with us. Uncle Mike has a bed for you."

I looked up at her and pleaded with my eyes. "I know you don't believe everything I've told you lately, but I need you to trust me right now. I have to see what's beneath this mattress."

She looked at me and nodded her head. "Okay, Jonah."

We stood side by side and pushed with all of our strength to heave the mattress up against the wall. I almost lost my balance and collapsed beneath the monstrous weight.

We stood back and stared at what was left beneath the mattress. I looked up at my mom and smiled. Her eyes looked as if they were about to explode out of her head.

More money than I had ever seen lay in front of us. It was dollar bills stacked in ones, fives, twenties, fifties, and hundreds! There were more stacks than I could count.

"Mom," I said, gasping for air. "Is this enough of what we need?"

She smiled and wrapped her arms around me. She screamed like she was at a rock and roll concert. That was awesome!

"It's more than enough," she said in a broken voice. "We don't have to leave!" She let go of me and danced around the room, laughing in a way I'd never heard. She was the happiest I'd ever seen her.

I reached down and touched a stack of cash to make sure it was real. This kind of thing didn't happen to kids like me. I had never even won a game of duck, duck, goose.

It felt like gold in my fingers. I couldn't wait to tell Fox that I didn't have to dig a hole to China. We could be best friends forever now.

MONDAY NIGHT

My mom cooked my favorite dinner that night—fried chicken, mashed potatoes, and buttery biscuits. She danced around the kitchen and hummed a happy tune I'd never heard. She banged the pot lids together like they were cymbals.

I stood there and smiled while I watched her, knowing she could keep living her childhood dream. She thought she had lost this house and its memories forever, but now it would always be hers. Nothing could take away her happiness.

Someone tapped on the front door.

"See who that is!" my mom shouted, dancing to her own beat. "Maybe they heard me singing and want my autograph!" She threw her head up, laughed like a crazy person, and whipped the mashed potatoes.

I shook my head. I didn't have the heart to tell her that her singing was worse than mine when I was in the shower.

I opened the front door and froze.

Fox stood on the other side on all four paws. That reminded me of the first time I had seen him. He was magnificent with his bright brown hair and aqua blue eyes and wide smile. I nearly collapsed like I had that first night.

"You shouldn't be here," I whispered to him. I turned to see if my mom had noticed him. She wasn't any the wiser—she was doing the salsa dance like a zombie.

"I smell chicken," Fox said. "I'm starving."

I crossed my arms and shook my head at him. He knew better than to come there when my mom was around. It was for his own protection. "I'll bring you some later. Wait for me out back."

"Did it come from the magic box?" he asked.

I knew he was talking about the refrigerator. I hung my head. "Yes." I started to close the door.

He licked his lips then slid through the

doorway right past me. What was he doing? I had no idea how my mom would react when she saw him.

I ran into the kitchen and waved my hands in front of her to get her attention. She stopped dancing but swayed her shoulders from side to side. "Loosen up," she whined. "Don't be a party pooper." She started to dance again but stopped when she looked over the kitchen counter.

Fox was staring at her with his bright blue eyes. She grabbed my chest and held me back. "Don't move," she whispered. "It could be dangerous." She was breathing hard.

"What are you talking about?" I asked her. "This is Fox. I told you about him the other night."

She pushed me behind her toward the back door. "That fox is not your friend. It's a wild animal and could have rabies." She reached into her pants pocket and pulled out her cell phone.

"Hello?" she said into the receiver. "Mike? Get here as fast as you can with your gun."

This was not going well. I had to find a way to make her believe everything I told her about Fox. I couldn't lose my best friend. I snatched the cell phone from my mom and threw it across the room.

"Jonah!" she shouted. "Why did you do that?" She took a deep breath. "It's okay. You've been under a lot of stress."

"He's my best friend, Mom," I told her. "You can't hurt him."

She opened the door and motioned for me to slip out. "He's a wild animal, Jonah. He's not a pet. He's not a dog." She was doing her best to convince me as she pushed me out the door. "If he was then he'd have a collar. Where's his collar?"

My uncle Mike would be there any minute, and he wouldn't hesitate to shoot Fox. I had to stop this before it was too late. "Tell her!" I shouted at Fox. "Tell her the truth!"

Fox stared at me for a moment then looked around like he wanted to make sure no one else was watching. He stood up slowly on his two hind legs and looked squarely at my mom.

"I don't know," he said. "Where's *your* collar?"

My mom shrieked and put her hands on her head. I was glad she didn't fall over because I wasn't sure if I was strong enough to catch her. Her mouth was wide open, and her chest heaved up and down.

"It's okay, Mom," I assured her, nodding my head slowly—the same way she did at me when she wanted to make sure I understood something. She tried to grab me as I walked around her and over to Fox. I stood by his side and faced her. "I need you to trust me."

She put a hand on her chest and waited for her breathing to slow down. Her legs were wobbly, like she wouldn't be able to stand much longer. She cleared her throat and looked back and forth from me to Fox.

"What do you want with us?" she asked Fox in a quiet voice.

He pointed at the kitchen. "Chicken from your magic box."

She looked confused before she stared back at me. "Jonah?" I had no idea what she was going to ask me. The only thing I knew for sure was that we were running out of time. Uncle Mike would be there soon with his gun.

"Yes, ma'am?" I gulped.

My mom took a deep breath. "Go get another plate for your friend."

I smiled at her and laughed. She smiled back.

"Are we gonna stand around and talk?" Fox asked with his two front paws up in the air. "Or are we gonna eat some chicken?"

My mom shook her head and laughed. She walked over to me and Fox. "I trust you, Jonah. I've always trusted you." She hugged me and bent down to face Fox.

"You're a cute little guy, aren't you?" She stroked his head and rubbed his ears.

"Right there," he said. "Yep. Yep. A little to the left." I laughed at the huge smile on his face while his tail whipped back and forth.

Then my mom said the one thing that let me know everything was okay. "Any friend of Jonah's is a friend of mine. Welcome to our home."

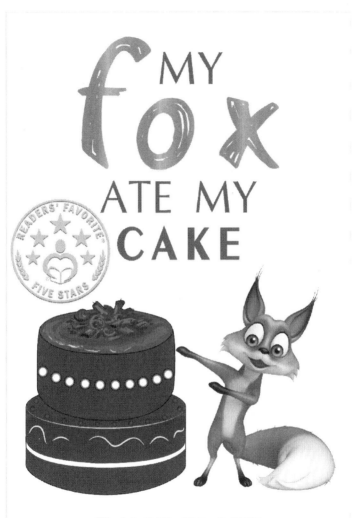

MY
fox
ATE MY
CAKE

READERS' FAVORITE
FIVE STARS

DAVID BLAZE

CONTENTS

FRIDAY AFTERNOON

I stared across the rickety old table and into the eyes of my sworn enemy—Shane Connors. The school bully had grown another two inches taller and three times meaner than the first day I met him. I wanted to crawl under the table and hide forever.

It was my twelfth birthday party and my mom had invited half of the school to surprise me in my backyard. I was surprised alright. Shane had been standing in the middle of everyone, pounding his fists together and laughing at me. It was my fault he was there. I never told my mom about him and the homework assignment I wrote for him.

She had set the backyard up with tons of games she thought the kids would love, like Poop the Potato—where two kids raced with potatoes between their legs then 'pooped' the potatoes into buckets. Seriously? I wasn't exactly the coolest guy at school, but whatever reputation I had was destroyed with the word Poop.

I glanced across the yard at my house and through the sliding glass door. All of the adults were inside doing whatever adults do. My mom looked back at me, smiled, and gave me two thumbs up. I love my mom and I'd do anything for her, but she had created my worst nightmare on my biggest day.

She had put together another table covered with every kind of candy you can imagine. She called it a candy buffet. Chocolate, licorice, mints, gummies … everything! The candy was piled so high that it would take weeks to eat it all.

But there was one problem. One *major* problem.

My mom had decided whoever won each game would win a handful of candy. It sounded fair, but Shane won every game. He had a plastic bag full of candy he kept waving in front of our faces. Every other kid complained to me that they couldn't get any.

I flinched when Shane stretched his arm across the unsteady table. He rested his elbow on the table and raised his hand straight up. "You're going to lose, Jonah," he snickered. "You know why?" He flexed his arm and stared at his biceps. "Because that's what losers do, Jonah." I bit my lip because I didn't like being called that name and he knew it.

This was an arm-wrestling contest, and he had already beaten every other kid there. He was so big and strong that it was a joke to think anyone could win against him. I'd be lucky enough to walk away without a cast on my hand.

I looked around at all the kids surrounding us in a circle. There were at least thirty of them. Most of them were on my side of the table. My mind screamed for one of them to take my place. My heart raced in fear. This didn't feel like a birthday party at all!

I took a deep breath and put my elbow next to Shane's on the table. I locked my hand with his and sat up straight. Maybe I could lessen the impact of my hand being crushed.

My cousin Dana leaned across the table and asked if we were ready. I nodded. She had light brown hair tied back in two ponytails and huge dimples when she smiled. But she seldom smiled. She was only seven years old and was always in charge of everything. Some people would call her bossy. I wondered how we could come from the same family. "Go!" she shouted.

I tightened my grip and pressed against Shane's hand as hard as I could. My only goal was to walk away without someone calling an ambulance for me.

But that didn't happen.

My hand didn't sway one way or the other. I looked back into Shane's eyes, confused. He was sweating and pushing as hard as he could. Was this really happening? I wouldn't have thought it in a million years, but I was as strong as him.

Dana looked at me and almost smiled. She shouted my name. "Joe!" I'm glad she didn't call me Jonah. I have my reasons for being called Joe. Dana turned to each side and shouted, "Joe! Joe! Joe! Joe!"

The other kids joined her and chanted in unison, "Joe! Joe! Joe! Joe!" I felt stronger every time they shouted my name. Shane's hand began to sink toward the table. This was really happening! I was going to beat him!

"You can do it, Joe," Melissa assured me from the side. She was pretty with her huge smile and long, brown ponytails. I remembered the first time I met her in school a few months ago. She gave me hope. I wasn't allowed to have a girlfriend yet, but if I was, I'd want it to be her. "I believe in you."

For the first time ever, I saw fear in Shane's eyes. I'll never forget how embarrassed he was after reading the paper I wrote for him at school. I had avoided him every day after that until now. I thought for sure he would beat me up.

Shane's hand was only inches from the table. I was about to win. Why had I been so afraid of him? I needed to be more like Dana. She was small and young, but she wasn't afraid of anyone. I smirked at Shane as I prepared to tap his hand on the table.

But that didn't happen either.

Shane lurched forward. A sharp pain shot

through my leg. Not the kind of pain that makes you want to find an aspirin. This was the kind of pain that made me want to scream like a fox!

I lost my concentration. Shane slammed my hand on the table then jumped out of his seat and threw his arms up in victory.

I fell out of my chair and grabbed my leg. It was swelling up like a basketball. The pain was unbearable. I panted so hard I could barely breathe. I wanted to vomit. I pointed at Shane. "You cheated."

Melissa kneeled next to me. "Are you okay?"

I shook my head. I took a few deep breaths and let my heartbeat slow down. "He kicked me," I complained. "I was going to win, and he kicked me."

Shane towered over me and laughed. It reminded me of the first day I met him. He had shoved me down and stood over me just like now. "You should've never messed with me," he barked. "Now you're going to pay."

Before I could respond, Dana jumped in front of Shane and pushed him back. He didn't move far because she was so much younger and smaller than him. "Back off, you big lug!" she shouted. "Leave him alone!"

Shane looked past her and down at me. He howled like this was the funniest thing he'd ever seen. "You can't even fight for yourself," he spit at me. "A little girl has to do it for you. How pathetic!"

One kid in the crowd chuckled. Everyone else stared with blank expressions. None of them were brave enough to stand up to this monster, but my little cousin was. I stood up slowly and balanced my weight on my good leg. I was as wobbly as the table we were just sitting at.

Dana turned to face me and held her palm out. "I've got this," she said confidently. And I knew she did, so I nodded. I stood close because I wasn't going to let anything bad happen to her. "You know what else is pathetic?" she asked as she faced Shane again. He looked like a mountain in front of her. "It's pathetic when it takes a little girl like me to beat a big girl like you."

Everyone laughed and cheered for Dana. They pointed at Shane and said things like, "She called him a girl!" and "He's a big girl!" They hooted and hollered until Shane grabbed his bag of candy and marched right past me.

"You're dead meat," he promised me before he disappeared back into the house. I had no doubt he meant every word.

Dana grabbed my hand and held it up as high as she could. "Winner!" she declared. I knew she meant I was the winner of the arm-wrestling match, but I had won so much more. Everyone cheered for me.

I looked over at the huge table of candy, knowing I had won the next handful. It was too far for me to walk until the throbbing in my leg went away. "Melissa, get two handfuls of candy for me, please."

She gave me a confused, weird look. I could tell she was disappointed I was willing to break the rules. We were only allowed to take one handful when we won. "It's okay," I told her. "It's my party, so it's my candy."

She sighed before walking to the table and doing exactly what I asked. When she returned, she shoved her hands toward me full of candy. "Just take it," she said, shaking her head. "You're not the person I thought you were."

"I'm sorry," I replied, feeling like I had lost a friend. I pointed at all the kids around us. "But that candy's not for me. It's for everyone else." They had been complaining all afternoon that they couldn't get any candy because Shane kept winning it all. This was my way of making things right.

The kids rushed to Melissa and accepted the candy from her. She wouldn't stop smiling at me. I had a feeling we were still friends.

"Let's hear it for Joe!" Dana shouted, standing by my side and holding my arm up again. Everyone chanted with her like before.

"Joe! Joe! Joe! Joe!"

It was a wonderful feeling, and I wish I could say the rest of the day was as awesome. But even after everything that had happened with Shane, it was all about to get ten times worse.

LATER FRIDAY

I tried my best not to smile when my mom and Uncle Mike walked into the backyard, holding a huge chocolate cake and singing "Happy Birthday". I was trying to look cool around my friends, but I was too excited to hide it. Officially twelve years old and one year away from being a teenager. Almost there!

My mom set the cake down on the same rickety table I had arm-wrestled Shane on. Where was he at? His dad, Mr. Connors, stood behind my mom and uncle with all the other parents. He had a smelly cigar in his mouth the last time I saw him. He tried to take this house away from us when we moved into it and my mom couldn't pay my late great-grandma's property taxes. I didn't trust him.

The other kids hovered over me and the cake. They were starving because the candy they got wasn't much at all.

"Make a wish, Jonah," my mom said. She was the only person allowed to call me that name. I only wanted one thing at that moment. I wished

Fox was there to share this day with me. My stomach hurt just thinking about it. My best friend couldn't be there for his own protection.

After I blew the candles out, my uncle cut the cake and handed it on small plates to the kids. They devoured it right away and begged for more. I could only laugh.

"Why are you limping?" my mom asked.

I had forgotten about my bad leg. I didn't want her to know about Shane and worry about me. I also didn't want my uncle to hear that Dana challenged a guy ten times her size. My mom had done a lot to make this party happen and surprise me. I wasn't going to ruin it for her. "I banged it against that table," I told her, pointing at it.

"It's pretty bad," she said, sounding concerned. "Come inside when you're done, and we'll clean it up." I looked down at it. It was as red as an apple. "Before you do anything else, someone wants to wish you a happy birthday. He's pretty shy." She motioned for me to step away from the other kids. I sighed and threw my hands up. We had been playing games in the backyard for what felt like hours and I could barely stand up. Now some kid wanted to wish me happy birthday? It had to be Shy Steve. That guy always sat by himself and avoided everyone.

I hobbled behind my mom past the outhouse and chicken coop. I remembered the first time I saw Fox there. I thought he was a dog—even with his brown hair that was almost orange, chest and tail that were white, and paws as black as night. I had fallen flat on my butt when he stood up on two legs and talked to me like a little kid. Ha!

My mom stopped by the back fence and faced me. "What?" I asked her. "Why are we here?" I knew the answer when I saw bright blue eyes peering through the bushes.

It was Fox!

"I'll give you two a few minutes," my mom promised. She smiled and headed back towards the party. We were well out of view of everyone. This was the one gift I wanted. I hadn't seen Fox in months. He had been searching for something.

He leaped over the fence and stood in front of me on his two hind legs. It amazed me how much he moved like a human. I was worried because he wasn't smiling anymore and had a serious look on his face. "If you dig a hole over there," he said, pointing to the far end of the fence, "you'll make it to China." He rubbed his chin and smirked. "And you know what they have in China?"

"Gold!" we both shouted at the same time. I couldn't stop smiling. He had tricked me once, but I researched it on the internet. You can't dig a hole to China.

"And why?" he continued.

"Because they have rainbows!" we said together. We both fell down laughing. My sides hurt as much from laughing as my bad leg hurt from Shane's kick. Fox kept rolling over and jumping up and down. I had missed this. I wished he could stay with me, but he was a wild animal. I was grateful for any time I could spend with him.

"I want to give you this," Fox said. I sat up when he handed me a wrapped present. "It's not much, and your mom helped."

It was awesome that he got me something for my birthday. He couldn't go into stores or even be seen in public. We agreed it was dangerous if other people found out what Fox could do. I opened the package to find a silver bracelet. "Thanks, Fox!"

"We're best friends, right?" he asked me. Of course we were. I couldn't imagine my life without him.

"We sure are," I promised him.

He wiped his forehead with a paw. "That's a good thing. Because otherwise I would look ridiculous in this." He had a bracelet just like mine beneath his paw. My mom had somehow fitted it for him.

I was grateful to have him in my life. I don't know how I ever lived without him. I couldn't explain our friendship to anyone else, but I never wanted to lose it.

I turned when a twig snapped behind me.

Shane was standing there with his cell phone pointed at us. It took a second for me to realize he had recorded Fox talking to me. My heart stopped. This couldn't be happening! "I knew you were a freak. I've got you now," he threatened.

I faced Fox, pointed at the fence, and shouted, "Run!"

He leaped over the fence and disappeared back into the woods. I stared into the bushes and tried to figure out how to explain this to Shane. Surely he had a heart and wouldn't put Fox in any danger. I had to convince him to delete that video on his phone. I took a deep breath, prepared to beg my sworn enemy, and turned back to face him.

He was gone!

I watched him race past the outhouse and back into the crowd of kids and parents.

He was going to tell all the other kids and adults what he saw and then show them the proof. I ignored the pain in my leg and ran after him. I had no idea what he planned to do with that video, but it couldn't be good. I had embarrassed him more than once and he wanted to destroy me.

The backyard was crowded with kids and

adults when I reached it—talking, laughing, pooping potatoes—none of them realizing my whole world was about to fall apart. I scanned through the crowd until I saw Shane next to the candy table by the back door.

He was with his dad, Mr. Connors. I couldn't breathe. Shane had his cell phone in front of his dad's face, playing the video he had recorded. They both looked up and stared at me.

I couldn't move. I was paralyzed.

Mr. Connors grabbed Shane and headed out of the yard. I couldn't let that happen.

"Stop!" I yelled. Everyone froze and stared at me. Then Mr. Connors did something I never expected.

He reached back to the candy table, grabbed two huge bowls full of candy, tossed the candy into the air and in front of me. "Candy for everyone!" he shouted.

The kids were scattered all over the backyard, but it only took a second for all of them to run in front of me and snatch the candy. They pushed and shoved. They were animals! And they completely blocked me!

I fought my way through the crowd, one kid at a time, desperate to get to Shane and his dad. Time was running out.

When I made it to the candy table, they were gone. The phone was gone. The video was gone. My hopes were gone. Tires squealed from the front yard. Shane and his dad were long gone.

"Is something wrong?" my mom asked, standing in front of me. "There's a lot more candy. And you have to eat some of your cake." She was the only person who could help me now. She had saved me more than once.

"Yep," my uncle Mike said, walking up to us with a plateful of cake in his hands. He had frosting all over his lips. "No one bakes a cake like your mom."

I tried my best not to cry, but I couldn't help it.

"Jonah," my mom said, "what's going on?" I could tell her because she knew about Fox. But I couldn't tell my uncle. He almost found out about Fox the same night my mom had, but we decided not to tell him. He was, after all, a hunter. The fewer people who knew we had a walking, talking fox the better.

"They know," I told my mom.

She gave me a confused look until I nodded at her. Then her eyes got big. "Who?"

I shook my head and balled my fists in anger. "Mr. Connors and his son." My stomach ached. "They recorded it."

Her eyes got even bigger. She searched through the crowd and realized Shane and his dad were gone. She cleared her throat and said, "Okay." She turned to my uncle. "We need to get everyone out of here. The party's over."

He stared at his plate and complained, "But I just started eating this cake." She grabbed him and turned him toward the kids and adults.

"Everyone, listen up!" my mom shouted into the crowd. "Thank you for coming today. I hope you had fun. We have a family emergency we need to handle. Please gather your things and leave as quickly as possible."

Some kids groaned. Their parents grabbed them and left one by one. My uncle Mike rushed them out, not even knowing why. I was amazed at his and my mom's ability to get everyone out so quickly, especially since there was so much candy and cake left behind.

Melissa grabbed my arm on her way out. "Is everything okay?"

I wished I could tell her the truth. Other than

my mom, I trusted her more than anyone else. "I hope so."

"Alright now," my uncle Mike said, "keep it moving." He ushered her and her mom out of the yard.

Less than a few minutes later, the only people left in my backyard were me, my mom, my uncle, and my little cousin Dana. "Does this mean we get all the candy?" Dana asked.

My uncle Mike huffed. "No, it doesn't, young lady," he assured her. He looked back at my mom. "Does it?"

She was deep in thought and staring at the chicken coop. When she got like this, she couldn't hear anyone or even sense anything around her. She was formulating a plan.

My uncle grabbed her shoulders and shook her. "Sis? Mind telling me what just happened?" She was lost when she came out of her trance.

Then the one voice I didn't expect to hear interrupted everything.

"This doesn't taste like chicken," Fox complained, standing behind my uncle. He had cake all over his face and was trying to lick it off.

Why was he revealing himself? I was worried about what was going to happen when my uncle turned around. No one could be prepared for what he was about to see.

"Look, kid," my uncle said, turning around, "the party's oooooooo... Oh, my gosh! Is that fox standing up and talking to me?"

Fox winked at me and raised his paws toward my uncle. "Sneak attack!"

Dana stepped forward and yelled, "Awesome! A talking fox!"

I didn't know if my uncle would accept Fox. I didn't know what was going to happen with that video Shane recorded. All I knew was one thing—Fox was in danger, and I'd protect him as long as I could.

FRIDAY NIGHT

Fox agreed to stay inside with us until we figured out how to deal with Shane and his dad. We didn't know what to expect. I was happy to have my best friend in the house again because he had disappeared for so long. I hated it, but he said there was something he had to do— something he had to search for.

I had done a lot of research about foxes and learned what they liked to eat. They liked chickens! I couldn't believe Fox had tricked me so many times so he could get to the chicken coop. But we solved that problem. My mom kept chicken in the fridge and freezer so Fox could eat some any time he was there.

Fox and Dana were in my room with me that night. My mom sent us there so she and my uncle could talk about Fox. They were brother and sister and loved each other, but there was a lot of yelling from the kitchen. I don't think my uncle approved of Fox at all.

Dana thought Fox was the most awesome thing ever. She kept petting him and talking to him like a baby. "Who's a good fox?" she said. "You are. Yes, you are!" Then she wrapped her arms around him and petted him. I don't think he was ever petted before, but he didn't have any problem with it. He rolled over on his back and let her rub his belly.

She lay down next to him and fell asleep within minutes. I put a blanket over her because I didn't know if my uncle planned to stay for the night. I guess she was exhausted from a long afternoon outside. We all were.

I yawned and stretched my arms out. "We should go to sleep," I told Fox. "I've got a feeling this is going to be a long weekend." I jumped on my bed. "You can sleep anywhere you want." I stood and took the top blanket off my bed, and laid it next to me on the floor. "This should be comfortable."

Fox shook his head. "I can't sleep here. This isn't anything like a den." He looked around the room like he was scared of it. I remembered the time I stayed in a hotel room with my mom. It was cool, but the bed didn't feel like mine, the room was freezing, the air conditioning made knocking sounds all night, and I could hear people talking outside. It was uncomfortable, and I didn't get any sleep.

"I have an idea," I said. I opened my closet and pulled out three more blankets. Then I stepped out of my room and grabbed two chairs from the kitchen. I don't think my mom or uncle even noticed me because they were still arguing.

Back in my room, I set one chair on each side. I pulled my bookcase out of the corner and dragged it next to my bed. I grabbed a handful of pins out of the billboard on my wall.

"What's going on?" Fox asked, scratching his head.

"Watch the magic," I told him. I grabbed a blanket, stretched it out, and then laid one end across one chair and the other end across the other chair. I put the back of it on top of the bookcase. That made it look like a tent. It had gaps of air in some spaces because the blanket couldn't cover everything. I grabbed the other blankets and stretched them high across other areas of the room and pinned them to the walls as high as I could. Most of the room looked like a huge tent now. Maybe like a crazy person built it—but still like a tent.

"Welcome to my den," I said to Fox. I lifted one blanket end off the floor and revealed the room within it. Fox wagged his tail and stepped inside with me. It was dark, but I had grabbed a flashlight. I had learned to do all of this with my friend Tommy in the second grade. I had forgotten how much fun it was.

I turned the flashlight on and sat it straight up on the floor. It lit up the new den. "What do you think?" I asked Fox.

"It'll do." He gazed up at the blankets above us and smiled. He was happier here. I understood there were too many distractions in a room he had never slept in.

"This is fun," I said. "Hey—wanna hear a riddle?"

Fox threw his paws up. "What's a riddle?"

I guess he still had a lot to learn. I was glad he chose me to teach him. "It's like a joke."

"What's a joke?"

This was going to be harder than I thought. "A joke is like a funny story. A riddle is like a funny question."

He scratched his head.

"Okay," I said, "let's try one." I laughed before I even asked the question. I had read the riddle in a joke book years ago. "What has four wheels and flies?"

Fox rubbed his chin and stared at me. "I

know the answer!" He smiled and said proudly, "It's a bird."

I shook my head. "Birds don't have wheels."

He blinked his eyes and pursed his lips. "What are wheels?"

I ran my hands through my hair. This was like trying to teach someone another language. "Cars and trucks have wheels. It's what makes them go." He still didn't understand. "Anyways, the answer is 'garbage truck.' A garbage truck has four wheels and it has flies—so it has four wheels and flies!" I tried to keep a straight face but couldn't stop laughing.

Fox looked at me like I was crazy. But he was a much faster learner than I thought. "I have a riddle. Wanna hear it?"

I made the mistake of saying, "Okay."

"Are you ready for this?" he asked. He laughed the same way I did before I asked my riddle. There was no way his could be better than mine. "What has four legs and farts?"

I tried to stop him, but it was too late. He let a fart rip that was so loud and so long that all the blankets around us flapped like there was a tornado!

And then there was the smell. It was trapped in the den with us. It smelled like tuna and broccoli and onions and vinegar and dirty feet and dirty underwear all mixed together. It was disgusting.

"Whew," Fox said. "No more cake for me."

I couldn't breathe. I could taste the foul smell in my mouth. I pulled my shirt up over my nose and sucked in as little air as I could. I was worried I was going to pass out.

My bedroom door opened. I flicked the flashlight off so no one could see us.

"I'll get her," my uncle said. He was talking about Dana. "See you in the morning, Sis." His footsteps were louder on his way out.

"I wonder where Jonah and Fox could be," my mom said. "I don't see them anywhere."

I held a finger over my lips for Fox to keep quiet. This was a good den and I put a lot of work into it. No one would ever find us.

"What's that smell?" she asked. I knew exactly what it was. Fox's smelly fart. "Is that … is that sour cream and onion?"

Fox and I burst out laughing at the same time. Sour cream and onion! I hoped I never had to eat anything that tasted like that horrible smell around us.

"Is someone in there?" my mom asked. I guessed the jig was up. She knew someone was in the den, and it was our own fault.

I lifted up the blanket closest to her and stayed hidden behind it. I disguised my voice to sound like Darth Vader. "What's the password?"

She huffed and said, "I don't know the password, but I have a pizza that's half pepperoni and half chicken. Do you know anyone who wants some?"

I reached out and snatched the pizza tray from her. Before closing the den blanket, I accidentally said, "Thank you," in my real voice.

"That was close," I told Fox. "She almost saw us." I flicked the flashlight back on. Fox licked his lips when he saw the chicken on his half of the pizza. We both laughed and munched on our den meal. I loved pepperoni and Fox loved chicken. My mom was the best mom ever.

Fox burped when he was done. I have no idea how his little body held so much gas. I yawned and reached out of the den for my pillow and a blanket big enough to cover both of us.

"Where do you go, Fox?" I asked him as I lay down and put part of the blanket over me. "When you don't come back for a long time." I had never asked him before, but I had a right to know the answer. I missed him when he was gone.

He was sitting down with his paws in front of him. He was silent for a moment, but he finally said, "Looking for my parents."

I never thought about Fox having parents, but of course he did. I sat up and asked him, "Where are they?"

The silence felt awkward. Fox's tail was limp by his side. I wished I had never asked the question and we could go back to laughing about farts.

"I was playing with my parents in the woods. Hide and Seek." He paused and smiled. "I was good at it. We would laugh and play and hug for hours." His smile disappeared, and his eyes focused on the floor.

"Two men with long guns came into the woods while we were playing." He cleared his throat. "There was a loud bang, and the ground jumped up next to me. My parents yelled at me to run as fast as I could to the den. I did, and they were right behind me."

He fell silent again, and I didn't know if I should say something. I waited for him to continue.

"When we got there, they told me to go in first." He took a deep breath. "They said they loved me and were proud of me." He looked back at me. "Before I could stop them, they shoved me inside and buried me in with dirt and leaves."

I could tell he was hurting. Why did I have to ask him about this? I had no idea what happened to his parents or where they were. I couldn't imagine living with both of them gone. I was lucky to have my mom.

"I screamed for my parents to come inside. The den became so dark and quiet." He laid his head on the floor. "And then I heard two more loud bangs." He took another deep breath. "I scratched at the dirt and leaves to get out, but it took me days. Once I made it, I couldn't find my parents anywhere."

My heart hurt for Fox. I didn't know if he understood what happened, but I had a pretty good idea. I wasn't going to tell him.

He sat up again. "I wandered around for weeks, searching for food and water. And then I found this place." His tail wagged a little. "I found you."

I tried not to yawn. I had to say something to him. "I'm sorry, Fox. No matter what happens, I will always protect you."

He stood up on all four paws. "Your mom's awesome. Where's your dad?"

I froze. I didn't expect that question to come up, and I wasn't prepared to answer it. I was afraid the other kids would think I was different. But this was my best friend. I was safe with him. He had just told me about the darkest moment in his life. Now I could tell him about mine.

I stared at my hands. "Two men in army

uniforms came to our house in the city a few months ago." It was raining hard that day. I remembered my mom crying and screaming when they knocked on the door. "They said my dad wasn't coming back."

Fox put a paw on my hand. "We're more alike than I thought."

I nodded. "My mom lost her job soon after that, and we moved here. We left everything behind, but I'll never forget my dad. He taught me three things: Honesty, integrity, and compassion. He's the greatest man I've ever known. I hope I can be like him one day."

Fox laid his head on my leg and yawned. "He was a great man. What was his name?"

I wanted to make sure his name was never forgotten. "His name is Joe."

I lay back down and pulled the blanket over me and Fox. He cuddled up to my side. He felt warm and comfortable. We were both exhausted. I wasn't even sure if half of what I said made any sense. I flicked the flashlight off. "Fox?"

"Yes?"

"It still smells like sour cream and onion in

here." I couldn't get the taste out of my mouth. It was disgusting.

"Nah," he said. "It smells more like farts." We both giggled.

I had one last thought before I closed my eyes and fell asleep. "I'm glad you're my best friend."

He yawned for the last time. "And I'm glad you're mine."

SATURDAY MORNING

My mom woke me up early in the morning and told me to get ready. She was crazy! First of all, how did she find me inside of that den? Second, I wasn't going anywhere without Fox.

"We're going to the farmers' market," my mom said. "Come on—the day won't wait for us forever." I was pretty sure the day would wait however long we needed it to.

"What about Fox?" I asked, pointing at him next to me. He was still asleep, and his tongue was sticking sideways out of his mouth. There was slobber everywhere.

"He'll be fine," my mom assured me. "Uncle Mike and Dana came back to watch him." She threw a T-shirt and a pair of jeans at me. "Get dressed." She walked out of the den and out of my room.

I slid the clothes on but didn't understand

why we were doing this. Our number one priority had to be to protect Fox—not to sell rotten eggs at the farmers' market.

Fox woke up and wiped the slobber off his chin. "Where am I? And is there any chicken?"

I shook my head and told him about what my mom had planned. He didn't seem to care one way or the other. He kept talking about how his stomach was growling and he needed chicken. Barbecued chicken, baked chicken, fried chicken, chicken pot pie, chicken soup, chicken and rice—he wouldn't stop talking about it.

I led him into the kitchen. My mom and uncle were sitting at the table, drinking coffee. "Haven't seen the two chairs that are missing, have you?" my mom asked. Sure, they were in my room. I had to keep them as long as Fox was with us so we'd have a den.

"I have no idea what you're talking about," I told her. She winked at me.

Dana ran into the kitchen and threw her arms around Fox. "Good morning!" she shouted. I couldn't believe how happy she was to see him. It was weird to see her like that when she was always so bossy. "What do you want to do today?"

He looked around at everyone in the room. "Eat chicken." I laughed because that's all he ever wanted to do. Dana would get bored with him soon enough.

My uncle shook his head and grunted. "This isn't right," he muttered. "It's not natural."

"Why can't we stay here?" I asked my mom. I didn't think it was safe to leave Fox with my uncle. He was a hunter and he didn't like Fox.

"We need to go," my mom said. "We don't want to draw any attention to ourselves. Everyone is expecting us to be there." She was right. We had made a lot of friends at the farmers' market and had a ton of loyal customers.

I didn't eat any breakfast because I felt sick

leaving Fox at home. I gave Dana instructions for keeping him entertained. He loved watching cartoons after he realized they weren't real and they weren't after him. My uncle Mike stared at Fox—I wasn't sure *he* wouldn't be after him.

One of the last things I heard when I walked out the door with my mom was Dana saying, "We can have a tea party."

As expected, Fox replied, "I have a better idea. We can have a chicken party."

***

"There's our table," my mom said when we got to the farmers' market. Everyone knew it belonged to us because my mom reserved it every Saturday for the rest of the year. It was the same wooden table we started at months ago when we didn't know anyone in town.

"Good morning, ya'll," Mr. Jim Bob said in his strong country accent. His table was right next to ours and full of fruits and vegetables he had grown in his own backyard. I never saw him without that big straw hat on his head. I wondered what his hair looked like—or if he even had any left.

FARM GROWN

"Good morning to you, Jim Bob," my mom replied, helping me set the eggs from our chickens on our table. We still sold half a dozen eggs for six dollars. I never understood why we didn't just say they were one dollar each. "Can I interest you in some fresh eggs today?"

Mr. Jim Bob shook his head and said, "I appreciate the offer, ma'am, but there's no way in God's green earth I'd ever eat your eggs again." He stared at me when I chuckled.

My mom had convinced him months ago to buy two dozen eggs because the chickens were farm raised. He was a hard sell because he could have gotten them cheaper at the grocery store. He was grateful to get the fresh eggs that came from chickens my great-grandma Rita had raised. But we didn't know Old Nelly's eggs were packed in his cartons.

"I was sick for weeks!" he reminded us for the thousandth time. "I had to eat my food through a straw." He exaggerated, but there was some truth to it. Old Nelly was my great-grandma's favorite chicken, but she only laid rotten eggs.

I looked into the crowd all around the park. I was hoping to find Melissa, she came most Saturdays and we would hang out. Sometimes we would share one of those hamburgers they grilled there. I was disappointed when I didn't see her. Everyone was wearing jeans and T-shirts. The most popular material of the day was flannel. I thought it was strange when we first came here from the big city, but now here I was wearing jeans and a T-shirt like everyone else.

"What are you doing with those eggs?" someone said from the side of our table. I smiled because I knew who it was. Mr. Hunter stepped over to me, smiled, and shook my hand. "Good to see you, Joe." He nodded at my mom. I wondered how he had that long, gray mustache and bushy eyebrows but no hair on his head.

"Leave him alone," Mrs. Hunter said when she passed him and hugged my mom. She used to have some brown in her hair, but it had turned completely gray. "He's got better things to do than talk to an old geezer like you."

He put his hands on his hips like he was offended. "Women," he said, shaking his head. "Can't live with them—can't live without them."

"Oh, you hush," she said, giggling like a teenage girl. They were very much in love. She pulled my mom aside and said they needed a minute to catch up.

"So," Mr. Hunter said to me, "have you seen the gas prices lately? Almost three dollars a gallon!" I had no idea if that was good or bad, but I quickly calculated. I got a weekly allowance for doing my chores, and it was enough to get two gallons at that price. It took a lot more than that when I filled the gas tank for my mom.

"It's better than the old days," he continued. "I had to walk ten miles through the snow and sandspurs just to get to school." I doubted that was true because sandspurs can't grow in the snow. I nodded at him like I was amazed and believed everything he said.

"Jonathan," Mrs. Hunter said to him when she came back to us, "leave that boy alone. Quit trying to turn him into an old geezer like yourself." I tried not to laugh. She hooked an arm around his arm. "Let the kid enjoy his childhood while he can." She winked at me and pulled him away.

Mr. Hunter threw his hands up. "Sorry, Joe. Don't forget what I said about women."

I wanted to answer him, but I realized several kids were staring at me. Another pointed at me. I had no idea what their problem was. I moved my tongue around my teeth to make sure there wasn't something stuck in them. I didn't find anything. I looked down at my zipper to make sure it was up—all good.

Melissa caught me off guard when she appeared right in front of me. "Why didn't you tell me?" she asked. She wasn't smiling, and I had no idea what she was talking about. I could only stare at her, confused.

She pulled a cell phone out of her pocket, pushed a button on it, then shoved it in front of my face. I was shocked and wanted to tell her to be careful, but I couldn't. I saw the one thing I didn't expect to see.

A video of Fox talking to me was playing on her phone. It was the same one Shane had recorded. My heart was beating fast. "Where did you get this?"

She put the phone back in her pocket. "It's all over the internet. It already has over two million views." The twang in her voice got higher. "What's going on, Joe?"

All I could do was shrug my shoulders—even with all of the evidence in front of me. I don't sweat much, but my shirt was soaking wet. Melissa was the one person I had wanted to tell about Fox. Now that was taken away from me. Now the whole world knew about him.

"Let me see that again," I said to her. I was scared to death about what would happen to Fox. I couldn't even think straight because my head felt like it was about to explode. I grabbed the phone from Melissa and asked her to give me a minute. I had to show my mom. She agreed.

My mom was with another customer when I reached her. "Happy chickens make better tasting eggs," she told the man looking at the cartons.

She told me to hold on for a minute when I tried to get her attention. She was busy, but there wasn't any time to waste. I yelled her name. "Mom!"

She gave me an ugly face that let me know I

was in big trouble. "I'll be right back," she told the customer. She grabbed me and pulled me aside. "Don't ever yell at me again. What's gotten into you?"

I put the phone in front of her face and let the video play, the same way Melissa had. My mom froze. I didn't think she was even breathing. "Mom? What are we gonna do?"

She snapped out of her trance and told me to get into the car because we needed to go home right away. I didn't argue. I grabbed the phone from her and gave it back to Melissa. "I'm sorry," I told her. "I'll explain everything later."

"What about my eggs?" the customer my mom had been with asked.

"Take them," she said. "You can pay me when you buy more next week.

SATURDAY AFTERNOON

My mom drove through town like a race car driver. She sped through every light. The tires squealed with every turn. I held on to my seat as tight as I could.

I ran to the house when we got there, not knowing what to expect. Uncle Mike didn't answer his cell phone when my mom called him from the farmers' market. I feared the worst. Maybe someone had seen the video and broken into our house. Maybe they had kidnapped Fox!

I threw the door open and nearly fainted.

Fox was sitting on the couch with my uncle, watching wrestling on TV. They were laughing and high fiving each other. I had thought for sure my uncle Mike would never accept him. "That's gonna hurt!" Fox shouted at the TV.

"Get a real job!" my uncle joined in.

My mom sighed and shook her head. "Boys will be boys." She walked over to the couch, tapped my uncle on the shoulder, and told him they needed to talk. He told her that he was busy bonding with his new friend and the wrestling match would be over soon.

She grabbed the remote control from him and turned the TV off. "Mr. Awesome Muscles was about to make his move!" Fox whined. "The world needs his awesomeness!"

My mom huffed and said to my uncle, "You ruined him."

Fox stood up on the couch and flexed his hairy arms. "My name is Mr. Awesome Muscles. Prepare to feel my awesomeness!"

I couldn't stop laughing. Fox didn't have a single muscle on his body. I was surprised he didn't run from the big men fighting in their underwear on TV. I remembered when he was scared of cartoons and hid behind the couch.

"Calm down, Mr. Awesome Muscles," my

mom said, trying not to laugh. She took out her cell phone and held it up for Fox and my uncle to see. She had found the video of Fox and was playing it.

My uncle stood up and said, "We have to do something." He looked at Fox like he was worried for him.

"I couldn't agree more," my mom said, turning to me. "Jonah, take Fox and Dana out back to feed the chickens. The grownups need to talk."

"But, Mom…" I said. I needed to be a part of whatever they were planning. I knew more about Fox than anyone else. And I had promised to protect him.

She came to me and put a hand on my shoulder. "Let us talk for a minute, Jonah," she said softly so only I could hear. "We have to figure out what's best for Fox." She nodded slowly to make sure I understood. "We need to review all of our options, and we don't want to scare him. He's fragile."

Fox yelled from the couch, "My name is Mr. Awesome Muscles, and I'm going to bring the pain!"

"Maybe not too fragile," my mom said, patting my shoulder. I realized she wanted Fox out of the house so he didn't hear anything discussed that might scare him. And she wanted to make sure I could protect him.

"Come on, Fox," I said. "Let's go outside and play. You've been cooped up in here since yesterday." My mom smiled at me.

Dana walked into the living room from the kitchen with a tray of chicken nuggets in her hands. "What did I miss?"

I stepped outside with Dana and Fox and wondered what was going to happen next. I feared my best friend was in terrible danger.

"I'm not cleaning this up," Dana said with her arms crossed. "Your party, your mess—you do it." I didn't know what she meant at first and why she was so feisty, but when I looked at the backyard I realized it was a mess from my birthday party the day before.

"Is there any more cake?" Fox asked. I ignored him because, after that nasty fart last night, I'd never let him eat cake again.

I looked at both of them like they were nuts. I held up the bag of chicken feed I brought with me. "We're just going to feed the chickens."

"Oh," Dana said, snatching the bag from me. "You should have said something sooner." She walked past us and kicked a balloon floating over the grass.

"You know what we should do?" Fox asked, rubbing his paws together. "We should find out what's inside that outhouse once and for all." He had a mischievous grin on his face that made me think he was up to something.

"You're not trying to trick me again—are you, Fox?" He had distracted me in the past so he could get to the chickens. I thought we had solved that problem, but old habits are hard to break.

"You have my word," he promised. "You know you wanna do it. I'll cover for you."

Dana came back to us. "What's taking you guys so long?" Her eyes were bulging out of her head like she was angry at us. "I'm not feeding those chickens by myself." She shoved the bag of feed back into my hands. "You do it."

"He wants to see what's in the outhouse," Fox told her. "But he's a scaredy-cat." I assured him that wasn't true. My mom wouldn't let me use the outhouse, and that made me want to see what was inside more than anything else.

"So you're a chicken?" Dana taunted me. "I get it. Everyone's scared of something." She nodded her head. "You're scared of an outhouse." She tucked her arms in and flapped them like wings. "Chicken. Bawk, bawk."

Fox licked his lips. "Mm, chicken."

I wasn't a chicken and told them as much. It was awesome to have a toilet outside. "I'll go in if you promise not to tell." They both nodded. Fox was standing with both front paws behind his back. I wasn't sure if he had a way to cross his fingers, but I was worried he did.

"Go on, chicken," Dana said, laughing. "Show us what you're made of."

I set the bag of feed down and marched to the outhouse. It was a wooden tower with a half-moon carved into it. I read on the internet that the moon had two purposes. In the old days, the half-moon meant it was for women. A star on the door meant it was for men. The main reason it was there was to let light in.

I took a deep breath and reached for the lock to open the outhouse door. I almost changed my mind because my mom told me to stay away from it. Maybe there was something inside I wasn't supposed to see. Maybe it was dangerous.

"Chicken!" Dana shouted. "Bawk, bawk, bawk, bawk." I turned to see Fox had joined her in flapping his arms and strutting around in circles.

I yanked the door open to show them I wasn't afraid. They'd have to eat their words.

Something green jumped out and attacked me! I ran from the outhouse as fast as I could, screaming for help.

Fox and Dana fell on the ground, laughing. They didn't care about me. My life was in danger, and all they could do was laugh.

"What's all that ruckus?" my mom asked, sticking her head out the back door. "I told you kids to feed the chickens."

"Joe's scared of a grasshopper," Dana said, laughing at my expense. "It jumped on him, and he can't stop screaming."

Fox nodded his head. "Look, I'm a chicken." He stood back up on his hind legs and flapped his arms.

My mom rubbed her temples. "Quit playing around. Go feed the chickens." She disappeared back inside, shaking her head.

The grasshopper jumped off of me and I was fine once I could breathe again. To be fair, I had no idea it was a grasshopper. All I knew was I was attacked. I should've listened to my mom and stayed out of the outhouse.

Dana and Fox joined me at the chicken coop. "Told you I wasn't a chicken," I informed them. They laughed at me.

"Mr. Awesome Muscles wouldn't have run," Fox said. "No sir."

I was glad no one else had seen what happened. And I hoped they never found out. Being in the sixth grade was hard enough already. "Just feed the chickens."

We grabbed handfuls of feed and threw it out to them as they wandered the fenced in area around the coop. Fox kept licking his lips.

As I watched the chickens eat, I realized Old Nelly wasn't outside. I didn't think Fox had anything to do with it, but I had to find out where she was. "I'll be back in a minute," I told Fox and Dana. "I need to check on Old Nelly."

Fox took a step back. "Good luck. She likes to throw those rotten eggs. Don't come back smelling like farts." It was a risk I would have to take.

I stepped into the chicken coop and looked for her. I looked high. I looked low. I found her perched in the back, eyes closed, breathing heavily. Something was wrong.

I had no idea what to do. I had to tell my mom. Did they have a doctor for chickens? I hoped so because this was my great-grandma's favorite chicken and the last piece of her we had left. It was funny she thought Old Nelly laid golden eggs.

I turned to head out of the chicken coop to see if my mom was ready for us to come back into the house yet. I hoped they had good news for what we planned to do with Fox. I'd do whatever they wanted to keep him safe.

"Wait," some woman said from the back of the chicken coop. My heart jumped. I swear there wasn't anyone in there with me. I turned back to see Old Nelly stepping off of

her rotten eggs. Her eyes popped open.
"Please wait."

If that had happened a few months ago, I
would have run out of there screaming for my
life. I should have believed it when my great-
grandma said Old Nelly talked to her.

"You have her eyes," Old Nelly said. I
didn't know who she was talking about. I
walked back to the old chicken. I kept my
distance in case she wanted to throw one of
her smelly eggs at me.

"Whose eyes?" I asked her.

Her breathing was hard, and she had a
difficult time speaking. "Rita's. You have
Rita's eyes." That was my great-grandma. My

mom always said I favored her.

"Do you need help?" I asked her.

She tried to laugh. "I'm not a spring chicken anymore. My time is near." I think she smiled at me, but it was hard to tell because I'd never seen a chicken smile. "Rita made this a wonderful life for me. I enjoyed our conversations."

I wanted to know more about my great-grandma, but Old Nelly was speaking slower and slower. I had one question I needed to know the answer to.

"How did you and Fox learn to talk?"

Her eyes were half closed like she couldn't keep them open. I was afraid I would never hear the answer.

"This place is magical," she said painfully. "I was chosen to be here." She took a deep breath. "So was the fox." The next thing she said left me with more questions than answers.

"So were you, Joe." She closed her eyes and didn't move again or say anything else. How did she know my name? How did she live so long? What did she mean I was chosen? Chosen for what?

I stepped out of the chicken coop and let the sun hit my face. I was so confused I couldn't sense anything else around me. I only knew Old Nelly for a few minutes, but I would never forget her and what she said.

"Kids!" my mom shouted from the back porch. "Come back inside!" A few seconds after that she shouted, "Was someone in the outhouse?"

I had no intention of answering that question. I joined Fox and Dana as we headed back to the house.

Fox sniffed my pants and said, "At least you don't smell any worse than you did before you went in there."

"Gee, thanks," was all I could say.

When we got back into the house, my mom had us sit on the couch in the living room. Fox had left some hairs behind on it. I picked them off, one at a time.

My mom and uncle stood in front of us. "We all know Fox was recorded talking in a video," my mom said. "That video has been seen by more than three million people now."

Dana faced Fox and put out a hand for a high five. "You're famous!"

My uncle said, "That's not a good thing. There's no other animal like Fox." He directed his attention to my best friend. "We don't know what this means for your future. You're going to receive a lot of attention."

Fox wasn't smiling. "I want to go home."

My mom sighed. "I don't think that's a good idea, Fox. People will be looking for you. Good people and bad people."

I could tell he was confused, and I knew he wanted to find his parents. "We'll take care of you. I'm sure we'll figure something out."

My mom agreed. "We need some time for this to blow over. We've already taken the first step."

I looked up at her. "What did you do?"

"I got in touch with Mr. Connors," my uncle said. "He assured me that he didn't know the video was online and he would never have allowed it. He's had his son take the video down." My mom showed us her phone. The link for the video was no longer available.

"This is good—right?" Fox asked.

"Yes," my mom agreed. "Mr. Connors wants to apologize for his son's behavior. I've invited them over for dinner tonight. We want to keep the peace."

I couldn't move. Shane was coming back here? In my house? I didn't trust him, and no matter what he said or did, I knew he had a mission to destroy me. Everyone around me was happy and relieved this was being resolved. I feared the real problem was only beginning.

SATURDAY NIGHT

I couldn't stop shaking as I helped my mom set the dinner table. I had goose bumps all over my arms like I did on my first day of school here in the country. I dropped a glass and it shattered on the floor. I was glad Fox didn't see any of that. I didn't want him to sense my fear. We had hidden him in the one place we didn't think anyone would look for a fox.

If I was rich, I would take Fox to Japan. I read about a village there where hundreds of foxes roam freely. You can run and play with them. Then he wouldn't have to worry about any of this and he could live with his own kind.

"Everything's going to work out," my mom promised. She grabbed a broom and dustpan.

I wanted to believe her, and I hoped she was right. I should have told her about Shane and how he bullied me, but there was too much going on. I didn't need her to worry about anything else at the moment.

I jumped when the doorbell rang. My sworn enemy was on the other side of the door with his dad. I wanted to leave the door locked and tell them to go away. But, instead, my mom told me to do the one thing that terrified me the most.

"Go let them in," she said. "I'll clean up this mess and get dinner on the table." I wanted to tell her that she could answer the door and I'd do everything else, but I didn't want her to know how nervous I was. I hoped I could get my uncle or Dana to do it, but they were at the dining table with their faces buried in their cell phones.

I took a deep breath, rolled my shoulders back, and headed for the front door. It wouldn't be that bad. They had already taken the video down. They wanted to make this right. Everything would be okay, like my mom said.

I opened the door and stared at the same face I had seen right there months ago. Mr. Connors was wearing the same striped suit he had on when he tried to take this house away from us for the IRS. The only thing missing was his smelly cigar. He was so big that I didn't see Shane behind him.

"Good evening, Joe," Mr. Connors said. "May we come in?"

Against my better judgment, I opened the door wide and let them in. It's not like I had a choice.

My uncle greeted Mr. Connors and led him to the dining table. Shane stepped in behind him and bent over to put his smug face in front of mine.

"You're dead meat, Jonah." He needed to come up with some new lines. Even though I had expected it, I swallowed hard.

"My name is Joe," I reminded him, slamming the door shut and almost catching his fingers in it. Maybe that would make him back off for the rest of the night.

My mom called everyone to the dining table because dinner was about to be served. Mr. Connors grabbed her hand and said, "I'm sincerely sorry for my son's behavior. That video should never have happened." I didn't like the way he was holding her hand. She slipped it away from him.

"But they're friends," he continued. He

redirected his attention to me. "And the boys were just having fun—right, Joe?"

I wasn't sure how to respond. Shane was definitely not my friend. And I never had fun with him. He had probably lied to his dad to save his hide.

Something didn't feel right. Mr. Connors didn't ask about Fox. He didn't even ask where Fox was.

The back door barreled open and slammed against the wall. I jumped. I had no idea who or what it was. But I saw the one thing that made my spine shiver. Shane and his dad were smiling.

A chubby man with a huge forehead and a hotdog nose walked right up to the dining table like it was his own house. He wouldn't stop laughing. "I got him, folks!" he shouted in the strongest country accent I'd ever heard. "No need to worry—I've got everything under control!"

Har!
Har!
Har!

My mom ran over and grabbed me. We both knew what he was talking about. But how? We had hidden Fox in the chicken coop. No logical person would look for him there.

"Who are you?" my uncle asked, standing up and challenging him. "What gives you the right to barge into this house?"

The man kept laughing. His tongue wouldn't stay inside of his mouth. "You don't know who I am? They know me around these parts!" He posed like he was a superhero about to get a picture. "I'm Tater the Exterminator!"

He held up a cage that he had been

holding by his side. Fox whimpered inside of it. Tater shook the cage and beat a fist against it. "Quiet down, you filthy animal!"

I saw Fox's blue eyes through the slits in the cage. He was in there—trapped, scared, alone. "It's Fox," I told my mom. "He's got Fox!"

Tater stared at me with empty eyes and laughed. "No need to shout, young man. Like I said, I've got everything under control." He shook the cage again. "This little guy ain't gonna bother anyone else. Guaranteed!"

My mom let go of me and stepped closer to the crazy man. "You can't take him," she insisted. "That fox is our pet, and he's not a danger to anyone."

Tater the Exterminator laughed at her and said that was impossible. "It's illegal to own a fox in the great state of Alabama!" He lowered his voice for the first time. "You seem like law abiding citizens who don't want any trouble." He shook his head like he was concerned. "I'd hate to report you to the police."

My mom glanced back at me like she was exhausted and shrugged. I couldn't accept that. This man couldn't leave our house with Fox.

"Mom, do something," I begged her.

Mr. Connors stood up from the table with Shane by his side. "I'm sure it's all just a big misunderstanding. I'll do whatever I can to fight this." I didn't believe him. Shane wanted to destroy me, and his dad was helping him do it.

"Don't worry, little guy," Tater the Exterminator said to me as he passed by with Fox in the cage. "This critter's gonna be relocated somewhere far away, where he can't bother anyone else." My mom grabbed me again and held me tight.

Shane and his dad followed Tater the Exterminator as they headed for the door. I knew they were all together. What were they going to do with Fox?

"Stop!" I shouted. My mom held me tighter as I tried to break free. "You can't take him!" My uncle Mike and Dana stood on either side of me.

"We'll get him back," my mom promised. "Whatever we have to do."

"I'll make some calls," my uncle assured me.

Shane turned and smiled at me. "I told you not to mess with me," he gloated. With that, he walked out the door with his father, Tater the Exterminator, and my best friend—Fox.

"No!" I shouted. I couldn't stop crying.

Shane slammed the door shut behind them.

"Come back!" I screamed. "Please come back!"

SUNDAY MORNING

I sat in the church pew farthest in the back, hoping no one would see me. My mom called people who sat there Back Row Baptists. They could call me whatever they wanted to that day—I didn't get any sleep the night before because I couldn't stop worrying about Fox.

My plan didn't work because every kid in church crowded around me. They wouldn't stop asking me questions about the video with Fox. They thought I was the coolest kid ever, but I didn't care. Being cool didn't matter if Fox was in danger.

"Back away from him!" Dana shouted from behind me. Her voice traveled through the whole church. Everyone turned around and stared at me. I wanted to sink to the floor.

Dana stepped into my row and told everyone to move their legs as she worked her way to me. I was in the middle. I was too tired to be embarrassed, so I closed my eyes and ignored everything around me.

"Take a hike," Dana said to whatever kid was next to me. There wasn't any argument and I felt her arms slide in by mine. Things got quieter. I hated to admit it, but I was glad I had a little bodyguard.

"Hey, Melissa!" she shouted. "Sit here!" I opened my eyes and looked around. Melissa always sat with her family, so I didn't expect that to change. Kids grunted as Melissa made her way through the row towards me on my other side.

Dana leaned across me and said to the girl next to me with too much makeup and a short dress on, "Hey, Blondie. You need Jesus. Go sit closer to the front." I couldn't move. Everyone was staring at me again and shaking their heads.

The girl stood up and said, "As if!" She shoved other kids' legs out of her way as she struggled to get out of the row when Melissa took her place.

Melissa was beautiful in her blue dress with colored polka dots. I wished I was brave enough to tell her that. She wouldn't look at me. She stared at the Bibles and hymnals shelved on the back of the pew in front of us. "Why didn't you tell me about the fox?"

I wasn't sure how to answer her. She seemed disappointed I had hid Fox from her. We were friends, but I didn't expect her to be hurt. "I didn't want you to think I was weird," I said.

She looked over at me and smiled. "Of course you're weird. Just be honest with me."

The church organ came to life and filled the sanctuary with music. I wondered if the organist knew more than one song. She played the same thing every Sunday.

"Brothers and sisters," the preacher said to all of us. I didn't catch much after that. The back row was warm and the lights were dim. I understood why so
many adults sat back there. It was the perfect place to close your eyes and go to sleep.

I didn't plan to do that, but my head fell forward every few seconds. I realized I was falling asleep and kept jerking my head back. But, sure enough, my head wouldn't stay still. There was nothing I could do about it. The pew was comfortable, and I was exhausted.

Then the preacher said the one thing that made me open my eyes and sit up straight.

"The wolf also shall dwell with the lamb, and the leopard shall lie down with the kid; and the calf and the young lion and the fatling together; and a little child shall lead them."

I rubbed my eyes and tried to process what he said. There was a question I had to ask him when the service was over. It became more important to me than anything else.

It was time to leave when the organist played the same song again. I jumped up and tried to avoid the kids crowding me. Was that how it was going to be for the rest of my life? I hoped not. "I need to get out of here," I told Dana. "I've got to talk to the preacher."

She nodded like she was accepting a mission. "Out of the way, heathens!" she yelled at the kids. "Move it, move it!" I wasn't surprised when they cleared the row.

I weaved my way through the old people and young people and regular members I saw every Sunday. After I got through the foyer, I stood in front of the preacher. He wore a black suit with a red tie.

"I need to ask you something," I said to him.

He put a hand on my shoulder. "Of course, Joe. Go ahead."

I felt silly asking it, but I had to know the answer. "Do foxes go to heaven?"

He smiled and squeezed my shoulder. "I like to think so. God created all of us. He created foxes, giraffes, hamsters and elephants—every living creature. I hate to think of a world without them." He let go of my shoulder and bent down to my height.

"It's important to love our animals as much as we can while they're here."

An old guy stepped up behind me and grabbed the pastor's hand. "Good sermon, brother. We need to talk about the budget."

I stepped out of the way and thought about what he said. I didn't want to think anything bad happened to Fox. I hoped he wasn't alone in some swamp or forest he had never seen. He was just a kid, like me. I was scared for him.

"What's going on, Joe?" Melissa asked when she stood by my side. "Be honest with me." I trusted her more than anyone else. I told her everything I knew about Fox, from the first day I met him.

She stopped me before I could finish. "Where is he now?"

I wished I knew the answer. I told her how Shane and his dad tricked my family. "Some guy named Tater the Exterminator took him. I don't know what to do. I have no idea how to find him." I searched for Tater the Exterminator on the internet, but he didn't have a webpage.

Mr. and Mrs. Hunter stopped next to me. "Hey, Joe," Mrs. Hunter said. "You're looking for Tater? He lives on Brown Street with his mom." She pointed to my right. "Big orange house—can't miss it. It's less than five minutes from here." She sprayed some perfume on her neck. It smelled like an old person.

I couldn't believe my luck. I knew where Tater the Exterminator lived. Maybe Fox was there!

"Tater is a disturbed young man," Mr. Hunter added. "A lot of loose screws."

Dana joined us and sniffed the air. "What stinks?"

"I've been meaning to pay Tater's mom a visit," Mrs. Hunter continued. "She's a lovely lady who's always left at home." She shook her head like she was angry. "Tater goes fishing on Sundays. He won't be back for hours." She snapped her fingers at her husband. "We should stop by and check on her."

He sighed and said, "Yes, dear." He rolled his eyes.

Melissa stared at me and nodded. I knew she was thinking the same thing as me. Maybe I could read other people's minds.

"You live across the street from us," Mrs. Hunter said to me. I realized that a few months ago when I knocked on their door and sold them all my chocolate. "You kids can catch a ride with us to Tater's house, and we'll drop you off at home—if your parents let you."

Dana pushed me forward and said, "What are we waiting for?"

SUNDAY AFTERNOON

I knew Tater's mom was as weird as him when we were all sitting around a hot fireplace, sipping hot chocolate while it was eighty-eight degrees outside.

"It's good to see you again, Mary," Mrs. Hunter said to Tater's mom. "How are you these days?"

I kept looking around the room for any evidence Fox was there. The walls were covered with hundreds of pictures of Tater from when he was a baby all the way until now. His mom must have thought he was the greatest kid in the world.

She rocked back and forth in an old wooden chair. Her eyes stared straight ahead. I suspected she was blind. She had fluffy pink hair that was oily and looked like it hadn't been washed in weeks. "No one comes to see me anymore," she complained. "No one cares."

"Maybe it's because her son is a lunatic," Dana whispered to me.

Tater's mom stopped rocking. "Who are the children? I love children."

Mr. Hunter shrugged and motioned for me to say something. Melissa nodded like it was my job to explain who we were and why we were there. I'm not proud of what I said. "We're friends of Tater."

Dana almost choked to death.

Tater's mom smiled and started rocking

again. "He loves animals and children. He'll be happy to see you."

Not if I could help it. I had to get out of that room and search the house for Fox or some clue as to where he was. I hated to be that close to the answer but feel trapped in my seat. I asked the one question that would get me out of there. "Where's your bathroom?"

"It's down the hall, honey," she said. "Second door on your right."

I didn't waste any time and headed for the hall. I waved for Melissa and Dana to follow me. They jumped up and followed without any argument. We were covered in sweat from the fireplace, so it was a relief to get out of there.

"Keep your eyes open," I told them. "We've got to find Fox." We opened the doors to every room and peeked inside. Nothing appeared unusual until we reached the last room with a sign on the door that looked like a kid made it.

I almost had a heart attack when I pried the door open. There were stuffed animals everywhere! A bear, lion, possum, squirrel, duck, beaver, rabbit, wolf—every animal you can think of. My heart wouldn't stop racing. With every step I took I was afraid I'd find Fox stuffed like one of those poor animals.

"Looking for something?" a man's voice said from behind us. Dana and Melissa shrieked. It was Tater the Exterminator! He closed the door and shook a finger at us. "You shouldn't be here." I didn't know what he planned to do with us, but I knew we were trapped in the room with a crazy man.

The girls held on to me. "Do something, Joe," Melissa pleaded.

Tater rolled his sleeves up. "I haven't decided if I should call the police or stuff you like one of these animals." He rubbed his chin like he was struggling with the decision. "The three of you would look good stuffed by the curtains," he said, pointing to the only window in the room.

Dana stepped away from me and towards him. I tried to stop her. "That's enough!" she shouted at him. "Quit being a big meanie!"

He stared at her for a moment then let his

shoulders slump. "I'm sorry. I'm not good with people."

"You need to be nicer," Melissa added. "People will like you better."

I didn't know what to say. Dana and Melissa had expected me to protect them, but I failed. They stood up for themselves and saved all of us. How was I supposed to be able to protect Fox?

"I remember you," Tater said, pointing at me. "You're the kid with the fox."

"Not anymore," I reminded him. "You took him away from me. Where is he? You're going to take us to him right now."

He shook his head. "I can't do that. It's too late."

I stopped breathing. My worst nightmare was confirmed. There was no way to save Fox. He was gone forever. It was my fault. I had failed to protect him.

"Joe," Melissa said, grabbing my arm, "you've got to see this."

My stomach churned. I was afraid she had found Fox stuffed like the other animals. She led me to a small metal table with papers and pictures on it. But one piece of paper stood out from all the others.

It was a flier, like the ones posted on the walls at school. Only this one wasn't about a dance, party, or fundraiser. Fox's picture was on the flier.

THE TALKING FOX was printed above the picture. It went on to explain Fox would be at the Grand Vulpine Hotel in Las Vegas giving a live performance that night at 8 p.m.

"I'm sorry," Tater repeated. "Mr. Connors paid me ten thousand dollars to capture the fox." He looked at Dana like he had to explain himself to her. "I needed the money to help my mom keep this house. I didn't mean to hurt anyone." He seemed truly sorry. And I knew a thing or two about trying to save a house.

Tater pointed to his ears and complained, "Everyone makes fun of me. I have huge ears that look like potatoes." I was confused. His ears looked normal to me but his hotdog nose was the right size for a hotdog bun. I wondered if any of us see ourselves the way we truly are.

"That's how I got the name Tater." He shook his head and sighed. "I don't want to be a mean person. I just want people to like me."

I wondered if that was why Shane had grown three times meaner. I had embarrassed him with that homework assignment I wrote for him. Everyone made fun of him for the first time in his life, and his reputation was never the same.

"We've got to stop them," Melissa said. She was talking about Mr. Connors and Shane. "They're going to exploit Fox."

I hoped Mr. and Mrs. Hunter were ready to leave. "We need to get out of here. I've got to talk to my mom." We were running out of time and I had to explain all of this to her. We had to find a way to get to Las Vegas and save Fox.

LATER SUNDAY

I jumped out of Mr. and Mrs. Hunter's car when we got to my house and ran to the front door screaming, "Mom! Mom!" The door swung open and her eyes bugged out of her head like she thought I was being chased by an alligator.

I couldn't breathe when I reached her, so I handed her the flier I brought back. She didn't say anything for a minute; then she stared at me and asked, "Is this a joke?"

"It's not a joke," Melissa confirmed as she joined me with Dana by her side. "We got it from Tater the Exterminator."

My mom's hair turned gray right then and there. "You did what?"

"He's a nice guy," Dana added. "He's just misunderstood because he has potato ears."

My mom looked more confused than

ever. She took a deep breath and tried to process what we told her. "Let me see if I understand this correctly…"

I knew right away we were in big trouble.

"You kids somehow met with Tater the Exterminator—when you clearly told me the Hunters were taking you out to eat?" Her face was turning red.

"We had hot chocolate around a nice fire," Dana said defensively.

We all jumped when Mr. Hunter honked his horn from the driveway. He and his wife waved at us like they just had the best time of their lives. They drove out of our driveway and into theirs across the street. I wanted to be in the car with them. I wasn't sure it was safe around my mom.

She glanced at the flier again and sighed. "Everyone inside," she ordered. "We've got a lot to figure out."

My uncle was sitting on the couch, watching wrestling again. I laughed when I pictured Fox there the day before flexing his puny arms and calling himself Mr. Awesome

Muscles. I missed the little guy. "Everything okay?" my uncle asked, not paying attention to us.

My mom handed him the flier. He glanced at it then set it down on the couch next to him. We all thought it was odd he didn't care while the wrestling match was still on. But then he jumped up, grabbed the flier again like he just realized what it said, and shouted, "What the heck?"

"This is not what Fox wants," I said to all of them. "He's scared and alone."

My mom stared at my uncle in a way I'd

only seen them do a few times. They had some type of secret communication between them that no one else could decipher. They developed it growing up as brother and sister. I wished I had the power to read people's minds.

My uncle nodded and said, "Las Vegas, huh? We need a plane and I've got a friend who owes me a favor." He winked at me. "Let me go make a call." He disappeared into the kitchen.

My mom took his place on the couch and patted the cushions for all of us to take a seat next to her. She laughed and couldn't stop. "This is not the weekend I had planned." We laughed with her. Everything was different with Fox in our lives. But everything was better.

"I hope he's okay," Dana said when the laughter died down. Her voice was sadder than I'd ever heard it.

Melissa wrapped an arm around her. "He will be. Joe will make sure of it." She smiled at me and it made me feel woozy. You would think the saying 'butterflies in your stomach' meant you felt awesome like you were flying. Nope! It felt more like I was trying to fly but instead doing a belly flop on the kitchen floor.

"Okay," my uncle said, standing in front of us now. "The good news is my friend can fly us to Vegas and get us there before the show starts. The bad news is he can only take two of us." He studied all of us on the couch. "Who's it gonna be?"

Everyone looked at me like it was my decision. I had to go because I couldn't let my best friend down. While everyone in that room wanted to help Fox, there was only one other person who loved him as much as me. "It looks like we're going to Vegas, Mom."

"Alright," my uncle agreed. "It's settled. My friend will meet you at the airport in twenty minutes. You need to leave now if you're going to make it in time." He shoved us out the door.

"Wait," my mom said to him. "What's your friend's name?"

I swear my uncle chuckled. "You'll know

him when you get there. And don't worry about anything. Me and Dana will take Melissa home and we'll lock up here."

He stopped me before I got to the driveway. "Bring him home, Joe. Whatever you have to do, bring Fox home."

The airport was extra windy when we got there. And my uncle was right. We knew his friend.

"Hope you didn't eat any of those eggs," Mr. Jim Bob joked. I wondered how that straw hat stayed on top of his head. Maybe it was glued. "They don't taste any good coming up a second time." He had plenty of experience with that after eating Old Nelly's rotten eggs.

"How safe is this plane?" my mom asked, knocking on it. The plane looked like it was made of plastic and weighed less than me. Okay, that's an exaggeration, but it didn't look like any plane I'd ever seen on TV. It was much smaller and there was a good chance it would tip over if the wind blew hard enough.

"This plane is safer than safe," Mr. Bob assured her. "I've been flying her for thirty-five years, and she's only crashed thirty-four times!" My mom didn't laugh. "C'mon now," he pleaded. "It's a pilot's joke. It's funny."

My mom grabbed my shoulders and made sure she had my full attention. "This is not going to work. We'll find another way."

We had less than six hours to get to Las Vegas. This was our best chance of making that happen. "We can't give up on Fox. He's part of our family."

She cracked her neck and rolled her shoulders back. "Let's do this."

Five minutes later, we were on the plane, riding down the runway, waiting for it to take off. The end of the runway was coming up fast, and we were still on the ground driving at a million miles an hour. I tasted my hot chocolate a second time that day. My mom shrieked.

Mr. Bob laughed hysterically when we took off at the last second. He shot the plane straight up into the air like a rocket. "Going up high to touch the sky! Yeeeeeeehaw!"

SUNDAY NIGHT

Four hours later, I was standing in front of the Grand Vulpine Hotel in Las Vegas with my mom. Well, not exactly in front of it. More like half a mile away because the line to get inside went on forever.

The hotel was like a mirrored tower. It was dark outside so I couldn't see myself in it, but I saw the one thing that took my breath away. It was a huge image of Fox lit up in lights along the front of the hotel. The lights flashed on for a minute to show my best friend then they flashed off. Every time they came back on I was amazed at how spectacular it looked.

"I hope we get inside," said the lady in front of us. "This is the hottest show of the year."

The big guy with her shrugged his shoulders. His hair was spiked and he had a tattoo of a spider on his cheek. "If we don't, then we don't. There's another ventriloquist across the street."

I asked my mom what a ventriloquist was. She said it was a person who made things that can't speak look like they were talking. It was like magic. This was good news. I wondered if everyone else thought Fox was controlled by a ventriloquist.

My mom glanced at her watch and said what I was thinking. "We can't just stand out here. We may never get inside." She pulled me out of the line and we walked around everyone like we were just passing by. There were young people and old people but no kids. Tall people and short people. White people, black people, Hispanics, Orientals. The whole world had come to see Fox.

A huge man covered with muscles was walking toward us. His muscles were so huge that his tank top barely fit across his chest. He was bigger than Mr. Awesome Muscles! He stopped every few steps and said something to the people in line. I heard what it was when we got closer to him. It was the one thing I didn't want to hear.

"Show's sold out," he barked. "Everyone go home."

My heart sank. My best friend was trapped inside the building in front of us. I don't want to sound weird, but I could feel how scared he was. He was just a kid who wanted to go home.

My mom marched right up to the muscle man and said, "We need to get inside. We've got a friend trapped in there."

He shook his head. "I couldn't let you in— even if your name was Donald Trump. There's not a seat left in the house." He stepped around us like we were invisible and kept telling people to go home.

I felt like crying but I refused to do it. I marched behind the big muscle man and tugged on his tank top. He seemed as tall as the hotel when he turned and faced me.

"What?" he barked.

"Please," I begged him. "We've got to help Fox."

He rubbed his eyebrows like he had a headache. "Sorry, kid. Even if every seat was empty I still couldn't let you in. You have to be at least twenty-one and have a picture ID." He squinted his eyes. "You don't look twenty-one to me." He started to laugh but stopped when I stared into his eyes.

"It's you," he said, his expression softening. "You're the kid in the video, the one who talks to the fox. What are you doing out here?" He motioned for me and my mom to follow him to the hotel. "We've got to get you on stage. This is your big night."

We weaved through hundreds or thousands of people to get to the back stage entrance. "Out of the way!" the muscle man kept shouting at everyone in front of us. "Superstar coming through!"

It seemed like hours before we were waiting in the wings to see Fox on stage. I peered through the curtains and saw the audience staring back. Some people were standing and some were sitting. There were more people than I'd ever seen in my entire life. I wondered how long was left until Fox was on stage and if we had time to stop it before it happened.

"Ladies and gentlemen," someone announced over the speakers above and around us. "Welcome to the Grand Vulpine Hotel and the hottest show on Earth. Here he is—the talking fox!"

The crowd went wild with cheers, whistles, and claps. I started to rush on stage and stop this, but another big guy stepped in front of me and blocked me. "We need you up front," he said to the muscle man next to me. "There's a fight." They both rushed away without saying anything to me.

When I looked back at the stage, I saw Mr. Connors pulling Fox on a leash to the center. Fox was thrashing all around, trying to break free. I wanted to run out there, grab Fox, and fly right back to Alabama, but my mom stopped me.

"Not yet, Jonah," she said. "If we do anything rash, they're going to kick us out of here." I hated that she was right.

"So, Fox," Mr. Connors said into a microphone. "How do you like Las Vegas?" That was an odd question. Maybe Mr. Connors and Shane had practiced a whole routine with Fox, but I doubted Fox agreed to any of it.

Fox didn't respond and lay down on the floor. He was shivering. A lot of people from the audience booed.

Mr. Connors yanked on the leash. Fox had to be choking. "I said, how do you like Las Vegas?"

Fox still wouldn't say anything.

My heart raced when Shane marched onto the stage from the other side. He walked right up to Fox and kicked him in the side! Fox yelped in a cry of pain that shattered my heart.

"Leave him alone!" someone shouted. The boos from the crowd got louder and louder.

That was enough. I couldn't stand by anymore. My mom nodded approval. Right before I set foot on stage, someone else grabbed my shoulders and stopped me. Really? Now?

I turned and saw the one face I didn't expect to see. It was Tater the Exterminator! He was toting a huge plastic bag over his back.

"Get your hands off my son," my mom growled.

He set the bag down and put his hands in the air. His hotdog nose stuck out like a sore thumb.

"Why are you here?" I asked him. If he had never come into our yard and our house, Fox wouldn't have been on that stage. He was just as guilty as Mr. Connors and Shane.

He put his hands down and sighed. "I made a mistake. I came to fix it." He looked back and forth from me to my mom. "You've got to let me go out there and make this right."

I was about to tell him no because it was my responsibility, but my mom put a hand on my shoulder. "Go on then," she told Tater.

He grabbed the huge bag from the floor and nodded. "Thank you." He brushed past me and right onto the stage.

"Stop!" Tater shouted at Mr. Connors and Shane. They both glared at him. "I came to return this." He opened his bag and dumped its contents on the floor. It looked like a lot of money. I guessed it was the ten thousand dollars Mr. Connors had paid him to capture Fox.

Mr. Connors handed the leash to his son

and walked over to Tater. "You fool. Do you think you're better than me? You'll never be anything more than a freak with potato ears." He faced the crowd and laughed. No one laughed with him. He returned his attention to Tater. "This is my world. There's nothing you can do about it."

Tater took a deep breath and looked back at me. I figured he was going to walk away and say he was sorry. I didn't know why any of us thought we could stop this. "I may not be able to do anything," he admitted, "but these guys can." He pointed to someone behind me.

Two cops passed me and marched onto the stage. "Charles Connors and Shane Connors," one cop said, "you're under arrest for kidnapping and animal cruelty." They slapped cuffs on both of them. "You have the right to remain silent," the second cop said.

Mr. Connors wouldn't stop laughing. He spit on Tater when the cop ushered him toward the stage exit. "You're going down with me!" he shouted. "You'll pay for this!"

"Maybe," Tater said, "but at least I tried to make things right."

I rushed onto the stage to get Fox. I couldn't wait any longer. My friend was scared and hurt. He had to know I was there for him. I kneeled next to him on the floor, unhooked the leash, and hugged him. He hugged me back.

"I knew you'd come for me," he whispered, smiling. He didn't want the audience to hear him.

I stood back up. "Was there ever any doubt?" He shook his head. "Let's go home, Fox."

My mom was talking to Tater when we joined her. "Why did you help us?"

He looked at Fox and smiled. "I forgot who I was. I forgot why I got into this business in the first place." He gazed into the crowd. "I love animals."

It was at that moment I realized they could hear everything we said. The crowd cheered for Tater and clapped. He had a huge smile on his face.

"I'm glad you're okay," I said to Fox. "Let's get you out of here."

"Wait," Fox whispered to me. I bent down close to him so I could hear. "There's something I want to say to them." His eyes were pleading like it was something important that would change the world.

I wasn't sure if it was a good idea or not. Everyone already knew he could talk. Now he could say whatever he wanted and not what someone was trying to force him to say. If he was brave enough to say something in front of thousands of people, I wouldn't be the one to stop him.

Fox walked back to the center of the stage on four paws. He faced the crowd. They gasped when he stood up on his two hind legs. He looked at me one last time and winked. Whatever he was going to say would be life changing.

The crowd was silent, waiting for his words.

That's when he shouted the one thing no one

expected. "I love Las Vegas!"

The crowd went crazy and chanted his name. "Fox! Fox! Fox! Fox! Fox! Fox! Fox! Fox! Fox! Fox! Fox! Fox! Fox! Fox! Fox! Fox!"

It had to be the greatest moment of Fox's life. I was so proud of him. Everything was exactly the way it was always meant to be.

I never expected it all to fall apart.

MONDAY MORNING

We got home early that morning. Like six o'clock in the morning early, thanks to Mr. Jim Bob's plane. My mom had suggested we get a hotel room in Las Vegas for the night, but I wanted to get Fox home so he could be comfortable in the den I made for him. And I had those bad memories about the last time we were in a hotel room.

My uncle Mike and Dana met us at the airport. Dana was so happy to see Fox that she ran up and tackled him. My uncle high fived Fox and flexed muscles with him.

We were all wide awake so we agreed to go back to my house to get something to eat and catch up with Fox. It was like a family reunion and no one would stop talking. You would think we hadn't seen Fox in years.

My mom wouldn't let me out of the car when we pulled into our driveway. Uncle Mike and Dana were behind us in their car. She rolled her window down and motioned for my uncle to come to ours.

"What's wrong?" he asked, standing by her window.

She pointed to the house. "I thought you said you were going to lock up." I looked at the front door. It was wide open.

"I did," he replied. He motioned for Dana to get out of their car and into ours. "Roll your window up and lock the doors. I'll find out why the front door's open."

My mom tried to stop him. "Wait," she begged. "We should call the police.'"

He glanced into the back seat where Fox was asleep with his tongue out. Even after all we had done to save Fox, it was still illegal to keep him. "No, we shouldn't." He walked past the car and into the house.

A lot of time had passed, and my uncle didn't come back out. My mom was crying. I feared something bad had happened to him. All of this was my fault—everything that happened over the weekend. If I had just written Shane's homework the way he wanted me to, none of this would ever have happened.

I opened my car door and raced to the house.

"Jonah!" my mom shouted.

I wasn't prepared for what I found when I stepped inside. Everything was turned over and broken. The TV was smashed. The couches were ripped apart. The pictures were shattered.

My mom rushed in after me. "Don't ever do that again! You almost gave me a…" She didn't say anything else when she saw the damage.

We both jumped when my uncle came out of the kitchen. "I don't understand," he said.

"They didn't take anything."

We all turned when Dana and Fox joined us. And that's when we saw it. Painted in big red letters above the doorway were the words GIVE US THE FOX.

I had thought all of this was over. But it looked like there would always be people looking for Fox. Like my mom said, good people and bad people. Mr. Connors and Shane were only the beginning.

"This is about me, isn't it?" Fox asked. He couldn't read but he was good at figuring things out. He looked through the trashed house. "All of this is because of me."

None of us could deny it, but no one wanted to admit it.

"Look," Fox said, "it's not safe for any of you if I'm here." He nodded his head at me like I didn't have any choice but to accept what he said. "I've got to disappear. They'll never stop looking for me."

"You can't go," Dana cried.

My uncle threw his hands up like he hated the idea but couldn't think of any other options. "Whoever these people are, they're going to come back." My mom reminded him that if the police were involved then Fox would be taken away for good. There was no upside. There was no way to win.

Her eyes sparkled. She held up a finger like she did whenever she had a good idea.

She stared at my uncle again in the way they secretly communicated. Why couldn't I read their minds? I hated being left out of a conversation that didn't even exist. I had a feeling they were discussing Fox's future. All I knew was I didn't want him to leave.

"I don't like it," my uncle finally said, "but everyone get into my car."

I wondered if we were going back to Las Vegas or running away. I didn't want to do either. This was my home and the one place I could guard my best friend. "What's going on?"

My mom motioned for me, Dana, and Fox to move toward the door. "I know someone who can help us."

Fox tapped her on the leg. "Mr. Awesome Muscles?"

She chuckled and said, "No, Fox. Not Mr. Awesome Muscles." She redirected her attention to me. "Do you remember how to get to Tater's house?"

Of course I remembered. He lived with his mom on Brown Street in the big orange house. I couldn't think of any reason to go there unless we wanted to roast marshmallows over their burning hot fireplace. "Yeah … why?"

My mom tried to close the front door after we were all out of the house, but the knob was busted. She sighed and followed my uncle to his car. "Tater may be the only person who can help Fox now."

MONDAY AFTERNOON

We sat around Tater's living room with his mom for hours. He hadn't returned from Las Vegas yet. Even though we sweated from the hot fireplace, his mom asked for a blanket to keep her warm. Her eyes didn't move.

"He's a good boy," she assured us about Tater. "He'd never hurt anyone." She rocked back and forth in her chair, nodding her head and smiling as my mom placed a blanket on her. "Thank you, honey."

I doubted Tater wouldn't hurt anyone. He killed bugs and captured animals for a living. And what about those stuffed animals in his room? It was like he collected them for trophies.

Fox waved his paws at me then rubbed his belly. "I'm starving. Do they have any chicken here?"

Tater's mom stopped rocking. "We only eat fruits and vegetables. You can have all the broccoli you want."

Dana stuck her tongue out and acted like she had to vomit. "I vote we get some fast food as soon as we leave."

Fox agreed with her. "We don't want slow food. We want fast food."

The front door opened, and Tater the Exterminator stepped in. He had on the same clothes as the night before.

Fox's whole body was shaking.

"Hey, Mama," Tater said as he closed the door and joined us. "Hey, everyone else. What are you doing here?"

"Christopher Joseph Allen," his mom said, standing up now. "Where have you been all night? I've been worried sick."

He rushed over to her. "It's okay, Mama.

Sit back down." He looked around the room at all of us. My uncle stood like a statue with his chest out. He was ready to protect us if Tater tried to hurt anyone.

Tater faced me and Dana. "Shouldn't you kids be in school?" Making sure Fox was safe was more important. And I can't lie—I was afraid to go back to school. I had no idea if Shane would be there or not. I wanted to see Melissa and tell her what happened, but that would have to wait.

"What's going to happen to Shane and his dad?" I asked him. I figured he knew the answer because he was the one who made sure they were taken away.

He put his hands in his pockets and shrugged. "It's up to the courts. For animal cruelty, they could be fined six thousand dollars and go to prison for a year." Mr. Connors had plenty of money. He had given Tater ten thousand dollars just to capture Fox. I wondered what happened to the money Tater dumped on the stage and left behind. If I was lucky, Shane would go away for a year.

He looked at Fox's body shaking next to mine. "It's okay," Tater promised him. "I'm not going to hurt you."

Fox calmed down a little, but Dana wanted answers. "What about all those animals in your room? You hurt them. All of them!"

Tater shook his head. "I bought those years ago on the internet. They remind me why I do what I do." He smiled at Dana. "I do everything I can to save them."

I was confused. I thought for sure Tater was a bad person who hurt animals. Sure, he was crazy. But maybe I had misunderstood him the whole time. After all, he did help us get Fox back.

"I was right about you," my mom said. She stood by his side. "We need your help."

Tater took his hands out of his pockets and laughed. "I'm not sure I can help anyone. I shouldn't have given that money back."

His mom stopped rocking again and said, "It was the right thing to do. We'll find another way."

My mom looked at both of them like she had no idea what they were talking about. I explained it to her. "They're going to lose the house. They needed that money."

Tater hung his head and scratched it. "Life is funny when you try to do the right thing. I can't win."

My mom cleared her throat and nodded at my uncle. I wasn't sure if they were talking to each other in their heads or not. "How much money do you need?"

"To stay here?" Tater asked. "About five thousand dollars. But that's not going to happen." He looked like he was about to cry. "Don't worry about us. We'll make it. We always do."

My mom took a deep breath and stared at Fox. He wasn't shaking anymore. "How much would it cost for you to do pest control at my house?" she asked Tater. "I hate ants and roaches."

He shrugged. "Your house is pretty big. I could do it for forty dollars a month."

My mom grabbed her purse off the floor. She pulled out her checkbook and wrote a check then handed it to Tater.

He looked it and whistled. "I can't take this," he said, handing it back to her. "It's for four thousand and eight hundred dollars. I don't accept charity anymore." His mom nodded her agreement.

My mom wouldn't take the check back. "It's not charity. You said you could provide my house with pest control for forty dollars a month."

He nodded. "Yes ma'am. But even if you prepaid me for a year, that would only be four hundred and eighty dollars for all twelve months."

She pushed his hand with the check back

towards him. "We're going to be living in that house for a very long time, Christopher. I've prepaid you for ten years." His mom smiled wide. "And you have a beautiful name. You should use it."

Tater—I mean Christopher—was speechless for the first time. He finally said, "There's no way I can thank you enough for this."

Dana jumped up from her seat. "You can start by getting some real food for us."

Fox nodded vigorously. "Fast food. Not slow food."

My mom held her hands out. "Just a minute. Christopher, we came here because we need your help. Fox is in danger and we have to find a safe place for him."

He stuffed the check into his pocket and nodded. "There's a wildlife sanctuary about thirty minutes from here." He looked at Fox. "I've taken foxes there before."

My mom looked at me and nodded. "Then that's where we're going. We'll get some fast food on the way."

Fox jumped off the couch and stood on his hind legs in front of my mom. "Chicken is fast. Broccoli is slow."

MONDAY EVENING

I felt sick when we arrived at the wildlife sanctuary. It was a huge place with acres of land and buildings for sick, injured, or orphaned animals. Christopher said he had brought all sorts of animals here for help, from skunks to bears. It was the right place for Fox, but I didn't want to let him go.

"Got another orphan, Christopher?" a lady in white shorts and a red T-shirt asked when we arrived. She had a pair of latex gloves on.

"Yep," he replied. "This one's special."

"They're all special," she said. "Let me have a look." She bent down and inspected Fox's hairy body. He was standing on all four paws in an attempt to blend in. She laid him down so she could check everything. The lady froze when she looked into his eyes. "His eyes are bright blue. I've never seen anything like this." She was about to see and hear a lot more things she'd never seen or heard before.

"Foxes are known carriers of rabies," she told all of us as she stood back up. "Have any of you been bitten or scratched?"

We all shook our heads. I didn't know what rabies were, but Fox never even had a cold.

"Okay then," she said. "We'll take him."

My heart dropped. There was a huge part of me that hoped they wouldn't take Fox. I wasn't sure when I could see him again. Christopher said visitors were only allowed in the afternoons when I was at school and on Saturdays when I worked with my mom at the farmers' market.

"I'd like to make a donation," my mom said. She pulled out her checkbook and wrote another check. The lady's eyes looked like they were going to pop out of her head when she saw how much money it was.

"Fox is different from other animals," my mom continued, nodding her head slowly to make sure the lady paid attention to every word. "His favorite food is chicken. He likes to sleep in a tent or den. And he loves to watch wrestling."

The lady raised her eyebrows.

"Exactly how much money was under my lumpy mattress?" I asked my mom. We had found enough money under my mattress to save our house months ago. I wondered how much was left over.

"There was enough, Jonah," was all she would say.

I tried to be happy for Fox because he had a chance to be with his own kind. He was lost without his parents and nothing would ever make up for that. But maybe this place would help him.

The lady stepped away to talk to Christopher. "Don't leave me here," Fox begged me. "I don't want to do this. I'm scared."

Dana ran over to Fox and hugged him. "I'll never forget you." She kissed the top of his head and went back to my uncle, crying.

My heart was being ripped to pieces. I wanted to grab my best friend and run away with him. I was leaving him behind in a world he wasn't familiar with. Were we doing the right thing? I didn't want to say goodbye. I was completely numb. How was I supposed to live my life not knowing how Fox was? How was I supposed to live without him?

"Maybe it'll be okay," Fox said, rubbing his side against my leg. "They don't serve chicken pot pie here, but I'll survive." He smiled and looked up at me with his bright blue eyes.

He was trying to make me feel better. He was the one whose world was being taken away from him, but he wanted to make sure I was okay. He had caused more trouble than anyone else in my life. And he was the best thing that ever happened to me.

He held out his arm with the bracelet. I held out mine. "Best friends," we said together. I tried not to cry. Fox stood up on his hind legs and hugged me. I never wanted to let him go. Mr. Awesome Muscles.

"He'll do well with the other two foxes," the lady said when she returned with Christopher. I could see the foxes partially hidden in the tall grass in the field across from us. They were bigger and older than Fox. "They've come a long ways since you brought them to us a few months ago."

Christopher nodded like he was impressed. "You did a good job. I wasn't sure they'd make it."

She smiled. "It's what we do. They were in bad shape after those hunters shot them." She paused and shook her head. "It still amazes me. They got away somehow and refused to die. It's like those foxes were fighting for something. Or someone."

Fox turned away from me and looked towards the other foxes. Then he said the two words I never thought I'd hear him say.

"Mom? Dad?"

He raced off toward them without looking back and leaped over the fence. The older foxes ran together toward Fox at the same time. Fox shouted their names over and over. "Mom! Dad! Mom! Dad!"

Fox had always believed he would find them. My heart was going to explode.

Fox and his parents jumped all around each other. They rubbed their sides together and licked each other's faces. Fox finally had everything he was looking for. Seeing them so happy made me miss my dad at that moment.

My mom hugged me from behind. "I'm here for you, Jonah. Mom's here."

"I miss Dad," I confided in her.

She held me tighter. "Your father loved you very much. And he would be proud of the man you're becoming. He'll always be with us. I can see him in you."

I took a few deep breaths and cleared my throat. "You're the best mom ever."

"I know," she said. "That's what it says on my mug at home." We both laughed.

The lady with the red shirt stepped up to us and handed me a shirt exactly like hers. "This is the only one I have. I'll order some more in your size."

I didn't understand. "What is this?"

My mom smiled. "It's for your after-school job. Uncle Mike will bring you here and I'll take you home after work."

My head spun for a moment. Did I hear that right? I could come here to see Fox after school every day? No way!

I ran to the fence Fox had leaped over and shouted his name. "Fox!" It sounded odd because they were all foxes, but only mine could talk. "I'm not leaving you here alone! I'm coming back tomorrow! I got a job here!"

He ran back to the fence with his parents. He grinned and wagged his tail when they reached me. "Guess you're stuck with me."

I grinned back. "I guess so. Nothing can keep us apart."

His mom and dad stood on all four paws on each side of him and looked up at me from the other side of the fence. They were tall and majestic. I could tell right away they couldn't talk or move like him. They sniffed my pants and licked my hands through slits in the fence. It tickled.

Fox leaped back over the fence and stood next to me with a serious look on his face. "You know what we should do? We should go to China."

I couldn't keep a straight face. I remembered when we first met and he convinced me it was possible to dig a hole to China. And when he came back a few days ago and we laughed about it. I don't know how I ever lived without Fox. "You're my best friend and the brother I never had."

"You welcomed me into your family," Fox said. "Now I welcome you into mine." I couldn't stop smiling.

My mom yelled my name. She was with my uncle, Dana, and my new boss at a table they set up outside. "We have cake!" she yelled. "Let's celebrate!"

"Cake?" Fox asked, licking his lips. "I want cake."

I remembered the last time Fox had cake. It had given him that nasty fart that smelled like tuna and broccoli and onions and vinegar and dirty feet and dirty underwear all mixed together.

I threw out my hands and shouted, "No!" I love Fox, but every kid has his limits.

MY
fox
ATE MY
ALARM CLOCK

DAVID BLAZE

CONTENTS

FRIDAY MORNING

I didn't feel safe at school. Sam sat behind me on the gym bleachers and blew spitballs at the back of my head. The big kid with a crew cut and a white tank top was Shane's best friend. He never forgave me for making the school bully go away.

"Everyone line up!" Coach Brown, the gym teacher, shouted. There were fifteen of us, boys and girls. Coach Brown wore a red workout jacket and a red cap. He had a clipboard in his hand and a whistle around his neck. He wasn't the nicest person in the world. He yelled at any kid who didn't move as fast as he wanted.

"Shane's coming for you, Jonah," Sam whispered from behind me. He laughed and jumped out of the bleachers to line up on the floor. I felt sick and thought about going to the front office to call my mom so she could take me home.

"Don't listen to him," Melissa told me, shaking her head. She was sitting right next to me. She wore a green sweatshirt and had her hair tied back in two ponytails. I was glad she was there because her smile made me feel better. "Shane didn't come to school today."

She was right. Miss Cox had called his name several times in English class that morning but he didn't answer. Today was the day he was supposed to return. I had looked all over the room, expecting Shane to pop his head up and attack me. He'd never forget the night he and his father were taken away by the police.

"Mr. Johnson?" Coach Brown said with his face right in front of mine. He called us by our last names. "I don't think you heard me." I realized I was still sitting down while everyone else was standing on the gym floor. I took a deep breath. Coach Brown was about to yell at me. "I said line up!" He blew his whistle as loud as he could. I wasn't sure if I'd ever hear anything again.

"We're doing the Presidential Fitness Program today and next week," he said. I saw the president on TV once. I wondered if he did any physical fitness or just made that program to torture us.

"Girls will go first," Coach Brown continued. He pointed at the metal pull-up bar on the other side of the gym. "I expect you to do at least three pull-ups." None of the girls moved. One of them shook her head and crossed her arms. Coach Brown blew his whistle and shouted, "Now! Move it!"

They ran to the other side. Coach Brown followed them. "I don't get paid enough for this," he muttered. He caught up to the girls and called them one at a time to the bar. I watched as some of them did two pull-ups. Some of them did one. And some did none at all—they just hung from the bar and fell down. I waited for Coach Brown to yell at them, but he had a soft spot for girls. He shook his head and told them to go sit down.

Melissa was the last girl standing there. "Let's go, Miss Morgan," he said. "I'm not getting any younger." That was true. He was really old—like thirty.

Melissa jumped up and grabbed the bar. I didn't expect her to do any pull-ups. She was the nicest girl I knew and a good friend of mine. I didn't think she could hurt a fly. I stared in amazement as she did one pull-up. Two pull-ups. Three pull-ups. Four pull-ups!

Everyone cheered for her. I shouted, "That's right! That's how you do it!" Coach Brown smiled for the first time in his life and patted Melissa on the back. She ran over to me and smirked. "Did you see that?" she asked.

I nodded and high fived her. "That was awesome. You're amazing, Melissa Morgan."

Sam laughed from behind me. "Jonah and

Melissa sitting in a tree…"

My face felt like it was on fire. I couldn't breathe. I liked Melissa a lot but I didn't know how she felt about me. She giggled and sat down.

"Boys!" Coach Brown shouted. "It's your turn." He waved us toward the bar on the other side of the gym. "Let's do this."

We ran over to him as fast as we could. None of us wanted to be the last person because that person was the weakest. I was the third boy out of eight.

Sam pushed us out of the way and said, "I'll go first." He cracked his knuckles and moved his neck from side to side. "I can do this," he said out loud to himself. "I'm the man." He jumped up to the bar and did five pull-ups!

He dropped down and rolled his shoulders back. "That's right," he said to us. "That's how a real man does it." Sam looked up at Coach Brown. "Right, Coach? I did five pull-ups and I only had to do three."

Coach Brown lowered his clipboard to his side. "Girls are supposed to do three." He took a deep breath and sighed. "Boys are supposed to do six." He pointed to the bleachers. "Go sit down."

A couple of guys laughed as Sam walked

away with his head hung low. I couldn't laugh because five pull-ups were more than any of the girls could do. I had never done pull-ups before but they looked hard, like something you'd see on *American Ninja Warrior* on TV.

I let the other guys go before me, hoping we'd run out of time before I got to the metal bar. Some of the guys did six pull-ups. Most of them could do three or four, like Melissa.

Before I knew it, I was the only person left. The pull-up bar was a mile high. I gulped. Coach Brown looked at his watch then stared at me like he had more important things to do. He waved his clipboard at the metal bar. "Let's go, Mr. Johnson. You can't do any worse than the girls."

My heart was racing. I couldn't move. I didn't want to be the one guy who couldn't do any pull-ups. The other guys would make fun of me for the rest of my life. I looked at the bleachers and realized no one was looking at me. They were talking and playing. Except for one person.

"You can do it, Joe!" Melissa shouted.

I smiled at her and nodded. I turned back to the bar. It was time to find out if I was the weakest link.

The gym doors opened with a loud crack that

echoed through the room. Everyone became silent. I turned and saw the one face that made me wish I had gone home. It was Shane.

He walked straight toward me. His shoes made a deep clickety clack sound that made my heart beat faster with every step. He looked taller than the night the police took him away. He stopped right in front of me and hovered over me like the Eiffel Tower.

He didn't say anything. He wanted to show me that he was back and there was nothing I could do about it. He was the king.

"Mr. Connors!" Coach Brown shouted. "Why are you walking into my gym late? I hope you have a note." Shane pulled a note out of his pocket and handed it to the coach without ever taking his eyes off me. I didn't know where he had been for the last few months, but rumors were his dad went to jail. Had Shane gone to jail too? Maybe he was a hardened criminal now.

"Mr. Connors!" Coach Brown shouted again. "Show everyone how to do pull-ups the right way." Shane didn't move. "Now, Mr. Connors!"

Shane turned from me without saying anything. He stepped up to the metal bar and grabbed it without jumping up. I watched in amazement as he did nine pull-ups! A lot of kids on the bleachers were talking about how strong Shane was and that they felt sorry for me.

Shane dropped to the floor and walked right back over to me. I was sure he was going to throw me to the ground like he did the first day we met. I closed my eyes. But nothing happened.

When I opened my eyes again, I saw Shane was on the bleachers, talking to Sam. No doubt they were planning how to destroy me.

"You're up, Mr. Johnson," Coach Brown said. "Make it quick."

Sam and Shane were staring at me. Melissa was the only other person paying attention. I turned to the bar and took a deep breath. Here went nothing.

I jumped up and grabbed the bar. My fingers

felt weird wrapped around it, like rubber bands. I held my breath and pulled myself up slowly to the bar, feeling it in my shoulders and upper back. It wasn't too bad. One pull-up done.

I went faster on the second one. It was easier that way. So then I did three. And four. Five. Six. Seven. Eight. Nine. This was too easy. I didn't understand why everyone else had trouble with this.

On my tenth pull-up, Coach Brown shouted, "Unseen force!" The room fell silent again. "Unseen force!"

I focused on the bar. Coach Brown counted out loud, shouting the numbers. "Eleven! Twelve! Thirteen! Fourteen! Fifteen! Sixteen! Seventeen!" They were getting harder to do. My shoulders were sore. I couldn't move as fast.

"Eighteen!" I wasn't sure I could do another one.

"Nineteen!" My back was on fire. I was breathing hard. Sweat fell from my face. There's no way I could do another one.

"Twenty!" I dropped down from the bar and rolled my shoulders back. They were sore but already getting stronger again. I had no idea where all that strength came from. I was not the weakest link.

A lot of the kids surrounded me and patted me on the back. They said things like, "That was dope!" and "Awesome!"

Melissa stood in front of me and smiled. "I knew you could do it, Joe."

We all turned when the gym doors cracked open again. I heard the clickety clack of Shane's shoes as the doors closed behind him. I was glad he left. Now that we both knew how strong I was he'd never bother me again.

I wish I could say I was safe then. But I was about to meet a much more powerful enemy.

FRIDAY AFTERNOON

My uncle Mike picked me up from school that afternoon. My little cousin Dana was sitting in the front middle seat of the pickup truck with us. She wouldn't stop smiling at me. It was weird.

"How was school?" my uncle asked. He stared straight ahead and waited for some kids to cross the road. He was talking to me because Dana didn't say anything. Her smile was starting to scare me. I figured she wanted something from me but was waiting for the right moment to ask.

"It was okay," I said, shrugging my shoulders. I wanted to tell him how awesome it

was, but that had to wait. Something was happening to me and I couldn't explain it. I had no idea how, but I was stronger than everyone else. And I had defeated
Shane all by myself. "I'm just happy I made it through another week of school."

He chuckled. "When you're a kid, all you want to do is grow up." He waved at the crossing guard as we pulled onto the main highway. "But when you get to be my age, all you want to do is be a kid again." He looked over at me for the first time. "Don't be in a hurry to grow up."

I wasn't sure if he was serious or not. All I knew was I wanted to see Fox. Thanks to the agreement my mom had made with the wildlife sanctuary a while back, I got to see Fox five days a week. My uncle Mike took me there after school every day for my part-time job cleaning animal cages. Sometimes I got to show visitors around the sanctuary and tell them about the animals.

"So, Joe," Dana said to me. Here it came. I couldn't wait to hear what she had been smiling about. "I haven't seen Fox in a while." She batted her eyes. "Think I could help you out today? Please, please, please, please, please, please, please, please?"

I sighed. I liked my little cousin, and she always stood up for me. She was tough as nails and didn't let anyone tell her what to do. But she liked to play with Fox and wouldn't be any help. That was a problem because there was a lot of work to do before the weekend. That's when the sanctuary was the busiest. It was a bad idea. "Maybe next time. There's too much going on right now."

She crossed her arms and stared at me with cold eyes. Her smile was gone.

"Oh, boy," my Uncle Mike said, shaking his head. "That was the wrong answer." He looked over at me and laughed. "Good luck with that."

Dana pinched my arm so hard I wanted to cry. "I'm going to help you," she assured me.

"Ouch!" I rubbed my arm. "You didn't have to do that." She was family and I'm glad she was on my side. But she didn't have to be so rough. I thought girls were supposed to be sugar and spice and everything nice.

She uncrossed her arms and said, "Sorry." She rolled her eyes and smirked. "You don't have to be a baby about it."

That was enough. I had to show her who the boss was. I did the one thing that broke her down and made her weak. I wasn't proud of it. I reached over with both hands and tickled her sides. She laughed so hard and squirmed so much that the whole truck shook. It was hilarious because she sounded like a monkey when she laughed.

"Stop, stop, stop!" Dana shouted, laughing like a crazy person. "I can't take it anymore!" So I did what any responsible kid would do. I tickled her harder.

I laughed with her until her leg jumped up and kicked the glove compartment. The compartment door busted open and a bunch of papers fell out.

"Alright, alright," my uncle said. "That's enough—both of you." He reached over and closed the door. "If I didn't know any better I'd think you were brother and sister. Geez."

I poked Dana in the side when my uncle

wasn't looking. It seemed like a good idea until she pinched me again. It felt like a bee sting. I held up my hands to show her I wasn't a threat anymore. She nodded her head like she agreed to it. I wasn't sure if I could trust her so I crossed my hands over my arms to protect them.

Thirty minutes later, we arrived at the wildlife sanctuary just outside of town. My heart raced in excitement when we got there. I remembered when my mom and I lived in Orlando. This was the type of excitement I felt when we went to Disney World or SeaWorld or Universal Studios.

"Have fun," my uncle said to me when the truck stopped. "Your mom already spoke with Miss Julie about the possibility of Dana helping out today." He turned his attention to Dana. "And you be on your best behavior, young lady."

I opened my door and Dana pushed me out. "Can't make any promises," she said before she jumped out behind me and closed the door. The windows were tinted, but I could see my uncle shaking his head as he drove off.

"Just remember I'm in charge," I told Dana as we walked into the main office. She was seven years old and liked to boss everyone around. But not today. No sir. I was in charge.

Dana didn't see things the same way. "Keep

281

thinking that."

"Welcome back, Joe," Miss Julie said when she saw us. She was wearing the red shirt and white shorts she wore there every day. I didn't have to wear my uniform today because it was casual Friday. "I'm glad you could join us, Dana. There's a lot of work to do."

Dana huffed, but I reminded her that she was there to help. "It's not my job," she complained, crossing her arms. "You do it."

I couldn't wait much longer to see Fox. He was probably in the fields with his parents. I wanted to tell him what happened at school and how I beat Shane. He'd love to hear about it after what Shane and his dad had done to him.

"He's in the learning center," Miss Julie said. I wanted to see Fox before I started working, and she understood he was my best friend. "Don't take too long. There's a lot of work and I've only got you for a few hours."

I grabbed Dana's hand and headed down the hall. The learning center was where we took visitors to teach them about the animals there. We had all kinds of animals: rabbits, deer, raccoons, and even a skunk. But most importantly, we had foxes. It was our job to help raise baby animals that were abandoned. Miss

Julie and other vets helped care for sick and injured animals too. They were all released once they were old enough or healthy enough to make it on their own. I had no idea why Fox would be in the learning center.

I froze when I opened the room door. Fox was standing on his hind legs at the front of the room, facing a squirrel, an opossum, a rabbit, and a raccoon. If that wasn't weird enough, he was standing behind a podium. The brownish orange hair on his body shined brilliantly in the room's light. He held out his paws for me and Dana to wait a minute.

He spoke to the animals. "And that's why farts smell like rotten eggs." He winked at me.

"Class dismissed." Nine months ago, this would have been unbelievable. It was only odd now because none of the animals could understand Fox, but they all wanted to be around him. He was one of a kind.

Dana ran up to Fox and hugged him. To her, he was like a walking, talking teddy bear. She never liked animals much but couldn't get enough of Fox.

"That was crazy," I told Fox. "They can't understand you. Only we can." He had gotten braver with humans ever since his performance in Las Vegas. Everyone who worked there knew he could talk. We did everything we could to hide his location from the world.

"Maybe not," Fox said. The best friend bracelet he shared with me glimmered around his wrist. I looked down at mine and smiled. It was the best birthday present I ever got. "But the fart joke was funny." I couldn't argue with him—it was hilarious. We both laughed.

Fox stumbled to the side and leaned against a table. I'd never seen him lose his balance like that.

"Are you okay?" Dana asked him.

He hit a paw against his head a few times. "The room's spinning. I just need a nap."

I was worried about him, but I had learned animals need as much as twenty hours of sleep a day. We don't see it in our pets because they change their sleeping schedules to match ours. But they do take "cat naps" throughout the day.

"You know what we should do?" I asked Fox. I waited for him to answer with me because it was an ongoing joke with us. "We should go to China."

Fox didn't say anything. He stared at me for a minute. Then he said, "Why?"

Now he was going to play along with me. "Because they have rainbows!" But Fox didn't say anything. He looked confused.

He banged a paw against his head again. "But we have rainbows here." I waited for Fox to joke with me but it never happened. His eyes moved from side to side.

Dana grabbed my arm. "Something's wrong."

Then everything fell apart. Fox stumbled again and fell flat on his back. I raced over to him. His eyes were closed like he was asleep. "Get Miss Julie!" I shouted to Dana. "Hurry!"

She raced out of the room. I sat beside Fox and held his head in my lap. "Please be okay. Please be okay."

Miss Julie ran into the room with Dana. "Stand back," she said. "Give him some room." She bent down and ran her hands over Fox's head and body. "He's burning up."

"Do something!" Dana cried to Miss Julie. I stood and wrapped an arm around her.

Miss Julie grabbed a small flashlight from her pocket that I'd seen her use with the sick animals. She shined it into Fox's mouth and eyes. Then she turned it off and sat on the floor. "I don't understand."

"What is it?" I asked, standing behind her. "What's wrong?" I was scared to death Fox was in trouble. He had already gone through so much. He didn't deserve this.

Miss Julie turned and looked up at me. "His eyes were blue. I know they were."

I stepped around her and looked into Fox's eyes. They were gray. I'd never seen them like that. He always had bright blue eyes. What did this mean?

Miss Julie took a deep breath. "I checked his pulse and his breathing. He's okay." That was a relief. "I'm going to get some fluids in him and keep him rested for now. And I'll get his temperature down." I wasn't sure that was enough. She placed one hand on my shoulder and the other on Dana's shoulder.

"I don't know what's wrong," she admitted. "But Christopher may be able to help."

Fox was in trouble and there was nothing I could do about it. I was stronger than ever before but what good was it if I couldn't help Fox? All I could do was wait until I heard some news from the one person who could help—Christopher, a.k.a. Tater the Exterminator.

FRIDAY NIGHT

I couldn't say anything when my mom picked us up that night. My whole body was numb. Dana wouldn't stop crying. I held her close to my side while my mom hugged us both.

I almost lost Fox once. I couldn't do it again. I remembered how scared I was the first day I met him. He stared back at me with his blue eyes, stood up on his hind legs, and talked to me. I remembered how much trouble he got me into while he tried to get to our chickens. I remembered how he stood up on stage in Las Vegas and showed the world who he was. And I remembered we would always be best friends.

"He's going to be okay," my mom said when she stopped the car at home. Her voice was broken. "We have to believe that."

I wanted to believe her. I jumped out of the car and headed for the house. I froze when an orange cat with brown stripes walked in front of me, stopped, sat down, and stared up at me. It had big, round, yellow eyes.

"How cute," my mom said. "It's an orange tabby." She kneeled and made a clicking sound

with her tongue. The cat didn't move. "Where did
you come from? Don't be afraid, little guy."

Dana stood next to my side. "Is that … is it possible?" I knew what she was thinking. Maybe this cat could do the same things Fox could. Maybe it could stand up like a human and talk to us. It didn't have blue eyes though. The cat stood on all four paws and stared up at me.

Then it did the one thing no one expected. It walked up to Dana and rubbed its sides against her legs. It purred so loud we could all hear it. It was super weird because Dana didn't like any animals except for Fox. I waited for her to kick the cat away.

Instead, she picked the orange cat up and put it over her shoulder. She patted its back and said, "I've got you, kitty cat. I'll take care of you."

My uncle pulled into the driveway in his pickup truck. He got out and stood behind Dana. "What in the world is going on?" he asked, scratching his head.

I shrugged my shoulders and kept walking toward the front door. "Welcome to the Twilight Zone." The cat was cool and all, but I had to focus on Fox. Miss Julie said she'd call me if anything changed with him. I planned to wait by the phone all night.

No one talked at the dinner table later that night. My mom had made baked chicken—Fox's favorite food. I kept staring at the phone, waiting for it to ring. Dana kept looking at the door, wanting to go outside and play with the cat. My mom and uncle kept looking at each other, talking silently.

I wondered if the night would ever end. The clock on the living room wall seemed like it was broken. It felt like hours waiting for a call but only minutes had passed.

I jumped when someone knocked on the door.

"Who could that be?" my mom asked,

wiping her mouth with a napkin. I didn't have any idea. She stood up and walked to the door. We all tried to see who was on the other side when she opened it. "Hello, Christopher. Come on in."

I was happy to see the exterminator who had once been a danger to Fox. I chuckled when I remembered how he thought he had big ears, but really, he had a long hotdog nose. He was wearing a green suit with a red striped tie that was way too long. We saw him every month when he sprayed pesticide around the house because my mom had prepaid him for ten years of extermination work.

"Hey, everyone," he said, waving at us. "I wanted to give you the news in person."

My heart sank. It had to be bad news if Christopher couldn't tell us over the phone. I gulped when he walked up to the dining room table. I figured there was nothing anyone could do for Fox. I was breathing so hard I had to use my mouth to get in enough air.

"He's going to be okay," Christopher assured us. He nodded at me. "He's weak, sick, and tired, but he'll make it through the night just fine."

I took a deep breath and sighed. I believed him. "What's wrong with Fox? What can we do?" My mom stood behind me and put her hands on my shoulders.

He crossed his arms. "I don't know yet. Julie contacted me because I know the best person who can help Fox now."

"Who?" my uncle asked. I forgot he was as worried about Fox as the rest of us were. He didn't approve of Fox at first, but they became friends after watching wrestling on TV together.

"I have a friend up north who may be able to help Fox," Christopher said. "He used to live around here but moved to Oklahoma a few years ago."

It didn't make any sense to me. I threw my

hands up. "If the veterinarians at the sanctuary can't help, what can your friend do?"

He unfolded his arms and looked around at us. "He's not like the rest of us. We call him the Fox Whisperer."

I put a hand on my forehead. He was crazy. I should have known it all along. I mean, the guy called himself Tater the Exterminator because he thought he had potato ears.

"Trust me," Christopher pleaded. "He's the right person to help Fox." He nodded at me again. He wanted me to believe him. "I already called him, and he's flying here tomorrow afternoon."

I didn't know what else to say to him before he left. Tater the Exterminator had a friend named the Fox Whisperer. Dana liked an orange cat that liked her back. And I was just a normal kid who was stronger than everyone else now. I didn't think my life could get any weirder. But it did.

SATURDAY MORNING

I didn't get any sleep the night before. I had a hard time standing up behind our table at the farmers' market. I argued with my mom that I needed to check on Fox and couldn't come today. She told me that he was in good hands and there was nothing we could do until the Fox Whisperer got there. And this would keep me busy and distracted. I was mad about it but there I was, selling eggs with her like I did every Saturday.

"Brave enough to try an egg today?" my mom yelled over to Mr. Jim Bob at the fruit and vegetable table next to us. I always saw him with that straw hat on and wondered if it was glued to his head. He wore a clean pair of overalls. I wondered if he owned any short pants or tank tops.

"Not on your life," he replied in his strong country accent. I didn't expect him to after he ate Old Nelly's rotten eggs. I missed that chicken. I would never forget she said I was chosen. I wished I knew what I was chosen for.

"Excuse me," a man I had never seen before said when he walked up to our table. He had light brown skin that reminded me of the Jet Li movies I used to watch with my dad. He wore a black suit without a tie. And there were two bigger men like him standing behind him like bodyguards. "How much are the eggs?" He picked one up and smelled it.

My mom didn't waste any time going into her sales pitch about how our chickens were farm raised. She said our eggs tasted better than store bought eggs. I didn't know if that was true or not. Eggs always tasted the same to me after they were scrambled. "It's six dollars for half a dozen eggs."

The man snapped his fingers. One of the big guys behind him handed him some money.

"I haven't seen you before," my mom told him. We knew everyone in that town after being there for almost a year. "You're not from around here, are you?" She smiled and took his money.

He didn't smile back. "I'm here on business from China." I wished Fox was there right then. I remembered how he liked to stand behind people and scare them by raising his paws and shouting, "Sneak attack!"

The man bowed and said, "You may call me Chen."

"Nice to meet you, Chen," my mom said. "My name is Julie." She pulled me close to her side. "And this is my son, Jonah."

I wished my mom would stop calling me that. "Please call me Joe," I told him.

He nodded and reached a hand out to shake mine. I froze when his hand touched my skin. It was as cold as ice. I'm not kidding. I don't remember touching anything that cold in my entire life. Goose bumps shot up all over my body. He stared at me with angry eyes. I stepped back. I had to get away from him.

"China," my mom said. "That sounds exciting. I hope we can go there one day." I hoped I never had to go there. I hoped I never had to see this man again.

I was relieved when Mr. Hunter stepped up to our table. I didn't think I'd be so happy to see the old man with a bald head and bushy eyebrows. "Hey, Joe. Is everything okay?" He looked over at Mr. Chen and the two big guys with him.

I was scared of Mr. Chen. How could I let Mr. Hunter know that? I should have blinked hard three times. But I didn't have to.

Mr. Chen snapped his fingers again. The big guys behind him moved to the side so he could turn around. "I need to go now."

My mom held up a hand. "Don't forget your eggs."

He shook his head and said, "Keep them." He looked straight at me and said something that made me swallow hard. "I'll see you soon, Joe." He turned and marched off with the two big guys following him.

I was glad Mr. Hunter showed up when he did. He had saved me more than once. Like when he bought all my chocolate. It seemed so long ago when I had tried to earn enough money to help save my great-grandma's house.

"What time is it?" Mrs. Hunter said when she joined her husband on the other side of the table. She smiled at my mom and said, "Hello, dear." She smiled at me too. "Hi, Joe." Me and my mom both smiled back at her and said our hellos.

"Look at that," Mr. Hunter said, holding his wrist up in the air and pointing at his watch. "It's my favorite time of day." He lowered his wrist and smirked at me. "Nap time."

I laughed. I don't think I've taken a nap since I was four years old.

"Laugh all you want," he said, crossing his

arms. "While you're mowing the lawn or doing chores, I'll be dreaming about lying on the beach and eating tacos."

Mrs. Hunter frowned and shook her head. "Unfortunately, he's not kidding." She jabbed an elbow into his side. "That's what happens when you become an old fart."

My mom reached for her pocket and pulled her phone out. She put it to her ear. "Hello?" she said, turning from all of us so we could keep talking. I liked the Hunters but I had to know if that was Christopher on the phone. He said he'd call as soon as his friend got into town.

"Uh huh," my mom said into the phone. "Yes. Okay." I hated listening to one side of a conversation. I could only guess what the other person was saying. "We'll be right there." She closed her phone and put it back into her pocket.

She was taking too long to tell me what was going on. "It was him, wasn't it?" I hoped it was so he could help Fox.

She placed a sign on the table that said FREE EGGS. Then she nodded and said, "Yes. Let's go." I walked away without looking back. "Sorry about this," my mom said to the Hunters. "We'll catch up later."

Mr. Hunter threw his hands up. "Where are you going so fast? What about the eggs?"

My mom raced behind me towards the parking lot. "Keep the eggs!" she yelled to the Hunters. "They're on the house!"

"I never turn down a free meal!" Mr. Hunter shouted back, rubbing his hands together. "Unless it's broccoli! I hate broccoli!"

SATURDAY AFTERNOON

I wasn't sure what to say when the Fox Whisperer asked me questions at the sanctuary. His name was Elan, which he explained means "friendly". He had darker skin than mine, like Chen's. Miss Julie told me that he was an American Indian. I had seen a lot of movies with my dad that had cowboys and Indians in them. But the Fox Whisperer didn't look like any of them. He wore jeans and tennis shoes, had an awesome haircut, and never stopped smiling.

"Were his eyes always bright blue before?" Elan asked me. I looked over at Fox. He was stretched out and asleep with a blanket over him on a table to keep him comfort-
table. I wondered how much Miss Julie had told Elan. She stood by his side and nodded at me.

"For as long as I've known him," I admitted. I had no idea if his eyes were bright blue before that. I never thought about it.

"How did you first meet him?" Elan pressed. I wasn't sure how much information to give him. Fox was sick and the Fox Whisperer was supposed to help him. That was his job, right?

"None of that's important," my mom said. She stood by my side. She could read my mind. We were both afraid Fox's abilities to walk and talk would be discovered.

"It's okay," Miss Julie said to us. "Elan's seen the video. He knows what Fox can do." I wished the video Shane had recorded never existed. It was the only reason Fox was there in the first place.

My mom said it was okay to tell Elan everything. "I met him at our chicken coop last year," I told him. I remembered how Fox had stared at me and smiled.

"Is that far from here?" Elan asked. I wasn't sure why that would make any difference.

"It's about thirty miles," my mom said. "In Andalusia."

Elan put a hand on his chin and paced around the room. He kept looking over at Fox. "I've been searching for a long time." What did he mean? What was he searching for? He was making me nervous the same way Dana did when she smiled at me.

"What are you talking about?" Miss Julie asked. She was checking Fox's eyes and throat again while he was asleep. His tongue was hanging out of the side of his mouth with slobber all over it.

Elan stopped pacing the room and looked around at us. "There were eight Indian tribes here in Alabama before we were forced to leave." He shook his head like he was disappointed. "Now there's only one."

I didn't understand. Why would anyone make them leave? I looked up at my mom. "That's not fair. Why did this happen?"

He smiled at me. "It was in the 1800s—long before you were born. The United States was young, like you." He stepped in front of me and put a hand on my shoulder. "You are pure and strong, Joe. Have your eyes always been blue?"

What was he talking about? I had brown eyes. He pulled a small mirror out of his pocket, just like the mirror Miss Julie had to check the animals with. He held it in front of my eyes. They were bright blue!

"Tell me something, Joe"—he winked at me—"have you noticed anything different? Are you faster, stronger, or smarter than you were before?"

I gulped. Months ago, I had almost beaten Shane at an arm-wrestling contest. And yesterday

I did more pull-ups than anyone else. And come to think of it, I was the only person in my sixth-grade classes to get straight A's—I had never done that before. I didn't want to tell Elan any of that because I was afraid I'd become a science project.

He bent down and looked into my eyes. "It's okay. You were chosen."

Goose bumps ran down my arms. I remembered Old Nelly saying those exact words to me in the chicken coop. I was stronger and smarter than I had ever been before. But why me? Why was I so special?

Elan stood back up and walked over to Fox. He stroked Fox's head. "There was one tribe you won't find any records of. I heard stories about them my entire childhood." His eyes became blank like he was remembering something. "They called themselves the Talking Dragons. They believed humans and animals could work together."

My mom held me close. "Is my son going to be okay? You have to do something!" She sounded hysterical, like she was about to cry.

Elan smiled at her. "He's going to be better than okay. There's nothing to worry about."

My mom held me tighter. "How can you

say that?" she shouted. "Look at what's happening to Fox!"

Miss Julie put her hands up in front of her. "We all need to calm down." Elan didn't come here because he had to. He just came to help."

My mom took a deep breath and stared at Elan. "What do we do?"

Elan nodded. "Fox's abilities come from the land he was on, the land owned by the Talking Dragons." He smiled at me again. He had a way of making me feel safe and comfortable. "Fox must go back to the land he was chosen by."

My mom let go of me and crossed her arms. "What about my son?"

Elan flashed his magic smile. "The land chooses those who are pure of heart. Joe is more special than you can ever imagine."

I didn't know if any of what Elan said was true. I hoped he could help make Fox better. It didn't matter if I was stronger or smarter if I couldn't share it with my best friend. I was about to find out for sure.

SATURDAY NIGHT

I looked at the outhouse as we walked past it. My mom, Miss Julie, and Elan were with me. Fox was in Elan's arms, wrapped in a blanket. My uncle and Dana waited for us in the backyard by the chicken coop.

I remembered the day I opened the outhouse door for the first time. I ran for my life when a grasshopper jumped out and surprised me. Dana and Fox had walked in circles, flapping their arms, making chicken sounds, and laughing at me. I was embarrassed that day, but I wished I could get it back.

Dana ran up to Elan and Fox. "Is he going to be okay?" she asked, walking backwards while facing them. She rubbed Fox's head. He was still asleep.

"We'll know soon," Elan promised. He turned to me. "Where did you meet him, Joe? Around here?"

I pictured Fox's bright blues looking back at me when I stepped out of the chicken coop nine months ago. "Yes." I pointed at the spot where Fox had stood on his hind legs and asked me where my collar was.

Elan laid Fox on the ground and took the blanket off him. Fox looked so young and healthy with his brownish orange hair, white chest and tail, and black paws. I didn't understand how he could be sick. "The land will decide what happens next," Elan said, stepping away from Fox.

What did he mean? I thought all we had to do was take Fox there and everything would be better. "You said this would help him." I tried not to cry. "It has to work."

"The land will decide," Elan repeated. He smiled at me again, but I could tell he was concerned. I wasn't sure he believed anything he told us about the land and the Talking Dragon tribe. He made everything up. He was another

crazy person like Tater the Exterminator.
I should have known better than to trust either of them.

"Maybe we should dance around him and chant like the Indians do," Dana said. I shook my head. My mom must have told her that Elan was an American Indian.

"That's not going to help," Elan told her. He wasn't smiling anymore.

The night got darker and darker. My legs were hurting from standing for so long, so I sat down in the grass. This was a waste of time. There had to be another way to help Fox. I wanted to grab him and take him to my room. But that wouldn't help.

Dana sat next to me. "He's going to be okay, right?" she asked. There were tears in her eyes. She didn't think this was going to work either. "Hey, what's going on with your eyes?"

I turned away from her. "Nothing."

She grabbed my head and turned it toward hers. "They're blue, just like Fox's." She probably thought I was a freak. "You're so lucky."

I didn't feel lucky. I needed to steer the attention away from me. "Where's your cat?"

Dana shrugged. "I haven't seen him since last night. He was a stray cat." Her eyes lit up and she laughed. "I've got a name for him if he comes back." Her shoulders shook every time she laughed.

"Spit it out," I told her. "What is it?"

She looked at me with serious eyes. "Peanut Butter Jelly."

I chuckled. "What? Why?"

She scooted in close. "Any time I spend with him… I can call it Peanut Butter Jelly time!"

We both laughed and started singing a song we heard on the internet. *"It's peanut butter jelly time, peanut butter jelly time…"*

I froze when I saw one of Fox's paws move. He was waking up. I stood and brushed my pants off. Dana bumped into me when she stood up too. My mom, uncle, Miss Julie, and Elan were on the other side of Fox. We all stared at him to see what would happen next.

It was slow. Fox stretched his legs out and yawned. His ears perked up. His eyes were still closed. My heart was beating fast. Did it work? Was he better?

Fox stood on all four paws, smiled, and opened his eyes. They were bright blue! He rose slowly on his two hind legs, raised a paw into the air, and said something that let me know everything was okay.

"My name is Mr. Awesome Muscles!"

I laughed and gave him a high five. Dana tackled him when she hugged him. My mom and Miss Julie both shook Elan's hand. He wasn't crazy after all.

Elan walked over to me and gave me a fist pump. "Trust the land." I nodded. I wasn't sure what the land had chosen me for, but it had saved Fox.

As I watched everyone hug Fox and talk with him, one realization hit me: he could never leave this land again. This is what gave him the power to walk and talk. It protected him. And without it, he would be sick. We couldn't be sure what would happen to him if he went away again. He couldn't go back to the sanctuary. I didn't know how to tell him that he may never see his parents again.

SUNDAY MORNING

I woke up because the sun was shining through my bedroom window and right into my eyes. I scooted further down the bed so the light wouldn't make me blind. That was better. A couple of birds were chirping outside. It made me smile.

Fox was asleep in the blanket den I had made for him months ago. I had never taken it down because I hoped he would return one day. I would have slept next to him on the floor, but he was restless and kept kicking me in the side. And his paws were like ice cubes when they touched my back.

I sat up and lifted the blanket closest to my bed. Fox was lying in the middle of the den on his stomach with all four hairy legs straight out like an airplane. He was facedown with his tongue sticking out. There was slobber all over my favorite pillow. Yes, I let him sleep on my favorite pillow. He could keep it now. Yuck!

I lay back down and thought about how perfect everything was. Fox was back with us and not in any more danger. He could stay there forever.

My mom threw my bedroom door open and rushed into my room. "Jonah! Get up right now." Her hands were in the air. "Why are you still in bed?"

I didn't know why she was so upset. I had plenty of time to get ready for Sunday School and church. My alarm clock hadn't gone off yet. I sat up and blocked the sun from my eyes. I looked over at my clock on the table next my bed.

Only, it wasn't there! Oh, no. Where was my clock? I jumped out of bed and said, "Sorry."

My mom had her arms crossed and was tapping a foot on the floor. She didn't like being late for anything. "Breakfast is on the kitchen table. Hurry up." She stormed out of the room, shaking her head.

I lifted the den blankets and yelled at Fox to wake up. He grabbed a sheet and pulled it up over his head. And that's when I saw it. My alarm clock was crushed and broken into pieces by Fox's back paws.

I snatched the sheet away from Fox. He crossed his legs and paws and shivered. "What is this?" I yelled at him. "What did you do to my clock?" It looked like he had smashed it with a hammer. My mom was mad at me because of what Fox had done. Some things never change.

He yawned and looked at the broken pieces. "Oh, that." He stretched his legs and stared at me. "You're not gonna believe this." I couldn't wait to hear it.

"So here I was," Fox continued, "sleeping nice and quietly, minding my own business." He sat up. "All of a sudden I heard screaming by your bed." His eyes got big. He pointed to the broken alarm clock. "It was jumping around like a bunny rabbit on five cups of coffee."

I couldn't help but laugh. Bunny rabbits don't drink coffee. At least I don't think they do.

"I pounced on the little monster," Fox said. "I defeated it." He stood on his two hind legs. I could tell he was proud of himself because he had saved me. "No thanks needed. Maybe some chicken, but that's all."

I threw on a pair of shorts and a tee shirt. "Come with me," I told Fox, heading for the kitchen. I couldn't be mad at him. He still had a lot to learn. Now he was back, we had all the time in the world for that.

"Glad you could make it," my mom said when we walked into the kitchen. "Eat your breakfast. Then wash up and get dressed for church." Her face was red. We had missed Sunday School. "There's no excuse," she muttered. "There's really no excuse."

I felt bad but it wasn't my fault. "Fox ate my alarm clock," I told her. I sat down at the table, grabbed the plate with my omelet and sipped on a glass of milk.

Fox sat across from me with his own omelet. "Traitor," he whispered.

My mom stepped behind Fox and rubbed his head. "You poor thing," she said to him. "You must be starving. You were gone for months and they didn't feed you properly." She nodded her head like she fixed something. "I'll make sure you always have chicken."

Fox ate the omelet with a big smile on his face. He winked at me.

I bit into my omelet and spit it out. It didn't taste anything like the eggs we normally ate. "What is this?" I asked my mom. "What did you put in my egg?" Was she trying to poison me?

She waved a hand like she was insulted by what I said. "It's a chicken omelet. It has chicken, onions, and banana peppers." Banana peppers? Who ever heard of that? "Oh, and I added a hint of cayenne and cheese."

Fox burped when he finished his omelet. "I like it." He looked at mine. "Are you gonna eat that?" I shook my head and pushed my plate across the table to him. Before he sunk his teeth into my omelet, he had the nerve to say to me, "Now that you have some free time, you can make me another chicken omelet."

My mom laughed with him. It wasn't funny. Fox wasn't the one who was starving. I was!

"Hey, Fox!" Dana shouted when she and my uncle walked into the house. She raced into the kitchen and kissed his cheek.

"We can't miss the wrestling match today," my uncle said to Fox from behind me. "World Championship. Mr. Awesome Muscles versus King Thunderbutt." He sounded super excited.

I didn't mind that Fox got so much attention, but I felt invisible. "I'm right here," I complained to them. "In case anyone cares."

My uncle squeezed my shoulders. Dana rolled her eyes at me. "Hey, Joe," she said, "you've got egg on your face." I wiped my face as fast as I could. There was nothing there. Dana and Fox laughed.

I had to laugh with them. "You got me." I let them talk all they wanted to while I got up to get ready for church. Dana would go with me and my mom. My uncle and Fox would stay there to watch the men in underwear fight on TV. I looked back at them and smiled. It was awesome seeing them together like this. We weren't all born from the same blood, but we were all family.

LATER SUNDAY MORNING

I was officially a Back Row Baptist. Dana and Melissa sat there with me every Sunday morning now. It gave us a chance to talk without being disturbed. Today, I needed to figure out what to do with Fox. He was healthy again, but he couldn't go back to the sanctuary.

Melissa was in her blue Sunday dress with polka dots. Dana wore a nice white dress. I wore slacks and a buttoned down white shirt. I wore a black tie with it—not the kind most guys wore. Mine was a clip on that snapped onto my shirt in a flash. The regular ties were like rope you wrap around your neck. No thanks!

I told Melissa about everything that had happened the night before. I had promised to be honest with her. And I needed her opinion. I would have asked Dana, but every time I looked at her, I started singing, *It's peanut butter jelly time,* in my head.

Before I could say anything, the one person I never expected to see there tapped me on the shoulder.

I turned around and looked up at my sworn enemy. It was Shane. He was smiling at me. What was he doing there? That was my one place to be surrounded by family and friends. It was the only place I could think clearly and feel safe. And now he was going to ruin it.

"Joe," he said, looking at me with a straight face. I was confused. He had always called me Jonah. "I'm sorry. For everything." I froze. I didn't believe him, and I had no idea how to respond.

His dad grabbed him and led him towards

the front of the church. I couldn't breathe. Mr. Connors and Shane were the ones who had put Fox in so much danger. They had no right to be there! They couldn't be trusted. My blood was boiling.

"Calm down, Joe," Melissa said, grabbing my hand. "Breathe. It's going to be okay." I wanted to believe her. But I was disgusted. I was breathing so hard that my chest hurt.

Dana scooted forward and put her hands together. "We should pray for Shane," she encouraged me. She closed her eyes. "Dear Lord, please let Shane trip over his feet and fall on his face. Amen." I couldn't help but say, "Amen," with her.

"Hey, Joe!" I jumped when Mr. Hunter stepped into my row and said, "Be sure to thank your mom for the eggs." I nodded at him before his wife grabbed him and pulled him away.

The church organist played the same song she did every Sunday. The service was about to start. From his seat up front, Shane turned and stared at me. I couldn't have been more uncomfortable.

The man in front of me stretched his arm over the pew and turned his head toward me. It was the man from China—Mr. Chen! His eyes were cold. "Hello, Joe. It's good to see you again." It wasn't good to see him. The two bodyguards he had with him at the farmers' market were sitting on either side of him. Shane didn't matter anymore. This man made me feel more afraid than anyone else.

"Brothers and sisters," the pastor said to the congregation. "God is good." Several voices said, "Amen." "Whatever you're afraid of today, give it to God." I swear he was looking right at me. "Fear not, my child. I am with you always."

I wanted to believe that more than anything, but I was surrounded by serpents. The people who tried to destroy me and Fox were only a few pews away. And the man who made me shake in fear was right in front of me. I thought about sneaking out and waiting for my mom in the car. With the doors locked.

"Love your enemies and pray for those who persecute you," the preacher continued. Dana had already prayed for Shane. That was good enough for me. The service was taking forever and I thought it would never end.

But then the organist played the same song again. It was time to disappear. "We need to get out of here, right now," I whispered to Dana. I grabbed Melissa's hand and pulled her along as Dana shouted for people to get out of the way.

Before we were out of the aisle, I noticed Mr. Chen and his bodyguards hadn't moved an inch. He was perfectly happy to sit there until everyone else left. What did this mean? Was I crazy? I had to be. Why would this man be any danger to me?

He turned and faced me again. "See you soon, Joe." He gave me a curt wave and faced the front again.

"Joe, wait!" Shane shouted from the front of the church. His dad held him back. "I have to talk to you!"

I wasn't going to fall for any of his tricks. He had pushed me down at school and kicked me at my birthday party. There was no telling what he would do to me in the church. He was despicable.

I pushed through the crowd until we were in the foyer again. The preacher stopped me. How did he get back there? He was just up front, preaching and singing.

"Is everything okay, Joe?" he asked me.

I didn't want to lie to him. "I thought so. But I don't know anymore." I had to keep moving. There wasn't any time to explain.

He put a hand on my shoulder. "We may not always have the answers, but we can always have faith. Sometimes we have to get out of our own way to see things clearly."

"Joe, wait!" Shane shouted from somewhere in the crowd.

I thanked the preacher and rushed out with Dana and Melissa. With any luck, my mom would meet us by the car and get us out of there. Everything was supposed to be better. Why did I feel like it was a lot worse? I wanted to get home and talk to my best friend.

I'm glad I got the chance to before I lost him forever.

SUNDAY AFTERNOON

I never expected what I found when I walked into my house. It horrified me. "What in the world?"

Fox was sitting at a princess table with four teacups on it. He motioned for all of us to join him for a teacup party. Dana had tried for years to get me to play with her, but I refused to do it.

"Out of the way," Dana said, shoving me to the side. She and Melissa joined Fox at the table. They pretended to pour drinks and sip on them. They talked in English accents. I won't lie—it looked fun. But I had to keep my cool image.

My uncle looked at me from the couch. He was watching wrestling. He shrugged his shoulders. "I did what I could."

"A fox has to do what a fox has to do," Fox explained. "I was promised a chicken party if I did this first." He pretended to pour himself another cup of tea and said, "Cheers!"

My mom walked in and closed the door

behind her. She smiled at Dana, Melissa, and Fox. "How cute! I'm gonna have to get my camera." There was no chance in the world you'd find me sitting at the table. "Joe," she said to me, "come join Uncle Mike
and me on the couch first. We need to talk."

That made me feel proud. I was asked to join the secret society of adults. The kids could play games at the princess table while the adults talked on the couch. How awesome was that?

My mom grabbed the remote from my uncle and turned the TV off. He grunted. "We need a plan," she said when we were on the couch. "What are we going to do with Fox?"

As far as I was concerned, Fox could stay with us forever. It wasn't legal for us to keep him, but no one had to know. "He still has the den I made for him. He knows all of us and we love him. He's our family."

My uncle nodded his agreement and tried to grab the remote from my mom. She slapped his hand away.

"I was thinking something else," my mom said.

My uncle rubbed his forehead. "Is that something else going to take more than three minutes?" She crossed her arms and stared at him. "I was just asking," my uncle said with his hands up for protection.

My mom shook her head and sighed. "I was thinking Fox's parents are getting better and they're going to be released soon." I hadn't thought of that. None of the animals were meant to stay at the sanctuary forever. "What if we can work it out so they're released back where they came from?"

I knew what she meant. They had come from somewhere around there, deep in the woods. Fox had said he wandered for days until he found the chicken coop. Their home couldn't be far from there.

"You're right," I told her. "That's the best idea ever. That way, Fox will always be close by." She smiled and messed up my hair.

I wanted to tell Fox the good news, but someone knocked on the door. "I'll get it," I told everyone. I was in such a good mood that nothing could bring me down. I'd get to keep seeing my best friend and he'd stay united with his parents forever.

Time stopped when I opened the door. I was wrong to think that nothing could bring me down. Things couldn't get any worse.

"Hello, Joe," Mr. Chen said to me from the doorstep. His bodyguards were behind him. He was wearing a pair of mirrored sunglasses. He took the glasses off and said, "Give us the fox."

All at once I remembered when we came home from Las Vegas. The house had been torn apart. The furniture was ripped to shreds. The pictures and TV were smashed. And someone had painted the words GIVE US THE FOX on the wall above the door.

These men were dangerous. I reached for the door to slam it shut, but Chen kept it open with his hands and kicked it down. He shoved me to the floor and marched right past me with his henchmen behind him.

"Where is he?" Chen shouted into the room. Then he saw Fox sitting at the princess table with a teacup in his hands. Chen smirked.

My mom and uncle jumped up from the couch and looked at the three men. I figured they were trying to determine if they could stop them.

Chen glared at them and snapped his fingers. One of his henchmen walked over to the couch and stood in front of my mom and uncle, daring them to try to stop him.

"If you hurt these children," my mom hissed, "I will hunt you down. You'll be sorry you ever walked into this house."

Chen laughed and said, "Promises, promises." He returned his attention to Fox. "I've been looking for you a long time. You have no idea how important you are." He snapped his fingers again.

His second henchman headed for the princess table where Dana, Melissa, and Fox were. Melissa shrieked. Dana stood up. "Stay away from him!" she yelled.

The henchman pushed her back into her seat. I got up to protect her, but Chen wagged a finger at me to let me know there was nothing I could do.

But maybe there was. I was chosen for

something. I was stronger and smarter than I had ever been before. This was why. The land had chosen me to protect everyone.

"Stop," Fox said. "Just stop." He stood on his hind legs and put his paws out. "No one has to get hurt." He looked at me and nodded. "We knew it wasn't safe for me to stay here." He looked up at Chen. "Just take me. Do whatever you have to. Leave them out of it."

He was sacrificing himself. I had no idea what these men wanted with him, but they proved they were dangerous. There's no way Fox could go with them.

Chen laughed again. "The fox is wise." He took two steps toward the table. "My employers in China are very interested in you."

The henchman grabbed Fox and held his legs together so he couldn't move. Melissa had a hand over her mouth.

"They're going to take you apart, piece by piece," Chen continued. "Like a clock. They're going to find out what makes you tick." I wasn't going to allow that to happen. I balled my fists and prepared to attack. But I never got the chance.

The back door in the kitchen barreled open

and slammed against the wall. "Who else is here?" Chen asked. No one answered because no one else was supposed to be there. We had no idea who it was. Chen snapped his fingers. The henchman who was standing in front of the couch headed for the kitchen.

He didn't have to. The chubby man with a huge forehead and a hotdog nose stepped into the room. It was Tater the Exterminator!

"Everything's going to be okay!" Tater shouted. He was carrying a big bottle of pesticide and waving the spray stick around. "I got all the ants, roaches, and termites for miles!" He wouldn't stop his crazy laugh with his tongue hanging out.

"Who are you?" Chen shouted.

Tater kept laughing. "You don't know who I am? They know me around these parts! I'm Tater the Exterminator!"

Chen nodded at his henchman. "Take him down." The man marched straight for Tater. I thought for sure he was going to hurt him. I was wrong.

Tater whipped his spray stick right in front of the man's face and sprayed the pesticide full force. The man screamed and scratched at his eyes.

One down.

"Fox!" I yelled. The second henchman turned to face me. Fox was locked in his arms. He could only move his head and tail. "His arms look like chicken legs." I pointed at the man.

Fox didn't do anything at first, but then his eyes lit up. He opened his mouth wide and used his razor-sharp teeth to chomp on the man's arm. The henchman screamed and threw Fox down.

"Enough!" Chen yelled. "You can't stop this!"

The front door busted open again. Three men in uniforms pointed guns inside. "FBI!" one of them shouted. "Nobody move!"

Chen tried to run for the back door, but
Dana stuck her foot out and tripped him. I
cringed when his face hit the floor like a brick.
Dana shook her head at him. "Don't ever disturb
my tea party again. I'm a princess."

It took a few minutes but the FBI agents
handcuffed Chen and his henchmen and took
them away. One stayed behind to ask us
questions. Melissa ran over to me and asked if I
was okay. I was, but I wished I could have done
more. I didn't use any of my gifts. But there was
one thing I had to do.

"I need to tell you something," I said to
Melissa. "We've been friends for a while." My
stomach felt like it was doing belly flops on the
kitchen floor. "I like you—a lot."

"That's sweet," she said. "I like you a lot
too." She blushed and giggled.

I couldn't say anything else because Shane

walked into my house. What was he doing there? Had he followed me? Why couldn't he leave me alone?

"Look us up in a few years," the FBI agent said to Shane on his way out. "We can use men like you. You did a good thing here."

What was the agent talking about? Mr. Hunter walked in and patted Shane on the shoulder. "Thank you, son."

"What's going on?" I asked when they walked up to me and Melissa. Why was everyone thanking my sworn enemy?

"I watch a lot of crime shows," Shane said. "I had a lot of free time after my dad and I were arrested in Las Vegas." I didn't care about his personal life. He probably watched crime shows so he knew how to commit crime.

"When we were in church," Shane continued, "I recognized the man in front of you. He's the most wanted man in America."

I gulped. The most wanted man in America had been following me and attacked my family? I didn't feel good at all.

"I saw him watching you," Shane said. "I knew you were in trouble." He shook his head. "I tried to get your attention, but I don't think you heard me."

I remembered him shouting my name in the church. I realized he wasn't staring at me. He was keeping an eye on Chen.

"Your friend's a real hero," Mr. Hunter said. He shook Shane's hand. "He told me everything after he couldn't get your attention in church. Honestly, I thought he was a crazy kid." He laughed. "He insisted we call the police. The rest is history."

Dana joined us. "That doesn't explain Tater being here."

Mr. Hunter and Shane both shrugged. No one knew why Tater showed up when he did, but we were sure glad he did.

"I was spraying your garden out back, like I do every third Sunday," Tater said to my mom and uncle. "I heard those bad men barge into your house. I looked through the window and saw you were in trouble." He pounded his fists. "I wasn't gonna let them hurt my friends."

My mom hugged him. "I always had a good feeling about you, Christopher."

I searched the room for Fox. He liked to be the center of attention, but I didn't hear anything from him. He was sitting at the princess table, staring at the teacups.

I sat across from him. "Hey, buddy. Are you

okay?"

He looked at me but didn't smile like he usually did. "I can't do this anymore. I put you in danger."

I had good news for him. I told him what I had discussed with my mom and uncle. He could go back to his old home with his parents. It had to be nearby. And he could see us whenever he wanted to.

I expected him to be thrilled. He wasn't. "I want my old life back," he begged.

"I'm confused," I told him. "I just said you can have it."

Fox sighed. "You don't understand. As long as I can walk and talk, you'll always be in danger."

I took a deep breath. He was talking about returning to the wild and being the way he used to be. I couldn't accept that. He was my best friend. I would lose him forever if he was nothing more than a wild animal. It didn't make any difference anyways. He'd be sick without his powers.

"None of this is your fault," I assured him. "I'm sorry, but there's not a way to go back."

"Actually," someone said from behind me, "there may be a way." I turned and looked up to see the American Indian, Elan, smiling at me with a laptop in his hands. "Christopher called me and said it was an emergency. It's time for me to tell you everything."

Everyone gathered around the table. Elan looked at the group. "I haven't been completely honest with you." I knew it! He made everything up about the Talking Dragon tribe and the land having power.

"You lied?" my mom asked. "Why?"

He shook his head. "I never lied." He focused on Fox. "I have been searching for you and this land my entire life. I am the last tribal member of the Talking Dragons."

My head wouldn't stop spinning. I lived on historic American Indian land that no one else knew about. And the last member of that tribe stood in front of me. It should have been a dream come true.

SUNDAY NIGHT

My stomach twisted inside and out as we walked past the outhouse again. We were about to say goodbye to Fox forever.

I was surrounded by so many people that Fox had touched. It wasn't just my mom, uncle, Dana, and Melissa. There was also Elan, Miss Julie, Tater, and Mr. Hunter. Ms. Julie had brought Fox's parents. Shane lurked behind everyone like he was ashamed. This was like going to a funeral.

We stopped in front of the chicken coop, where this all started. It was bittersweet. I wanted the best for Fox, but I didn't want to lose him.

"Form a circle around Fox," Elan said. Fox's parents stood on either side of him.

Melissa grabbed my hand and squeezed it. I wrapped my other arm around Dana's shoulders. She was crying.

"So," Dana said through tears, "now are we supposed to dance or chant something?" She tried to laugh but it turned into a cough.

"I know you're all worried," Elan said. "And I can't lie. I've never done this before." He smiled wide at us to make us feel calm. "But we're doing this so Fox can live his life the way it was meant to be. It's what he wants."

My mom and uncle were on the other side of the circle. They both wiped away tears. My uncle and Fox were wrestling buddies. My mom treated Fox like he was one of her own children.

Shane and Mr. Hunter were on my right. Shane had always been my enemy and had helped kidnap Fox to destroy me. But something had changed in him. He had helped save Fox. It was weird to think we might be friends one day. Mr. Hunter didn't know Fox very well, but he had always supported me.

Christopher and Miss Julie were on my left. They had proven to be the most valuable to Fox. They helped him and his parents. I had misjudged Christopher at first. I laughed when I remembered he thought he had potato ears, when he really had a hotdog nose.

"You'll want to say your goodbyes to Fox," Elan said. "Once he returns to his natural state, he may not remember any of this or any of us."

I waited for everyone else to hug Fox and tell him goodbye. There were a lot of tears. It was hard to stand there and watch. I tried to swallow but I couldn't. My throat wouldn't move.

"I'm gonna miss you," Dana said to Fox with tears in her eyes. "Thanks for the tea party. No one else ever did that for me." She bent down and hugged him.

He winked at her. "I hope you don't think I forgot." She shrugged. "You owe me a chicken party." They laughed and waved goodbye.

My mom was the last person to speak with Fox before me. "You're a good fox," she said. "No matter what happens, always remember we love you."

Fox hugged her leg. "You're a second mom to me. Thank you, Mom." My mom held her chest when she walked away. I thought she was going to fall over.

And then Fox was standing alone in the center. It was my turn to say goodbye. I forced my legs to move toward him. They felt like cement.

We faced each other but didn't say anything for the longest time. I was cold and sweating. My heart wouldn't stop racing. I couldn't breathe. I wanted to beg him to stay.

"You know what we should do?" Fox asked.

"We should go to China," I replied, trying not to smile.

Fox shook his head. "No, we shouldn't. Not

after today." We both burst out laughing. He was right. He raised his paws into the air and said, "Sneak attack!"

We both fell on the ground laughing. Just like the old days. "Thank you for everything," Fox said. "I mean it."

I stood up with him and hugged him. "Thank you for being my friend." I held out my wrist with the best friend bracelet he had gotten me for my birthday. He held out his. "Best friends forever," we said together.

I stepped out of the circle. Fox's parents stood by his side again. He was doing the right thing. He was a good fox.

We all clasped hands when Elan spoke in a language we had never heard. I guessed it was the language of his ancestors, the Talking Dragons. I didn't take my eyes off Fox. I had to see if anything changed about him.

Nothing happened until a few minutes later. I watched Fox's eyes change from blue to brown.

Elan stopped talking. He told us to give Fox some room because he might not recognize us and become scared. We broke the circle and gathered in one group. Fox looked at us like he was confused. Like he was trapped. His wide eyes seemed afraid of us.

"Fox!" I called out. "It's me, Joe. Remember?"

Fox stared at me then he turned and ran off into the woods. His parents followed him. He was afraid of me. He didn't recognize me. It was like I never existed to him. I covered my eyes and cried more than I ever had before.

My mom held me and kept saying, "Shh. It's going to be okay." I wished I could believe her. Dana cried in my uncle's arms. That made me cry harder.

A few minutes passed. Or maybe hours. Melissa patted me on the arm. "Joe. Look."

I turned and followed her gaze. Fox was walking slowly out of the woods. Everyone backed away to let me stand in the open all by myself.

As Fox got closer, he inched slower and slower on his four legs. I wasn't sure he recognized me, but he sensed we had a connection.

I stayed still as he came closer and sniffed my shoes and pants. He looked skittish, like he would run if I moved even a little. He stopped sniffing when he saw the bracelet on my wrist.

He looked back and forth from his bracelet to mine. He was remembering. "Best friends forever," I whispered. He licked my hand, bowed his head, then turned and ran back into the woods.

He remembered me! Not completely, but our bond would never be broken.

"Do you think we'll ever see him again?" Dana asked when she joined me. Melissa was with her.

"I hope so," I told her, smiling.

The adults and Shane were talking behind us. We were all sad and excited. Fox would always be a part of our lives.

"Look!" Dana shouted. The stray orange tabby walked around her legs and purred. "It's Peanut Butter Jelly!"

"That cat's been out here all night," Melissa said. "I saw him by the chicken coop earlier. He stared at Fox the whole time he was talking to us." She faced Dana. "Why would you call him Peanut Butter Jelly?"

Dana and I laughed and started singing, "*It's peanut butter jelly time, peanut butter jelly time...*"

The orange tabby meowed while we sang. I think it wanted us to stop. It walked away from us and towards the woods. And then it did the one thing I never expected.

Peanut Butter Jelly stood up on his hind legs and looked back at us with bright blue eyes he didn't have before. "This whole night was weird," he said. "Foxes can't talk."

DAVID BLAZE

CONTENTS

THURSDAY MORNING

I didn't know the answer to Miss Turner's math question when she tapped on my desk. I smiled, swallowed hard, and shrugged my shoulders. I wanted to run out of the classroom and go home.

"Does anyone else know the answer?" she asked all the kids around me. She was the youngest teacher at the school and had a pretty smile with bright white teeth. I wished I could smile back. I stared down at my desk. I was good at every subject but math. I hated it.

Jennifer stood up behind me. Of course she

knew the answer. She was the president of the Mathletes, the school math team. She only wore blue dresses like every day was a tea party. She had matching blue ribbons in her blond hair. "I do, Miss Turner," she said. I didn't have to turn around to see her glaring at me. "The answer is four. Everyone knows that. Well, almost everyone."

The other three girls around me laughed. They were all on the math team. Jennifer's math army surrounded me.

"Everyone settle down," Miss Turner said. She leaned in close to my ear and whispered, "Melissa, meet me at my desk after class." I didn't know if I was in trouble or not. I sank into my chair.

She stood at the front of the classroom and faced all eighteen of us. "I hope you've all had a chance to work on your math assignment. It's due tomorrow."

I felt like a deer caught in headlights. The assignment had been given to us weeks earlier. I hadn't even started on it. I thought I had a lot of time to figure it out and get it done. But now it was due tomorrow and I had no idea how to do it!

The class bell rang. I sat at my desk as the rest of the kids walked past me. Jennifer and her math army stopped in front of my desk. "We're competing in the county math championship tomorrow night. You should come watch us win." She flipped her hair back and snapped her fingers for her army to follow her out. "Maybe you can learn something. But I doubt it."

I knew she was being mean, but my daddy had taught me to be nice to everyone. "I hope you win."

Amanda stayed at my desk when the other girls walked away laughing. She was the only girl on the math team who was nice to me. She wore big glasses and dressed like we had a school uniform. "Don't listen to her. She's having a bad hair day." We both chuckled.

"Amanda, let's go," Jennifer commanded. Amanda smiled at me then joined the rest of her team by the door. The other girls kept pointing at me. They whispered to each other and laughed. One of the girls laughed so hard that she coughed and couldn't stop. I felt small.

"Are you okay, Vanessa?" Miss Turner asked her. "That's a nasty cough." She rushed over to Vanessa.

"I'm fine," she said, still coughing. "It's only a cold."

Miss Turner stood by Vanessa's side and put a hand on her forehead. "You're burning up. Go see the school nurse." She looked at her watch. "I've got to head that direction for a minute. I'll go with you."

I hoped she was okay, but I was glad I didn't have to talk to Miss Turner now. I hadn't started on the math assignment and wouldn't get it done by tomorrow. I'd have to stay home and hide under my bed all day.

"I'll be right back," she said to Vanessa. "I need to talk to Melissa."

She marched to my desk and stood over me. "I know you're having a hard time in this class. Let's get you some extra help." She put a hand on my shoulder. "I'll talk to your dad."

I smiled at her as she walked out of the room with Vanessa. I missed my dad. I wished I knew when he was coming home. He was an electrician. He went to Puerto Rico to help them get their electricity back after Hurricane Irma took it away. He was like a superhero.

I stood and put my math book in my backpack. One other person could help me. He had blue eyes and was the smartest person I knew. He was my friend Joe.

THURSDAY AFTERNOON

I headed straight for Joe's house when I got off the school bus. He lived on the street next to mine. We used to hang out after school together, but he was never around anymore. He was always with Shane. It was super weird because Shane used to be the school bully. He was eleven years old like Joe and me, but he was so tall that he looked like he was supposed to be in high school.

I stared at the yard before I walked into it. Patches of grass and patches of dirt filled the yard. The house was older than my dad. A chicken coop was in the backyard. Joe's great grandma Rita had lived here for a long time. He and his mom moved in last year.

I brushed my hair back with my fingers and straightened my clothes before I knocked on the door. I smiled as the door opened. I hoped Joe was on the other side.

"Joe's not here," his little cousin Dana said with her arms crossed after she opened the door. She had beautiful bright brown hair. She didn't live here but spent a lot of time with Joe and his mom. She was a tough kid and took karate lessons, but she was nice if you were nice to her.

"Where's he at?" I asked her. "I need his help." I felt desperate. My dad helped me when he was home. My sister was supposed to be taking care of me, but she was in college and always busy. Joe was my last hope in getting the math assignment done.

"I don't know," she said, shrugging her shoulders.

I wanted to cry. Dana was seven years old. I couldn't ask her for help. "Can I talk to your aunt?" Miss Johnson was an adult. She could help me.

"She'll be back in a minute," Dana explained. "She went across the street to ask Mrs. Hunter something. You can hang out here if you want. I have pizza rolls." She paused. "But they're mine. Don't touch them."

"Come and get em!" a high-pitched voice shouted from behind her. "Pizza rolls for everyone!" My favorite cat in the world, Peanut Butter Jelly, poked his head out from between Dana's legs. He was laughing his head off.

I laughed with the talking tiger striped orange tabby. The brown stripes on his orange fur were beautiful. His blue eyes appeared green in the right light. It was hard to believe he'd only been here for a few weeks. It was harder to believe he could talk like you and me.

"Those are my pizza rolls!" Dana complained.

"They were," Peanut Butter Jelly said, standing on his hind legs and rubbing his belly. "They were nice and warm going down my throat. Now they're safe in my belly."

"What!" Dana shouted. She brushed him out of the way and marched back into the house. "This better be a joke!"

Peanut Butter Jelly looked up at me and whispered, "April fools."

I shook my head and laughed. "It's not April, Peanut Butter Jelly." It was February. He had learned so much from us since the first day he stood up and talked. I had always wanted a cat. I wished he could live with me. PJ was independent, but he was okay with me calling him my cat.

"Maybe it's not April," he said, "but it should be." He winked at me. "And don't call me Peanut Butter Jelly anymore. I'm not a little kitten." He puffed his chest out. "I've got hair on my chest. Call me PJ."

I was confused. "You have hair on your

entire body."

Dana stormed back over to us. "That wasn't funny." She had a plate full of pizza rolls in her hand. She shoved the plate in front of me. "Hold this. But don't touch my pizza rolls. Don't you dare touch them." I didn't argue with her. It was useless. I didn't want the pizza rolls anyways.

Dana reached into her pocket and pulled out a metal pen. It looked like the one Miss Cox had in her English class. She called it a laser pointer. Whenever she pointed it at the chalkboard, a small red ball of light would appear.

"I've got something for you," she said to PJ. She pressed the button on the end of the pen and pointed the pen at a wall in the living room. A red ball of light appeared on the wall.

PJ faced the wall and got down on all four paws. His tail waved back and forth slowly. "We meet again, evil red ball. I will defeat you." He didn't realize Dana was controlling the light with her pen. And that it wasn't evil.

Dana waved the pen back and forth. The red light moved from one side of the wall to the other. PJ's head moved in rhythm with it. His tail waved faster and faster. He lifted his rear end into the air like he was ready to attack.

"You can run but you can't hide," PJ mumbled. "It's go time!" He raced toward the wall like a wild animal. He jumped up and swatted at the red light when he reached the wall. It moved faster than him. Side to side. He kept swatting at it like a crazy cat.

I burst out laughing. There was no way for him to catch the ball of light. Dana smirked at me and yawned as she waved the pen one last time. Then she pressed the button on her pen again. The ball of light disappeared.

PJ spun in circles. "Not again! I will find you. And I will win." He ran from room to room. "Why does this keep happening to me?" he yelled.

Dana closed the door behind us. "That should keep him busy for a few hours." She snatched the plate of pizza rolls back from me. "Come help me feed the chickens." She headed for the kitchen. The back door was in there.

I set my backpack down on a dining room chair. I opened the backpack and pulled out my math book. I laid the book on the table so Miss Johnson would see it when she came home.

The three-page math assignment was stuffed in the middle of my book. Miss Turner called it an assignment, but it was really a math test. And it was worth half of the grade for that class. If I failed the assignment, then I would fail the class. That's why I was desperate.

"Hurry up," Dana commanded. For a little kid, she sure was bossy. She set her plate of pizza rolls on the kitchen counter. Then she opened the back door and waited for me to join her. I shook my head and followed her out the door. She shoved a bag of chicken feed into my hands as soon as we stepped outside.

"Last person out the door feeds the chickens," she said. She marched toward the chicken coop. I sighed and followed her past the outhouse. I chuckled when I remembered the first time Joe opened it. He ran away screaming after a grasshopper jumped out at him.

We stopped at the chicken coop. Five chickens were walking around the fenced area. The rest were inside.

"We don't have all day," Dana complained. She pointed at the bag of chicken feed and nodded at the chickens. "Hurry up."

I threw out a handful of feed. More chickens came out of the coop. "I miss him," I said to Dana.

She put her hands in her pockets. "Who?"

I missed my best friend. "Joe." I couldn't look at her. I felt lost without him. I passed him in the halls at school sometimes. He didn't talk to me like he used to.

Dana huffed. "Me too. He's different since Fox left." PJ wasn't the first animal to talk on this land. Fox left weeks ago to return to his parents. Joe was heartbroken about it. Fox had been his best friend.

"Most nights," Dana continued, "he sits out here and stares into the woods." I hated to hear that.

Dana sat on the grass and folded her legs. She took a deep breath and closed her eyes. She became calm and still, like she was in another world. I thought it was weird but didn't say anything. I wondered what she was learning in the karate class.

She missed Fox as much as her cousin Joe did. "Let's go back inside," she said after a minute. "Hopefully PJ didn't burn the house down."

I smiled and walked with her back into the house. I froze when I saw the kitchen table. My math book was wide open, and the three-page assignment was spread over the table. What had PJ done? "No, no, no, no, no." I was sure he had destroyed it in his search for the red ball of light.

I ran to the table and grabbed the papers. They were okay. I breathed a sigh of relief and opened my backpack again. The math book and papers would have to stay in there until Miss Johnson came home. One of the papers caught my attention.

"What is this?" I whispered.

Dana sat at the table and stuffed another pizza roll into her mouth. "It's a sheet of paper." She winked at me when I glanced up. I held the paper in front of me and looked over the other two sheets. Every math problem had an answer next to it – even the bonus question about seconds, minutes, and hours on a clock. Someone had filled in the blanks.

"Where's it at?" PJ asked when he raced into the kitchen. "I will catch that red ball. It can't hide forever." He looked beneath the table and opened all the cabinets.

It felt foolish, but I had to ask him. "Did you do this?" I held the homework out to him.

He stood on his hind legs and looked at the papers. "The math game? It wasn't very fun." He held his paws out. "No one wins."

I didn't think I could trust his answers to be right. Dana agreed with me. "What do you know about math? You chase a ball of light and think you're going to catch it."

"I'll catch it," PJ promised. "Wait and see." He motioned to me. "Cats know everything about math. We have to know how high to jump. How fast to run. And how many naps to take."

I had no idea if the answers were right, but this was a talking cat. How many cats can talk? Maybe, just maybe PJ was a math genius.

"Twenty," Dana said, laughing. "You take twenty naps a day. You're so lazy."

I put the math book and papers into my backpack and zipped it closed. It would take most kids hours, or even days, to do the math work PJ had done. Or in my case – forever. I wasn't sure what to do.

"My aunt will be home soon," Dana reminded me.

My heart was racing. Was it crazy to think I could turn these papers in to Miss Turner tomorrow? They were already done. No one would ever have to know a cat had done the work.

"I'm going home," I told Dana. "My sister is waiting for me." That wasn't true. My sister never waited for me. She was out with her friends.

"Okay," Dana said. "I'll let Joe know you were here. Kissy, kissy." I blushed. Dana knew I liked Joe. I hung out at this house way too much.

"Bye, Melissa," PJ said. "Call me if you find that ball of light."

As I walked home, I couldn't stop sweating. I felt excited and guilty about the idea of turning in the math papers. I had never cheated in my life, but I was about to fail that class. Maybe PJ was the answer to all my problems.

LATE THURSDAY AFTERNOON

I set my backpack on my bed when I got home. My sister Angie wasn't there yet. I hoped she'd come home soon because I needed her advice. She was eight years older than me. She'd know what to do.

I sat on my bed and stared at the backpack. Tomorrow morning, I could open it in class and hand the math assignment to Miss Turner. The answers were probably wrong but at least she'd think I tried. I didn't want her to be disappointed in me.

The only other thing I could do was tell Miss Turner I didn't do the assignment. If I admitted that, I'd fail the class. She'd call my dad when he came back from Puerto Rico and have a meeting with him. I'd have to go to summer school. My life would be over.

I heard Angie's old car pull into the driveway. I raced into the living room and waited by the front door. My big sister had been in Miss Turner's class years ago. She'd know what to do.

"Hey, sis," Angie said when she walked in. "I've got a date tonight and I need to get ready." She wore a cute pink dress.

I stood in front of her so she couldn't get around me. She would lock herself in the bathroom for hours doing her hair and putting on makeup. "I need your help."

She sighed. "What is it?"

I raced into my bedroom, unzipped my backpack, and pulled the assignment out of my math book. Angie was standing in front of me when I turned around. I handed the papers to her.

"What's this?" She shuffled the three pages. "I remember this stuff. I was never any good at it."

I guess it ran in our genes. "Me either. A cat did it for me." She had never met PJ. I wasn't sure how she'd react.

Angie stared at me. I didn't know what she'd say next. She didn't say anything. She burst out laughing. "Whatever you say." She looked back down at the papers. "This looks good. It's better than I could have done." She handed the papers back to me. "I'm proud of you."

I was speechless. My sister had never been proud of me. She usually called me names or ignored me. It felt wrong that she was proud of me for something I didn't do.

"Are you okay, sis?" she asked. "What do you need help with?"

I sat on my bed. I wanted to tell her the truth. I wanted to tell her that PJ could walk and talk. I wanted to tell her that I was like her and couldn't understand the math homework. But I realized I couldn't.

I laughed when I wondered what would happen if she believed a cat had done my homework. She'd put me in a home for crazy people. Everyone knows cats can't do home-work. They can't even talk.

"Everything's fine," I told her. "You should get ready for your date." She smiled and walked out of the bedroom.

I put my backpack on the floor and laid back on my bed. I had no idea what to do. I mean, I knew what the right thing was. But was the right thing the best thing? Why did life have to be so hard? I wished I was an adult.

I almost convinced myself to get up and tell Angie that I was there the night PJ stood and talked for the first time. There was something magical about the land Joe's great grandma had left for him and his mom.

I yawned as the room got darker. I closed my eyes and tried to figure out what I was going to do tomorrow. My stomach felt like it was twisted inside and out. I wanted to do the right thing. I wasn't sure if I could.

FRIDAY MORNING

I was the last person off the school bus that morning. I felt sick when I thought about walking into Miss Turner's class. I didn't want to get out of my seat. The bus driver stared at me through his rearview mirror. I knew he wanted me to get out of my seat. He had a big frown on his face.

I took a deep breath, stood, and picked my backpack up from the floor. It felt like it weighed a thousand pounds. I slid it onto my back and walked slowly off the bus. Daddy had taught me to smile when I felt sad. I'm not sure it did any good.

I felt invisible as the kids around me went into the school. Some of them were excited and didn't stop talking. Some of them bumped into me and kept going without saying a word. Some of them looked as sick as I felt.

I passed by the gym and saw Coach Brown yelling at a kid. He always wore a red cap and had a whistle around his neck. I don't think he liked kids. Most of us were afraid of him.

Before I reached Miss Turner's room, Jennifer stepped in front of me. "Hey, Melissa," she said in a sweet tone. Her math army wasn't complete. Tracy and Amanda were with her, but Vanessa wasn't. "You have a great smile."

I wasn't sure why she was being nice. She had been mean to me ever since the second grade. "Thank you," I told her. "I love your hair."

She turned to Tracy and laughed. "Doesn't she have a great smile?"

"Sure," Tracy said. "If you count her pretty teeth, that's the number of times she'll have to take sixth grade math class before she passes it." They both laughed at me and walked away. Amanda whispered, "Sorry." I wanted to get back on the school bus.

I stepped into Miss Turner's class with my head down. I knew what I had to do. I sat at my desk and set my backpack on the floor. I opened the backpack and pulled out my math book. The three-page assignment was inside of it.

Jennifer kicked my chair from behind. "It was nice knowing you," she laughed. Tracy laughed with her from the desk on my right side. Amanda shook her head. I waited for Vanessa to laugh on my left side, but she wasn't there. The math army was a soldier short.

"Welcome to class," Miss Turner said from the front of the room. "I hope you all had a chance to complete your math assignment." Several kids groaned. "I've got a video for you to watch while I grade them." She pointed to a TV on a cart by her side. "Go ahead and pass your papers forward, please."

Jennifer kicked my chair again. "Here you go," she said. "Don't count the papers. It'll take you all day." She shoved her papers against my arm. I turned and grabbed them. I knew there were only three pages.

Miss Turner was standing over my desk when I turned back around. "I'll take those." I gulped and handed them to her. She looked at them. "Where are your papers, Melissa?"

I stared at my math book. The papers were inside. All I had to do was pull them out and hand them to her. She would never know a cat had done the work. I could get away with it if I wanted to.

But I couldn't do it. I was scared and ashamed when I looked into Miss Turner's eyes. I took a deep breath so I could speak. "I don't have it."

Jennifer jumped out of her seat and stood up. "I did my work, Miss Turner," she said. "It was hard but smart people like me can do it." She looked at me and shook her head like she felt sorry for me. "It's not Melissa's fault she's not smart. She was born that way."

My hands were shaking. I wanted to cry. Miss Turner's face was redder than mine. "Jennifer, get your things and sit by my desk." That's where she made us sit whenever we were in trouble. "What you said was mean and hurtful. Apologize to Melissa right now."

She huffed and said, "I'm sorry you're not any good at math."

Miss Turner guided Jennifer to the desk by hers. She straightened her clothes and came back to my desk. "I'm sorry about that, Melissa. None of what she said is true. I'm going to speak with her parents."

All the kids in that room were staring at me. I had never been so embarrassed in my life. There was only one thing I could do to save myself. I opened the math book and pulled out the three pages. I handed them to Miss Turner. "I thought I forgot them, but here they are."

She looked over the papers and smiled at me. "Thank you, Melissa. I knew you could do it." I sank into my chair when she collected the other papers. *What had I done?*

Miss Turner turned the TV on and played a boring movie about the history of math. At least it was better than doing schoolwork. The people it spoke about had weird names, like Archimedes and Pythagoras. The only name I recognized was

Albert Einstein. I think he invented the light bulb. Or was that some other guy?

Miss Turner smiled and winked at me when she sat back down at her desk. I hoped my papers were the last ones she would grade. PJ had probably made up the answers. I crossed my arms over my desk and put my head down. I just wanted the class to end. The anticipation was too much.

"Melissa!" Miss Turner called out from her desk. I looked up at her. My heart beat a million times a minute. She had figured everything out. "Come here for a moment, please."

Tracy chuckled when I stood up. Several boys shouted "ooh" like I was in trouble. My head was spinning. I focused on Miss Turner's desk and took one step at a time toward it.

"Did you have any help with this?" Miss Turner asked when I stood next to her. She was tapping her red marker on my papers.

My lips felt like they were stuck together. My tongue felt like a big ball of cotton in my mouth. "Yes," I finally said. That wasn't a lie. PJ had helped me by doing the whole thing. "I asked my sister for help." That also wasn't a lie.

She stopped tapping her marker. "I have to

ask – did your sister do any of this work?" Her lips were as red and as straight as her marker. My sister had been in the class years ago. She had barely passed the class.

I looked Miss Turner straight in the eyes. "My sister didn't do any of the work. She didn't help me at all."

Miss Turner looked down at my papers again and grunted. She seemed angry at me. It was my fault I hadn't studied harder. I should have asked my dad for help when he was here. "I see," she said. She sounded disappointed. "Go sit back down, please."

Jennifer chuckled from the other side of Miss Turner's desk. I forgot she was there and hadn't noticed her. The leader of the math army had figured I wasn't any good at math. She had heard everything and now she knew it for sure.

I wanted to cry when I walked back to my desk. It was obvious the answers were wrong. I was about to fail this class, and I had never failed anything before. Why did math have to be so hard?

The TV was talking about a guy named Isaac Newton. Whoever he was. I put my head down on my desk again. My life was over. My daddy was going to come home from Puerto Rico and find out I wasn't the smartest girl in the world like he thought I was.

Thirty minutes later, Miss Turner turned the TV off. I sat up straight and stared at the chalkboard behind her. I couldn't look her in the eyes anymore. I felt ashamed.

"Most of you did well," Miss Turner said. "One or two of you will need some extra help."

Jennifer made a fake coughing sound. Then she said my name fast and fake coughed again. The whole class laughed.

"Quiet down," Miss Turner said. Her face was red again. "A few of you got a perfect score." Jennifer and Tracy both cheered. They always got perfect scores. "But only one person got the bonus question right."

Jennifer stood up behind Miss Turner. She

was all smiles. She waved at the class like she was accepting an award for being the smartest person alive. I felt sick. I couldn't watch her gloat while my life was falling apart. I had to get out of that room.

"That person," Miss Turner said, sounding chipper, "is Melissa." She smiled at me and nodded her approval. The room became silent. No one believed it. How was this possible? I couldn't move.

Jennifer's smile disappeared. Her eyes were so big that they looked like they were going to explode. She sat back down and didn't take her huge eyes off me.

The class bell rang. The kids around me rushed out of the classroom. I would have run out with them, but Miss Turner blocked my way. She looked back and forth from Jennifer to Tracy and Amanda.

"I know it's short notice," Miss Turner said to me, "but the Mathletes could use your help tonight."

Jennifer shot out of her seat. "No!" Her hands were on her hips. Her eyes were redder than a hot volcano.

"Vanessa is sick," Miss Turner said. "The

county championship is tonight. You can't play without a fourth person." Jennifer kept shaking her head. "It's not what anyone planned for, but it's the only way you can play."

Why wasn't anyone talking to me about it? The girls didn't want me on the team and I didn't want to be on it. I wasn't any good at math! "I don't think I can make it," I said. "My dad is in Puerto Rico." My sister or Miss Johnson could take me, but they didn't need to know that. I put my math book into my backpack and stood to leave.

"I understand," Miss Turner said. "But you need a few more points to pass this class." She put a hand on my shoulder. "I'll award those points to you if you participate in the competition."

I bit my lower lip. I couldn't fail this class – not now. I'd have to stand next to Jennifer, Tracy, and Amanda and keep my mouth shut. I hated it but what else could I do? "What time does the competition start

FRIDAY AFTERNOON

I held my breath when I knocked on Joe's door again after school. I couldn't believe I had agreed to be a part of the math competition. What was I thinking? I hoped Joe was home so he could give me some tips.

Miss Johnson answered the door. "Hey, Melissa," she said, smiling. "Come on in." She waved for me to join her inside the house. I was glad to see her, but disappointed Joe wasn't there. She must have gotten off from work early for the weekend.

"I've got you now," PJ said from the living room. He was circling slowly around a pink ball of yarn. I shook my head. He pounced on the yarn then batted it away. "Get back here!" he yelled. The yarn unraveled as it rolled down the hallway. He chased after it and pounced on it again.

"It never gets old," Miss Johnson said, chuckling. "Come with me to the kitchen, Melissa. I made chocolate chip cookies." She didn't have to tell me twice. I loved cookies. Chocolate chip was my favorite.

"Joe's not here?" I asked.

She shook her head and told me to take a seat at the kitchen counter. She put a plate of cookies and a glass of milk in front of me. "Joe will be back Sunday night. He's staying with his friend Shane for the weekend." She paused. "And Dana is with her dad."

I felt lost. The cookies smelled great, but I couldn't eat any of them. My stomach was twisted in knots. In a few hours I was supposed to be in a competition I knew nothing about.

"Is everything okay?" Miss Johnson asked. She sat in the chair next to mine and wrapped an arm around me. Her eyes were wide like she was concerned. "You can talk to me."

She was a great mother to Joe and a great aunt to Dana. I could trust her, but I couldn't tell her everything. I couldn't tell anyone everything. "I have a friend who didn't tell the truth about something."

HELLO
I AM A...

STORYTELLER

"I see," Miss Johnson said. "And how does your friend feel about this?"

"She's scared and confused," I replied. It felt weird talking about myself like I was someone else. I hoped she didn't realize I was talking about me. "Now she's got to do something she's not comfortable with to cover up her lie."

Miss Johnson took her arm from around me and looked me straight in the eyes. "I don't know what your friend lied about, but I think she'd feel a lot better if she told the truth."

I huffed when she said that. "Everyone will laugh at her if they find out what she did." They would all know I wasn't any good at math. I was so bad at it that a cat had to do it for me!

"Are you going to eat any of those?" she asked, pointing at my cookies. I shook my head. I lost my appetite when I thought about the Mathletes. She stood, grabbed the plate of cookies, and covered them with plastic wrapping. "Tell your friend not to worry about everyone else. It's important she feels good about herself."

She sat back down next to me. "The problem with lies is that you often have to tell more lies to cover the first one up. Then you tell so many that you can't remember what the first one was." She nodded slowly at me, like she wanted to make sure I understood what she was saying. "In the end, you're only hurting yourself. And you may lose the trust of the people you lied to."

She was right. I think she knew I was talking about myself. Joe was lucky to have her as a mom. "Thank you," I whispered. My throat was tight.

PJ walked into the kitchen on his hind legs. His head was as high as my stomach. "That yarn won't bother you anymore," he said to us. "I took care of it. You're welcome."

Miss Johnson reached over and rubbed his head. "You must be starving. Are you ready for your Meow Masters?" She stood and walked over to the kitchen sink. She opened the cabinet beneath it and pulled out a bag of cat food.

PJ jumped up and down. He kept licking his lips. "You know what I like!" he shouted. "Give it to me!" I had to laugh. He could eat whatever he wanted. PJ was addicted to Meow Masters.

He got down on all four paws when Miss Johnson put a bowl of it in front of him. PJ shoved his face into the bowl. He ate it so fast that food went flying all over the floor. When he was done, he burped the way that only a cat can. It sounded like he was coughing up a hairball. A nasty, wet hairball. He wiped his lips with a front paw.

"Mind your manners," Miss Johnson scolded him.

He stood and apologized. He put a paw on my leg. "I want to be a Meow Master. That would be the life." He was talking about the cat food commercials on TV. The Meow Masters were cats that could do the impossible. They were like ninjas. They could catch balls of light.

PJ scratched at my leg. "Did I win the math game?"

"What math game?" Miss Johnson asked.

I stood and said, "Look at the time. I need to get home."

Miss Johnson handed me the plate of cookies. "Take these with you." She walked with me to the front door. "Your friend sounds like a smart girl. I'm sure she'll do the right thing."

I hugged her. "She will."

PJ scratched at my leg again. "Did I win?"

I looked down at him and smiled. "We both won."

LATE FRIDAY AFTERNOON

I was surprised to see my sister Angie when I got home. She had never been home this early. "What are you doing here?"

"I've got a surprise for you," she said with a huge smile. She looked excited. I had to stop her. When she got excited, it was hard to get her to stop talking. I had to make her understand the truth about my math problem.

"Hold on to that thought," I told her. "They want me to compete in a math contest tonight."

My sister's eyes got big. "The school?"

I nodded at her. "I'm not going to do it, though." On the way home, I had decided not to go to the math competition. It was dishonest, and I would look like a fool.

Angie grabbed my shoulders. "You have to do it!" She looked like she was out of breath. "No Morgan girl has ever been able to do that."

She hugged me. It was awkward because she hadn't hugged me in years.

I pulled away from her. "Daddy doesn't need to know anything about this." I was already going to be in enough trouble when I told Miss Turner the truth on Monday. "Just leave it alone." I had to put this fire out before it started.

Angie put her hands in the air like she was surrendering to the police. "What's wrong, sis?"

I could only shake my head at her. I wanted to cry. I didn't have any problem telling her the truth. I didn't want to have to face my daddy. I couldn't bear the thought of him being disappointed in me.

"Don't be mad at me," she said, "but I called

him last night and told him about your math assignment." I couldn't breathe. On most days we couldn't reach him in Puerto Rico. "I'm proud of you. I knew he would be too." She put her hands down.

I had never felt so guilty in my life. Daddy was proud of me for something I didn't do.

"So you see," Angie continued, "you have to go to the math competition." She was smiling again. "We're both proud of you."

I put my hands in my pockets. My head was spinning. I could go to the competition. It was only for one night. I would let Jennifer and her math army answer the questions. Then all of this could go away. I would never have to lie again, and no one would get hurt.

"It's at the school gym in a couple of hours," I said. I felt exhausted. "You can drop me off."

"Yea!" she squealed. "We're the Morgan sisters. I'll be with you every step of the way." She danced around the room like she had just received the best news in the world.

I shook my head and sighed as I watched her excitement. I was sure no one would be at the gym to watch the competition. There was nothing to worry about. Tonight wouldn't be bad. I just wanted it to be over.

FRIDAY NIGHT

I froze when I walked into the school gym with Angie by my side. The bleachers were full of parents, grandparents and people I had never seen before. They stared at me. I was sure they were secretly laughing and pointing at me. It was my worst nightmare.

Joe's mother called my name and stood up from the bleachers. She smiled, waved, and walked toward me. I turned to Angie. "How did she know I was here?"

Angie shrugged. "It's because I called her and told her about tonight. You spend a lot of time at her house. I thought it would make you happy."

I jumped when Miss Johnson tapped me on

the shoulder. "Hey, Melissa," she said. She looked around the gym and at the tables that were set up in the middle of it. "Does this have anything to do with the math game PJ asked about?"

I wasn't sure what to say to her. I couldn't think straight with all the noise around me. Everyone was talking. All I could focus on were the tables. Two long wooden tables were laid out straight in the middle of the gym. Four chairs were under each table.

"Did you talk to your friend about her lie?" Miss Johnson asked. She was staring into my eyes. I had never felt so guilty in my life. My stomach felt like it had been punched.

"Welcome to the Covington County Math Competition," a man's voice said through the speakers in the gym. "Contestants, please take your seats."

I wanted to throw up. Miss Johnson smiled at me, nodded, and headed back to the bleachers. "You're going to do great," Angie said to me. "Smile!" A bright light flashed in my face when she took a picture from her cell phone.

I was shocked when Amanda came from behind me and linked her arm around mine.

"Come on," my friend said. She pulled me toward the tables. "I'll tell you how this works." I didn't have any choice but to follow her.

When we sat at the table, we were facing the crowd in the bleachers. There must have been hundreds of people. It wasn't supposed to be like that. "I didn't think anyone came to these competitions," I said to Angie.

"It's usually just the parents," she said. "But this is the biggest competition of the year." She looked around me to the table lined up with ours. On the other end were four kids I didn't know. "They're from the Catholic school, Saint Gertrude's."

Jennifer and the rest of her army sat on the other side of me. "I see you decided to show your face," she said. "Stay out of my way." She rolled her eyes and flipped her hair right into my eyes.

"Here's how it works," Amanda continued. "There's a red buzzer in front of us." I looked at the table before me. There was a red buzzer for each contestant. A sheet of paper and a pencil was next to each buzzer. "If you know the answer when the moderator asks it, press the button. You can calculate on that paper if you don't know right away."

I had a feeling I wouldn't be pressing the button at all. The only things I'd be drawing on the paper were unicorns. I like unicorns. "What if I don't know the answer?"

Amanda laughed. "That's not a problem. Jennifer answers all the questions on this team." That didn't seem right or fair, but who was I to argue? "The first team to get ten points wins."

I looked into the audience and smiled. Everything was going to be okay. I could sit there and act like I knew what I was doing. No one would ever know any different because Jennifer would do all the work. I would pass Miss Turner's math class. Nothing could go wrong.

"Hey, sis!" Angie called out from behind me. I hadn't realized she never sat in the bleachers. "Before we left home, I told you I had a surprise planned."

I turned to tell her to sit down. I didn't need her embarrassing me in front of all these people. But that's not what happened. The one man I would have never expected to be there was facing me.

"Daddy," I squealed. I jumped out of my seat and ran to hug him. I was full of mixed emotions. I was happy he was back from Puerto Rico. But I felt horrible that he would see me behaving dishonestly.

"I love you, baby girl," he said. "I'm so proud of what you've done." He looked at the table and into the crowd. "Now go show everyone what you can do."

I stumbled back to my seat. My daddy had a huge smile as he sat on the first row of the bleachers with Angie. He gave me a big thumbs up. Seeing Daddy there made me feel like the worst person in the world. There's no way that night could get any worse.

"Is everyone ready?" the same voice I heard on the speakers asked. A man in a black suit was standing at the center of the tables, between the two teams. He spoke to the audience. "For the first time ever, this math competition will be broadcast live on Channel 9."

A woman with a huge TV camera stood right in front of me. I couldn't move a muscle. My face felt like it was cemented in place. I didn't want to be famous — not like this! The woman walked past me and filmed the other contestants.

"The team that wins tonight will be declared the county champions," the moderator continued. "That team will move on to the state championship." He cleared his throat. "Here is the first question: If three out of five teachers gave you homework today, what percent of teachers didn't give you homework?"

Before I could even think about it, Jennifer hit her buzzer. How was that possible? She stood and faced the crowd, though I don't think she was supposed to. "If three out of five teachers gave us homework, then forty percent of them are awesome and didn't give us homework."

The moderator cleared his throat. He looked as surprised as me. There was no way Jennifer could have gotten the answer right. Not that fast. "That's, uh, that's correct. One point for Waterfalls Middle School!" That was the name of our school.

Jennifer waved to the crowd like she was a princess. She made sure to smile big for the TV camera. She sat back down and said to me, "That's how you do math." It didn't look like she had done any math at all.

"Here is tonight's second question," the moderator said. I grabbed my pencil and prepared to draw a unicorn. "If you double the number of books in your locker and add five more, you'll have twenty-three books. How many books do you have in your locker?"

I had three books in my locker. And the latest edition of *Girl's World Magazine*. I had a feeling that wasn't the answer he was looking for.

A boy from the other team hit his buzzer. Jennifer looked around me and glared at the kid at the far end of the table. He wore big green glasses and a green bowtie. He stood with his mouth opened wide. He looked like he was going to pee in his pants.

"If I have twenty-three books then I need to subtract the five that were added," he said. "That gives me eighteen. Since the number was doubled, I need to take away half of that." He stood and stared back at Jennifer with confidence. "I have nine books in my locker." He put his arms in the air. "Boo-yeah!"

Amanda nudged me. "He's cute," she whispered.

"That's correct," the moderator said. "One point for Saint Gertrude's!" He looked directly into the camera. "Ladies and gentlemen, we officially have a math war." The crowd in the bleachers cheered. Jennifer crossed her arms and sat back. I got the feeling no one had ever challenged her. I smiled.

The next hour was exhausting. Jennifer

would get an answer right. Then the kid on the other team would get an answer right. It went back and forth like a seesaw. I didn't think it would ever end. The front and back of my paper was full of unicorns.

"It's a tie!" the moderator shouted. "Both teams have nine points. Whichever team answers the next question correctly first, wins!" He grabbed a glass of water and swallowed it all in one gulp. He wiped his brow like this was exciting and exhausting. I didn't care. I was trying to figure out how to tell my dad the truth about everything when this was over.

"The final question is: What is the total number of times that the hour hand, minute hand, and second hand go around a circular clock in one day?"

A buzzer on my team's side went off first. A buzzer on the other team's was right behind it. That team groaned. Jennifer's math army cheered and crowded around me. I had no idea why. But then I did.

The buzzer in front of me was lit up like I had hit it. But I didn't. Jennifer's hand was on it. "What did you do?" I asked her. Why would she destroy the team's chances when she knew I wasn't any good at math?

"I was wrong," she said. "We need you here." The other girls agreed with her. "The final question is the same one that was on Miss Turner's math assignment as a bonus. You're the only one who got it right." She put her hand over mine. "Let's win this."

Amanda chanted my name softly. "Melissa, Melissa, Melissa." Then the other girls joined her. ""Melissa, Melissa, Melissa." My dad and sister stood from the audience and chanted with them. "Melissa, Melissa, Melissa." Then everything fell apart. More than half of the people in the bleachers chanted my name over and over. "Melissa, Melissa, Melissa." It was deafening.

My whole body shook. I couldn't think. The TV camera pointed at the people cheering for me. Then it focused on me. I had no idea what to say. I had no idea what the answer was.

"We need an answer," the moderator said, "or Saint Gertrude's will have the chance to steal."

I tried to remember the answer I had seen on the math assignment after PJ filled it in. I could only think of one number. "The answer is four."

The moderator sounded excited. "That's…" He shuffled through the papers in his hands, like he was looking at the wrong one. His voice deepened. "That's incorrect."

The cheering stopped. The room fell silent. Except for a cricket. A cricket chirped somewhere in the gym and wouldn't stop. I waved the camera away and put my hands over my face.

"I knew you were a fraud," Jennifer spat at me. "You're going to pay for this."

The moderator leaned over and whispered, "Sorry, kid." Then he stood up straight and talked to the camera. "And now for the nail-biting climax. Saint Gertrude's, what is your answer?"

The kid at the end of the table stood again. He was shorter than I thought he was. And he was cute like Amanda said. "The hour hand goes around the clock two times every twenty-four hours. The minute hand goes around twenty-four times. And the second hand goes around 1440 times." He smiled big and pointed at Jennifer. "The correct answer is 1466. Boo-yeah!"

"That's correct!" the moderator shouted. "Saint Gertrude's wins!"

Half of the audience cheered. Jennifer and her math army stood, shook their heads at me, and stormed away from the table. Amanda wouldn't look at me. I grabbed her hand as she walked by.

"I could use a friend right now," I told her. She had been my friend when the other girls weren't. I would forever be known as the girl at school who lost the math championship. My dad and sister had believed I was someone that I wasn't. I was scared and lost. It was all my fault.

"I don't understand," Amanda said, pulling her hand away from me. "You knew the answer, but you blew it."

Miss Johnson stepped out of the bleachers, nodded at me kindly, and left the gym. I should have listened to her. Maybe I could save my friendship with Amanda. I had to tell her the truth.

"I didn't know the answer," I admitted. I watched her eyes to see how she would react when I told her about PJ. "My cat did my math homework."

It was at that very moment I realized the TV camera was pointed directly at me. The woman behind the camera lowered it when I said that. She looked confused and amazed. I stepped over to her. "You can't show that on TV."

"Sorry, kid," she said. "This is live TV."

I rubbed my eyes and put my hands on my head. No one was supposed to know about PJ. It had caused too much trouble when people found out Fox could walk and talk. Maybe it was okay. I didn't really have a cat. I liked to think of him as mine.

I turned back to Amanda, but she was gone. She was at the table with the winning team, talking to the boy who had been nervous at first but was confident when he got the answers right. I was afraid I had lost my friend forever.

I took a deep breath as my dad and Angie approached me. They would tell me that they were proud of me because I had at least tried. But I wasn't sure what they would tell me when I explained to them how I got here. I smiled at them, prepared for my whole world to collapse.

LATE FRIDAY NIGHT

I had a heart attack when I got home with my daddy and Angie. We went in the front door, turned the lights on, and a bunch of people shouted at us, "Surprise!"

Daddy held Angie and me back to protect us. But then he put a hand on his chest and laughed. "You guys!" he shouted. I recognized the Hunters and a few of Daddy's friends. Miss Johnson was there too. Now I knew why she had left the gym in such a hurry.

They crowded around my dad and said things like, "Welcome home!" and "Good to see you!" It took me a moment to realize this was a party for Daddy. He had been in Puerto Rico for months. I shook my head at Angie. No doubt she had planned this.

"Sorry you didn't win tonight," Miss Johnson said to me when she broke away from the crowd.

Everyone else was listening to my dad tell stories about his time in Puerto Rico. "But at least you tried."

I wanted to tell her that I hadn't tried. I owed her that much because she had warned me what could happen if I lied and continued to lie. I had to explain it wasn't a friend that needed help — it was me. I took a deep breath and cleared my throat.

"Speech, speech, speech, speech!" Mr. Hunter shouted. He was an old guy with a bald head and long curly mustache and bushy eyebrows. A lot of kids thought he looked scary, but he was sweet. Miss Johnson turned to face him and shook her head. He was holding up a cocktail glass. All the adults had one.

Daddy held out a hand for Mr. Hunter to hush. "Alright now," he said, chuckling. "I'm happy to be back home with my family and friends. I was given the opportunity to help some of the people in Puerto Rico. They didn't have electricity and couldn't enjoy what we do every day. Some of them are still in trouble. I don't deserve praise. It's our responsibility to help each other."

"Hear, hear!" Mr. Hunter shouted. The adults raised their glasses.

Daddy put out a hand again. "There is one person in this room who deserves praise." He scanned the room until he locked eyes with me. "My daughter Melissa – the math genius!"

They stared at me. The room felt like it was caving in. They smiled and waved their glasses at me. I thought I was going to pass out.

"Wait," I said. I couldn't do this anymore. Daddy had to know the truth. "Daddy, I'm not a math genius." The lights were so bright they were blinding me. "I'm failing my math class and I cheated on my test."

The room fell silent. Mrs. Hunter grabbed her husband's shoulder and said, "It's time to go, dear. Let's let them talk about this." She nodded at me and pulled him along. The others in the room said their goodbyes.

I turned to Miss Johnson to apologize to her, but she was gone. I hoped she didn't leave because of me. I looked back at Daddy and Angie. He looked confused and hurt.

"I don't understand," Daddy said. "You're on the math team and you were in the competition. What's going on?"

I did my best not to cry. "I'm sorry, Daddy. Please don't be mad." My hands were shaking. He had always taught me to be honest. I couldn't tell him a cat had done my homework. That would make me look like a bigger liar. "I'm not good at math. I don't understand it. A friend did my homework for me."

His face was blank. It looked like the life was sucked out of it. He told me the one thing that hurt more than him being mad at me. "I'm not mad. Just disappointed."

That's when I cried. He came to me and wrapped his arms around me. "This too will pass," he said. "I don't want you to feel lost. We'll find you a math tutor." He put his hands on my shoulders and made sure I was looking at him. "I'm not disappointed about the math. I'm disappointed you lied."

Angie stood next to us. "I hate to leave but

I've got a date." I could tell she was uncomfortable with me crying. I wondered if she really had a date. Daddy nodded at her.

"Thank you for telling me the truth tonight," he said to me. "Tomorrow you must tell the truth to everyone you lied to." Two more people needed to know. One was Miss Johnson. The other was my math teacher Miss Turner but she'd have to wait until Monday. The twisting and churning in my stomach wouldn't stop.

SATURDAY MORNING

I kicked a rock across the dirt road as I walked towards Joe's house. My math assignment was in my right hand. I had told Daddy the truth about how I aced it. He was disappointed I had cheated but was proud of me for telling the truth. Now he wanted me to tell Miss Johnson the truth. I hoped I could catch her before she went to the farmers market.

I froze when I got close to the yard. News vans were parked all over the dirt and grass. One was for local Channel 9. The others were national news services.

I ran into the yard. Miss Johnson didn't want anyone to know about PJ. The reporters had to be here because of PJ, but I had no idea how they knew he was here. This was all my fault. I had to do something.

Reporters and camera people stood in front of the house. Miss Johnson stood in the doorway, facing them. She was silent as they kept asking her questions like, "Is it true? Can the cat do math?"

Miss Johnson motioned for me to come into the house. I was behind the reporters and cameramen and would have to squeeze between them. They turned and looked at me.

I felt sick when I saw a man who looked like Chen, the most wanted man in America. The FBI had taken him away when he threatened Fox and put us all in danger. He was the main reason Fox had left. When the man saw me, he pulled a cap over his eyes and walked away.

"Hey, that's the girl!" one of the reporters shouted. They crowded around me like cereal in a box. They asked so many questions so fast that I couldn't understand anything. I wanted to scream for help.

Miss Johnson reached through the crowd,

grabbed my hand and pulled me to the front door. "Back off, vultures!" I stood behind her and shivered. "She's just a kid!"

"We've all seen the video of the talking fox," a female reporter in a red dress said. It had been all over the internet. "Is there a cat here that can do the same thing?" A bunch of microphones were shoved in front of us.

"No comment," Miss Johnson said. "I want you off my property right now." She crossed her arms. "Don't make me call the police."

A few of them grunted. The microphones disappeared. "Let's go," the female reporter shouted to the crew with her. "Just another false lead." They turned and headed back to their vans.

"Hey!" Miss Johnson shouted at the reporter. "Who told you there was a cat here that could do math?"

The reporter shrugged. "It was an anonymous tip." She shook her head and frowned. I felt bad for her because the tip was right. But who else knew PJ was here? And why would they do that?

Miss Johnson started to shut the door, but a man called out, "Hang on there just a second."

He wore a gray suit with a blue tie. He smiled big, holding a briefcase in one hand and a hat in the other. He didn't look like the other reporters.

"I tried to be nice," Miss Johnson said. "You reporters are not welcome here. Get off my land."

He held out his hands and stepped closer to the front door. "I'm not a reporter." He reached into a pocket on the front of his shirt and pulled out a card. "My name is Jason Peters. I represent Meow Masters cat food."

PJ appeared out of nowhere. He brushed

past me on four paws and stood next to Miss Johnson. He looked up at Mr. Peters and meowed when Miss Johnson took his card.

"I know this is a stressful time with the media," Mr. Peters said. "But I can help."

Miss Johnson read his card. She uncrossed her arms. "How can you help?"

He smiled. "Meow Masters gets its success from cats that do impossible things." He winked at PJ. "I'll let you in on a secret." He looked around to make sure the reporters were gone. "None of it's true," he whispered.

I chuckled. Everyone knew the cats couldn't really do what they did on the commercials. They couldn't fly. They couldn't brush their teeth. And they couldn't catch balls of light.

"Everyone thinks this cat can do math… let them think that!" He waved his arms like he was excited. "We'll put your cat in his own commercial. It's good TV."

Miss Johnson handed his card back to him. "I'm not sure it's a good idea. Thank you, though." PJ meowed loudly and hit her leg with a paw.

Mr. Peters grunted and put the card back into his pocket. "That's a shame." He looked down at PJ. "I could have made you a star, little guy. And you would have had a lifetime supply of Meow Masters." Mr. Peters' eyes got big after what happened next.

PJ looked back at me and then up at Miss Johnson. His eyes glossed over when he stared at Mr. Peters next. He slowly stood up on his two hind legs and said, "When can I start?"

SATURDAY AFTERNOON

"Dana and her father are coming over," Miss Johnson told me. "My brother is concerned."

Mr. Mike was a good guy. He loved to watch wrestling and made sure we were all taken care of.

"What do you have there?" Miss Johnson asked, pointing at the papers in my hand. I forgot I had them. I didn't want to tell her the truth, but I owed it to her.

"This is a math assignment I had." We walked into the kitchen. She turned the oven on. "Remember that I told you about my friend? The one who told a lie?"

She rubbed her chin. "Yeah. Did she get a chance to tell the truth?"

I shrugged. "Not to everyone." I took a deep breath. "I don't have a friend who lied. It was me." I held up the papers. "I didn't do this homework. PJ did."

She looked behind me at PJ as he walked into the kitchen. "You can do homework?" she asked him. She acted surprised, but she winked at me. "You can't even use a litter box."

"It's not my fault," PJ complained. "You try pooping on litter. I'd rather dig a hole out back." I couldn't stop laughing. PJ insisted on going outside like a dog. He had been a stray cat when he found this home. It wasn't so bad. He helped keep the grass green.

"I want to do the commercial," PJ said. "Being a Meow Master is my destiny."

Someone knocked on the front door. "That better not be another reporter," Miss Johnson said. She turned the oven off. She walked out of the kitchen and through the living room towards the front door.

"You're okay if I go?" PJ asked, walking alongside Miss Johnson. "I'll get you a front row seat to all the action." He was purring. "I won't forget you when I'm famous."

Miss Johnson stopped walking. "Listen to me, PJ." She sounded exhausted. "I know you want to do it, but it's not safe." She patted his head.

PJ didn't say anything when she continued walking. I wasn't sure if he was mad or sad. He walked away slowly on all four paws. His tail was between his legs.

"Come on in," Miss Johnson said after she opened the door. "Where's your key?" Mr. Mike and Dana came inside. Mr. Mike had on a pair of shorts and a tank top. He looked like he just rolled out of bed.

"I don't know," Mr. Mike said. "Maybe your cat ate it." He smirked. "Look who we dragged in with us." He used his thumb to point behind him. He headed for the couch and turned the TV on. The Native Indian Elan smiled big when he walked in. He was the last member of The Talking Dragon tribe. I hadn't seen him since the night he helped set Fox free to return to his parents.

"I'm happy to see you all again," he said. He was handsome with his short hair and bronze skin. He had his satchel and laptop with him. "I heard rumors about a cat doing math. Is he here?"

"PJ!" Miss Johnson yelled.

Dana stood by my side and shuddered. "I hate it when she does that." I agreed. Nothing is scarier than an adult yelling your name.

"You changed your mind?" PJ asked when he raced into the room on his hind legs. He covered his mouth when he saw Elan. "I remember you," he said. "You were there the night I first talked."

Elan bent down so he was the same height as PJ. "It amazes me how spectacular you are. You walk and talk like you've been doing it your entire life. And now you're a math genius?"

PJ looked over at Miss Johnson. "I like this guy. He knows what he's talking about." His eyes got big and watery. He was cute when he did that. "I'm spectacular — like a Meow Master."

"You're not going," Miss Johnson repeated. PJ's eyes went back to their regular size and dryness.

"Meow Master?" Elan asked, standing back up.

"It's a cat food commercial," she replied. She shook her head with every word. "They want PJ to talk and do math in it."

"You're gonna be famous!" Dana squealed.

Elan stood by Miss Johnson's side. "You can't do that," he said to PJ. "Something has changed with this land. It was silent for hundreds of years." He looked at each of us. "First there was a talking fox. Now there's a talking cat." He put a hand on Miss Johnson's shoulder. "And a boy who's stronger and smarter than all of us."

He was talking about Joe. I remembered when Joe did twenty pull-ups in P.E. class. No one thought he could do more than one.

"Don't forget about the chicken," Dana said. Joe was the only person who had heard Old Nelly speak. His great grandma claimed to have talked to her for years. She claimed Old Nelly could lay golden eggs. The whole town knew Old Nelly could only lay rotten eggs.

"I didn't know why this land gave them power," Elan continued. "I didn't know what it had chosen them for."

"What?" PJ asked. "What did it choose me for?"

Elan winked at him. "I believe you were chosen to protect this land."

"From what?" Dana asked.

Elan shrugged. "I don't know yet. I fear something dark is coming."

That reminded me of the man with the cap. I stood in front of Miss Johnson to get her attention. "I saw a man when we were outside with the reporters. He looked like the man who wanted to take Fox to China."

Mr. Mike stood from the couch and faced me. "Chen? You saw Chen?" His face was red.

"I don't know," I admitted. "Maybe." He looked like Chen, but he had a cap on. He pulled it over his eyes and left before I could confirm it. I bit my lower lip. "The reporters surrounded me."

"This is bad," Mr. Mike said. He walked around the couch and stood by my side. "Real bad. We need a plan."

Miss Johnson stood in front of us. "Everyone calm down. We all saw Chen get taken away by the FBI." She nodded her head slowly again to make sure we understood every word. "There's no way it could have been him. He's in prison for the rest of his life."

Mr. Mike's face was still red. "You remember what he wanted to do to Fox? He wanted to take him apart piece by piece." He looked down at PJ. "What if he wants to do the same thing to the cat?"

PJ cleared his throat. "Wait a minute. You're saying this wacko may be in town? I'm going to hide in the litter box."

"Shane got a card from that FBI guy, didn't he?" Mr. Mike asked. "After he helped him catch

Chen?" I nodded. Shane made sure he contacted the FBI when Chen was here the last time. "We can get in touch with him and clear all of this up." One of the agents had been impressed with Shane and left a card with him for a job when he got older.

"It's settled," Miss Johnson said. "We'll give Shane a call and see if he's still got that card." She nodded at all of us and smiled.

Elan said his goodbyes. I was sure we would see him again. Mr. Mike tried to call Shane but had to leave a message. PJ hid under the couch. He still wouldn't touch the litter box.

Miss Johnson put her arms around me and Dana. "Try not to worry, girls. I'm sure we'll be fine."

I wish she had been right.

SUNDAY MORNING

I sat in the back row of church because that's where Joe always sat. Angie and my dad sat with Miss Johnson at the front. I turned every time I heard someone come through the foyer, hoping it was Joe.

"He's playing video games," Dana said next to me. "You know how boys are." I smiled weakly. She knew me too well. I took a deep breath and faced forward. I wasn't sure I'd ever see Joe again.

I thought about PJ. I felt bad he couldn't do the commercial like he wanted to. Instead, he was at Joe's house with Dana's dad, watching wrestling. PJ didn't understand wrestling and thought it was silly.

The church organ came to life. I don't know why, but the organist always played the same song – *How Great Thou Art*. Her hair was gray, and her fingers were long and bony. She was the sweetest woman in the world. No one ever complained about the song.

"Brothers and sisters," the preacher said from the front of the church. The choir was seated behind him. "This is the day that the Lord has made." Several people said 'Amen'. "Let us rejoice and be glad in it." In any other church, the organist would have played that song then and there. Not ours. She was eating an apple.

"Proverbs 22 says that the Lord detests lying lips," the preacher continued. The room felt hot at that moment. I was sure the air conditioner was broken.

Someone put their hand on my shoulder. My heart jumped. Was it Chen? I turned and smiled at my best friend. "Joe," I whispered. The land had changed him. He was leaner, and his smile was brighter. He sure was cute.

He smiled and walked around the pew to join me. I panicked because there wasn't anywhere for him to sit. Dana was on my right. Sally was on my left. I didn't know Sally very well, but she was always in trouble at school. She pulled the fire alarm last week.

"Hey, Sally," Dana hissed as she leaned across me. "How many times do I have to tell you? You need Jesus. Go sit up front."

Sally crossed her arms. "I'm tired of you bossing me around. I'm not going anywhere." I cleared my throat, hoping they'd leave each other alone. I could sit anywhere, as long as it was next to Joe.

Dana reached over and pinched Sally's leg. Sally shrieked. Half of the church looked back at us. "Go, go, go," Dana said. Her face was as stern as a rock.

Sally stood and huffed. "You'll pay for this, you little demon." Her voice was broken. I could tell she was in pain. She held her leg and scooted out of the row.

Joe took her place next to me. "Sorry I'm late," he said.

"There's so much to tell you," I replied.

He nodded. "I heard about PJ." He leaned

against my arm. "Don't worry. I'm not going to let anything bad happen to him." I knew he meant it. Joe had done everything he could to protect Fox. "Shane has been trying to contact the FBI agent all morning."

"The Lord delights in people who are trustworthy!" the preacher shouted out. "All those who ask for forgiveness and change their ways will receive it."

I turned to Joe. "I needed your help with a math assignment." I didn't want to complain, but he had to know.

"I wasn't trying to avoid you," he assured me. "I feel lost without Fox."

Dana leaned across my lap when the organist played *How Great Thou Art* again. It was time to go. "Kissy, kissy," she teased. She smacked her lips together. Joe and I both blushed.

"Let's go check on PJ," Joe said. He stood and motioned for us to follow him. "He's always getting into trouble."

SUNDAY AFTERNOON

I went back to Joe's house with his family. Miss Johnson cooked spaghetti on Sundays. I asked her once how she made it. She said she made it with love. And tomato sauce.

Mr. Mike was sitting on the couch, watching wrestling. A big guy named Mr. Awesome Muscles was flexing his muscles on TV. He kept talking about how awesome he was.

"Where's PJ?" Joe asked.

Mr. Mike looked back at us. "Oh, hey." He brushed a hand at us like we were disturbing him. "He had to relieve himself."

Joe shook his head and said, "I'll be right back." If PJ had to use the bathroom, then he was out back somewhere.

"Melissa, come help me with lunch," Miss Johnson said to me. "We need to chat." I wasn't sure what she wanted to talk about, but she never asked anyone to help her with the spaghetti. It was a secret family recipe handed down from her grandmother.

"What did your father say?" she asked, putting oven mitts on her hands. She opened the oven and slid in a pan with garlic bread on it. "When you told him the truth?"

"He wasn't happy about it," I admitted. I hated seeing the disappointment on his face. "But he was glad I told him the truth." I was glad he heard it from me and not from TV.

"Good," Miss Johnson said. She winked at me. "You can always come to me for help if you need it." I smiled because it was true. She would never judge me and always help me.

"He's not out there," Joe said when he walked in through the back door. "I can't find PJ anywhere." Joe's face was flush. He looked out of breath.

"Maybe he came back in," Miss Johnson said.

431

Her face had creases in it, like she was thinking hard.

"Not a chance," Mr. Mike said, walking into the kitchen. "I've been here the whole time. PJ went out the back door and has not come back."

Miss Johnson ran her hands through her hair. "Shane hasn't heard back from the FBI?" she asked Joe. He shook his head. "I don't know what to think," she continued. "I'm afraid Chen has something to do with this."

"We've got to do something!" Dana cried. "PJ's just a cat. A crazy, stubborn cat."

"Meow Masters — saving the world one cat at a time," a deep voice said from the TV in the living room. I peeked around the kitchen doorway and saw the Meow Masters commercial playing on TV. A Persian cat was flying in a cape like a superhero. It looked real.

"What about the commercial?" I asked everyone in the room.

"What about it?" Mr. Mike said.

I focused on Miss Johnson. "PJ wanted to make one of those commercials." I pointed to the TV. "What if he actually went to make one?"

"Maybe," Miss Johnson said. "I wouldn't put it past him."

Someone banged on the front door. "Who can that be at a time like this?" Miss Johnson asked. We all walked to the door, discussing what to do about PJ. Dana wanted to lock him in his litter box.

Shane was on the other side of the door when we opened it. "Where's he at?" he asked. He walked past us. "We need to keep PJ in this house."

"What's wrong?" Joe asked.

Shane held out a cell phone. "I got a call from the FBI. Chen escaped last week."

Five minutes later I was in the backseat of Miss Johnson's car with Joe by my side. Miss Johnson was driving, and Shane was in the front passenger seat. Dana stayed at the house with Mr. Mike in case PJ came back.

"He's going to be okay," Joe said to me. "He has to be."

"It's right up here," Shane said, watching the GPS on his cell phone. The FBI had given him the address of the Meow Masters commercial filming. We didn't know if PJ would be there, but it was our only hope. No one knew how to find Chen.

I looked through the windshield. A big white

screen was up ahead outside. PJ was in front of it with a camera crew. A security guard waved us down before we could get any closer.

Miss Johnson rolled her window down. "Is there a problem, officer?"

"You folks need to turn around," he said, tipping his hat. "This is a closed set." He smiled big and pointed at the road behind us.

Miss Johnson turned the car off and took the keys out. "We're not going anywhere." I gulped. Daddy had taught me to obey the police. "Our cat is over there, and he's in danger."

The security guard took his hat off. "Look, ma'am, I don't want any trouble." Sweat covered his forehead. "Turn the car back on and go home."

She looked back at Joe and me. "Open your

doors and get out." She opened hers first and stood in front of the guard. Then she cocked her arm back and threw her keys toward the white screen. "Whoops."

"Wait a minute," the guard said. "Do not leave your vehicle. Stay in your seats."

Joe opened his door next. I looked over at my door, but I couldn't get myself to open it. I didn't want to get in trouble for not listening to the guard.

Joe stepped out and reached for my hand. "Come on," he said. "Let's go save that crazy cat." I realized he was right. PJ was in danger and it was our job to protect him. What was there to think about? I grabbed Joe's hand and stepped out.

"Hey, you kids, get back in the car!" the guard shouted. He looked scary. He carried a gun and had handcuffs. He rubbed the sweat off his forehead and threw his hands in the air like he had given up.

"Sorry," I whispered.

He shook his head at me. "Hey," he said. "You're the girl." He smiled for the first time. "The one from TV." His face lit up. "Yeah, you were in the math competition."

I wanted to bury my head. I didn't want to be remembered as the girl who lost the math competition. All I could do was nod.

He rubbed his chin and shrugged. "That cat's a pain in the butt. Go get him."

Joe held onto my hand and pulled me toward the white board. "Let's go." His mom nodded at us. We ran toward the screen and cameras. It wasn't that far. We'd be there in less than a minute.

We passed through two cameramen. PJ was in front of the screen, holding a can of Meow Masters. "Meow," he said, licking his lips. "It's delicious." I never expected what happened next. It changed everything.

"Do it again, you stupid cat!" Jennifer screamed at him. Yes, it was the same Jennifer that was the leader of the math team. The same Jennifer that said I would pay for losing the math competition. How could this be happening?

"Look who's here," she said when she spotted me. "The world's biggest loser." She shook her head and laughed. "Let me tell you what's going on since you're not smart enough to figure it out."

I didn't have time for her games. PJ was in danger and we had to get him out of there. "PJ," I said to him, "let's go. Don't let her treat you like this."

PJ didn't move. "I'm about to be famous." He shook his head. "I can't leave now." He looked at Jennifer. "Let's keep filming."

Jennifer snorted. "You see, he belongs to me now." She smirked and winked at Joe like he belonged to her too. "Did you ever wonder how the reporters found PJ? How Meow Masters found him?" I did, but now I knew.

"Your good friend Amanda told me that you spend a lot of time at Joe's house," she continued. "It doesn't take a genius to figure out where a talking cat could come from. Joe already made the mistake of posting his talking fox all over the internet."

"That wasn't me!" Joe shouted. Shane had recorded the video of Fox talking to Joe, without him knowing about it. That was before they were friends, and Shane was trying to destroy him.

"You two are a cute couple," Jennifer said. "And dumb." She walked over to me and stared into my eyes like she wanted to pick a fight. "I called every news station I could and told them about PJ. Then I struck a deal with Meow Masters. I told them I would get them a cat that could do math, but only if they let me direct the commercial." She smiled like she was proud of herself.

Joe stepped between us and faced Jennifer. "Back off." She laughed and stepped back. "PJ," Joe shouted at him, "Chen is back and he's after you."

Jennifer faced PJ. "Don't listen to them. No one is after you." She walked over to him and petted his head. "They just want to hold you back. I can make sure you get a lifetime supply of Meow Masters. And we'll get you a sports car. Every cat will know your name."

PJ purred. His eyes were frozen, like he was dreaming of all that food and driving his own car. But then his eyes drifted to me. He sighed. "Cats can't drive," he said to Jennifer. "And don't ever talk to my friends like that again." He smiled at me.

That's when I knew everything was going to be okay. We'd take PJ back to Joe's house, protect him, and live happily ever after. But life doesn't always go the way we planned it.

One of the cameramen threw his camera down and rushed toward PJ. I recognized him as the man from China, Chen. He reached for PJ's neck and grabbed him by the scruff. He held PJ up in the air. PJ couldn't move, like he was paralyzed.

Jennifer ran off, screaming.

"Let him go!" Joe shouted. His shoulders were squared, and his fists were out. My heart was racing.

Chen laughed. "There's no one to help you this time." He studied PJ's fur. "I'm going to find out if there really is more than one way to skin a cat."

"No, you're not," Miss Johnson said from behind me. I was happy to hear her voice. Joe could protect me, but no one can protect you more than a mom. "You're going to put the cat down and walk away."

Chen shook his head. "You should leave before you get hurt." He held PJ in front of us like a trophy. "This cat isn't worth it. He's just a mangy animal with a big mouth."

"No," Joe said. "He's family."

Shane appeared behind Chen. We hadn't noticed him in all the commotion. He was holding the camera Chen had thrown down in both hands. "Hey!" he shouted at Chen.

As soon as Chen turned, Shane whacked him across the head with the camera. Chen fell like a chopped tree. PJ fell out of his grip and landed on all four paws. "Don't mess with my friends," Shane said, standing over Chen's body.

The sound of sirens filled the air. Police cars sped down the road toward us. Helicopters hovered over us. Maybe there would be a happy ending after all.

"Thank you," PJ said, standing on his hind legs. He stood between me and Joe. "I don't know what I was thinking." I patted his head.

"We all make mistakes," Miss Johnson said. "That's okay, as long as we learn from them." She smiled at him and nodded her head the way she always did when she wanted to make a point.

"I did learn something," he replied. "I learned it's too dangerous for you to be around me." He stared into the distance. "I'm a stray cat. I'm supposed to be alone — that's what cats do."

"You're my cat!" I cried. "You can't leave." He didn't want to believe he belonged to anyone, but he owned a piece of my heart. I didn't want to lose him.

"The power you have — the power to walk and talk — that comes from our property," Joe said. He sounded sad. His heart had been broken when Fox left. Though he had never bonded with PJ, I didn't think his heart could take much more. "If you leave, you'll become sick and even worse."

Miss Johnson put one arm around me and the other around Joe. She was still behind us. "You're not a danger to us," she said to PJ. "You're a blessing to us. You make our lives better and fill our home with happiness. We smile when you chase lights on the wall and fight with balls of yarn."

PJ smirked. "I am a pretty swell cat. Let's go home."

The FBI took Chen away. They thanked Shane for his assistance. They said he'd make a good agent one day. I could breathe again because PJ was safe. I thought that was end of this. But it was only the beginning.

SUNDAY NIGHT

Dana hugged PJ as soon as we got back to Joe's house. "Don't ever do that again," she told the cat. The microwave made a beeping sound in the kitchen. Dana darted her eyes at each of us. "Those are my pizza rolls. Nobody touch them."

Mr. Mike waved at us from the couch. He was watching wrestling again. Mr. Awesome Muscles was fighting for a championship belt. "I wish Fox was here," he said. "He would have loved this."

Joe sighed and walked past me into the kitchen. I heard the back door open and close. I suspected he was going to disappear again.

"Hey, Melissa," PJ said, "come check this out." He waved a paw for me to follow him. He led me to the bathroom hallway, where his litter box was at. It was a waste of money. He would never use it. "Look inside," he said.

It was an unusual request. I didn't want to stick my head inside a dirty litter box. But, it was unused. There was nothing to worry about. I was confused by what I found.

"Hey," I said. "Isn't that my math assignment?" I recognized my name on the front page. The paper was laying on top of the litter. "There were three pages. Where are the other two?"

PJ smirked and said, "You don't want to know." They say curiosity kills a cat. I was curious, but I was a human. I looked deeper into the litter box. Two lumps were buried in the litter. I had a pretty good idea what they were.

"That's disgusting," I said, sticking my tongue out and holding my stomach. I would never look at homework the same way.

"Thank you," he said, smiling. "It's some of

my best work." He put a paw on my leg. "And thank you for looking out for me. You are a true friend." I smiled back at him and played with his ears.

Miss Johnson walked into the hallway and joined us. "What are you two so happy about?" she asked. She crossed her arms like she thought we were up to no good.

I winked at PJ. "My cat ate my homework." I burst out laughing with him. It wasn't an excuse. It's what really happened.

Miss Johnson raised her eyebrows like she was confused. "Alright, then," she said. "Melissa, can you go check on Joe? He's asking for you."

I nodded at her. I would do anything for Joe. Miss Johnson thanked me when I walked past her and headed for the back door. I stopped and looked back at PJ.

"Don't worry," he assured me, "I'll be here when you get back." That was what I needed to hear. I walked through the hallway and into the kitchen.

"These are my pizza rolls," Dana said again. "Don't touch them." I shook my head and opened the back door. Dana giggled when I looked back at her. As tough as she was, she was like a baby sister to me. I smiled at her.

I stepped into the backyard and walked past the outhouse. I wondered what I was going to say to Joe. He didn't talk to anyone anymore. Months ago, he had told me that he liked me — really liked me. I later admitted the same thing to him. My stomach was full of butterflies.

I sat next to Joe on the green grass close to the chicken coop. Joe was staring into the woods behind the fence in front of us. This was where we had last seen Fox.

"He's never coming back, is he?" Joe asked. He kept staring into the woods. I wanted to sound positive, but we both knew the answer. Fox had been kidnapped by Shane's dad one time and almost tortured by Chen another time. Now he was back with his parents.

"No," I said, leaning against his shoulder. "But he's safe because of you." I wanted to be honest with him. "Fox gave up his ability to walk and talk so we wouldn't be in danger. It was the right thing to do."

"I'm afraid," Joe said, leaning on my arm now. He was strong and fast. He had nothing to be afraid of. "I heard Elan was here. He said something dark is coming."

We both jumped when the chickens went crazy in the coop. They were distressed and squawked loudly like a predator was attacking them. Joe stood and shouted, "Mom! Help!"

She rushed out of the back door. Dana was behind her with Mr. Mike. "Stand back!" Miss Johnson commanded. "We don't know what's in there. It could be a dangerous animal." We were all scared after what Elan had told us. The chickens cackled, "kuh-kuh-kuh-KACK!"

Miss Johnson slowly stepped into the coop with Mr. Mike. We all followed her, even though she told us to stay back. *Curiosity kills a cat*, I thought again.

I froze when Miss Johnson stopped and put a hand over her mouth. "I don't believe this," she whispered, sounding confused. I came from around her and stood by her side with the others to see what she was talking about.

An animal with brownish orange hair had its

back to us. The end of its tail was white. I gasped when it turned to face us. It had the same blue eyes as Joe. I knew right away who it was.

Fox stood slowly on his two hind legs and looked at all of us, one by one. His eyes stopped and focused on Joe. "I heard you were in trouble," he said in his childish voice. "I came back to help."

MY
fox
Begins

DAVID BLAZE

CONTENTS

EARLY ONE MORNING

"You're not like the rest of us," a kid fox said to him. "You don't belong here." Five other kid foxes were with him. They all had bodies of brown hair with white chests and white-tipped tails. They looked like him.

He wanted to play with them. They had been kicking a pine cone around the forest, keeping it away from each other. It looked like fun. "I want to be your friend."

"Look at you," the first kid fox said. "You walk on two legs like a human." Another kid fox snickered. "And your eyes are weird. They're bright blue. You're a freak." The other red foxes had brown, orange, yellow, or green eyes. They

453

laughed at him.

His tail sank to the ground. He watched as the kid foxes ran off, kicking the pine cone. He'd probably never see them again, and he was glad. The forest was huge.

"Little Fox, where are you?" his mama called from their den. He didn't have a name yet, but he knew she was talking to him. The red foxes were not given names until they did something great.

He ran to the den on his two hind legs. "Here I am, Mama."

"Don't run off like that again," she scolded him. "You know it's dangerous out there." Her eyes narrowed. "Don't go out unless one of us is with you." She nodded at his dad.

"I'm sorry, Mama," he said. "I just want to be like the other kid foxes." He felt trapped in that den, like his parents were ashamed of him and didn't want the other foxes to see him.

She nudged his hand. "What other kid foxes?" His tail was still down.

"I saw them out there," he said. He pointed outside.

"What?" his dad asked. He was a quiet fox and didn't speak much. "Did they hurt you?" Little Fox shook his head. His dad didn't trust anyone but his own family.

"They were just playing a game with a pine cone," Little Fox assured him. He looked down. "They wouldn't let me play with them."

His mama rubbed her head against his leg. "Little foxes can be mean sometimes."

"And trouble," his dad added. "Lots and lots of trouble."

Little Fox crossed his arms. "They said I walk like a human." He had no idea what a human was. He guessed it was a monster that nobody liked. If that's what a human was, then it was the right word for him.

His mama glanced at his dad. He took a deep breath and said, "Okay. It's time."

Little Fox put his arms in the air. "Time for what?"

His mama smiled. "It's time for you to learn the truth."

MID-MORNING, Part 1

Little Fox followed his dad through the forest for miles. "Keep moving!" his dad yelled at him over and over. Little Fox stopped every time he saw something new. Beautiful flying creatures surrounded them. His dad called them butterflies. Small, red creatures bit his paws. His dad called them ants. Little Fox didn't like ants.

They stopped when there were no more trees in front of them. A great wall of silver string stood in their way. "It's a fence," his dad said. "It's meant to keep us out."

"Out of what?" Little Fox wondered aloud. His dad pointed through the fence at piles of wood standing up in a perfect square. It was tall and wide. It was colored pink with blue trim.

"That's a chicken coop," his dad said. Little Fox didn't know what that meant. "It's where chickens live. Lots of them."

Little Fox's stomach growled. He loved to eat chicken! He licked his lips. So that was where chickens came from. He had always wondered how they magically appeared on his plate for dinner. He reached for the fence to climb over it.

His dad bit his tail and pulled him back. "Wait," he said. "That's not why we're here."

Little Fox threw his paws up. "Why not? We're foxes and those are chickens in there." Why had his dad taken him all the way out there? Was it a lesson to teach him not to disobey his parents again?

A loud bang came from farther beyond the fence. Little Fox jumped. It sounded like wood slamming against wood. "Lie on the ground and stay quiet," his dad told him. Little Fox hated to do it because he preferred to stand tall on his hind legs.

What he saw next took his breath away. A creature much taller than him walked on two legs toward the chicken coop. It had a soft, kind face like his mama's—but much rounder. The only hair it had was on its head, and that was gray. The top half of its body had pink cloth over it. Its legs were covered in thick blue cloth.

"What is that?" Little Fox asked his dad. It was the most amazing thing he'd ever seen.

MID-MORNING, Part 2

His dad growled softly. "That's a human."
That was a human? It wasn't scary at all! Little
Fox watched as the human walked to the chicken
coop and opened the door with one hand. The
human had a bucket in its other hand.

"Come out, my little friends," the human said
in a soft voice. "It's time to eat."

Little Fox's ears perked up. He had never
heard the human language, but he understood
every word she said. He looked at his dad. "Did
you hear that?"

His dad nodded. "Their language is ancient.
"There's no way for us to understand them." He
shook his head. "The human may have seen us

and warned the chickens."

Little Fox was confused. How could his dad not understand the human? Little Fox knew he was different than the other red foxes, but this didn't make any sense. "She's going to feed the chickens," he told his dad. "She told them to come out."

His dad huffed when dozens of chickens walked out of the coop. The human reached into her bucket and threw out grains to the chickens. They happily pecked at the grains.

Little Fox's dad stared at him. His dad probably thought he was weird, just like the little red foxes did. There had to be something wrong with him.

"Good morning, Rita," a different human voice said. Fox looked up to see the human kneeling in front of a chicken. "It's a beautiful day," the chicken said.

Little Fox choked. The chicken spoke human! He stared at it with big eyes and saw the chicken had the same bright blue eyes as him. He couldn't believe it!

"Yes, it is a beautiful day, Old Nelly," the human said. She looked up into the sky. "Looks like we might get rain later." She nodded at the chicken. "It will be good for the grass. It could be greener."

"Did you hear that?" Little Fox asked his dad. "Old Nelly speaks like a human!" His dad continued to stare at him.

"We need to go," his dad said. "It's not safe here."

Little Fox did not want to leave. They weren't in any danger—he was sure of it. "I can talk to the human. I can ask her to be our friend."

"NEVER talk to humans," his dad said in a deep voice that scared him. "They cannot be trusted." He stood slowly and quietly on four paws. "I don't want to hear another word about it. Let's go."

"But—" Little Fox said.

"NOW," his dad commanded.

Little Fox looked back at Rita and Old Nelly. They talked and laughed like they were best friends. He wanted to be a part of that. Maybe this was the one place he would be accepted.

He walked away quietly on four paws with his

dad. Little Fox only stopped when another red ant bit his paw. Red ants were mean! He couldn't stop thinking about Rita and Old Nelly. One day he'd find a way to talk to them.

LATE MORNING, PART 1

"He can understand the humans," Little Fox's dad told his mama. They were in the den and sitting in a circle. "I was afraid of this."

"The human is like you, Mama," Little Fox said. "She's nice and pretty." Sure, the human looked different than them, but she wasn't scary.

His mama stroked his head. "You are special, Little Fox. You're going to do great things."

His dad stood on four paws and huffed. "He's going to put us in danger." He walked in circles around the room. "He must not be allowed to talk to the humans." His face was like stone, and his voice was deep again. Little Fox shivered. "We are red foxes!"

His mama stood. "Little Fox, go outside and

play. Don't go far. Make sure I can see you." She stared at him until he stood. "I need to talk to your dad."

Little Fox watched as his dad continued to walk in a circle. His chest heaved up and down. Little Fox had never seen him so angry. He listened to his mama and ran out of the den.

"What happened today doesn't change anything," he heard his mama say back in the den. "He's still a fox. And he's still our son."

Little Fox didn't hear his dad say anything. He imagined his dad was still walking in circles and shaking his head. He didn't understand why his dad was so angry about this. There wasn't any reason why red foxes and humans couldn't be friends.

Little Fox jumped when he heard a rustle to his right. He looked over and saw a strange animal smaller than him looking at him. It was black with a white chest, a white streak of hair down its back, and a head full of white hair. It also had bright blue eyes!

Little Fox looked into the den and saw his parents weren't watching him. His dad was walking in circles and his mama was trying to calm him down. Little Fox knew he had to meet the strange animal. He could step away for a minute.

"Hi," Little Fox said to the animal in the human language. He had never spoken it before, but it was easy. He suspected the animal with blue eyes could understand him. "I want to be your friend."

LATE MORNING, PART 2

"Hi!" the animal said to him. He sounded
like a kid. He stood on his hind legs just like
Little Fox and waved. "I'm Stinky the skunk.
Sure, we can be friends."

Little Fox smiled. Stinky was his first friend!
"You can call me Little Fox." He wondered why
his new friend was called Stinky. "How did you
get your name?"

"It's a joke," Stinky said. "The other skunks
call me that to make fun of me." He shrugged his
shoulders. "Skunks are supposed to stink,"
he continued. "When we're scared or in danger,
we spray a stinky liquid at our enemies." He
laughed. "It sticks to them, and they can't get the
smell off for a long time."

Little Fox wondered what it smelled like.

"Does it smell like farts?"

Stinky laughed. "It's worse than that. You can't wash the smell off of you. It's disgusting."

Little Fox wasn't sure it could be worse. "One time, my dad asked me to pull his finger." He shuddered when he recalled the nightmare. "I wasn't sure why he asked, but he farted when I pulled his finger."

Stinky's mouth was wide open like he was amazed. "Your dad is my hero."

One thing didn't make sense to Little Fox. He put his paws in the air. "If skunks are supposed to stink, then why is your name a joke?"

Stinky shrugged. "I can't spray my enemies like the other skunks. When I get scared or nervous, I run away." He looked down at the ground. "The other skunks don't like me. I hope we can still be friends."

Little Fox put a hand on Stinky's shoulder. "Of course we're friends!" They were both different. They were the only animals he knew of that could walk upright and speak human. Stinky and Little Fox were connected somehow.

"Get out of here, skunk!" Little Fox's dad

shouted from behind him. He bared his teeth and growled. Stinky didn't speak the red fox language, but the sharp teeth and deep growl explained everything.

The hair on Stinky's head stood straight up. He turned around and ran away faster than a streak of lightning.

"Dad!" Little Fox shouted. "That was my new friend!"

"Your mama told you to stay near the den," his dad said. "You don't listen, and that's going to get you into trouble one day." He shook his head. "Come with me."

Fox looked through the woods to see if he could spot Stinky. As fast as the skunk ran off, he was a mile away by then. Had Little Fox lost the only friend he ever had? He sighed. "Where are we going?" he asked.

His dad walked past him. "We're going back to the chicken coop."

EARLY AFTERNOON

Little Fox stood tall on two legs with his dad next to him in front of the silver fence again. The chicken coop was closed, and the chickens were inside. His dad hadn't said a word on the trip there. "Do you want me to talk to the human?" Little Fox asked.

His dad grunted. "Forget about the human. We're going to hunt."

Little Fox had never hunted before. He thought about Old Nelly. Nothing could happen to the chicken. She was like him. "I'm not hungry," he said. His stomach growled.

His dad looked up at him. "I won't always be able to take care of you. I need to know that you can take care of yourself."

Little Fox gulped. His dad had never talked to him like that. Little Fox couldn't imagine his life without him. He wanted to prove to his dad that he wasn't so little anymore. "What do I have to do?"

His dad nodded. "I've been watching this place for weeks. The human sleeps in the afternoon." He motioned to the chicken coop. "I want you to catch one of those chickens."

Little Fox cocked his head. "Me? Aren't you going to help?"

His dad shook his head. "You can do this. I know you can."

Little Fox gulped. He jumped up and grabbed the top of the fence. He pulled himself over and fell flat on his back on the other side. It hurt more than the red ant bites. His dad appeared upside down. "I'm okay," Little Fox said.

He turned over and stood on four paws so he could move with stealth. When he got to the chicken coop, he used his paws to unlatch the door. It creaked open.

Little Fox stood up on his two hind legs. Inside the coop were chickens on the right and on the left. Some were up high on shelves and some were down low. They were everywhere. Jackpot!

"Rita!" Old Nelly yelled. "Help! Fox!"

The chickens went crazy. They screamed, "Kuh-kuh-kuh-KACK!"

The loud bang of wood against wood came from farther in the yard. The ground shook as Rita's footsteps raced toward the coop. Little Fox got down on four legs and turned to see her pointing a long, skinny wooden object at him. "Oh no, you don't!" she shouted at him. "Get away from my chickens!"

Little Fox couldn't move. His chest pounded hard. His heart felt like it was going to explode. His legs shook.

Rita stepped closer to him. "You're scared, aren't you?" She lowered the long wooden object. "You're just a kid, a fox cub."

Little Fox wanted to tell her "Yes," but he remembered what his dad had said. *NEVER talk to humans*. But was he right about humans being dangerous?

"You have beautiful blue eyes," Rita said. She patted his head. "You can understand me, can't you?"

Little Fox was happy she already knew. He was about to say, "Yes," when his dad raced up behind Rita. His dad bared his sharp teeth and growled at her. She dropped her gun and fell to the ground.

"Let's go!" his dad shouted to him. "Now!"

Little Fox looked at Rita. She nodded at him. "It's okay," she said. "Come back and see me when you're older. I have much to tell you."

Little Fox winked at her and ran off with his dad.

MID-AFTERNOON

"What happened?" his mama asked when they got back to the den. She was making up the beds.

"It didn't go as planned," his dad said. "But Little Fox was brave. I'm proud of him. He stared danger in the face."

Little Fox was happy his dad was proud of him. But he didn't want his dad to think he was in danger. "Rita—the human—wouldn't have hurt me. She wants to help."

"There you go with that nonsense again," his dad said. They were both on four paws. His dad put his face right in front of his. "She wants to help? She pointed a gun at you."

"What?" his mama said. "You let a human point a gun at my baby?"

"Not now, dear," his dad said. "Listen to me,

Little Fox. Guns are used to hunt red foxes. Humans hunt us the same way we hunt chickens." His voice got deep again. "That human is not your friend. She cannot be trusted."

"But—" Little Fox said.

"You need to take a nap," his dad said. "It's been a long day. Go lie down."

Little Fox looked to his mama for support. She shrugged her shoulders like there was nothing she could do. "You never listen to me," he said to his dad before he stomped to his bed.

His mama tucked him into his bed. "I know it's hard to see it sometimes, but your dad just wants what's best for you. He loves you more than you will ever know."

Little Fox wasn't sure about that. His dad thought he was weird like the other red foxes did. At least that's what Little Fox believed.

He yawned. He wondered what it would be like to talk to Rita. She had the answers to why he was the way he was. Why was he so much like a human?

He fell asleep and dreamed of chasing chickens. Only, he didn't hunt them. He played with them.

LATE AFTERNOON

"Wake up, Little Fox," his mama said. "It's almost dinner time."

He yawned and stretched his paws. It was fun playing with the chickens in his dreams. "What are we eating?" he asked.

She patted his head. "Your dad is out looking for food." Little Fox knew his dad wouldn't go back to the chicken coop. They'd eat what they did most days—crickets, caterpillars, beetles or grasshoppers.

"Go wash up in the river," his mom continued. "We don't want your grubby paws all over the food." He looked at his paws. They were black with dirt and mud.

"Really?" he asked. He had never been allowed

to go to the river by himself. It wasn't far away. His dad had built the den years ago so they would be close to water. "What will Dad say?"

She kissed his cheek. "Don't worry about your dad. I'll take care of him."

Little Fox jumped out of bed and headed for the den exit. "I'm going now…" He waited for his mama to stop him. "I'm stepping outside…" She had to be kidding about letting him go to the river. "I'm going to the river—"

"Bye, Little Fox," his mama said. "Come right back when you're done."

Little Fox shrugged and raced out of the den before she changed her mind. He ran to the river on four paws. He was much faster that way than on two paws. *Stealth mode,* he thought. *I'm super-fast!*

He stopped at the river and stared at his reflection in the water. "You look like the other foxes," he said to his reflection. "Why do you have to be so different?" His mama had told him that he was born with green eyes and took his first steps with four paws. His eyes turned blue the first time he stepped out of the den and into the forest. He stood and walked on two legs that same day. The land had changed him.

Little Fox turned and fell into the water when another reflection appeared next to his. Looking closer, he noticed it was his friend Stinky the skunk!

"Don't worry," Stinky said. "I'm the cleanest skunk around." He smiled and laughed.

Little Fox climbed out of the water and shook his body dry. He remembered Stinky wasn't like the other skunks. "It's no fun being different, is it?"

Stinky shrugged. "My mom says it's okay to be different. I don't have to be like the other skunks." He dipped a paw into the water. "Besides, when the right time comes, I'll find a way to stop my enemies if I have to."

Little Fox chuckled and splashed water on Stinky. "You better never spray me!"

Stinky splashed water back on Little Fox. "You better never pull your dad's finger around me!" They laughed and jumped into the water, splashing it all over each other.

EARLY EVENING, Part 1

Little Fox's dad was waiting for him outside the den when he got back. "Come with me," his dad said. He walked into the forest without looking back. Little Fox was scared that he was in trouble.

They walked for miles in a direction Little Fox had never been. The sun was getting lower. All four of his legs were sore. He was sure his dad was punishing him. "I'm sorry, Dad," he said.

"Shh…" his dad said. He stopped walking. "Listen." Soft chirps filled the air around them like a chorus. "Those are crickets." Little Fox turned in circles. It sounded like the crickets were everywhere. "I found this place earlier," his dad continued. "I want you to help me catch the crickets for dinner."

Little Fox stood on his hind legs and scratched his head. If his dad was here earlier, then why didn't he get the crickets himself? "You want me to help you?"

His dad looked up at him. "This is what red foxes do." He took a deep breath. His face softened. "You're my son. You're smart and you're fast. I can't do the things you can. What I can do is protect you and show you how to survive."

Little Fox nodded. His dad hadn't spoken this way to him before. He had always been a stern dad and never complimented him.

A loud bang filled the air. It was like wood hitting against the wood at Rita's place but louder. The crickets became silent. The dirt between Little Fox and his dad jumped up and stung them.

"Fox hunters!" his dad yelled. "Run!"

Little Fox couldn't move. He was more scared than when Rita stood over him. They were surrounded by trees. He couldn't see hunters anywhere. His legs shook again.

His dad bit his leg. Little Fox fell to four paws. "Run home to your mama," his dad said quickly. "You're faster than me. Warn her." Little Fox knew he had to keep his mama safe. "Don't look back. I'm right behind you."

Two humans walked toward them. They had long guns like Rita's in their hands. "Run!" his dad shouted again.

Little Fox took off as fast as he could. He hoped his dad could keep up with him. They had to protect his mama. He knew he wasn't supposed to look back, but he wanted to make sure his dad could keep up.

Little Fox slowed down. His dad wasn't with him. His dad had run in the opposite direction. He was running straight for the hunters.

BANG!

Little Fox turned toward his home and ran as fast as he could. "Mama!" he shouted over and over. "Mama! Mama! Mama!"

EARLY EVENING, PART 2

The trip to the land of crickets had taken hours, but Little Fox was back at the den in minutes. His mama stood outside with a worried look on her face. "Where's your dad?"

Little Fox could only think of one word. "Hunters." He focused on his mama's eyes. "He tried to stop them!" Little Fox cried. "He was supposed to be right behind me. He's supposed to be here."

His mama rubbed her head against his. "Okay," she said. Her voice was weak, like she was exhausted. "Okay, okay, okay." She looked back at the den and shook her head. She cleared her throat. "We need to get to the river." Her voice was stronger than ever. "They can't follow our tracks in the water."

Little Fox took a deep breath. "What about Dad?"

She shook her head at him. "He's not coming back."

They jumped when a large animal ran out of the trees toward them. "Dad!" Little Fox shouted. "I knew it! I knew you'd make it!"

His dad collapsed in front of them. "They're coming," he said, out of breath. "I slowed them down as much as I could."

Little Fox's mama examined his dad's leg. It had been shot. "We've got to get to the river," she said again. "It's our only chance."

"There's not enough time," his dad said. "There's only one thing we can do." He whispered something into her ear. She stared at Little Fox and nodded her head.

"Let's get back into the den," she told Little Fox. "We'll have to hide in there." He didn't question it. She always knew what was best. They'd hide in there until the hunters went away. "Hurry, go. There's no time to waste."

Little Fox jumped into the den and waited for them. The hunters would never find them there. It would all be okay.

He coughed when dirt and mud hit his face. He looked up into the den opening. It was a hole in the ground that led to their underground house. His parents were standing over it and pushing the dirt and mud and rocks inside. "What are you doing?"

"It was always supposed to be you," his mama said. She kept pushing more dirt into the hole. "You're the greatest thing that's ever happened to us."

Little Fox couldn't stop coughing. "Let me out!" he shouted. He realized they were blocking him in so the hunters couldn't see him. "Mama, please don't leave me." She didn't say anything; she just kept pushing more dirt in.

"Dad, you don't have to do this!"

His dad stopped filling the hole for a moment. "My son, I believe in you. I always did. Unite the humans and the red foxes." With that, he pushed in a larger rock. The hole was completely blocked. The den was as dark as a night without a moon or stars.

"Let me out!" Little Fox shouted. "I can help!"

BANG! BANG!

"No!"

EARLY EVENING, PART 3

Little Fox froze. He listened for his parents, but they didn't say anything else. All he heard was the footsteps of humans.

"We hit them both, Billy," one of them said. "They won't make it far."

"Well, well, well… What do we have here, John?" He stomped on the ground above Little Fox. "I believe we have a foxhole."

"Looks like it's covered up," John said. "I reckon they were hiding something." He stomped on the ground too. "Maybe other foxes."

Little Fox's heart raced. His parents were gone and now the hunters would find him. He was trapped in the den. There was nowhere for him to run.

"Forget about it," Billy said. "If there are foxes in there, they'll never get out."

"That's not the point," John argued. "The Boss is paying us a lot of money to wipe out all the animals in this forest. I'm going to get every cent I can."

"Wait a second," John said. "Is that a skunk?" They both jumped. "Why is it walking toward us?"

Little Fox perked his ears up and listened for smaller footsteps. Was that Stinky? He wanted to tell his friend to run.

"Maybe it's not a foxhole," Billy said. "Maybe it's a skunk hole."

"I doubt it," John said. "They usually live in tree hollows or logs."

"More money for us," Billy said. "Do you want to shoot it or should I?"

Little Fox heard Stinky on the ground above him. The skunk stopped there and faced the hunters. Why didn't he run?

"He's cute," John said. "Not smart though. He's just sitting there. Poor guy." Little Fox heard a clicking sound. "I've got it."

What was Stinky doing? He needed to run

like he always did! Little Fox felt the ground shift. Was Stinky turning around to run away? Good! *Run, Stinky! Run!*

Little Fox heard a gushing sound, like the river.

"Nooooo!" John shouted. "He sprayed me in the eyes! Get it out! Get it out of my eyes!"

"It's all over me!" Billy screamed like a girl fox. "It smells so bad! I can't breathe!"

Yes! Little Fox thought. *He did it. Stinky did it.*

The ground vibrated when Stinky ran off. "Get him!" John shouted. "Get that skunk!" The footsteps were heavy on the ground above Little Fox as the hunters ran after Stinky.

Little Fox laid his head down in the darkness and whined. His parents were gone. Stinky was in danger. And someone named The Boss wanted to wipe out all the animals in the forest.

MID-EVENING

Little Fox stood and felt for the dirt and rocks in front of him. His parents were out there somewhere. The hunters had shot them, but his mama and dad were fighters and wouldn't give up easily. They would have gone to the river.

He put one paw in front of the other and scratched at the dirt to pull it away. It was easy until he hit rocks. It was harder to dig them out. He carried them deeper into the den so they weren't in the way.

The more he dug the more dirt and rocks he found. It didn't seem like it would ever end. There still wasn't any light.

Little Fox was exhausted. He lay down again to rest. He had no idea if it was day or night.

When he woke up, he dug again and carried rocks until he was exhausted. He was fast, but he wasn't strong like his dad.

Time disappeared. He would dig, carry rocks, dig some more, and carry more rocks. Then he would sleep for hours or days, he wasn't sure. Every now and then he'd find a cricket or worm in the dirt. The worms were disgusting. They were slimy. But he was starving. He had to eat them.

Dig. Carry rocks. Dig. Carry rocks.

Light! There was light! Little Fox dug faster. More and more light came through the hole. He could feel the wind. He was almost out!

One big rock was in the way now. It covered half of the hole. It was too heavy for him to move it. Little Fox was determined. He couldn't let his parents down. He reached through the half hole and tried to pull himself out. He sucked in his chest and squeezed through the hole.

Freedom! The sun shined bright. It had to be the afternoon. Little Fox ran on four paws to the river. "Mama! Dad! Mama! Dad!"

He ran up and down the river, shouting their names. They didn't answer. Little Fox stared at his reflection in the water. He hit the water as hard as he could to make the reflection disappear.

He went back to the den. The sun was low. He squeezed into the den and waited. He did the same thing day after day. He searched the forest for his parents. He went to the land of crickets so he could eat. He taught himself how to catch crayfish in the river. He learned to survive on his own—like his dad had taught him.

The hunters didn't return. He couldn't find his parents or Stinky anywhere, but he wouldn't stop looking. Days, weeks, and months passed. Then, one day, he realized his parents weren't coming back. There was only one thing left for him to do.

Rita, he thought. *I've got to talk to Rita. She'll have the answers.*

A NEW DAY

Little Fox stared through the silver fence at the chicken coop. It was closed. The sun was bright. Rita would be out soon. He smiled when he heard wood slamming against wood. She was coming.

But wait. There was a different human this time. He was shorter than Rita. He appeared to be a kid. He wore black cloth with orange beneath it.

Where did he come from? Where was Rita?

The kid opened the chicken coop and stepped inside. Little Fox wasn't sure what to do. He needed to talk to Rita, but this other human was there. Could this human have the same answers? Little Fox sighed. There was only one way to find out. He jumped over the fence.

The kid froze when he came out of the chicken coop. He stared at Little Fox. Little Fox stared back. He stood on all four legs—he didn't want to scare the kid. He smiled.

The kid picked up a stick. Little Fox prepared to run. He didn't want to be hit by a stick. The kid threw the stick into the grass and shouted, "Fetch!"

Little Fox understood the human language, but he wasn't sure what that word meant. He figured it meant "get away". He couldn't give up now. He needed answers. Little Fox shook his head no.

"What are you?" the kid asked. "You're not a dog. If you were, then you'd have a collar." He walked toward Little Fox. He held his hands out for some reason. "This is nuts," the kid continued. "You've got to be some kind of dog. Where's your collar?"

The kid stopped right in front of him. He stared into Little Fox's eyes like he was amazed by them. Little Fox wondered if humans wore collars. He stood on his two hind legs. "I don't know," he said in his human voice. "Where's *your* collar?"

The kid fell backward and scooted away from Little Fox. It was too soon to talk to the human. Little Fox wished he had waited for Rita.

"Jonah!" another human shouted from the yard. She sounded like Rita but younger. "Where are you? You better not be in the outhouse!"

The kid sat on the ground and stared at Little Fox. He looked as scared as Little Fox felt when Rita had pointed the gun at him. Little Fox would have to fix this later. The other human could be coming.

Little Fox walked on his hind legs to the kid. "I'm a fox," he said. "Don't tell anyone you saw me here." He winked at the kid to show him that he wasn't dangerous. Then Little Fox ran to the fence and jumped over it. He'd have to figure out what to do later. Maybe the kid could give him the answers he needed. And maybe, just maybe, the kid could be his friend.

MY fox ATE MY REPORT CARD

REPORT CARD	
ENGLISH	C
HISTORY	B
SCIENCE	B
MATH	B
ART	A
GYM	A

DAVID BLAZE

CONTENTS

FRIDAY MORNING

I smashed a handful of clay on the table in front of me with a bang. Every kid in the art class stared at me. The past few months had been hard without Fox. My grades in school had slipped and I hadn't even realized it. At least not until I got my report card in Miss Cox's class earlier.

Sam hovered over my shoulder. "You're supposed to be the smart one," he said. He must have seen my report card on the table, because he shouted, "Hey, everyone! Joe got a C in English!" He reached around me, snatched it, and held it up for the class to see.

"Pipe down!" Miss Pendleton shouted. She was the oldest teacher at school. She wore a long skirt that went up past her waist and to her chest. She glared at us from her desk.

I grabbed the report card from Sam. He wore his usual tank top to show off his biceps. He laughed at me and returned to the group at his art table across the room. He high fived one of them.

"No Mama, nooo!" Sam shouted in a high-pitched voice. The class laughed. He looked around and smirked. He slammed his own handful of clay on his table. "I didn't mean to get a bad grade! Please don't hurt me!"

The class kept laughing. I could only shake my head. He picked up the clay and slammed it down again and again onto the tabletop. It sounded like a kid getting spanked with a wooden spoon. The class laughed louder and louder until Miss Pendleton shouted, "Knock it off!"

Melissa bumped her shoulder against mine. "Hey, Joe. Don't listen to him." She put a thumb down. I loved her smile and bouncy ponytails. I smiled back and nodded.

"English is my best class," I told her. "I write for the school newsletter." I tapped my fingers on the table. "I don't know how I'm going to tell my mom about this."

Melissa waved her hands at me. "I didn't pass Math. Remember?" She bit her lower lip. "I'm the one going to summer school."

I nodded. "You win."

She chuckled. "It doesn't feel like it." She looked over my report card. "Show your mom. She'll understand." I wasn't sure about that.

"Do you like my flowerpot?" Melissa asked. I couldn't tell her the truth. Melissa didn't have any artistic talent with clay. Her flowerpot looked like a soccer ball had exploded.

"It's beautiful," I lied.

She smiled. "It's for my dad," she said.

Sam came by our table again and laughed his head off. "Your dad likes flowers?" He shook his head. "Real men don't like flowers." He made sure to stop by every student and tell them about Melissa's dad.

Melissa shrugged her shoulders at me. "My dad likes to keep fresh roses. They were my mom's favorite." She rubbed her eyes. "Stupid allergies."

Before I could say anything, Miss Pendleton tapped me on the shoulder. I gulped. She was not a nice person when she was mad. All I could see was her skirt when I turned to face her. It was as high as my head.

"Tell me that you're done, Jonah," she said. Her arms were crossed. "I've got to get this work in the kiln tonight."

The rest of the school called me Joe. No matter how many times I reminded Miss Pendleton that I didn't like being called Jonah, she still forgot. I wondered how old she was. "It'll be a minute or two," I assured her.

"Well, what are you making?" she asked. "A salad bowl?" She flinched like she was disgusted. "I hate salads!"

I looked at my work and had to agree — it did look like a big salad bowl. But that's not what it was. "I need more time," I told her. "It has to be perfect."

She squeezed her eyes and shouted, "Look at me! Does it look like I'm getting any younger?"

"No!" Sam shouted from across the room. The class laughed with him again.

Miss Pendleton waved her fists like a crazy person. "That just burns me up!" She marched to her desk, huffing and puffing with every step.

Melissa nudged me. "I like salad." She smirked. "Taco salad!"

I tried not to laugh because, well, it wasn't

funny. "You've been hanging around the cat too much," I told her. She laughed hysterically.

"I'm a Meow Master," she mocked, chopping her arms in the air like a karate expert. I laughed with her. PJ had kept our lives interesting while Fox was gone. Crazy cat.

I looked at the clock on the wall behind Miss Pendleton. Five minutes were left in class. I stared at my report card as I put it into my backpack. I wasn't sure I could give it to my mom. But that wasn't my greatest fear.

I needed to see Fox so he could give me an update. He and his parents had been searching our land and the forest. Something dark was coming. They were doing whatever they could to keep it away from us.

FRIDAY AFTERNOON

I jumped into my Uncle Mike's pickup truck in the school parking lot. My little cousin Dana was in the middle seat. She smirked at me and punched my arm. I flinched. She was a lot stronger than she thought she was.

"Play nice," my uncle warned. He turned from the steering wheel and winked at me. "She's a sweet little kid." Sure, a sweet little kid with the strength of a rhino!

"Cry quietly in the corner." She burst out laughing. I rubbed my shoulder and shook my head. It was a good thing she was family and I liked her.

"How did you do on your report card?" my uncle asked.

I gulped. "I did okay."

He nodded and smiled at me. "Of course you did. You're the smartest kid I know." He pulled out of the parking lot.

"Hey!" Dana shouted. "What about me?" She crossed her arms.

My uncle cleared his throat. "I mean he's the second smartest kid I know." He looked straight ahead.

I sat back and closed my eyes. It was a thirty-minute trip out of town to the wildlife sanctuary. I hadn't been there in a while but was ready to get back to work. I couldn't wait for summer. I could be there with the animals all day.

Something jumped into my lap and slapped me in the face with a wet tongue. I screamed. My eyes shot open. Fox's bright blue eyes stared back at me.

"Fox!" I shouted. I wrapped my arms
around him. His brown and orange fur was
warm and comforting. "What are you doing
here?" I looked behind the seat and realized
he had been hiding there.

"Sneak attack!" he said in his childish
voice. He licked my face again. I laughed with
him and Dana.

"Miss Julie wants to see Fox," my uncle
said.

I didn't know why she wanted to see him.
Fox was as healthy as an ox. Hey, that rhymes!
I held him closer. Fox had been through way
too much in the last year. I hoped there was
nothing wrong with him.

"Don't worry," Dana said. Her eyes were
wide like everything was fine. I was glad she

was there. "I won't tell your friends that I slap you around." She was being playful and having fun. At least I hope that's what she was doing.

"We're getting close," my uncle said. He nodded at me. "Dana will help you today and Fox will... do whatever he does."

Fox faced my uncle. "Don't make me bring the pain, Mary. Do not unleash Mr. Awesome Muscles."

My uncle stopped the pickup truck in front of the animal sanctuary. He turned to Fox. "My name isn't Mary."

Fox wiped a paw across his lips. "It will be when I'm done with you." Dana high fived him. Fox had learned a lot from her. Too much.

My uncle narrowed his eyes. "Sunday afternoon. You and me on the mat." I rolled my eyes. Fox and my uncle loved to watch wrestling on TV. Last week they dressed like wrestlers. Fox wore bright red underwear. It was ridiculous.

I hopped out of the truck with Fox and Dana. I didn't bother to tell Dana that I was in charge once we got inside the sanctuary. That never went over well. I jumped when my uncle honked his horn.

"Be good," he shouted out his window. "Give Fox a bath. He smells like pickles!" My uncle laughed and drove off.

Fox stood on his hind legs, sniffed his armpits and shuddered. "He's right. Don't stand too close."

I wasn't prepared for what I saw when we walked into the sanctuary. Animals were in cages all over the floor. Squirrels, opossum, rabbits, raccoons — too many to count! They were laid out like they were injured or worse. Miss Julie ran around the room, shouting into her cell phone. She closed it when she saw us.

"Come in, kids," she said, out of breath. "Go into the back and find as many cages as you can. We're going to need all of them."

Dana grabbed my hand as we looked over the animals. None of them were moving. "What's wrong with them?"

Fox sniffed at their cages. He looked at me and Miss Julie with sad eyes. "We have to help them."

Miss Julie focused her eyes on me. "You haven't been here in a while." She was right. When Fox had returned to his parents in the forest, I didn't want to be around the other animals. They reminded me of him.

"Christopher has been bringing in animals like this for more than a week," she continued. She and my mom called him Christopher, but I would always remember him as Tater the Exterminator. "They've been shot." She turned her head away from us. "I haven't been able to save all of them."

"I don't understand," I said. "Fox and his parents have been watching the forest. They were supposed to warn us." I looked at him. "How did you miss this?"

Miss Julie held out a hand. " It's not their fault. The Conecuh National Forest is 84,000 acres. It reaches from here to Florida." She shrugged. "There's no way Fox and his parents could watch all of it."

Dana let go of my hand. She put her arms around Fox. "You can't go back into the forest. You can't."

"Elan is flying here in a couple of days," Miss Julie said. "He's visiting his brother in Los Angeles." I gulped. The American Indian had warned my family that darkness was coming.

"An old friend wants to see you," Miss Julie said to Fox. He was standing on his hind legs. He put his paws in the air like he was confused.

Miss Julie's face softened. "Christopher found a young skunk a few weeks ago. He's your age." Fox's ears perked up. "He has a broken paw, but it's healing much faster than I expected." She smiled for the first time that afternoon. "He reminds me of you."

A kid skunk stepped into the room on

hind legs, just like Fox! He looked around at us with bright blue eyes then stared at Fox. "Don't pull your dad's finger!" he shouted.

Fox ran right past me and tackled the skunk. They jumped around each other and laughed like they were old friends.

"Who is that?" Dana asked me. I shrugged, wondering the same thing myself.

"This is my friend Stinky!" Fox shouted. He wrapped an arm around the skunk and chuckled.

Dana crossed her arms. "Why is his name Stinky?"

Fox and Stinky burst out laughing. "Don't ask," Fox advised.

The front door opened behind us. Tater

the Exterminator walked in with another cage in his hand. A rabbit was laid out in it. "Where should I put this one?" he asked. That's when he saw me and Dana. "Oh, hey kids."

I barely recognized him. He had lost a lot of weight and combed his hair over his forehead. I remembered him as a chubby man with a huge forehead and a hotdog nose. At least he still had the nose. You could see it from a mile away.

Dana shrunk away from him and stood close to my side. We would never forget the day he had barged into my house and taken Fox away. He had changed since then. My mom trusted him, so I trusted him too.

"What are we going to do?" Miss Julie asked Tater. "We're running out of room." Her voice was weak. Her shoulders were low.

Tater shrugged. "It's déjà vu." Miss Julie nodded. Tater stared at Fox. "The same thing happened last year when your parents were shot."

Miss Julie cried. She cleared her throat and said, "I'm sorry."

"It's got to be the same hunters," Tater continued. He put a hand on his forehead. "It doesn't make any sense, though. They're not taking the animals. They're leaving them."

Fox and Stinky whispered to each other. When they were done, Fox looked at me and raised his chin. That meant he wanted my attention later. He didn't want Tater to know. Fox was afraid of him.

"It's like they want to wipe out all the animals in the forest," Tater said. He shook his head and set the cage down. His face was creased and red.

"They're looking for something specific," Miss Julie said. "And they're not going to stop until they find it." She waved her hands like she had no idea what to do. "Elan will have answers," she assured us.

I hoped Miss Julie was right about Elan and wrong about everything else. Somehow the hunters knew Fox wasn't the only creature with blue eyes that could walk and talk.

FRIDAY NIGHT

It was quiet at the kitchen table. My mom sat at one end and my uncle sat at the other. Dana sat across from me. Fox searched the refrigerator for any leftover chicken. PJ was taking a nap. I used to think he was lazy, but cats sleep up to twenty hours a day.

"Let's see your report card, Jonah," my mom said. She rubbed her hands together and smiled like she was excited. When we first moved to Alabama, grades dropped because I missed a lot of school. I got straight A's on the last report card.

Thunder roared outside. I hoped I wasn't going to be struck by lightning. "I left it in my locker," I said. "I'm sorry. I'll get it Monday." Her eyes narrowed. I had to change the subject. "What are we going to do about the animals?"

She leaned back and crossed her arms. I wished I could read her mind. I hoped she believed me. "I can't believe someone's hurting them." She shook her head and huffed. A vein in her forehead looked like it was ready to explode.

"Pass the salt, please," my uncle said. He rubbed his hands together. My mom had made his favorite dinner — pork chops and french fries. He had the last porkchop. This was his third helping. My mom glared at him. "What?" he asked. "I said please."

The refrigerator door slammed shut. Fox came to the table and sat next to me. "All I ask for is a little chicken," he complained. He stared at my uncle's plate. "That looks good."

My uncle pulled his plate closer. "Salt? Please pass the salt?"

"I don't want it anyways," Fox said. "It doesn't taste like chicken."

Dana laughed. "How would you know? You don't eat pork chops."

Fox leaned across the table and winked at my uncle. "I licked it earlier."

My uncle looked down at his plate. "Never mind. Keep the salt." He pushed his plate forward and stared at Fox. I had a feeling the wrestling match between Fox and my uncle was going to be epic. I'd have to get a front row seat.

I raise my chin to Fox. He had wanted my attention earlier at the sanctuary. "What were you and Stinky talking about?" The skunk looked like his foot was better, but Miss Julie wanted to keep him for two more days. She was concerned about infection.

Fox nodded at me. "I've always been able to talk and walk on two legs." He spoke slowly. "I've done it since the first time I stepped out of my parents' den."

"You don't have to be a showoff," Dana

said. "I can rub my belly and pat my head at the same time." And that's what she did.

"He's not showing off," I said. I realized what Fox was telling us. I looked into his blue eyes. "You didn't get your powers from my great-grandmother's land like Elan thought. They came from somewhere else."

"The forest," my mom whispered. "I should have seen it. There could be more like you." We already knew of two animals like him.

Fox nodded. "My family was hunted by two men." He stared at the wall across from us. "Stinky saved me."

I grabbed his arm to get his attention. "The hunters. It's the same men leaving the injured animals behind today, isn't it?" I could see in his eyes the answer was yes.

My uncle stood. "This is good. We can work with this." He put his hands on the table. "What did they look like?"

Fox shrugged. "I only saw them from a distance." He stared at his paws. "My parents buried me in the den." He looked at my uncle. "I didn't see them up close, but I heard them."

My uncle walked over to Fox and knelt next to him. "Think. What did they say?" His voice was high like he was frustrated.

Fox leaned away from him. "You need a breath mint." He waved a paw in front of his nose.

My uncle stood and grunted. "What did they say?" he repeated.

Fox looked at me. "Tater was right. They're hunting all of the animals in the forest."

My uncle threw his hands up and returned to his chair. "That doesn't help us," he complained. "We already knew that."

Fox pounded a paw on the table. "Hold on to your britches, Mary." He was talking to my uncle. "The names of the hunters are Billy and John. They're being paid a lot of money."

My mom smiled and cheered. "You're a smart fox!" I agreed with her. Fox remembered names he had only heard once. And he hadn't seen their faces.We looked at him, confused. "Who is paying them?"

"I don't know," Fox admitted. He stared at the wall across from us again. His face froze like he was lost in thought. "They said the boss was paying them a lot of money."

"The boss?" my mom asked. "That could be anyone. Do you guys know any hunters named Billy or John?" We shook our heads. "I'll check with Christopher. He knows a lot of hunters."

"It could be Chen," I said. "He could be the boss." I hoped I was wrong. The man from China had tried to kidnap Fox twice before.

I jumped when there was a knock on the front door. "Fox, go into the bedroom," my mom told him.

"I know the drill," he said. "I'll go mess with the cat. He hates it when I do that." Fox got out of his seat, went into the hall, then into my bedroom.

I went to the door with my mom. Shane was on the other side, standing in the rain when we opened it. He was the tallest kid at school but at least he finally stopped growing. Once my enemy, he was now my friend.

"Get in here," my mom told him. "You're soaking wet." He stood there, letting the rain fall on his head and shoulders.

"My dad…" he said, looking lost. "I didn't know how to tell you. I'm sorry." I was worried. I motioned for him to come in, but he shook his head.

"He got out of prison a few days ago,"

Shane continued, "but he didn't come home." I couldn't move. It was obvious who the boss was. Shane's dad, Mr. Connors, didn't know I had the same blue eyes as Fox. It happened after he went to prison. He didn't know what I could do. He couldn't find out. He was far too dangerous.

"Get in here," my mom said again. She grabbed his arm and pulled him inside. "I'm not going to let you get sick." She pointed to the hall. "My brother has some spare clothes in the guest bedroom. Go dry off and put them on." He was way too tall to fit into my clothes.

My mom went back into the kitchen with me. "Charles Connors is out of prison," she told my uncle before she sat down.

"Mystery solved," he said. 'We need to figure out a plan." He took a deep breath. "I'm sorry for earlier," he said to Fox. "You've been a big help."

"No problem," Fox said. "I'm sorry I called you Mary." He smiled. "And I'm sorry I lied. I didn't lick your porkchop."

"What?" my uncle asked. He pulled his

plate close again. "Salt? Please pass the salt?"

SATURDAY MORNING

I glanced at the man standing at the table next to us. He had a brown beard and mustache. My mom and I had been coming to the farmers market for a year. Mr. Jim Bob had always been at that table with his fruits and vegetables. This didn't feel right. Where was Mr. Jim Bob?

"Good morning!" the stranger shouted to us with a smile. He walked around his table and came over to our table full of eggs. He wore a brown leather belt with the biggest buckle I had ever seen. It was silver with the image of a cowboy holding his hat in the air while riding a horse.

"Good morning," my mom said. "It's nice to see a new face." She reached out a hand and shook his. "I'm Julie." She wrapped an arm around me. "This is my son Jonah."

I squeezed out of her grip. "Joe," I told the man smiling at me. "My name is Joe."

"Joe," he whispered, crossing his arms. His smile disappeared. His eyes narrowed. "I've heard a lot about you."

I gulped. What had he heard? The last stranger who knew who I was had nearly destroyed my world. Was I in danger? I leaned against my mom and put her arm back around me.

"Uncle Max!" a familiar voice shouted from the crowd. I looked around the stranger and saw Melissa wearing sunglasses and with a drink in hand. She ran to the stranger and hugged him.

My fists tightened. I didn't know this man. I didn't trust him. What had he done to Mr. Jim Bob?

He pointed at me and shook his head. "So," he said to Melissa, "this is the guy you have a crush on?" Her face turned red. She covered her forehead with a hand. "What?" her uncle asked. "You talk about him all the time."

My mom chuckled in a way I hadn't heard in years. "It's nice to meet you, Max."

He winked at her. "I wanted to surprise my niece." He looked at the table next to ours and nodded. "I was talking to the guy running that table. We're both into airplanes." I'd never forget that crazy flight straight up into the air with Mr. Jim Bob. "He asked me to watch his table while he went to the restroom."

"You're not from around here, are you?" my mom asked. "You don't have a country accent like the rest of the city."

"He lives in Florida," Melissa said. She nudged him. "It must be nice to live in Orlando. You need to take me with you so I can go to Disney World."

"We're from Orlando!" my mom shouted. She took her arm from me again and walked around the table. "I love the sun and rain there. I miss the way the city lights up at night."

Mr. Max smiled. "I love it there." He looked into the crowd. "We could talk about it while we eat. Are you hungry?"

My mom chuckled again. "I could eat. They have hamburgers here." She motioned to me and Melissa. "Watch the tables. We'll bring you some food back." And just like that, she disappeared into the crowd with Melissa's uncle.

"That was weird," I said to Melissa. I didn't know what else to say to her. She talked about me all the time?

"Yeah," Melissa agreed. "Way weird." She smiled at me. "Did you show your mom your report card?"

I shuffled the eggs. "Not yet. I'm waiting for the right time."

"You should do it today," she said. She took off her sunglasses and set her drink down. "It's like pulling off a Band-Aid. It will sting a little at first, but you'll feel a lot better."

"Maybe," I said. I cut my knee once when I fell in a parking lot. It left a scar. It didn't hurt anymore, but it would be there for the rest of my life.

"How's my cat doing?" Melissa asked.

"PJ sleeps all day," I complained. "He only comes to life when you're around. You're his favorite person." Melissa liked to think of him as hers. I didn't mind. It was cool to have a talking cat, but I had been through so much with Fox. He was my best friend.

"You're a lot happier," she said. I wasn't sure what she meant. Happier than what? "Since Fox came back." I couldn't argue with her. I was lost when Fox had disappeared into the woods with his family for months. I couldn't lose him again.

"What's wrong, Joe?" she asked, standing between me and the eggs on the table. "You're quieter than usual."

I shrugged my shoulders. "It's silly." I couldn't shake the feeling that bad people were looking for me. Melissa put her hands in the air like she wanted me to tell her everything. I told her about the animals being hunted.

"That's not the worst part," I confided in

her. "I don't want to be paranoid, but I think they're after me." I watched her eyes to see how she'd respond.

Melissa squinted her eyes like she was confused. Her face relaxed after a minute. "It's because you're like them, right? Fox and PJ?" I nodded. She tapped her chin with a finger. "Your eyes are bright blue like theirs. You're faster and stronger than you were before."

I nodded. "I feel like I'm being watched." I was embarrassed to admit it. I sounded like a crazy person. "I've got to find out who The Boss is."

"We've always stuck together," she said. "I won't let anything happen to you. They'll have to get through me first." She put her hands on her hips.

I believed her. I hoped I wasn't being paranoid. She winked at me and went to Mr. Jim Bob's table when a customer walked up to it.

That's when I froze. Two men in camouflage pants and jackets sat on a park bench in the middle of the crowd. They faced me and whispered to each other. They stood and walked away as soon as they realized I saw them.

I shook my head and took a deep breath. It had to be my imagination. No one was after me.

I wish I had been right.

SATURDAY AFTERNOON

"Help!" Fox shouted from inside my house. "Somebody save me!"

I jumped out of the car and raced toward the house. I shouldn't have gone to the farmers market. I should have known better than to leave Fox in the house. Now he was in trouble and it was my fault.

"Jonah, wait!" my mom shouted after me. Her mouth was open, and her eyes begged me not to go. I couldn't wait. I had to save my friend.

"Don't hurt him!" Dana shouted at someone right before I shoved the front door open. Nobody better have touched Fox or my little cousin. I would give up everything to protect them. I was ready to do whatever I had to do.

I froze when I saw what was in front on me. My heart raced, and my chest was pounded. A large blue mat covered the living room floor. Dana and PJ were standing on the outside of it, staring at the two bodies wrestling in front of them. My Uncle Mike had Fox pinned on the mat.

"One!" Dana shouted. She banged her fist on the mat. "Two!" She banged it again.

"Come on, Fox!" PJ shouted. "We've gotta win! You can do it!"

Dana raised her hand to bang it one more time. But before she could, Fox opened his claws and scratched my uncle's hand.

"Ouch!" my uncle shouted, jumping back. He squeezed his hand a few times and stared at it. "That really hurt. You broke my skin." He shook his head and nodded at Dana. "It should be against the rules."

Fox stood and smirked. He turned his neck from side to side until it cracked. "There are no rules. My name is Captain Awesome Muscles, and this is war."

My mom rushed into the house behind me. "What's going on here?" she asked.

I turned and looked at her. "Children," I said, shaking my head. I got my breath back. "They're children."

My uncle grunted and pounced on Fox again. He pinned my best friend to the mat like before. He turned his head away from Fox's armpits. "You still smell like pickles," he complained.

"I haven't had a bath this week," Fox admitted. He grinned and raised his armpits to my uncle's face. "Smell it! Smell it!"

Dana jumped down on the mat and banged her fist. "One!"

My mom closed the door behind her. "I'm going to make lunch," she said as she walked past me to the kitchen. "Any requests?"

"Chi…cken," Fox grunted. He stretched one of his paws out as far as he could while it was pinned. I couldn't understand why at first.

"Tag me in!" PJ shouted. "Come on! Come on!" He jumped up and down impatiently. Fox grimaced and reached out a little farther. Then it happened. PJ tapped his paw.

PJ jumped onto the mat on his two hind legs. He jumped from side to side, one leg to the other. "Gotta get the blood flowing," he said. He nodded at Fox as my best friend rolled out of the ring.

Fox noticed me for the first time and winked at me. I smiled at him and shrugged. A minute earlier I thought he was in danger. Thank goodness he wasn't. I would always do what I could to keep him safe.

Dana clasped her hands in front of her like she was holding a microphone. "Crazy Karate Cat steps into the ring," she announced. PJ put his paws together in front of him. It looked like he was praying. He bowed to my uncle like he was in a karate tournament.

"Let's see what you're made out of," my uncle said. He stood with his legs open wide and his hands in front of him. PJ didn't have a chance. All my uncle had to do was reach out and grab him. At least that's what I thought.

My uncle shot out his hands to grab PJ. At that very moment PJ did a somersault between my uncle's legs and ended up behind him. He turned to face my uncle's back and shouted, "Karate chop!" He threw a paw into the back of my uncle's leg like he had a black belt in karate.

My uncle fell to his knees and groaned. "Wow," I said. "PJ's gotten really good." Dana had been training him with what she learned in her karate classes. PJ had wanted to be good at karate. I didn't know he was serious about it.

PJ bowed to me. "Thank you, young grasshopper. I am a Meow Master."

My mom walked out of the kitchen and laughed. "I don't want to know what happened." She motioned to Dana. "Come help me set the table. Let's let the boys be boys."

Dana put her hands on her face and shook her head. "It's not my job," she whispered so my mom couldn't hear her. "You do it." What she didn't know was my mom could hear everything.

"I heard that, young lady," my mom said. She turned to my uncle. "Better get your daughter."

He stood and brushed his knees off. "Why? She reminds me of you at that age."

My mom chuckled. "I know. That's the problem."

PJ jumped from leg to leg again. "Are we doing this or not?" He punched his fists in front of him at an invisible punching bag.

"We're done here," my uncle said. He

rubbed his knees. "I'm going to need some ice."

I watched him hobble into the kitchen. PJ and Fox went with him. They teased him a lot, but they respected him. I hoped I could be like my uncle one day.

What PJ had done was amazing. My uncle was much bigger than him. With one blow of PJ's paw, my uncle fell. I never thought I'd say it, but I'd be happy to have him by my side if we were in trouble.

That day was coming much sooner than I expected.

SATURDAY NIGHT

Melissa and her uncle Max came to our house for dinner that night. My mom had invited them. Melissa's dad had returned to Puerto Rico for a few days. He was an electrician and wanted to make sure there weren't any more problems after Hurricane Irma last year.

"I'm glad you could join us," my mom said to Melissa. "I can't let you survive on burgers and tacos while your dad is gone." She winked at Mr. Max and led them into the kitchen.

"That's not fair," Mr. Max complained. "I do a lot more than order burgers and tacos." He winked back at my mom. "I also order pizza."

I was seated at the kitchen table with Dana and my Uncle Mike. "This is my brother Mike," my mom said, pointing to him. "And this is my niece Dana," she continued, pointing to her. "You already know Jonah. Go ahead and take a seat. Dinner will be ready in a minute."

"Joe," I reminded Mr. Max. "Please call me Joe."

He nodded at me. "You got it, Joe." He pulled out the chair next to mine. "I'll sit here." Dana was on the other side of the table. My uncle was at the end.

"Sit next to me," Dana said to Melissa. She patted the chair by hers. "Girl power." Melissa smiled at me and joined her.

My uncle stood and reached his arm past me. "It's nice to meet you," he said to Mr. Max. The man from Orlando shook his hand. "What do you do for a living?" He sat back down.

"I'm a writer," Mr. Max said. He had my full attention.

"Did you hear that, Jonah?" my mom asked. She opened the oven to check on the chicken she was baking. "He's a writer, too."

Mr. Max turned to me. "What do you write?" I wasn't sure how to answer him. I had sent articles to magazines, but none of them were published. My throat was dry, and my ears rang.

"He writes for the school newspaper," Melissa said. She smiled at me again. "And he wrote an amazing paper about friendship." I mouthed the words 'thank you' to her.

My mom set a pan of baked barbecue chicken on the table. She came back with a big pot of mashed potatoes and another pot full of corn. "Help yourselves," she said as she sat at the other end of the table. "Make sure you save a piece for Fox."

Mr. Max raised his eyebrows. "Who's that? A friend?"

My uncle stood and stabbed a chicken leg quarter on the pan with his fork. "That's right. He's a family friend." He put the chicken on his plate and scooped a spoonful of mashed potatoes from the pot. "And he smells like pickles."

Dana burst out laughing. I couldn't stop myself from laughing with her. My mom's face turned red.

Mr. Max raised an eyebrow. My uncle shrugged at him like he had no idea why we were laughing. "So," my uncle said to him, "what do you write?"

We helped ourselves to the food on the table. Dana swatted a spoon at me when I reached for the corn. "I'm a travel writer," Mr. Max said. "I go all over the world and write about different cities and countries." I didn't know writers could do that. I stared at him in awe.

My mom's face lit up. "Any time you

come through Alabama, you can stop here for a home cooked meal." He smiled at her and nodded.

My uncle stopped chewing his food. He looked back and forth from my mom to Mr. Max. "Has anyone heard from Elan?" We looked at him, shocked. He changed the subject, but Mr. Max didn't need to know about this. "Another family friend," my uncle said to him.

My mom stared at my uncle like she wanted to burn a hole into his head. He stared right back at her. They had a way of talking to each other silently, but I didn't want to imagine what they were saying.

"We need to talk to Elan," my uncle said out loud. "We're in danger." He ate a forkful of mashed potatoes. He looked like he was happy with himself. My mom and Mr. Max weren't smiling at each other anymore.

"I can have a friend of mine install an alarm for you," Mr. Max offered. He sounded like he wanted to help. "It'll make you safer if you're worried about being robbed." I remembered the one time our house was trashed but nothing was taken. The words 'GIVE US THE FOX' were painted above the front door.

I did a double take when PJ walked across the kitchen floor toward Dana and Melissa. He was on four paws. We had instructed him to stay in the back bedroom. I suspected Fox had convinced him to come out and get a piece of chicken.

"We don't need an alarm," Dana said. She patted PJ's head. "Our cat hears everything. He'd let us know if there was a burglar." PJ walked past her and jumped into Melissa's lap.

Mr. Max scoffed. "What's he going to do? Meow loudly?"

PJ stood on his hind legs on Melissa's lap and put his front paws on the table. Whatever he was about to do wouldn't be good. "I'll karate chop the bad man," he said. "I'm a Meow Master."

Mr. Max jumped up out of his chair. It fell behind him and crashed on the floor with a loud thud. "We're leaving," he said to Melissa. His chest heaved up and down like it couldn't get enough air. "Put the cat down."

Melissa set PJ on the floor and stood. "Uncle Max," she said, "I told you about PJ." She put her hands on her head. "He really did help me with my math homework."

"Let's calm down," my mom said. "We can talk about this." She didn't take her eyes off Mr. Max.

He looked around the table at all of us. "I thought it was just a story. You know, for fun." He cleared his throat and said to Melissa, "I forbid you from coming here anymore. I have to talk to your father. Let's go. Now."

Melissa put hands in the air. "These are my friends. Don't do this." She shrugged her shoulders at me.

Mr. Max pointed to the front door. "I'm doing this for your own good. I have to protect you." He kicked his chair away.

Melissa looked at me with tears in her eyes. "I'm sorry." She pushed her chair out and followed her uncle to the front door and out of the house. I couldn't move. Did I lose a good friend? Would I ever see her outside of school again?

SUNDAY MORNING

I sat in the back row of the church. Dana was on one side of me and Shane was on the other. His father sat in a pew at the front of the church. I couldn't believe Mr. Connors had the nerve to come to church after what he did to Fox and the other animals. I kept an eye on him.

I didn't get any sleep the night before. I kept thinking about Melissa. I remembered the first time we met in school. I didn't think I'd ever get used to her country accent, but now I didn't notice it.

I turned each time the church doors

opened, hoping she was there. Fox was my best friend, but Melissa was my favorite human. I hoped her uncle changed his mind. I didn't want to lose my friend.

It didn't help that terrible things were happening that I couldn't stop. With so many animals being hunted in the forest, I couldn't protect all of them. I knew I couldn't. I was losing hope.

The church organ came to life. I didn't recognize the song being played. For months *How Great Thou Art* had been played at the beginning and end of service. Now we had a new organist because Miss Sally had arthritis and couldn't play anymore. I didn't like change.

"Brothers and sisters," the preacher said from the pulpit. "I feel in my heart that a troubled soul needs to hear this today." He raised his arms to the side of him. "The name of the Lord is a strong tower. The righteous run to it and are safe." I swear he was staring at me.

I don't remember much after that. When the collection plate got to me, I put in fifty cents. That was ten percent of my allowance. The people around me shook their heads whenever I didn't put anything in the plate. So, I came prepared.

The organist played another song I hadn't heard before when it was time to leave. When we stood, I looked for Melissa again. I knew she wasn't there, but it was still disappointing each time I looked.

As we stepped out of the aisles to leave, Shane's dad stood in front of me. I gulped. The man was as big as a house. I didn't respect him. He had kidnapped Fox and forced him to put on a show in Las Vegas.

And he had tried to take away my mom's house. Now he was hurting all the animals and calling himself *The Boss.* "Jonah," he said.

I wanted to push him out of the way. "My name is Joe," I reminded him. "You're gonna pay for what you're doing. I'm gonna make sure of it." He stared at me with a blank expression. I turned from him and pushed through the crowd.

"Joe, wait up!" Shane shouted after me. He was my friend, but I couldn't be around his father. I squeezed between people to get out. I had one foot out of the foyer when the preacher grabbed my arm.

"Hi, Joe," he said. "I've been praying for you." He smiled. "Is everything okay?"

I looked through the crowd behind me. I didn't see Mr. Connors anywhere. I felt bad for the question I needed to ask, but I had to know the answer. "How are you supposed to love your enemies when they want to hurt you?"

He put a hand on my shoulder. "That sounds impossible, doesn't it?" I was glad he understood. I nodded. "You love your mom with all your heart, don't you? You'd do anything for her." I nodded again.

"I don't think you have to love your enemies the same way," he continued. "But you should respect them as human beings. I like to think we'd push them out of the way of a moving train." I chuckled. He was right. I couldn't let anyone get hurt if there was a way for me to stop it.

"Thank you," I told him. "I understand."

Dana grabbed my hand and pulled me toward the exit. "Come on, Joe," she begged. "We have to see what my dad and Fox are doing. The big wrestling match is on TV!"

SUNDAY AFTERNOON

Fox and my uncle were screaming at the TV when we got home. They had a big bowl of popcorn between them on the couch. The championship wrestling match between Mr. Awesome Muscles and The Millennial Kid blasted from the TV.

My mom sighed and said, "I'm gonna take a nap with PJ. There's too much testosterone in here." Fox and my uncle didn't notice her as she walked past them to her bedroom.

"I'm starving," Dana said. She punched my shoulder. "What do you have to eat?"

I put a hand on my shoulder and held it there. I'm not sure why. It's not like my shoulder was going to fall off. But it hurt. "There's some meatloaf in the fridge. YOYO." Whenever my mom wasn't there to cook, she told me to eat YOYO — You're On Your Own. That meant I had to eat leftovers.

"Whatever," Dana said. "I should've gone home." As she passed the couch to the kitchen, she stopped behind my uncle. He didn't know she was there. She shouted "BOO!" into his ear. He jumped up and spilled the bowl of popcorn all over the floor. Dana continued walking to the kitchen, laughing the whole way.

"Not funny!" my uncle shouted after her. "Grab me a drink while you're in there."

Dana kept walking. "It's not my job. You do it."

I didn't care much for wrestling, but I wanted to see what The Millennial Kid could do. He was the youngest guy in wrestling history. He wasn't covered in muscles like most of the older wrestlers. He didn't wear a mask. And he was as popular as Mr. Awesome Muscles.

Fox didn't say anything when I sat next to him. He held out his fist. I pounded it with my fist in what we called a fist pump. It wasn't hard, and it didn't hurt. It's what we did to greet each other since he couldn't shake hands.

Mr. Awesome Muscles dove from the top of a post in the ring. He flew straight for the Millennial Kid! There wasn't any hope for the Kid. Mr. Awesome Muscles was twice his size.

Mr. Awesome Muscles crushed The Millennial Kid and pinned him to the mat. The count was 1. It looked like he would stay the champion. Then the count was 2. Half of the crowd cheered for him. The other half yelled for The Millennial Kid to get up. The referee raised his hand to count to 3.

The TV shut off.

Fox and my uncle both jumped up and shouted, "No!"

My mom stepped in front of the TV. She had the remote control in her hand.

"Why is there popcorn all over my floor?"

She pointed down at the mess. "There's no excuse for this."

"Are you kidding me?!" Fox shouted.

"Turn it back on!" my uncle begged. He tried to snatch the remote from my mom, but she swung it over her shoulder before he could reach it. He got down on his hands and knees and threw handfuls of popcorn into the bowl as fast as he could. "This can't be happening!"

My mom handed the remote to me when my uncle finished. "I'll leave you in charge." She yawned as she walked away. "There's too much noise for me to sleep."

"Turn it on, man!" Fox shouted into my ear. I shook my head and turned it back on. None of us believed what we saw and heard on the screen.

"In the biggest upset in wrestling history," the announcer said, "the Millennial Kid has beat Mr. Awesome Muscles to win the world championship!"

Mr. Awesome Muscles shook the Kid's hand and hugged him. He handed the Championship belt to the Kid himself. It was like he was handing the Kid his dynasty and approved of it. The crowd cheered for both of them.

The Millennial Kid put his shirt back on. He accepted the championship belt and held it high in the air. The crowd roared. "We witnessed history today!" the announcer shouted.

I turned the TV off. None of us said anything. My uncle stood and pointed at Fox. "Ha, ha, ha! My guy won!" He danced in circles like he had scored a touchdown.

Fox crossed his arms. "He cheated."

My uncle kept laughing. "No one likes a sore loser."

Dana came into the living room with a

ham sandwich in her hand. She took a bite. "What did I miss?"

"Mr. Awesome Muscles lost," my uncle said. "That means my guy won. Fox's guy lost."

Fox jumped off the couch and headed for the kitchen. "At least my hair isn't turning gray."

Dana choked and spit out a mouthful of her sandwich. My uncle put a hand on his head. It used to be completely black. Now gray hairs were sprinkled throughout it. "Gray hairs are a sign of wisdom," he explained. "That's how I knew my guy would win!"

I chuckled. I loved my family, even though they were crazy. We were honest with each other, even when it hurt. It was time to face the truth. I had to tell my mom about my report card.

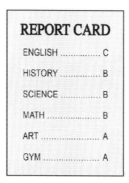

REPORT CARD

ENGLISH C

HISTORY .... B

SCIENCE .... B

MATH .... B

ART .... A

GYM .... A

SUNDAY NIGHT

I closed my bedroom door and stared at the backpack on the floor by my closet. My report card was inside of it. I had never gotten a C before. I was hard for me to breathe. I needed to take it out and show it to my mom. I owed her the truth.

I sat on my bed and considered my options. I could give it to her tomorrow after school. I wouldn't have to worry about it tonight. Or I could give it to her now and get it over with. My stomach churned.

I had called Melissa's house. She would know what to do. Her uncle answered and said she wasn't available. I wanted to ask him if he changed his mind about PJ, and if Melissa could come over. He hung up before I could do that.

My Uncle Mike and Dana had gone home for the evening. Fox and PJ chased each other around the house. My mom yelled at them to stop sometimes and laughed about it at other times. I wished I could get Fox's attention. He ate my homework once before. I wished he'd eat my report card too.

I stood and grabbed the backpack. I had an idea.

I opened the backpack and pulled out a piece of paper and a pencil. I was going to write my mom a letter telling her the truth. I wouldn't have to talk to her about my bad grade. I could apologize ahead of time in writing and promise to do better. Why didn't I think of this earlier? I'm a writer!

That's what I did for the next ten minutes. When I was done, I breathed easier. I didn't feel like the world was going to end. Don't get me wrong. My stomach was weak. But I felt like I could face the truth.

I opened my bedroom door. I smelled

hamburgers cooking in the kitchen. That's where my mom would be. I clutched my letter and report card, took a deep breath, and headed for the kitchen.

"I hope you're hungry," my mom said from the kitchen counter. "I added extra garlic to your burgers, the way you like it." She winked at me.

I gulped. I set the report card on the table first then the letter on top of it. I hoped my plan worked. If she saw the report card first, then I had a lot of explaining to do.

"What do you have there?" my mom asked, smiling.

I walked over to the oven behind her and grabbed the spatula on the counter. "I'll flip the burgers." My back was to her. "I need you to read the letter on the table."

She crossed her arms. It was probably my imagination, but she seemed angry already. She said, "Okay, Jonah." I turned and watched her walk to the table. She moved slowly, like she was afraid of what she'd find.

The hamburgers sizzled. I flipped them so they wouldn't burn. When I looked back at my mom, she set the letter down and picked up the report card. I was dizzy again.

I focused on the hamburgers and moved them an inch in every direction. The sizzling was so loud I thought I was going to go deaf. The smell was so strong I couldn't breathe. My throat was tight. I couldn't swallow.

I jumped when my mom grabbed the spatula. "That's enough, Jonah. They're done." Her expression was blank. I couldn't tell what she was thinking or how angry she was. Would I be grounded for the rest of my life?

"Look at me, Jonah," she said. I couldn't

stop staring at the hamburgers. My mom grabbed the pan and turned off the burner. She set the pan on the counter. My fingers trembled. She sighed.

"A lot has happened this year," she said. "We left our friends behind when we moved here." I missed my friends in Orlando, but I wouldn't have met Fox if we hadn't moved. "The IRS wanted to take this house away from us." Thank goodness we still had it.

Fox and PJ raced into the kitchen and ran in circles around us. My mom put a hand on her forehead. "And plenty of unexpected changes." Fox and PJ ran back into the living room. My mom and I both chuckled.

"One thing will never change," she said. "You'll always be my son and I'll always love you, no matter what." She put her arms around me and squeezed tight. "I don't want you to feel like you can't talk to me. You'll get through this and do better next time."

I shivered and cried. I was relieved but felt guilty for hiding this from my mom. "I'm sorry, mom. I'm supposed to be smart. I don't know what happened."

She held me at arm's length. "Listen to me, Jonah. You are smart. You passed your classes, and you've always done well." She walked back to the kitchen table and grabbed the report card. "This doesn't define you. You don't always have to be the best." She set it down. "I just ask that you do your best."

I promised her I would. I wasn't sure if it would happen in the next day. I had to reveal my clay project to the art class. I could tell the class what it was, but I didn't know if anyone would understand why I made it.

MONDAY MORNING

When I walked into school that morning, I held my breath. I didn't know how to act around Melissa when I saw her. I didn't know if she was allowed to talk to me. I wanted to talk to her more than anything.

"Are you okay?" Shane asked when I passed him in the halls later. I remembered the first time I met him in this same hall and he shoved me to the floor. I never thought we'd be friends.

"Not really," I said.

He stopped me. "What's up? You raced out of church yesterday."

Kids passed us on both sides. A few bumped into me. None of them apologized. "Your dad ...the animals ... Melissa." The class bells rang. I shrugged at Shane. "We'll talk after school." I headed for the art room. It was time to face Melissa.

"Hi, Joe!" Melissa shouted when I stepped in the room. She waved for me to join her at her table.

"Stop shouting!" Miss Pendleton yelled. "That just burns me up!"

I met Melissa at her table. She smiled at me. I smiled back. "I called my dad and told him what happened," she said. "I told him how PJ did my math homework for me that one time." She chuckled. "He was silent for a long time, but then he asked to speak to my uncle."

"I'm guessing it was good news," I said. Her dad must have told her uncle that we could still be friends. I was glad. I took a deep breath and relaxed.

Miss Pendleton knocked a fist on our table like she was knocking on a door. "Since you like to talk so much, your table can go first." Our clay projects were laid out in front of us. She had taken them out of the kiln that morning.

"Wait!" Sam shouted. "Let me go first!" He held his project over his head. "My project is dope!"

Miss Pendleton rolled her eyes. "Go ahead. This should be fun."

"Ladies and gentlemen," Sam said, standing at his table. "I present to you — Professor Mug!" He held his clay mug out. It didn't look special. It was a big cup that was uneven and without a handle.

He turned the mug around. The class burst out laughing. The other side of the mug had two big eyeballs and a long tongue sticking out of it.

"Professor Mug is the worst teacher there is," Sam continued, shaking his head. "He doesn't say anything." Sam looked around the class and nodded at each of us. "His mouth is always full of clay."

I couldn't hold it in. I laughed and laughed and laughed! His mouth was full of clay? His mouth was made of clay!

"I could have been a doctor," Miss Pendleton muttered. "Fifty years...I've wasted fifty years." She rubbed her temples. "Melissa, you're up. It can't get any worse."

I nudged Melissa to let her know it would be okay. She nodded. She picked up her clay flowerpot from the table. "This is my flowerpot. I made sure it's big enough to hold dozens of flowers." She shrugged like there was nothing else to say.

"It's for her dad!" Sam reminded the class. "Her dad likes flowers!" He laughed. Some kids chuckled with him. The others were silent. They were scared to show their projects to the class.

"My mom was in the hospital for a long time," Melissa said to Sam. "My dad and I took her fresh roses every day." She didn't say anything after that. She couldn't. I helped her set the pot back on the table.

"This is how they remember her," I told Sam. He didn't laugh any more. He turned his head from me.

"Okay," Miss Pendleton said. "Jonah, you're up."

I grabbed my project from the table and

held it up. It wasn't perfect, but it was the best
I could do. Before I could say anything, Sam
mumbled, "Nice bowl." It looked like a large
salad bowl and I could have told them that's
what it was.

I flipped the project over and put it on
top of my head. It fit perfectly. Two sides
were longer than the rest to cover my ears.
The front covered my eyebrows. The back
covered the top half of my head.

"Sometimes life is scary," I said. "We're
afraid." I remembered my first day at this
school. "It's easier if we cover our heads and
protect ourselves. That way no one can hurt
us." I took the helmet off and set it on the
table. I hadn't planned what I said next.

"We don't need a helmet. What we need are our friends and family to remind us that we're stronger together. And we'll always be safe." I looked at Melissa and smiled. She smiled back.

The rest of the kids presented their clay projects one by one. My favorite was a volcano. Terry had spread a packet of ketchup from the cafeteria on the sides of it. The worst one was a little blob Nicole called a rock. I don't think she put any effort into it.

Sam made sure to stop by Miss Pendleton's desk when class was over. He held up his mug to her, eyeballs and tongue facing her. "Professor Mug says 'Give Sam an A! He did good with clay!'"

"Fifty years," Miss Pendleton muttered again. "Fifty years."

I felt a lot better when I left school that day. Melissa and I would be okay. The clay project was done. I didn't have anything to hide from my mom. Life was good.

If only I had known I was going to face my greatest fear when I got home.

MONDAY AFTERNOON

I couldn't believe my eyes when I walked into my house. The two men I had seen watching me in the park were standing in the living room with their hands in their pockets. One was dressed in a blue suit and the other in a black and red suit. My mom was talking to them and laughing. I wanted to tell her to run.

"Jonah," my mom said when she saw me, "come over here for a minute." She waved for me to join them. I wished my Uncle Mike was there. He had dropped me off to take Dana home because she wasn't feeling well.

I walked over cautiously. I didn't trust the men.

"This is Mr. Thompson and Mr. Pool," she said, pointing at them. I suspected their first names were Billy and John, the hunters. "They're new in town and looking for a place to stay. They may move across the street into the Hunters' old house." Mr. and Mrs. Hunter had moved up north to live in their vacation home. I missed them. They had bought all my chocolate when we first moved here.

"Also," my mom continued, "Miss Julie brought a young skunk named Stinky by. She said your best friend would know the best place to release him." I nodded. Stinky and Fox had been friends in the forest.

Both men stood and faced me. "Nice to meet you, Jonah," the one called Mr. Thompson said. He reached out a hand for me to shake it.

"My name is…" There was a knock on the front door. "I'll get it." I needed a distraction.

It only got worse when I opened the door. Shane's dad was on the other side, smoking a cigar, and staring at me. It was like the first time I met him, when he had threatened to take away our house.

"What are you doing here?" was all I
could say. Did he come to gloat? Were these
his henchmen in our living room? They were
on a sick mission to destroy all the animals. I
knew he was The Boss. I didn't know if there
was any way to stop him.

Shane stepped up from behind Mr.
Connors. "Hear him out, Joe. He's not here
to hurt anyone." His hands were clasped like
he was begging me.

I crossed my arms. I didn't want to hear
anything Mr. Connors had to say. It could all
be lies and threats. That was all he ever said to
us.

574

He pulled the cigar out of his mouth. "It will only take a minute, Joe. You don't ever have to see me again after this."

I doubted it was true. I looked back at my mom and considered getting her attention. She was still talking and laughing with the two men sitting on our couch now. They didn't look dangerous. "Go ahead," I told Mr. Connors.

He cleared his throat. "I've made a lot of mistakes. I've hurt a lot of people. I hurt you. I hurt the fox." He put a hand in his pocket. "It was wrong. I was wrong." He looked me in the eyes. "I can't make up for what I've done. But I'll spend the rest of my life trying to."

His shoulders sunk. I wanted to believe he was telling the truth, but how could I? The Boss stood in front of me, lying to my face. He had hurt my best friend in the past and he was hurting the other animals now.

"He's telling the truth," Shane said. "His sponsor told me how much he's changed." I huffed. "I'm serious," Shane continued. "My father is donating his time and money to help others."

I was confused. None of this made sense. I looked at Mr. Connors. "Call it off. Stop the hunters." I pointed to the men on the couch. "You know who they are. Get them out of here."

Mr. Connors — The Boss — glanced at the men on the couch. He shrugged and put his hands in the air. "I don't know what you're talking about. And I have no idea who those men are."

As much as I didn't want to believe him, his eyes told me what I needed to know. He was telling the truth. He was not The Boss.

Was I dreaming? He wasn't The Boss? The men on our couch weren't the hunters? Was there a boss? Were there hunters? Living in a world with talking animals was driving me crazy. I needed to lay down.

"Are you okay?" Shane asked.

I nodded. "I'll call you later." I turned to Mr. Connors. His face was drawn like he was exhausted and weak. He was truly sorry. All I could do was whisper, "Thank you."

Shane grabbed his dad's arm and pulled him toward the driveway. "Call me, Joe," he said. And then they were gone.

I closed the door and turned around. What I saw made me more scared than I had been in my entire life.

Mr. Thompson was standing behind my mom with one hand around her waist and the other over her mouth. She had tears in her eyes.

"Mom!" I shouted.

"Tell us where the fox is," Mr. Pool said. He stood over the couch and straightened his clothes. He spoke slowly and clearly. "Don't make us hurt your mom."

I thought as fast as I could. They couldn't hurt my mom! I wouldn't let them! I was strong, and I was fast. Was this the reason the land had given me these powers? The men weren't close enough together though. I could stop one, but I couldn't stop both at the same time. I wished Shane would come back.

I saw beautiful blue eyes peer from the bedroom door down the hallway. It was Fox. I wanted to tell him not to come out. But I knew who he was. He would sacrifice himself to save my mom.

"He doesn't live here," I told the men. "The law doesn't allow it." The bedroom door opened wider and PJ stepped out on four paws. He walked toward the living room. What was he doing?

"Maybe not," Mr. Thompson said. "But you know where to find him." He stepped over to Mr. Pool's side. "Your mom wouldn't tell us. But you will when we hurt her."

PJ entered the living room. He walked over to Mr. Thompson, rubbed his sides against his legs, and purred. Then he sat in front of him and smiled.

"Get away from me!" Mr. Thompson shouted. He bent down and kicked PJ halfway across the room. PJ landed on his feet. Mr. Thompson stared at him. "Your eyes… they're blue. You're one of them."

Fox raced out of the bedroom and stopped in front of my mom and the bad guys. He stood on his hind legs. "Take me," he said. "Leave them alone."

No. This couldn't be happening. There had to be a better way. I was tired of my friends and family getting hurt. I was tired of Fox sacrificing himself for us. I had to do something.

"Now!" Fox shouted. PJ raced toward the bad guys and ran in a circle around them and my mom. Fox chased after PJ, like he had the day before. They ran faster and faster in circles around them. Mr. Thompson reached out for them, but they were too fast.

Fox and PJ finally stopped, huffing. Fox was back in front of them and PJ was behind them. "I've got you now," Mr. Thompson said. He reached down to grab Fox by his neck.

"Karate chop!" PJ yelled. He threw a paw into the back of Mr. Thompson's leg then twisted and threw the same paw into the back of Mr. Pool's leg. They both fell to their knees.

My mom broke free and ran over to me. She wrapped her arms around me and pulled me toward the door.

"Now, Stinky!" Fox yelled. The skunk ran out of the bedroom and stood in front of the bad guys.

"Hey," Mr. Pool said to Mr. Thompson. "Isn't that the skunk from the forest? The one that sprayed us?"

"At your service," Stinky said. He turned around, balanced himself on his front paws and raised his rump into the air.

"No!" Mr. Thompson shouted. "Not again!"

Liquid shot out of Stinky's rear end like a water hose. He waved his rump back and forth from Mr. Pool's face to Mr. Thompson's face. There was so much stinky skunk spray that it didn't look like it would ever end.

"It smells so bad!" Mr. Pool shouted. "I can't breathe!"

"My eyes!" Mr. Thompson screamed. "It's burning my eyes!"

They jumped up, scratching at their faces and eyes. My mom pushed me behind her and opened the front door. "Get out!" she yelled. They stumbled over themselves and raced out the door. My mom pulled her cell phone out of her purse and took a picture of their license plate.

She closed the front door and locked it. She hugged me close. "Thank goodness you're safe," she said. She dialed 911, put the phone to her ear, and walked in circles.

"Not bad, huh?" PJ said. He stood on his hind legs with Fox and Stinky next to him. "I've got moves."

I patted his head. I'm glad he was there.
I put my palms together in a praying position
and bowed to him. "You are a Meow Master."

"You did ok," Fox said. "For a cat." He
laughed and patted PJ on the shoulder.

I patted Fox's head too. "You were
willing to give yourself up for my mom.
That's amazing, Fox. Thank you." He blushed
and swatted a paw like it was nothing.

"What about me?" Stinky asked. "I helped."

I rubbed his head, making sure to stay away from his backside. "You saved the day," I told him. "We couldn't have done this without you. We are forever your friends." He had the biggest smile a skunk could make.

"What do we do now?" PJ asked. "The bad guys are out there."

I hadn't thought that far ahead. My mom had a picture of the bad guys' car. She gave that information to the police on the phone. In the best-case scenario, the bad guys would be caught that night. "We prepare ourselves," I said. "We don't know what's coming next."

I thought I had the answers. But it turned out I didn't have any of them. I had no idea who The Boss was. I hated to think it was someone I knew. Why were they determined to hurt me and my friends?

I would have all the answers before the night was over.

MONDAY EVENING

Two policemen came and took statements from me and my mom. It was hard explaining to them what happened. We couldn't say anything about Fox, PJ, or Stinky. My mom told them two men broke into our house. She sprayed them with pepper spray and they ran off. It wasn't 100% the truth, but it was close enough that the cops could look for the bad guys. I agreed with everything she said.

Right as the cops were leaving, the American Indian Elan came into our house. He shook my hand right away. "How are you doing, Joe?"

I was relieved to see him. He was our best chance in saving the animals in the forest. He was the last member of his tribe, The Talking

Dragons. He was the only one who understood why some of the animals had blue eyes and the ability to walk and talk like humans.

"It's been rough," I admitted. "Have you seen Miss Julie?"

He nodded. "I stopped by the wildlife sanctuary. We'll save as many as we can." He put a hand on my shoulder. "How about you? Have you noticed any changes?"

He was referring to my blue eyes and how they affected me. For whatever reason, the land had chosen me to protect it. Elan was fascinated by this because the land had always chosen animals. I wasn't sure where I fit in, though. I was faster and stronger than before I had the blue eyes. But I hadn't done anything with it yet.

I shook my head.

"Elan," my mom said, "it's good to see you." She gave him a shoulder hug. "I'm glad you're here."

A man I didn't know stepped into the house and stood next to Elan. He had caramel colored skin like Elan and was the same height. He looked just like Elan but had a short beard and mustache. "This is my brother, Waya," Elan said.

"Nice to meet you, Waya," my mom said, shaking his hand. "I'm Julie." She pointed to me. "This is my son, Jonah."

I shook my head. How many times did we have to do this? "Please call me Joe," I said.

Waya chuckled. "Hello, Joe. Elan has told me a lot about you." Elan shrugged like he was sorry. "I'm very happy to know you."

"Elan," my mom said, "You said you were the last member of your tribe. I'm confused."

Waya put his hands out and said, "It's true. My brother and I are the last of The Talking Dragons." That didn't make any sense. If there were two in the tribe, how could one be the last? "I didn't believe in what The Talking Dragons stand for and left the tribe many years ago." He pulled out his wallet and handed me a card. "I'm a record producer in Los Angeles now."

"He lost his way," Elan said, wrapping an arm around his brother. "But he's coming back."

"Elan has been writing me letters for the past year," Waya said. "Crazy talk about how he found the land of our ancestors. How he found a talking fox." He shook his head like he couldn't believe it. "But then I saw a video on the internet with a talking fox and a boy — you." He nodded at me. Thanks a lot, Shane. "I had to see it with my own eyes."

PJ walked into the room on four paws and looked at Waya. "There's my favorite cat," Elan said. He pointed to Waya. "This is my brother. Show him what you can do."

PJ looked over at me. His eyes were darker. I sensed he was scared. He turned around and walked out of the living room.

"What was that about?" Elan asked. "PJ loves to talk about himself."

My mom shrugged. "It's been a long day. He's tired."

"Can we see the fox?" Waya asked. "It will prove to me once for all that my ancestors were right. This is sacred land that must be protected."

I waved at him. "Follow me. Fox took a skunk named Stinky back to his home in the forest earlier. Fox is saying his goodbyes." I walked into the kitchen and to the back door. I held it open and let the others out first.

PJ stopped me before I went outside and joined them. "What's wrong?" I asked him. It was weird how he walked away from us without saying a word.

"It's here," PJ said. "The darkness." He stood and put a paw on my leg. "You can't sense it?" Nothing was out of the ordinary. I shook my head.

"Did he ask to see Fox?" PJ asked.

"Yeah," I said. "He's Elan's brother. He's from the tribe sworn to protect Fox and all animals that walk and talk." I scratched his head. "We were chosen, PJ. You, me, Fox, and Stinky."

PJ tapped my leg three times. "His name is Waya. Do you know what that means?" I shook my head. "Waya means 'wolf.'"

My mom shouted from the backyard, "Come on, Jonah!"

I took PJ's paw off my leg so his four paws were on the floor. "I don't know what you're getting at," I told him. "Your name is PJ, which we shortened from Peanut Butter Jelly. We still love you." I stepped outside and reached to pull the door closed.

"Wolves attack red foxes," PJ said before I closed it. I ignored him. Waya was probably the name Elan's brother was given when he was born.

I walked past the outhouse and toward the chicken coop. It didn't look like Fox had returned yet. My mom, Elan, and Waya were standing by the fence when I joined them.

"Their powers came from this land," Elan said to his brother. He motioned around us. "This is where our ancestors lived and thrived."

Waya turned to me. "The fox was the first one in this generation to have the power. It started with him. Where is he?"

I shrugged. "He's disappeared for months at a time before." I felt like I had to explain further. "His parents are out there." My mom nodded.

Elan turned his head from side to side. "Does anyone else smell smoke?" We sniffed the air but none of us smelled anything.

Waya sighed. "If a man wanted to destroy all the animals, it wouldn't do any good to hunt them. This forest is way too big for that." He turned and looked at me. "It would be quicker to burn the forest down."

"Don't say stuff like that," my mom warned. "I don't want to imagine anyone is that sick." She leaned against the fence. "It would burn down the houses around it, including mine."

"I didn't mean to upset you," Waya said. He faced Elan. "We should get going. We can come back tomorrow, if that's okay." My mom nodded.

"It was nice to meet you, Joe," he said to me. "I'm sure we'll see a lot more of each other." He shook my hand again and studied my eyes. "Amazing."

"Come on, big brother," Elan said. "We'll get some fast food on the way home."

"No way," Waya said. "Let's go to a steak house. I'm paying."

Elan chuckled. "If you insist. You're the boss."

"That's right," Waya said. He winked at me. "I'm The Boss."

MY

fox

MY FRIEND

FOREVER

DAVID BLAZE

CONTENTS

LATER THAT NIGHT

Ashes fell from the sky like snowflakes as smoke rose up from deep within the forest. There was no question about it—Waya was The Boss. He was here to destroy the forest and every animal in it.

"Fox!" I yelled into the trees, afraid for my furry best friend's life. We had been through so much together. It couldn't end like this. I didn't care what the fire could do to me—I was going to get him out.

Waya stood in front of me and put a hand on my shoulder to hold me back. "It's too late. This will all be over soon."

"Let me go!" I shouted at him. "I have to save him!"

My mom beat her fists against his arm. "Get away from Jonah." For the first time in my life, I didn't care that she didn't call me Joe. I just wanted her to stay away from this evil man.

Waya's brother, the American Indian Elan, pulled Waya's hand off me and pushed him back. "What is this?" he asked. "What are you doing?"

"Tell him!" I shouted at Waya as my mom pulled me away and hovered over my body. "Tell him the truth!"

Waya shook his head at Elan. "I'm tired of you always following the ancient ways. I won't allow it anymore." He stepped forward and poked Elan in the shoulder. "After I burn the heart of the forest, all of this Talking Dragon foolishness will be over."

"He can't hurt Fox," I cried out to Elan. "Don't let him do it."

"It was you," Elan said to Waya. He looked like he felt sick. "You're the one who's been hurting the animals. But why?"

"Not me," Waya said. "I'm not a hunter. I hired two local yahoos to take care of it, but they failed. I've come to handle things myself."

Elan put his hands on his head. "Why didn't I see this? You fought hard to get out of the tribe.

Now you think you can end it by burning the heart of the forest."

"Some of the animals can talk—so what?" Waya said. "Human life is more valuable. I'm not going to let you waste your life like our ancestors did."

"All lives are valuable," Elan argued.

"We're brothers!" Waya shouted. "You should have followed me."

A large white van drove slowly through the backyard and right up to us. I nearly passed out when the driver door and front passenger door opened, and two men stepped out with rifles. They were Mr. Thompson and Mr. Pool, better known as John and Billy the hunters.

"What's going on?" Elan asked. "Why are they here?"

"I'm sorry it's come to this, brother," Waya said to Elan. "But I can't let you get in the way." He motioned for John and Billy to come to him. "Take them inside," he told the hunters, "and tie them up."

I gulped when John pointed his gun at my mom. Billy pointed his at Elan. "Let's go," John said to me, knowing I would do whatever he said to keep my mom safe.

I wanted to run into the forest and save Fox but there's no way I could leave my mom's life in danger. It wasn't fair! Both choices had consequences. "Fox!" I shouted into the forest as I walked toward the house with tears in my eyes. "Fox!"

EARLY THE NEXT MORNING

I laid on my stomach on the cold living room floor and stared at a speck of dust. My hands and feet were tied behind my back like a chicken about to be fried. My mom lay on one side of me and Elan on the other.

"Someone should mop this floor," my mom said, trying to distract us from the horrible predicament we were in. None of us had slept all night as we worried about Fox and the forest. "Fox tracked in mud again."

I remembered the first time I had let him into the house. The only rule I had given him was he wasn't allowed to pee on the carpet. He had promised he wouldn't if I wouldn't.

"Your eyes are still blue," Elan said to me.

"What?" I asked. His words were an odd thing to say.

"Your eyes," he said, turning his head toward mine. "They're still blue." My eyes had been brown until last year. They turned blue on the day I had met Elan. He was known as the Fox Whisperer.

"What good does it do?" I asked. It had made me faster and stronger but here I was, laying on the floor as helpless as a baby.

"The heart of the forest is alive as long as your eyes are blue," he said. "It chose you for a time like this.

Fox, PJ the cat, Stinky the skunk, and I all had blue eyes from the forest. The animals could talk, and PJ had even learned Karate. What good did it do us to be chosen? Fox's life had been in danger since the beginning. But they were all part of my family now, and I'd always protect them.

"Why is your brother doing this?" my mom asked Elan. "I thought your people were supposed to protect the animals."

Elan sighed. "Waya has always gone his own way. He's not a bad person, just misguided."

"Holding us hostage and setting the forest on fire seems like something a bad person would do," my mom said. Her voice was slower and deeper than usual.

The room fell silent and felt uncomfortable.

"He's searching for the heart of the forest," Elan finally said. "He won't burn the forest down at one time because it will draw too much attention."

"What do you mean?" I asked. He kept talking about the heart of forest. Maybe Fox and the other animals would be okay.

"The heart of the forest pumps life into every tree, every flower, and every animal," he advised. "It chooses which animals will protect it." He winked at me. "It chose you."

I had been trying to figure out for more than a year what he meant when he said I was chosen. I was faster than all the other kids in school and won every race. I was also the strongest, surprising everyone (even myself) when I did twenty pullups in gym class. None of that helped anyone. At least now I knew what I was chosen for. "What do I have to do?"

Elan smiled. "The forest will guide you."

PJ ran into the room and skidded to a stop on four paws. His mouth was wide open as he stood on his two back paws and looked over us laying on the floor. "It's not my fault. I was taking a cat nap and they caught me off guard." He ran to my mom and attempted to karate chop the rope around her hands. "You'll be proud of me. I karate chopped my way out of the cage they put me in."

"Thank goodness you're okay," Elan told PJ.

"Where are they?" my mom asked.

PJ took a deep breath and focused his paw on the rope. "I am a Meow Master. I can do this." He struck his paw at the rope, but it didn't break.

"Hey!" my mom shouted. "Where are they?"

PJ gave up and stepped back to look at me. "The hunters … they want Stinky. They're going to make him pay." I wasn't surprised by this because the friendly skunk had sprayed them in the face twice.

"What about Fox?" I asked. I was concerned about Stinky, but Fox was my best friend.

PJ shrugged. "I don't know. It all happened so fast." He stared into my eyes like cats do. "I tried to warn you. Waya means 'wolf'." He shook his head. "Wolves attack red foxes."

Two car doors slammed shut outside. We all fell silent and stayed still. My heart beat faster and faster. I feared that Waya and the hunters had returned to gloat about how they had destroyed the heart of the forest. And maybe, hopefully not, they had hurt Fox.

I jerked my head when someone banged on the front door and the knob turned from side to side. How was I supposed to use my power if I couldn't even get off the floor?

The door barreled open and light flooded into the room.

"Julie!" my uncle Mike shouted. "Joe!" He ran to my mom and began to untie her. "What happened?"

"My brother," Elan said softly. "He did this."

My little cousin Dana stepped into the house and stared at everyone. "What in the…"

"I tried to help," PJ said.

"Help Joe," my uncle told Dana as he unraveled the rope from behind my mom. "I've got your aunt and Elan."

I expected her to say that it wasn't her job, but she came to me and fiddled with the rope. "Thanks,"
I told her.

My mom was finally free. She joined Dana in untying me as my uncle helped Elan. "I hope Fox is okay," she whispered.

"What?" Dana asked, looking around the

room. "Where is he?" I looked up at her and shook my head. She sat down and wrapped her arms around her legs. "He's okay. I know he is. He's got to be."

I stood when I was finally free and marched toward the back door. I passed the refrigerator that Fox had once called a magic box. He was somewhere in the forest and I was going to get him out.

"Jonah, wait!" my mom shouted after me.

A LITTLE LATER
THAT MORNING

I stood in the backyard and looked up as ashes fell all around me. There were more of them than the night before and they fell faster. Wherever the fire was in the forest, it was getting bigger.

My mom and uncle walked up from behind me and gasped. She nodded at him and communicated in the silent way they had as brother and sister. He pulled his cellphone out of his pocket and pressed three numbers.

"This is an emergency," he said quickly into the phone. "The forest is on fire." He searched through the trees and threw his hands up before he nodded at my mom and asked, "What's the name of it again?"

"Conecuh," she told him.

"Right—Conecuh National Forest," he reported back to the person on the other end of the phone. I imagined it was a dispatcher for the cops and firemen. "I know a lot of people camp here. No, I don't see a fire. There are ashes everywhere." His face turned red. "Look, there's a crazy man who's trying to kill all the animals in the forest."

Dana and PJ stepped up to my side. "Do you see Fox?" she asked. I shook my head as my uncle pulled the phone away from his ear and squeezed it in anger.

"Hello?" he shouted into the phone angrily. "Hello?" My mom snatched it from him and stepped away.

"Hi, my name is Julie Johnson," she told the dispatcher. "I live at 2468 Cocomo Drive. Yeah, we've seen lots of smoke coming from somewhere in the forest since last night." She stared at the ground as she listened. "Right. It seems worse today. I'm concerned about my house and those around mine." She nodded like she understood the dispatcher. "Okay, thank you." She hung up and handed the phone back to my uncle.

"What'd they say?" I asked.

"The fire department is being dispatched to investigate," she replied. That should have made me feel better, but I had learned at the animal sanctuary that the forest was over 84,000 acres. If it wasn't a huge fire and Waya was controlling it with small burns, it could take forever to find the source.

"That's not good enough," I told everyone around me. "We've got to do something now." I started to walk toward the forest before my mom stopped me.

"Hold on there, Mr.," she said. "I know you're concerned about Fox. He's with his parents. They're not going to let anything bad happen to him." I wanted to believe her, and I knew his parents loved him, but the hunters who were searching for him were the same hunters who had shot his parents just a year earlier. "We're gonna have to let the police and fire department handle this."

Elan blew out a deep breath, sounding concerned. "I hate it, but your mother's right. The fire. The hunters." He shook his head. "My brother."

"We need to come up with a plan to keep

this house safe," my uncle said to my mom. "At the very least, we should clear out all your valuable possessions and take them to my place for now. We can load them up in the back of my truck."

My mom motioned for him to step aside so she could speak with him privately. I imagined they were discussing how she and I would move in with him and Dana if we had to, just like when we had first moved here.

"What happens when your brother burns the heart of the forest," I asked Elan.

He turned his face from me like he didn't know the answer or didn't want to tell me. He returned his attention to me and said, "It pumps life into every tree, every animal, and every flower. I don't know for sure what's going to happen, but when it's gone..."

"Hey, Elan," my mom called out. "Come here for a second."

He smiled weakly and patted me on the shoulder before joining them. He didn't have to complete his thoughts because I knew he was thinking the same thing as me.

"What was that about?" Dana asked. "The heart of the forest?" I didn't know why she didn't understand but realized she and my uncle hadn't been there when Elan had explained it.

"It gave me these blue eyes," I said. "And Fox, and PJ, and Stinky."

She looked from me to PJ and said, "That's what gave you guys the power to be faster and stronger." She focused on PJ. "It's what gave you your big mouth."

"Big enough to eat a whole bag of pizza rolls," he said, licking his lips. "Don't be jealous."

She pointed a finger at him and opened her mouth to argue but stopped and stared at me. "If the heart of the forest pumps life into you guys then what happens when it can no longer pump?"

I gulped because I knew what the answer could be. I hadn't stopped thinking about it since Elan had walked away. I looked back at him, waiting for him to explain, but he was in a circle with my mom and uncle in a private conversation. "If a heart stops working…"

"Maybe your eyes just won't be blue anymore," Dana said quickly. Her mouth stayed partly open, like she didn't believe her own words and was afraid of what might happen to me.

I could only think of one thing to do. The forest had chosen me to protect it. I was fast and I was strong, fast enough and strong enough to race through the forest and push danger aside. Fox, PJ, and Stinky had been chosen too but I couldn't put them in anymore danger.

I looked back at my mom, uncle, and Elan one last time. Elan glanced at me and winked before my mom stole his attention away again. "You know I love you, right?" I said to Dana. "You're my favorite cousin."

"Whoa," she said, putting her hands up. "Don't act all weird. Wait. I'm your only cousin."

"Tell my mom and your dad not to worry," I told her. "I know what I'm doing. At least I think I do."

She shook her head. "It's not my job—you do it. If you're about to do something crazy, I want in."

I smiled and winked at PJ. He winked back like he knew what I was about to do and that I had to do it alone. That's when I did the only thing that made sense to me.

I stepped past Dana and raced toward the back fence.

I ran past the outhouse where I had once been attacked by a grasshopper. Dana and Fox had only laughed at my misfortune.

I ran past the chicken coop that Fox had tried

to raid so many times until we had provided him baked chicken from our magic box. He loved it more than live chicken and would never go back to that.

I remembered the time I ran through the yard in the opposite direction to stop Shane after he had recorded Fox talking to me. I never thought that Shane and I would be friends one day.

The fence was in front of me now and coming up quickly as I ran faster. It was an old wooden fence with chicken wire and at least five feet tall. I could clear it. Maybe.

Here it comes.

Deep breath.

And jump!

I don't know how, but I made it. My shoes landed on the ground on the opposite side of the fence with a thud as I bent down to balance myself with one fist. I stood back up slowly, turned, and looked back to see my mom looking at me in the distance. I didn't want to disobey her, but I had to do this. I kept running into the smoky forest.

"Jonah!" my mom shouted. "Jonah!"

EVEN LATER
THAT MORNING

I had never been on this side of the fence. Elan had told me that the Conecuh forest had been named by Indians many years ago. It was Fox's world and the home of hundreds or thousands of other animals. The trees were mostly slash pines, but longleaf pines were being planted throughout the forest to attract red-cockaded woodpeckers. I had learned in school that the forest had been cleared of long leaf pines almost a hundred years ago, and that had put the woodpeckers in danger.

I ran as fast as I could through the brush

because there was no time to waste. Fox had always run at an angle to the left whenever he jumped out of my yard and over the fence. I followed the same path. I chuckled when I thought about one of the times Fox had headed this way to clean himself off in a body of water after the chickens had thrown their eggs at him. Yeah, he had smelled like farts.

There, ahead.

I slowed down as I saw a large rock surrounded by dirt. Was it possible? Fox had told me the story of how his parents had buried him in a hole they lived in and covered it with a large rock to protect him from the hunters when he was younger.

I stopped at the rock and looked around, making sure Waya and the hunters weren't anywhere close. Sensing it was safe, I pushed the rock away and stood back.

A deep hole in the dirt seemed to go down and back as much as six feet. I imagined it branched off into other tunnels leading to rooms. I wondered if Fox had his own room. I pictured the days or weeks he had clawed his way out and couldn't find his parents. The only good thing about it was it had led him to me. And he was eventually reunited with his parents.

I jumped when a squeaky voice behind me said, "What are you looking for?" I turned with my fists up, ready to fight. The black and white skunk Stinky stared back at me and smiled.

"You scared me," I said with a hand over my chest. "Where's Fox?"

The friendly skunk shrugged and said, "He lives with his parents deep in the forest. It's not safe here anymore."

"Can you take me there?"

He jumped up on a log beside the rock and focused on the trees ahead of us. "There's a lot of smoke in that direction."

"I know," I told him. "The forest is in danger." *And so are you. The hunters want revenge for what you did to them.*

"I can take you there," he said reluctantly, "but bad things happen when I get scared." He looked back at his tail. "Bad smells happen."

I chuckled and shook my head. "We need to move fast. Lead the way."

A twig snapped behind us.

"Thought I'd find you here," came a squeaky cat's voice. We turned around and saw PJ's smiling face.

"You can't be here," I told him. I couldn't put any more of my friends in danger. "You have to go back."

He stood on his hind legs and put his paws up in the air. "Wait a minute. You want to save Fox and you want to save the forest. You can't do it alone." He crossed his arms in front of him in a karate pose. "I am a Meow Master. The forest didn't just choose you. It also chose me, Stinky, and Fox. We are the guardians of the forest."

I hated to admit that he was right. I just didn't want to see any of them get hurt. We had to stop the hunters and Waya and protect the heart of the forest from them. The only problem was none of us knew where it was or even what it looked like. And we didn't know where the bad guys were.

"Where's my mom?" I asked. She had to be close if PJ had found me.

"She won't be here any time soon," he said. "The fire department showed up and they're not letting anyone into the forest."

"Then how'd you get here?" Stinky asked.

PJ cocked his head and stared at him like that wasn't a smart question. "I'm a cat. And a Meow Master."

I turned to Stinky and sighed. "Lead the way."

It wasn't long before we came to a lake. I knew there were swamps in the forest, but this lake was crystal clear. Stinky laughed as he jumped into the shallow water by us and swatted some of it at PJ.

The hair on PJ's back stood straight up as he jumped. I tried not to laugh because I knew how much he hated water. "I'll get you back," he hissed at Stinky.

"Sorry," he said, sounding sincere. "Me and Fox used to play here. It was so much fun."

That's when I saw the reflection of flames on the water. I looked across the lake to the other side and watched fire crawl up the pine trees.

"Waya is close," I whispered.

"Fox…" Stinky said, patting me on the leg. "He lives on that side of the lake."

I didn't hesitate and began to race to the other side. But something stopped me. Something that changed my life.

Two men who looked a lot like the American Indian Elan stood in front of us. They literally popped up from out of nowhere. They wore clothes I didn't recognize. Brown robes wrapped around their bodies with cotton belts. They had thin lines of orange and pink paint on their faces. They appeared to be old and didn't look dangerous, just sad.

"You found it," one of the men said to me. "We knew you would come back one day."

I had no idea what he was talking about. "What? Who are you?"

"We have a message for you from the heart of the forest," he said, placing a hand on my shoulder. "Save them. Save them all."

The other man reached into the water and splashed some of it into my face the same way Stinky had splashed PJ. "Remember who you are." I closed my eyes to shield them from the water then quickly wiped the water away with the sleeve of my shirt and reopened my eyes.

The men were gone.

"Where did they go?" I asked Stinky and PJ.

"Who?" Stinky asked.

PJ squinted his eyes. "What are you talking about?"

I scratched my head and sighed as I stared at my reflection in the water. Was I going crazy?

Remember who you are.

I poked my reflection and let the water ripple

around it. "I've been here before," I realized. "We all have."

"Okay, I admit it," PJ said. "I peed in the lake once."

"Ewww," Stinky replied. Then he blushed and said, "Me too."

"I was here when I was a baby," I thought out loud. I don't know how I remembered that. My great-grandmother Rita had brought me here and cleaned me off in the water. "We've all touched the water." That's when it clicked for me. "This lake is the heart of the forest. It pumps life into every living creature in it."

"It can't be burned," Stinky said. He was right. Waya was burning the forest for no reason.

The fire beyond the lake grew wider and closer. Smoke began to surround us. I could feel heat from the flames. I knew at that moment that Waya had lost control of the fire or had lost his mind and decided to burn everything down. I didn't know if the fire department could stop it before it consumed everything around us.

"We should go," PJ suggested in a rush. "I don't like water and I don't like fire. There's no way for us to stop it." Stinky nodded vigorously and coughed.

"Maybe there is," I said, realizing the forest never wanted me to save the trees and bushes and flowers. It valued something more than itself. It wanted me to save the animals.

"Go back and tell everyone where the fire is," I told PJ. I wasn't going anywhere until I knew Fox was okay. "Take Stinky with you. Make sure the firemen know."

PJ put his paws up. "Wait. What are you going to do?"

I looked from him to Stinky. They both appeared to be afraid. "I know what I have to do now." I waved them away and yelled, "Go!"

PJ seemed hurt and confused but backed away slowly as the flames got closer. "You don't have to do this," he said as I took my shoes off and stepped into the shallow end of the lake. He huffed and coughed. "We're coming back for you!" he shouted as he rushed off with Stinky.

The fire was close now, too close. It wrapped around the lake and was only yards away, scouring the trees and leaving destruction behind.

I took a deep breath and put my hands by my sides. Memories flooded my head, memories that were not my own. My great-grandmother had been in love with a Talking Dragon many years earlier and maybe married to him. He had taught her the ancient ways of his people. He had taught her to tame the heart of the forest.

I saw it all in my mind like a lucid dream. Again, I saw my great-grandmother bring me to the lake. She was standing me up in the water and showing me hand motions to communicate with it.

Now I was ready. My cheeks were hot from the flames around me. I took five more steps into the water, until it was waist high. This is what I had been taught. I raised my hands as high as I could into the air.

"May the heart guide me and restore peace," I whispered, words my great-grandmother had repeated to me hundreds of times before I could even walk. This moment was why I was gifted strength and speed. I prayed that I wasn't wrong about this because if I was, then all would be lost.

EARLY THAT AFTERNOON

With my hands in the air, using all the power and speed the lake had given me, I drove them down as fast and as hard as I could into the waters beside me.

The lake parted in a complete circle around me, and all its water spread out and flew high up into the air in a wide arc. It hovered for just a moment over the forest like a big bowl of Jell-O. Hundreds of animals stood around the naked trees and stared at me. I was relieved to see that they all seemed okay.

The world was still and silent for a split

second before the water fell and crashed over the trees. It saturated every tree and doused every flame. By the time it hit the ground, the water was nothing more than rain that lasted for less than a minute.

I spun and looked around at all the trees. Dense smoke filled the air, but the fire was gone and couldn't come back any time soon because everything was wet. But then I looked down and my heart sank.

There was no more lake. There was no more heart of the forest. What did it mean for me and the others? Was my strength and speed gone? Was my life in danger without the heart?

The smoke began to clear, and three figures emerged in a haze. They weren't human. One smaller animal walked on four paws in front of two larger animals.

I took a step back, completely unprotected in the barren lake, and maybe unable to defend myself. I put my arms up as the smaller animal got closer and stood up on two legs.

"Fox," I whispered as he became clear. I laughed and cried at the same time as I ran toward him. We crashed into each other because he ran toward me too. We both fell and laughed. I was flat on my back when he jumped on top of me and bounced up and down on my stomach.

"You should stop eating cake and eat more chicken," he teased me.

I wrapped my arms around him and hugged him so close that I could feel his bones. "You should stop eating chicken and eat more cake."

His parents walked up to us and shook their heads. They didn't have the ability to talk like him, but it was easy to tell that they thought we were silly.

"Hey," I said to Fox as I sat up, "you can still talk." I rubbed my hands on the dry land beneath me. "How is that possible?"

Fox shrugged. "What do you mean?" He didn't know what the heart of the forest was or what it did.

"My eyes, what color are they?"

"I'm not going to tell you that they're pretty," he said, chuckling. "I'm not that kind of fox."

"What color?"

He looked at me funny and said, "Blue, Joe. Your eyes are blue." He put his face close to mine, looking concerned. "So is your tongue."

"What?" I stuck my tongue out as far as I could and tried to look down at it. Fox laughed and pointed at me.

"I can't believe you looked!" He fell and rolled on the ground. "I can't believe it!"

I shook my head. "You better be glad we're friends."

"Friends forever," he confirmed.

Footsteps trampled through broken branches around us. Not just in front of us. Not just behind us. All around us. I stood next to Fox and his parents, prepared to fight or run, knowing it had to be either Waya and the hunters or the firemen.

I gasped when a black bear walked out of the forest in front of us. It just stood there and stared. Two little cubs appeared by its side.

On the right, a herd of deer appeared and surrounded the side of the empty lake.

Behind us, a team of hogs snorted.

On the left, a flock of turkeys gobbled and danced around each other.

Small shadows appeared from above. The sky was full of sparrows and doves and woodpeckers, cawing and chirping.

"What is this? I whispered.

The bear and its cubs growled and roared. The deer pounded their hooves on the ground. The hogs snorted and grumbled. The birds fell silent and glided over us.

Fox patted my leg. "They honor you."

"What? Why?"

"You saved them, Joe," he said. "You saved us all."

I felt like crying. "I'm nobody."

The bear cubs ran away from their mama and raced to me. I tried not to freak out when they reached me and climbed up my legs. They ended up in my arms, held close to my chest. The mama bear stood back and watched.

"You're somebody to those little monsters," Fox said, shaking his head. "They keep trying to steal my chickens." He stuck his tongue out at them and they stuck theirs out at him.

"I need to go back," I told Fox. "I have to let my mom know that I'm okay and you're okay." I looked down at the cubs. "But it's not safe here while Waya and the hunters are in the forest. We don't know where they are."

"I'll go with you," he said. "All of these animals around us — this is what we've been doing for thousands of years. This is our life. We're not afraid of it."

The cubs fought to get out of my arms and crawled back down my legs. They raced to their mama and disappeared with her into the woods. The deer and hogs and turkeys settled back into the forest. One sparrow remained flying above us.

"Let's go," I told Fox. "I've got to think of way to explain all of this to my mom."

LATER THAT AFTERNOON

The ground was squishy as we trekked through the forest. I let Fox lead the way since I didn't know how to get back. I felt tired and weak for the first time since I had these blue eyes. Did I lose my powers?

"When we get back to your house," Fox said, "I'm going to eat some baked chicken then fried chicken then microwaved chicken."

I yawned and covered my mouth. "I'm going to take a nap."

Another twig snapped behind me. I didn't turn around because I figured it was one of the cubs. If I showed it more attention, then it would never leave me alone. I didn't want it to think that I wanted it to follow me to the house because while my mom had accepted a talking fox, I wasn't so sure she'd accept a cub that would grow up to weigh 660 pounds.

"It's good to see you again, Joe," said a man's voice I was afraid to hear. I froze then turned around to face Waya. He didn't have any weapons in his hands. "I don't want to hurt you."

"Where are your friends?" I asked, not trusting him.

John and Billy the hunters stepped out of the woods on both sides of me. "You rang?" John asked.

Fox tapped me on the leg. "You don't have a phone. Someone else must have rang him."

"You shouldn't be here, kid," Waya warned. "Bad things can happen in the forest." He didn't notice the mama black bear behind him, standing tall, towering over him.

"You're right, they can," I told Waya, pointing behind him. He turned and looked up at the massive bear that growled at him.

"Shoot it!" he shouted to John and Billy. "Shoot it, you fools!"

They raised their guns and prepared to fire,

but not before the bear cubs swung out of the trees and slapped the guns out of their hands. Hogs rushed out of the brush and knocked the hunters flat on their backs. They laid there in pain, unable to move.

"It can't get any worse than this," Billy said. That's when PJ and Stinky showed up.

"The cavalry has arrived," PJ said, saluting me. "Orders, sir?"

"Spray them," I ordered. "Spray them good."

PJ turned to Stinky and stepped to the side, next to Fox. "Prepare to fire, soldier." Stinky turned around and raced his rump to the back and top of the hunters' heads.

"Fire!"

Stinky let out a huge stream of stinky liquid that covered John and Billy's faces and heads.

"Why does this keep happening?!" John shouted.

"It smells and tastes so bad!" Billy complained.

Waya turned from the bear. "You may have won this time, but you're no better than these filthy animals."

I smiled at the mama bear as she got down on all four paws and lumbered back into the forest with her cubs in tow. I remembered how all the animals had surrounded me at barren lake. It had been the greatest feeling in the world. Maybe Waya was right and I wasn't better than any of the them. "I hope not."

"Jonah!" my mom shouted from close by. She ran down the path toward me. Elan, a policeman, and a bunch of firemen were with her. She hugged me then held me back as the firemen walked past us. "You're always running into danger. You've got to stop."

Maybe she was right, but I was glad I did it. "I have so much to tell you."

"What is it?" she asked.

"Let's go home," I said. "I'll tell you after my nap." Elan patted me on the shoulder as he passed me with the cop.

"Why?" Waya asked Elan as the cop hand-cuffed him. "Why are you here? Why do you have to keep following the old ways?"

"You're my brother," he said. "No matter what you do, I'm always going to be here for you." The cop pushed Waya forward and past us.

"Your little friend took care of everything for me," he called back, laughing. "He destroy-ed the heart of the forest."

PJ karate chopped Waya in the knee as he walked by. Waya hobbled away while the cop pushed him forward.

"It's true," I told Elan. "I had to destroy the heart to save the forest and the animals. I'm sorry."

"Don't be sorry, Joe," he said. "I'm sure you did exactly what you were supposed to do. Sometimes I think there's Talking Dragon in your blood."

I remembered the vision I had of my great-grandmother with a Talking Dragon that she loved and maybe secretly married long ago. Maybe I really did have Talking Dragon in my blood.

As we all headed back to the house to rejoin my uncle and Dana, I wondered if Melissa would be there. I hoped she would. And I wondered if she'd like me anymore if my powers were gone. What if I was just regular Joe again? What if I wasn't strong anymore? What if I wasn't fast anymore? Who was I?

"Hey, Joe," Elan said from behind me as we entered the yard. Melissa was there with Shane and Dana! My Uncle stood back and grinned. Dana ran up to me and kicked me in the shin.

"Next time take me with you!" she shouted before turning back and walking away with Fox and PJ. Yeah, she was still my favorite cousin.

"Joe," Elan called out again as I walked up to

Melissa and Shane.

Fox gave me a thumbs up and smiled before he entered the house to raid the magic box. He really was my friend forever.

I turned one last time to face Elan. Maybe the heart of the forest was gone but at least I was lucky enough to have such great friends and family. "Sorry. Yeah?"

He smiled and nodded. "Your eyes are still blue."

THE END

If you enjoyed reading this series by David Blaze, you may also like the first book of his new series, Epic Kids. Please enjoy two free chapters in the next few pages…

ONE

MY LUNCH TRAY
HAS WINGS

I wasn't sure what to do when the cool new kids at school asked me to sit at their lunch table. I had just set my tray down at my usual spot, you know, the not-so-cool table where one kid is always picking his nose and another is wiping greasy pizza hands all over his shirt.

"Do you think you're cool, Jake?" Omar Kim asked from my table. He had long black hair tied back in a ponytail and wore a bright tie-dye T-shirt. "You're not cool." He scooped a spoonful of mashed potatoes, splashed it in gravy, and then swished it through the air like a boomerang. "Get on the gravy plane! Yeah!"

I sighed and glanced at the cool table behind me, where two kids stared at me and waved, waiting for me to join them. It didn't seem real because no one ever picked me for anything.

I wasn't good at sports and was always the last kid chosen for teams in P.E. Well, I wasn't chosen—I was the last kid left. Just yesterday, I tried to throw a baseball to second base, but it went sideways and nearly took Coach Michael's head off.

I wasn't that great at school either. I never went home with a perfect report card … I was more of an A, B, and sometimes C student. Okay, mostly C's. And I only got A's in one class—English.

Then there's the school bus situation. Every day was a challenge to find a seat because other kids claimed the seat next to them was reserved. The only thing it was reserved for was their lunches and selfish backpacks.

"See you later," I said to Omar as I picked my tray back up from the table and turned around. He had a habit of making me feel like I would never amount to anything. I hadn't been picked before today, but now it was time to find out what it felt like.

Five seconds later, I was sitting at the cool table, across from the new girl named Amanda. She had long blonde hair and shiny green eyes. She had to be a year or two older than me (I was twelve) because she looked more mature than all the other girls in sixth grade. I didn't know much about her other than she started at this school last week with two boys who were always by her side. One of them was stuck in the lunch line, glaring at me like I'd better run for my life before he got his monstrous hands around my neck.

"Don't worry about him," Amanda said with a straight face. Easy for her to say, but I sat far enough back from the table to make for a quick escape if necessary. The guy in the lunch line was named Darryl. He had arrived here on the same day as Amanda, but I don't care what anyone says, he wasn't a sixth grader like the rest of us, he couldn't be. I wondered if he had repeated the second grade, third, fourth, and fifth. He was over six feet tall and looked like he needed to shave his hairy face.

"Jake doesn't belong here," the only other kid at the table said, shaking his head at Amanda and waving me off. I wasn't sure what he had against me, and I couldn't figure out how he fit in with the other cool kids. He was the last one who had arrived here with Amanda. His name was Tony; he was the yin to Darryl's yang at a noticeably short four feet tall and had the biggest forehead I had ever seen. "He's not like us."

Amanda held up a hand for him to be silent.

He huffed like a frustrated kindergartener and stood up to point at my usual table. I turned to see Omar and the other guys flinging mashed potatoes and gravy at each other, laughing and snorting like happy pigs playing in filthy mud. "That's where he came from. Those kids are morons."

"Back off," I warned him. "Those are my friends." I was surprised when he sat back down without an argument. He squinted at me and kept eating his lunch.

"I've been watching you," Amanda said to me. "You always stand up for others. Why?"

I shrugged and said, "I'm not better than anyone else."

She caught Tony's attention and nodded.

"So," he said to me reluctantly, wiping the sides

of his mouth with a napkin, "we're all going to see the latest *Party Marty* movie tomorrow morning in Spring Rock." Spring Rock was the town next to ours and more than thirty miles away. He shook his head slowly like he felt sick by what he was about to say next. "You should come with us."

I was dying to see that movie, but there was a major problem with their plan that made it impractical. "We have school tomorrow."

Tony snickered and put his palms up in the air like he didn't understand what the problem was. He looked around the cafeteria then leaned across the table and motioned for me to come close. "We're not coming to school tomorrow."

Amanda nodded to confirm what he said was true. I felt conflicted because I'd never skipped school and had perfect attendance. Teachers loved me. What would they think of me if I missed a day?

Tony pointed back at my usual lunch table. "Unless you want to stay here and hang out with your weird friends."

Omar was piloting his spoon full of mashed

potatoes and gravy through the air again. "Get on the gravy plane!"

I took a deep breath. Could I even consider skipping school? There was a rumor that a teacher guarded the movie theaters to catch any kid trying to escape from class. And if a kid was caught, they were kicked out of school forever. We all knew it wasn't true, but no one was brave enough to test that theory. Besides, I was the kid who always did what he was told to do. I was the kid who stayed out of trouble. But ... I was also the kid who felt like I didn't belong where everyone thought I was supposed to be.

"This is never going to work," Tony warned, tossing his fork onto his tray and crossing his arms. "He's not ready." Amanda stared at him with cold eyes to silence him. It seemed odd to me that he always obeyed.

"What do you want to do?" Amanda asked me, smiling wide while her eyes sparkled again. "I really want you to come with us. You have to be there."

I looked into her eyes, wondering how today

went from being a boring school day to a day when I considered doing something I would never have considered before. "I think that—"

A large shadow loomed over the table. I turned to the side and looked up to see Darryl's hairy face.

"Get out of my seat," he demanded. He set his tray down on the table and stood there, staring down at me, waiting for me to stand up and leave. I felt sick because I didn't want to cause any trouble, but I also didn't want to be condemned back to the uncool table.

"He sits here now," Amanda informed him in a stern voice.

"You can't do this! I won't allow it!" Darryl raised a fist to his chest then threw it forward like he was tossing a Frisbee.

That's when things got crazy.

My lunch tray flew off the table and up into the air, higher than my head, then spun around and floated before it dropped and crashed back onto the table in front of me. Milk splashed all over my face and shirt.

I jumped out of my chair and backed away

from the table while my chair crashed to the floor behind me with a loud thud. Every movement in the lunchroom seemed to happen in slow motion as kids turned to look at me. My heart and breathing stopped. What I had just seen was impossible!

The lunchroom fell silent; then all the kids pointed at me and laughed, not knowing what had happened before I was dripping wet in milk. At any other time in my life, I would have been embarrassed, but all I could think about was the floating tray. If Darryl and the other new kids were capable of that, then what else were they capable of?

"What's going on here?" the vice principal, Mr. Spradley, asked, standing behind Amanda and shaking his bald head at me. He had a bushy gray mustache to match the gray suit and tie he wore every day. His steel eyes felt eerily familiar to me. Something you should know about Mr. Spradley is some days he loved kids and other days he hated kids. You could never tell what kind of day it was by looking at him because he always smiled.

Amanda stared across the table at Darryl with eyes that told him to be silent. Tony put his hands behind his head, leaned back in his chair, and chuckled. Darryl grabbed the chair from behind me, placed it back at the table, and sat on it, reclaiming his spot. And me? I stood there, lost and confused, milk dripping off my nose, not sure if I could form any words after what had happened.

"You," Mr. Spradley said, pointing at me. "Get your food and go stand up front." That's where he sent all the troublemakers during lunch. They had to face the kids in the cafeteria while standing up, holding their trays, and eating whatever they could without dropping it. I had never expected to go up there.

I tried to explain what had happened, but my mouth was dry, and words felt like rocks scraping against my throat.

"Save your breath," he advised. "I don't want to hear a word out of you. Get up front."

"But—"

"Now!"

I glanced at Darryl, Tony, and Amanda, hoping one of them would say something to save me. Amanda mouthed that she was sorry, and I believed her. I believed she was the only good person at the table I wished I had never sat at.

Maybe Omar Kim was right—I wasn't cool.

I brushed past Mr. Spradley and headed to the front of the cafeteria with the other dozen kids he had sent up there. I lost my breath when I turned around to face the tables filled with kids. Hundreds of them watched me on display as a convicted troublemaker.

I didn't touch my food and waited impatiently for lunch hour to be over, shifting my weight from one leg to the other so they wouldn't both go numb at the same time. Ten minutes were still left on the clock. Every second was longer than the last one.

Darryl kept turning his head back and forth as he glanced at me then argued with Amanda. I had no idea what his problem was with me or why Amanda seemed to like me. All I knew was he had made my lunch tray fly like a magic carpet, and he didn't look like a magician.

As I watched them, I realized there was something different about the new kids, something magical, something epic. Maybe it made them dangerous, but I had to know more about them. Even after what had just happened, I was drawn to them like cheese to pizza. I had to be part of their group.

There's no way I could skip school though. The teachers would faint, and my mom would send me to school in some foreign country. Everyone expected me to be good and do well all the time, but I hated it. Once, just once, I wanted to do something no one ever expected me to do.

"I didn't do anything wrong," I said to Mr. Spradley as he marched across the lunch line of delinquents.

He smiled wide and reached for the microphone on the podium he used so the whole lunchroom could hear him. "Hey, everyone!" he shouted in a cheery voice. "Because of Jake, you are all now on silent lunch. Enjoy." He set the microphone back down and said to me, "I told you to save your breath."

All the talking and laughing and horse playing left the lunchroom like a vacuum cleaner had sucked it out. Hundreds of angry eyes stared at me as if they wanted to rip me apart. I gulped and tried not to look at anyone.

Omar jumped out of his chair and ran through the crowd of kids like he was being chased by angry hornets. His tie-dye T-shirt made it hard to miss him. Bits of mashed potatoes and gravy flew off his body with every hurried step. When he reached the front of the cafeteria, Mr. Spradley held his hands out and stopped him.

"There's no running in here!" he shouted like Omar wasn't right in front of him. "Where do you think you're going?"

Omar's face turned blue. He bent over and chunked at least a gallon of vomit all over Mr. Spradley's pants and shoes.

Mr. Spradley stepped back and put his hands up high in the air. "Go on," he said in disgust. "Get out of here."

I couldn't help but laugh. That turned out to

be a huge mistake. My laugh was the only noise in the lunchroom because everyone else was still silent. But, come on, Mr. Spradley deserved it!

He used two fingers to motion for the janitor to come over. That guy had messy blond hair that draped over his ears and into his eyes like a surfer. He looked like he was still in high school. "Hey, Janitor Whatever-Your-Name-Is, get a mop and bucket for Jake." Mr. Spradley crossed his arms and glared at me. He shook his legs to get off as much of the slimy mess as he could then headed for the bathroom. "This floor better be shining like pure gold by the time I get back."

The noise in the lunchroom grew loud again as soon as he was out of sight. The janitor took my tray, shoved a mop into my hands, and rolled a mop bucket up to my feet. "Do what I do," he suggested, nodding down at the vomit. "Imagine it's spaghetti." He stepped away but turned right back around and held up a hand. "Don't eat it though. I made that mistake once."

My stomach churned. I dipped the mop in the bucket then chased the vomit as fast as I could. It spread over the floor like a raging river, right to Amanda's table.

She shrieked when it nearly touched her shoes. I jammed the mop under the table and stopped the vomit stream. She was standing in her chair when she thanked me.

"Looking for one of your relatives down there?" Tony asked me, smirking.

"What?"

"You know, like your aunt." I didn't have any idea what he meant and decided he was looney. "Your aunt," he repeated. "A-N-T." He burst out laughing as the teachers came into the lunchroom to let us know it was time to head back to class. "See you later, cleanup boy."

Amanda and Darryl stood up and faced me. "So, what did you decide?" she asked. Darryl crossed his arms and stared at me without an expression.

I didn't know what she meant at first but then remembered she had wanted me to go to a movie with them tomorrow. I wanted to go, but it wasn't possible. It went against everything my mom had taught me.

Mr. Spradley walked back into the lunchroom with clean, damp pants. "I can't believe that happened," he complained to the janitor. "These kids…" He stared at me and shook his head.

"Want some spaghetti?" the janitor asked him.

I shrugged at Amanda and said, "I don't think I can go. Sorry." As I walked away with the other kids, all I could think about was how badly I wanted to miss just one day of school and hang out with the cool kids.

TWO

PLAYING DODGEBALL
WITH A JAGUAR

As soon as I walked into my computer class, Miss Causey caught my attention. "Jake, come here for a minute." The odd thing about her was she was super short and big, and her boyfriend, the school resource officer, was super tall and thin. "Why were you sent to the front of the cafeteria?" she asked, concerned.

I wasn't sure she'd believe me if I told her about the flying tray, or even if I believed it myself, so I summarized it as best as I could. "I sat at a different table today." I looked to the back of the room where Darryl was. "Not everyone liked that."

She put a hand over her chest and blew out a breath of air like she was relieved to hear I hadn't robbed the lunch ladies. "I knew you couldn't do anything bad. You're the best student I've ever had. I'd clone you a hundred times if I could."

I wondered if a hundred clones of me would wear the same clothes and eat the same food. Eh, who cares? I wondered if one of them could be cool and do something bad. I was tired of being good all the time and making adults happy while other kids mocked me.

"I can be bad," I whispered. Miss Causey must have heard me because she chuckled like it was absurd. I put my head down and headed to my seat while kids jeered at me for making them sit through silent lunch.

"Be careful," Tony warned the class. "He might get angry and do extra homework!" The whole class laughed until Amanda stood up and told them to leave me alone.

I thanked her and took the empty seat next to her that belonged to Omar. One of my regular lunchroom buddies had told me in the halls that Omar had gone to the nurse's station then was sent home with the flu. If I had to guess, he had the mashed potatoes and gravy flu (and maybe Mr. Spradley had it now too!).

"Don't listen to him," Amanda advised me.

"He's always got a bad attitude."

"Then why do you hang out with him?" I asked.

She opened her mouth to say something but was interrupted by Jennifer, another popular girl, as she walked by.

"Hey, Amanda." Jennifer glanced at me and rolled her eyes. "You don't have to sit next to him," she said in a strong whisper, like I wasn't supposed to hear it but she meant for me to anyway. "There's an empty seat by me."

I sank in my chair.

"I'd rather sit by my friend," Amanda responded.

Jennifer rolled her eyes at me again and stomped off to her desk.

"You didn't have to do that," I told Amanda.

"I wanted to." She smiled softly.

I smiled back because she made me feel important. I was still hurt by what Jennifer had said though. I guess it didn't matter who I hung out with, I still wouldn't be cool to the rest of the world. "I wish I was popular like you," I mumbled.

Amanda chuckled. "It's not as great as you think it is." She looked down at her desk and sighed. "I wish I could go back in time and change everything."

I was shocked to hear her say that because her life seemed great to me. I didn't know her very well, but it seemed like everyone wanted to be her friend and would do whatever she asked them to do.

If I could go back in time, I'd go all the way back to kindergarten and start being cool. I'd learn every sport and practice them every day until I became really good at them. I'd hang out with the kids I knew were going to be cool one day, so I'd be cool by association.

"I didn't mean to get you in trouble earlier," Amanda assured me. "Darryl is very protective and—" She clutched her chest like she was having a heart attack then pulled up on the necklace that was tucked beneath her shirt. At the bottom of it was an emerald that glowed bright green. "Oh, no."

"What?" I asked as she tucked the emerald

quickly back under her shirt so no one could see it. The gem was beautifully spectacular, something I'd show the whole world if I had it, not hide it away. The light in Amanda's eyes was gone, and her face was drawn as if she had received the worst possible news.

The fire alarm suddenly screamed its deafening roar. Orange and red lights flashed around the room.

"Everyone up!" Miss Causey shouted over the fire alarm. "Line up in an orderly fashion and let's head to the courtyard." We had practiced this drill twice every month during the school year, but no one said it was going to happen today. Maybe there really was a fire this time, but I suspected whatever was wrong had something to do with Amanda's glowing emerald.

Before I could stand up, Darryl appeared behind Amanda and threw a coat over her head as he led her out of the room urgently. Tony tagged along right behind them and knocked me down before I could get out of my seat. I had to catch up with them to find out what was going on.

By the time I got up and reached the door, the hall was flooded with kids from classes all over the school. Amanda and the new kids were nowhere in sight. What was Amanda being protected from?

I fought through the crowd until I finally spotted them separating themselves from everyone else and slipping into the gym. I squeezed and pushed through as many kids as I could until I reached the gym and slipped in just like the cool new kids.

The gym was empty. Basketball hoops stood at both ends of the floor and empty bleachers sat on both sides. I had seen Amanda and the others come in here, so I knew they had to be close. Maybe they were in a locker room behind the basketball nets. I decided to check the boys' room first because, well, it'd be too weird being caught in the girls' locker room.

Just as I stepped into the room, I heard Amanda scream from somewhere behind the gym. I raced to the rear door that led to the outside track and pulled the door open hastily.

I froze in disbelief when I saw what was outside

in front of me.

The largest cat I had ever seen bared its sharp, powerful fangs and roared at Amanda, Darryl, and Tony. The cat's coat was yellow and orange with black spots like a jaguar but that was crazy— jaguars didn't live anywhere near here.

Darryl stood in front of Amanda to protect her with his hands out in defense. Tony was running away across the track like an all-star athlete.

I'm not sure why, but I had an overwhelming desire to protect Amanda. No one outside seemed to realize I was standing in the doorframe, watching them in suspense. I grabbed the only weapon I could find close by—a dodgeball.

I threw the dodgeball as hard as I could at the jaguar, who was in my direct path. I'd like to say the jaguar fell over then ran away when the ball hit it, but honestly, the ball never made it there. It hit the ground before it reached the jaguar and bounced right over the monstrous cat.

That's when I faced the scariest moment of my life (at that time).

The jaguar swiveled its head toward me and

smiled with its fangs dripping hot saliva. I'm not kidding. The cat smiled like it was happy to see me, like I was the one it wanted to tear apart. It roared again and sprinted toward me like a freight train.

I froze. They say your life flashes before your eyes right before you die. That's a lie. It's more like everything moves in slow motion. I could see and hear every footfall of the jaguar as it barreled toward me. I watched Amanda's mouth open wide and her arms wave back and forth in what seemed to take minutes instead of seconds.

"Jake!" I finally heard Amanda's voice shout. "Run!"

I turned around and forced my feet to move faster than they had ever moved before across the gym floor. The jaguar roared behind me, its breath on my heels. My heart beat faster than any heart was meant to beat. My ears felt like they were on fire.

But I was going to get out. I was going to survive. I had to.

That's when my sneakers squeaked on the floor,

and I tumbled onto my knees and arms and face. I instinctively huddled my limbs together like a baby in its mother's womb to protect myself. There was nothing else I could do but wait to be eaten alive.

I watched in slow motion as the jaguar jumped into the air to pounce on me. Its fangs were beautiful and huge as they came down toward my head.

The jaguar unexpectedly yelped, and its body rose up into the air like my lunch tray had then soared across the gym and slammed into the wall like it had been hit by a semi-truck.

I sat up as Darryl stood over me and kept an eye on the jaguar. It got back up slowly on its four paws and shook its head like it was trying to get water out of its ears. The big cat looked around the gym at me and Darryl like it had never seen us before. It seemed confused about where it was and how it got there. After searching for a way out, it walked cautiously through the open back door.

Darryl reached out a hand to me and helped me up. He nodded like he respected me now. "It's not your job to protect her," he advised me. He stepped to the side to show Amanda behind him. "It's mine." He guided her out the way they had gone before.

"Are you okay?" Amanda shouted back at me.

Darryl kept guiding her. "Is he okay?" she asked him.

The janitor stood at the gym entrance with his mouth wide open, apparently having seen me run through the gym. "Dude, that was awesome. You were almost cat food."

I didn't say anything to him. I wasn't sure I could or even if I could ever move from that spot again. Every cell in my body felt numb.

Tony walked in and shook his head at me. "A dodgeball? Really?" He walked away slowly backward and snapped his fingers. "Tomorrow. Forget about school. We're gonna blow your mind!

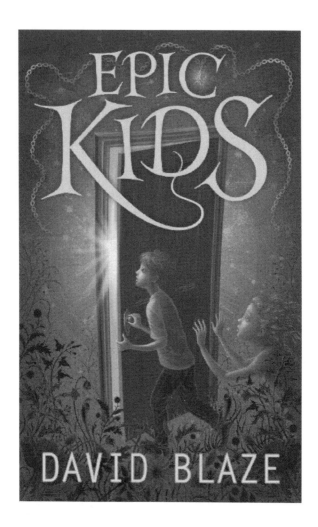

If you enjoyed the My Fox complete series, please tell your friends and family. I'd also appreciate it if you'd leave a review on Amazon.com and tell me what you think about my best friend, Fox.

You can keep up with everything I'm doing and contact me at:

www.davidblazebooks.com

Be sure to click the Follow button next to my name (David Blaze) on Amazon to be notified when my new books are released.

And you can follow me on Facebook. Just search for David Blaze, Children's Author. Be sure to like the page!

See you soon!

Made in the USA
Coppell, TX
05 October 2020

39214406R10367